KING OIL

by Max Catto

Simon and Schuster : New York

48793

SBN 671-20481-5
Library of Congress Catalog Card Number: 72-101868
Designed by Irving Perkins
Manufactured in the United States of America
By H. Wolff Book Mfg. Co., Inc., New York, N.Y.

*The voice of my beloved! behold, he cometh
Leaping upon the mountains, skipping
upon the hills.*

—SONG OF SOLOMON

🎎🎎🎎🎎🎎 ONE:

The Barbarian

I

HE WOULD remember everything that happened that morning till the day he died. The crunch of wheels in the cobbled yard, the snort of unsavory mules, the massed gabble of his father's servants . . . and he raced out of his tutor's room into the radiant sunshine of Seville.

The first thing he saw was an arm poking out of Pancho Guzman's decrepit coach. Next a leg, then huge shoulders, until the whole body had prized itself free like a fetus from the womb. Miguel watched with frozen fascination. He knew nothing about *Americanos*, except that they had just emerged from the self-inflicted cruelty of a Civil War, that they were endowed with a natural brutality, that there was some explosive force forever driving them on to new frontiers so that one day they would all crowd up against the Pacific and stream like mad lemmings into the sea. Or so Miguel's tutor said.

They were furiously hostile to the Mexican *rancheros* whose lands had been properly granted by letters patent of the King of Spain. He had an uncle in El Paso, which had once been Spanish and now was not.

11

Miguel's second impression was: big, big, big. The man stretched himself with a chuckle and the sound of a creaking hinge. Miguel's father, Don Alonso, was already out to greet him effusively. A most hospitable soul. Señor Dibbler, Miguel had been told, was from somewhere in Texas—Mexican name, surely?—with a letter of introduction from Don Alonso's second cousin, who was a neighboring *ranchero* across the Rio Grande.

It turned out that anyone within three hundred miles of one's hacienda in Texas was a neighbor. How unbelievably vast!

"Señor," Don Alonso cried out, "where is your baggage?"

"At the inn."

"I will have it collected. You are staying with us. How is Jaquindo, my dear cousin?"

"Who?"

"You have just brought me his letter of introduction . . ."

"Oh, Jake. He's well. Lost a lot of cows with tick fever. Haven't seen him this side of six months." Frank Dibbler—it was his *Yanqui* name—stared about the ancient courtyard, then over at Pancho Guzman's equally ancient coach; it stank, of course. In 1867 all coaches stank.

Then he stared into Miguel's eyes. He spoke a coarse, but quite intelligible Spanish.

"*Muchacho*," he said friendlily. And grinned.

The boy bowed. He was twelve years of age and had been very well brought up. "Señor," he said gravely, "I am Miguel de los Sanchez y Sotomayer . . ."

"Do not confuse our guest with your volubility," Don Alonso said. Then with the true courtesy of an *hidalgo*, "Enter my home, señor. Consider it yours."

The man gave him a sidelong glance. Did he doubt his sincerity? He made Miguel's father, who was plump, round and dapper, look very small. He spat the dryness of the ride from Cádiz delicately out of the side of his mouth and said, "Dusty, don't you think?"

12

"Ah," Don Alonso said apologetically, "forgive me. A drink, of course!"

"Tequila?"

It made Miguel's father chuckle. "This is not Mexico. You will find our brandy good."

While Don Alonso read his cousin's letter commending Señor Dibbler they sat in the paneled hall. There was always a fire burning, for even in summer the stones struck chill. The household staff crept obsequiously about. Miguel's mother had died at his birth. There was a senile majordomo to attend to things.

It was the first *Americano* Miguel had ever seen and he studied him intently. He walked oddly, he thought. A slight roll as if a horse moved under his buttocks. His eyebrows and lashes were bleached to the color of straw. His skin somewhat pitted, as if from the abrasive blast of wind and dust. His face very red, but the redness ending sharply at the brim of his hat. Did he eat in it? Sleep in it? And his hands . . . horny and powerful, calloused like a peasant's. This is a hard, maybe cruel, but humorously self-contained man, thought Miguel, who could think like an adult, and I would not like those hands about my throat. It was Señor Dibbler's eyes that affected him most. Very gray, very un-Spanish, they glimmered—except in his ironic moments—like cold wet stone. And always aloof: as if fixed dreamily on something only to be seen in the privacy of his skull.

He wore a short embroidered Mexican jacket and flared trousers that didn't seem to belong: as if he had dressed for a ball at which he wouldn't be at ease. They were terribly out of date. And too small for his bulk. They were split here and there at the seams. Nobody in Seville wore such things anymore. Fashion must take a long time to percolate to Texas, Miguel thought.

Something else about him . . . Miguel leaned forward rather impolitely to sniff. An odd smell. The man was impregnated with it. He would learn in time to come that it was the smell of sagebrush and prairie grass.

13

And suddenly—why?—Miguel heard his father, reading his cousin's letter, give a small gasp. Actually there were two letters, one very formal, recommending Señor Dibbler, the other heavily sealed for Don Alonso's private eye. It was this that caused Don Alonso to stare with incredulity at his guest. Not for a long time would Miguel know what it contained. Don Alonso thought: *Madre de Dios,* but this large *Yanqui* is blunt!

The letter said: "You have no conception of the vastness of this continent, nor of the quality of the men who open it up. Do not expect high Castilian manners in Señor Dibbler. They are not there. He is of the earth, earthy. His father—I do not tell you this to disparage him—was an illiterate backwoods Kentuckian who came into Texas after they stole it from us (and they did, did they not?) to dispossess the Indians violently of their land. His son, this Frank I commend to you, has inherited his ambitious streak and has vastly increased his spread. It is truly colossal. He is the largest landowner in the Panhandle of Texas, and his cows, so I believe, are numberless. Rich—he must be, surely—very rich.

"He is a man of great self-sufficiency. Not of gentle blood, as you may guess: but gentle blood is soon spilled in these harsh plains. It is not a country for delicate men. Do not underestimate him. He is ruthless, I hear. Quick and cruel in vengeance, hard on his *vaqueros,* the cowmen, but curiously gentle with the Indians, perhaps because of conscience: it is their ancient hunting ground he owns.

"Do you know how long it takes to ride round his spread? On a good horse? Three days.

"Now I tell you in confidence why I have referred him to you, my dear cousin. He will make no bones about it with you. His tongue is blunt. He seeks a wife. Why not here, in Texas? The women in this wilderness are rawboned and coarse. I have sought to interest him in one or two of our Mexican gently bred girls, but it is a curious propensity of this arid land that it breeds in women the vestige of a moustache. And bosoms! The bottoms! Alonso, this man has a high taste for the sex, and what

14

he seeks may only be found amongst the angels of paradise. But if you can guide him toward some fertile—and *this* is important!—lady who does not fear a cruel sun and a wild wind in the old Indian prairies . . .

"Yes, what I am trying to tell you is: he requires sons. Many, many! He has illusions of grandeur. He will found a dynasty. So he says.

"How is your dear son, Miguel? Give him my fondest . . ."

But Don Alonso read no further. He stared at Señor Dibbler with raised brows. He found himself twinkling. He smoothed it suddenly from his face. Do not laugh, Alonso; this man probably has a primitive sense of humor. Like Miguel, he was vaguely intimidated by those impassive, wet-stone eyes.

And the smell? Don Alonso was too well-bred to sniff . . . what was it? The tang of the stable? Age-old deposits of unwashed sweat?

Be careful how you address him. Anglo-Saxon stock, of course, with its insane pride of race. Burned like a brick. And probably as hard. A heavy aggressive nose, a mouth that could no doubt tighten to a fleshless trap.

He stole a last glance at the massive hams of his hands, scarred beyond salvation. Don Alonso's hands were very delicate, almost feminine, and beautifully kept.

"Miguel," he said with the lightest hint, "tell the cook that there will be another to lunch." Miguel knew that what was to be discussed wasn't intended for his ears.

"Yes, Father."

"Be sure that she has the four-year-old Alicante chilled. You see, Señor Dibbler," he said cordially, "here we press our wines from our own grapes."

"Sound idea. I eat my beef off our own hoofs."

"You have many?" Cattle, he meant.

Frank Dibbler said placidly, "Enough."

He probably has herds of twenty thousand. He is too modest. This man is some kind of primeval magnate, Don Alonso thought. He waited for Miguel to go, then held his cousin's sealed letter aloft. He didn't know how to begin. "Señor Dibbler," he said diffidently, "my cousin's letter refers to . . ."

"I know what it says. Believe two thirds of it. It's as much truth as you can expect of one man."

"Señor, it contains certain indelicate insinuations . . ."

"They aren't insinuations. They're a cold statement of fact. I'm here to find myself a wife."

Don Alonso stared at him. He said curiously, "Señor, you are not an unattractive man. There must have been many opportunities in your own land . . . !"

"I've had my pick. I've tested myself against them. I know that I work." With that big body and no doubt violent loins, I am sure he does, Don Alonso thought. "I'm not interested in flesh. I want something out of a good stable," Frank Dibbler said.

"One does not go marketing for a wife like a heifer."

"It's what markets are for."

Don Alonso said rather helplessly, "Señor Dibbler, my friend, there is more to marriage than that. You do not think, if you will forgive me, that it is altogether too practical—perhaps too cynical—an approach? One selects a mate for life. There must be a community of interests. Mutual trust and respect." He was getting into very deep water. "Love is a frail flower. One begins with affection. One waits for passion to grow. The holy state of matrimony . . ."

"It's for bedding women," Frank Dibbler interrupted him calmly. "And that's another cold fact."

"Yes." Don Alonso winced. "It is one aspect of it." How brutally he comes to the point. "God help us," he admitted, "we are creatures of our lusts. But there are other aspects. It is for life, as I have just said." At least it was with Catholics, and Don Alonso, a devout son of the church, looked narrowly at the *Americano*, wondering if perhaps . . . but, no, if this prairie brigand had a religion it dwelt in his rigorous and demanding loins.

16

"What is it you have in mind?" Spoken like one cattle-breeder to another.

"I'll know it when I see it."

"Why Spanish?"

"They're fertile."

Ah, coming straight to his cousin's cruel point. He wants sons. Many, many! He will bed the poor woman prolifically. May the Mother of Heaven help her, when she is found.

Don Alonso turned the proposition over in his mind. His immediate instinct was to reject involvement. Too indelicate! Not for gentlemen! Certainly not for the Count of Fuende, Knight of Castile, Grandee First Class of Spain . . . but Don Alonso sometimes had the uneasiest feeling that the rolling titles, which had anyway been purchased in rather sordid commercial circumstances, were a little like a cracked bugle call sounding an old-fashioned cavalry charge. And studying the cool hooded eyes, watching him ironically, he changed his mind. Arranged marriages were as common as rainfall in Spain. It was, indeed, a natural and understandable approach. Women of good birth, shut off by the duenna from the hurly-burly of life, were unfitted to determine their future affairs. Matters of great importance could be involved. Estates to be linked, blood to be suited, dowries agreed. Don Alonso recollected that he himself had only twice set eyes on his dear wife, the late Countess—may she rest in the arms of the angels—before the ink of the marriage settlement was dry. Neither had regretted it. Respect and affection had come with time. She had given him devotion and a good son; what more could one demand of a wife?

He shrugged. His eyes gleamed sympathetically. "Señor," he said, "I will give the matter some thought." Perhaps there is some good widow of reduced means, some healthy woman of middle class—he can hardly expect gentle blood—who will be prepared to launch herself into a wilderness of painted barbarians . . . but a sudden practical thought struck him.

"You understand, señor? I cannot guarantee a dowry?"

17

"Her body'll be her dowry."

"Yes." And again Don Alonso flinched. Dear, dear heaven . . . well, it wasn't where marriages were usually made.

One last point.

"Señor Dibbler—may I call you Francisco?—this is a socially conscious country. You will not be offended? There are certain —well, say, ethnic requirements. Your family . . ."

And Frank Dibbler grinned sulphurously. "It's a mess. Scotch. Dutch. Maybe a dash of Lipan Apache." Apache? What was that? "Indian."

Madre mía. Was this the manure heap of which a great nation was to be made?

Don Alonso said faintly, "Tell nobody, if you have any hope of success." He had none, anyway. "Be advised by me, keep it to yourself. . . . Now let us have lunch. You must be hungry after your stupendous journey."

Four thousand miles? God give the woman courage. I would not go with him if all his cattle had horns of gold.

He retired after lunch for the siesta that was as necessary to him as morning Mass. He was awakened by the sound of voices and the swish of water. He went bewilderedly to the window to peer out. His guest stood dripping in the stable yard, stripped down shockingly to long skin-tight woolen underpants. His son, Miguel, chattering excitedly, wielded the pump. Don Alonso frowned; he could see the women servants giggling at the upper windows. He found himself staring at the brown beefy body. It was even bigger than he'd thought. As the man turned he saw the splash of an old red scar drawn viciously across the brawny back. A bullet? An arrow wound? Don Alonso felt the queerest sense of uneasiness, as if an aborigine had invaded his house.

But he had an obligation to his guest; he was a hospitable man. In the late afternoon, when the heat had gone out of the sky, he had his carriage harnessed for the usual fashionable drive about Seville. Let him see what a civilized city looks like!

18

The lamps had begun to glimmer, the streets thronged with siesta-sated townsfolk come to see the circus parade of the resplendent carriages of the rich. Not all of them rich; the Napoleonic wars had ruined many an ancient family. There was an old Marquesa who starved on cabbage soup so that she could maintain a coach and footmen in style. But Don Alonso didn't have to live on cabbage soup; he was comfortably off and he could afford two postilions to sit on the leading horses. Chic, if somewhat expensive, the carriage bore his coat of arms in gold leaf.

They trotted down the crowded Sierpes, alongside the park-like gardens by the river. The Guadalquivir, unfortunately, smelled a little. Languid hands waved to Don Alonso, teeth flashed. He kissed his fingers in reply. Above them towered the great houses of the nobility, with dark barred balconies where ladies of quality could watch the evening parade without being exposed to vulgar eyes. Don Alonso, with the warm summer breeze on his face, glanced slyly and proudly at his guest. He didn't seem unduly impressed.

The brown face had a sardonic look as if this ancient musty city, crusted with mouldering old churches, affected him like overripe cheese. Perhaps he preferred the Spartan harshness of his native plains? Don Alonso felt piqued. Then he sighed. It *was* old, musty and worn-out; everything had gone out of Spain into the New World, all the virility and passion of the Conquistadores; nothing remained but the dregs of history.

Terrible! Time has passed us by. The future belongs to these raw, half-tamed pioneers, he thought.

There he sat, monstrously large, sprawled on the soft upholstery of the carriage as if he would be more comfortable on the spine of a horse. He needs the civilizing touch of a decent European woman. We must do something to help him. Already Don Alonso was ransacking his mind for candidates. He was no matchmaker, but he had one or two possibilities lined up.

19

The Widow Garcia? No, no. That luxuriant moustache! He remembered his cousin's letter: the man is allergic to feminine moustaches. Doña Alvarado? Too long in the tooth, and built as solidly as a mule behind.

It was the feast of San Isidoro, the patron saint of Seville, and the gardens were packed. A choir of boys from the Cathedral sang in the square. Don Alonso ran his eyes along the chairs, studying the tall mantillas and the fluttering fans, then clicked his fingers to the coachman to stop. "Shall we walk a little?" he suggested to Frank Dibbler. He had something interesting to show him.

"Suits me."

"It will be a pleasure to introduce you to some of my friends."

They strolled by the assembly, Don Alonso wielding his cane to keep off the beggars with the traditional response, "God will provide." He scrutinized the señoritas as he bowed to them, cancelling out this one, considering that. His eyes narrowed. He stopped. "A most especial acquaintance," he whispered to Frank Dibbler. "Permit me to present you to Señorita Lopez," he said aloud, "one of our most distinguished families . . ." Her father was a small city official. A gray little mouse, up she perked, the pale eyes glimmering, the fan suddenly aflutter. She stared strangely at Frank Dibbler's outlandish clothes. Something of a barbarian, I know, Don Alonso thought, but look at his size: a woman would get quite a considerable quantity of man.

He heard her giggle. Pity about the simper; she *is* rather a foolish girl, he mused. But she has a little money. She was accompanied by her duenna, who was experienced in the matrimonial market. He met her eyes significantly, indicating the possibility of the *Americano* at his side.

"Señor Dibbler from Texas," he announced.

The duenna muttered with a disdainful grimace, "A *Yanqui?*" She was quite put out.

A husky chuckle from Frank Dibbler. He knows what I am

up to, Don Alonso thought. I hope he will help things along.

He was disconcerted to hear him say gravely, "Señora, in Texas it could be a shooting sin to call a man that."

Señorita Lopez peered at him. The fan stiffened. "The señor shoots?"

"Only infrequently, señorita."

Another agitated flutter of the fan. Don Alonso couldn't tell if she was alight with interest or unnerved. "I hear it is a most fascinating country," she said.

Frank Dibbler nodded indulgently. "All manner of fascinating things. Coyotes. Rattlers." Rattlesnakes? Don Alonso sighed. He *isn't* trying very hard to help. "And Kiowas," he said.

The duenna asked grimly, "What is a Kiowa?"

"Cousin to a Comanche."

"Savages?"

"We've tamed them a little. Very spirited people; they sometimes fall on a lonely homesteader and burn him out. Play-games mostly. Happens at the full moon," Frank Dibbler said.

It is finished. He has ruined his chance, Don Alonso thought. The duenna glared at him. Señorita Lopez shrank to nothing behind her fan.

"That was most inopportune," he said to Frank Dibbler as they walked on.

Another hoarse chuckle. "Thought I'd made quite an impression."

"You did. If you are so blunt with women you will go to your doom a bachelor," Don Alonso said.

But we will not give up hope. I am a Spaniard, and therefore tenacious. He was chuckling to himself. He was growing humorously intrigued. Something else he recollected in his cousin's letter: *this man has a high taste in sex.* Who hasn't? And what do most of us get? Just what is available in the market, which is better than nothing at all. He drew his guest across the garden; he had caught sight of a candidate that might . . . but he no longer had much heart.

21

"Doña Jerez de la Frontera," he whispered, "and her mother."
He pointed them out.

"Which is which?"

Can he be joking? "The one with the mantilla is the daughter." It was beginning to be hopeless. "It is a good provincial family."

And Don Alonso stopped at the park bench. He said to them graciously, "May I be permitted to present a visitor to Seville? Señor Dibbler from the American States."

Both were dressed in funereal black. The mother was thick, hard and enduring. She had endured two husbands; the daughter, too, was a widow. They came from Galicia where women usually outlasted men. Don Alonso had heard that Galician women were plentifully equipped with sex. He studied them. Either would be pretty sulphurous in bed. They had the same liquid sloe eyes, the quick marriageable glitter. Both are mad for matrimony, he guessed. The daughter cannot be more than thirty. He wondered pensively how much money she had.

Keep your fan up, Doña Jerez, he thought; do not let him see the warts on your chin.

She said coquettishly behind the fan, "The boys sing well, señor, do they not?"

Frank Dibbler glanced at them. They sang as sexlessly as sparrows. "I find them edifying," he said.

"You have visited our wonderful Cathedral?" Both women were great churchgoers.

He bowed. *Muy caballero.* "I have been here only a few hours. I am obsessed with the desire to see it. I shall not rest until I have seized an opportunity," he said. His Spanish was rough-edged, but with what Castilians called *gracia:* a nice decorous turn of phrase. It surprised Don Alonso. Where had he learned it?

"The señor favors our city with a long visit?" Doña Jerez's mother asked.

22

"Perhaps a week. Long enough to transact the business I have in mind," Frank Dibbler said.

Is that what he calls it? Business? Don Alonso was standing behind him. He raised his eyebrows discreetly to Doña Jerez's mother in a way that suggested: he is available. He saw both women's faces flash with interest.

"My mother and I would be delighted to show you our lovely churches," Doña Jerez said.

"You are too good."

"My uncle has a nephew in El Paso. You know it?"

"Intimately. It is a town of fascinating possibilities. I have a woman there," Frank Dibbler said.

The silence froze: it broke with the tinkle of ice as Doña Jerez's mother gasped. She could hardly believe her ears.

She said in a high voice, "The señor means a wife? You said a—?"

"Woman. We Texans are a lusty deprived race of men. It is lonely on the range. I go to El Paso to buy cattle, but cows are no solution to a man's pressing need."

She stared at him thunderously. "Señor, such language is not fit for my daughter's delicate ears . . ."

"Forgive me. I am unused to refined company. It is another unfortunate aspect of Texans. They are notoriously loose-tongued."

But Doña Jerez's mother made a falsetto sound. The daughter had already retired behind the fan. "Come," Don Alonso said, touching his guest's arm. He has dished his opportunity, he thought.

When they had gone some distance he said with a sigh, "Señor Dibbler, it seems that I am wasting my time."

"Don't say that. Keep trying."

"You are not mocking me?"

"I haven't come all this way to make fun of a generous man."

"What exactly is it you want?"

"I told you. I'll know it when I see it."

23

"Señor Francisco, my friend," Don Alonso said sincerely, "I fear that what you seek is not to be found this side of paradise."

"Could be so. I'm not the kind of man to be satisfied with second best."

Then you will have to make do with the women of El Paso, Don Alonso thought. He was done with the business. His cousin Jaquindo would be told sternly that it wasn't conducive to the dignity of an *hidalgo* of Spain. They had come round by the Cathedral. A grave, elderly gentleman had just issued from the great doors, accompanied by the archbishop. He stooped to kiss the Apostolic ring with the faintest air of condescension. Alonso went forward with a genial cry, "Luis."

It was the Duke of Estremadura. He waved back carelessly. "Ah, Alonso." He descended the steps. He moved with a stiff, erect back as if he had just removed his breastplate. What a pity the doublet and ruff had gone out, Alonso mused; they were made for him. He looked exactly like Velasquez's painting of his ancestor at the court of Philip II. His six sons followed him at a respectful two paces, like a feudal assembly. Good blood persists, Alonso thought; the family resemblance was remarkable. They even walked with the same stiff gait.

A shabby coach, its lacquer cracked, waited for them at the foot of the steps. The family was impoverished, of course; Alonso could buy them out without feeling the pinch. The crest emblazoned on the coach, unlike Alonso's rather garish adornment, was unobtrusive. The Dukes of Estremadura had no need to advertise themselves.

"It all went very well," the Duke said. Alonso suddenly remembered: it was the rehearsal for tomorrow's christening of the Duke's first grandson. "Alonso, you should have been there."

"You will forgive me. I had a duty to my guest," Alonso said. He acknowledged the range of sons, one by one, from eldest to youngest, like a schoolmaster mechanically checking in a class.

"Esteban." He was the father of the new arrival who would one day inherit the dukedom. I fear he has come into a world that will not think much of titles, Alonso thought. "Pedro. Bernardo. Philip. Jesús. Tomás." They bowed to him, but not too extravagantly.

Alonso was no upstart; one of his forebears had had money in Columbus's first voyage. But the Dukes of Estremadura went back into the dim history of Spain. They had helped drive out the Moors. They claimed to stem from the paternal root of El Cid.

"But you will be there tomorrow, Alonso?"

"Nothing will prevent me, Luis," Alonso said. He glanced about. One of the family was missing. Maria, the only daughter, the Condesa de Rojas. The title, especially granted by Queen Isabella, continued through the female line. "Where is Maria?"

A shadow crossed the Duke's face. He said stiffly, "She is indisposed." If that was the word for it. A difficult girl. No, a woman . . . at twenty-six, in Spain, girlhood was a long way behind. Probably on the shelf for good. *Por Dios,* Alonso thought ruefully, that tongue of hers. Volcanic!

He said tactfully, "I hope she will soon be well," thinking: she will be cured only when they stop up her mouth.

Then he saw the Duke gazing over his shoulder at Frank Dibbler. "Alonso," he said courteously, "you have not presented your friend."

Alonso hesitated. "Forgive me." He was in a quandary. He knew the Duke's aversion to *Americanos.* "Señor Dibbler," he said in a clear voice, adding in a mutter he was sure nobody heard, "from Amarillo." Then turning to Frank Dibbler, "It is my pleasure to present you to the Duke of Estremadura."

"Yes," he heard Frank Dibbler say gently. "My father knew him. They met."

Alonso's mind stammered: *What?* How could that be?

"We did?" The Duke gave Frank Dibbler a curious look.

"At shooting distance. I have a small parcel of land you once owned. About a hundred thousand acres."

The Duke continued to stare at him. "Where are you from, Señor?"

"North of Amarillo."

"Texas?" Everything was suddenly electric. Ah, Alonso sighed. It was such a long time ago. And they still remember. The Duke's eyes flashed. "Señor," he said fiercely, "I still own that land."

"Not now. Mine by right of possession. All registered in the land office of Santa Fe."

Alonso saw Esteban's eyes glint. The sons moved forward with hostility. Estremaduran blood, he thought; it bubbles at the drop of a hat.

"Señor," the Duke cried, "those estates were granted to my forefathers in perpetuity by the King of Spain . . ."

"Who took it from the Indians. Sets a nice legal precedent, don't you think?"

The Duke composed himself with an effort. "Esteban, stand back." The sons retreated. He was quite pale. "No matter." He shrugged. "It is all over now," he said. The family had also owned vast acreages in Mexico, and when Juárez had shot the Hapsburg Maximilian they had been lost, too. Everything gone! He said wryly, still staring palely into Frank Dibbler's face, "You live well off the land, señor?"

"I eat. I have cattle. I have something else. Oil."

The Duke frowned. "Olive groves? I remember none. They take a long time to mature . . ."

"Mineral oil. Under the earth."

"Ah, that foulness in the creeks," the Duke recollected. "It stinks. It poisons the cattle."

"It won't poison me. It'll make me rich."

The Duke sighed. He said grimly, "You are the guest of my friend, Don Alonso. I bear you no ill will, señor." He beckoned to his sons to follow. "You are welcome to Seville."

26

He waited for a moment, stiff-backed and imperious, looking expectantly at Frank Dibbler, but nothing happened, just a small indifferent nod. He shrugged again and led his sons into the coach. They sat in it as frozenly as waxworks, cruelly beaten down by fate. Alonso watched them drive off.

"Francisco, my friend," he said reproachfully, "when a duke leaves you are supposed to do something."

"What?"

"Well, bow."

"I nodded."

"It isn't the same thing." A primitive. He is lost to civilization, Alonso thought. He stared at him pensively. He suddenly twinkled. "Francisco," he said, "what is your religion?"

"I'm an honest man."

Alonso had met priests who weren't that religious. "Would you care to come to the Cathedral in the morning? It will be an impressive christening." It might even reclaim a hardened heretic . . . no, it would take more than a sonorous ceremony to do that.

Anyway, he expected him to refuse. But Frank Dibbler chuckled. "Might be amusing."

Alonso winced. "Francisco, the acceptance of a young soul into the bosom of Holy Church is not . . ."

"I'll still come."

"At ten. Very well." They walked back to the carriage. The dusk was purple. The lamps glowed like fireflies; a chapel bell tolled. It affected Alonso deeply. The choir boys were still singing in the square, the ancient Latin hymn *Mens humilis, vita quieta* . . .

Humility of mind, a quiet life. The recipe for a gentleman, Alonso thought. He looked sidelong at Frank Dibbler. His face was dreamy. Had he been religiously moved, too?

"Goddamn it. Absentee landlords. They pity themselves," he said. "My father was a Kentuckian." So Jaquindo had said. "Rode into Texas in '37. Broke up the sod, grew a little, starved a little. Bled more than a little, too. Fought off the Indians. I got powder burns before I was ten. Then ran a few cattle and opened up the range. He worked the land. Loved it. Died for it. I buried him in it with my own hands." Alonso stared at him. He was afraid to open his mouth. "He was a hard man. And I'm harder," Frank Dibbler said. "I *use* the land. That's custodian-ship. That's the possession that counts." Would he spit? He spat. "Not by some far-off Spanish grandee who never dripped sweat over a plow, never slept a night on the range."

Do not underestimate him, Jaquindo had said; he is a ruth-less man, and here it was displayed. The dour luminous face intimidated Alonso. He took off his beaver hat. The sweatband was wet.

Frank Dibbler suddenly grinned. "Something wrong, Alonso?"

"Nothing."

"You ever rode a cow pony until your balls were sore?"

"Never." Maybe that was why the *Americanos* had the land, and not the King of Spain. He muttered, "It is terrible to hear you say such things . . ."

"We're different animals, Alonso."

"Yes." God be thanked. Alonso took a deep breath; it was as if he'd patted a friendly brown bear and felt the quick snap of its teeth. They reached the carriage and drove silently back.

That night he had a fearsome dream. At first all he was con-scious of was space. Space of a vastness that was incomprehen-sible to his cramped European mind. The loneliness of it hurt like a wound. There was almost no sound, just the sad breath of a hot wind that blew steadily from the west. It trundled a kind of tumbleweed ahead of it like a child's hoop, and in the eye of his dream it went rolling on and on over the edge of the world.

There was a familiar smell to it, too—the tang of prairie and sagebrush he had smelled in Frank Dibbler. Alonso was very conscious of this in his dream.

28

The land was all burned up, a gray-green arid plain, and dust —dust, *por el amor de Dios!* It clouded the sun.

Hot, hot, hot. In the shimmering distance were canyons with weird rock formations, tall chimneys and eroded spires poking into the bitter blue sky.

Then—still tossing in his dream—he saw a squat figure come dragging out of the alkali dust, a flat-faced, reddish, bowlegged man. Of an incredible squalor. A tattered blanket and a breech-cloth. He had nothing but a mangy pony, as hollow-bellied as he was, and on he went, that Indian, vanishing hopelessly like a phantom into the emptiness of the plain.

And suddenly it all changed. The wind came blowing from a different direction, and now it was a blaster: a vicious north-easter that ripped the sagebrush out of the ground. What was it sheltering in the gulches? Cattle. Exactly like the cattle Alonso knew in Spain; long-horned, unspeakably bad-tempered, and there they huddled, bellowing hatefully into the wind.

It was a terrible land, a cruel land, and Alonso just wanted to escape it, but for some strange reason he knew that it had him trapped. He shouted out of his dream, "No, no, I will not . . ." and then, dry-mouthed, full of apprehension, he woke up.

A nightmare! It had been so real. He got up and washed his mouth out with wine. He was sweating. He was afraid to go back to sleep in case he should dream it again.

But he felt better when he arose. He drove with Frank Dibbler to the Cathedral after breakfast. He eyed him half-fondly. He didn't know why he liked him. Perhaps because he got on so well with Miguel, who sat chattering with him in the carriage. Alonso looked again at his outlandish unfashionable clothes. It would be a very distinguished gathering, with the Bishop of Seville anointing the child. The entire social register would be there. Everybody dressed up to kill! He would have offered to loan Frank Dibbler one of the latest frock coats with black silk facings and a gray beaver hat, but nothing he possessed would remotely fit him. Big, big!

"Miguel," he reproved his son softly, "do not bother our guest."

"Father, did you know that mustangs bite like dogs . . ."

"You are not likely to ride one." Miguel had a gentle Spanish barb of impeccable ancestry. "You will talk Señor Dibbler's head off."

"Had a pony that did that, too. Talked my head off." Frank Dibbler grinned. "Horse-language."

I am prepared to believe it. Anything is possible in that outrageous country, Alonso thought.

They were a little late. They could hardly get into the Cathedral. They had to cram themselves behind a pillar; they could just see the Duke's family gathered importantly about the font. The service would be as prolonged and sonorous as semiroyalty deserved. The dresses of the women, a little daring with today's mode, sparkled; the nave was a forest of tall mantillas. Gold-braided uniforms slashed the religious gloom. The Virgin watched them. Alonso stared at the dust-laden sculptures, the vast interior streaked with light from the glorious windows. It uplifted his soul. He glanced at Frank Dibbler, hoping to see him begrudgingly affected too. He stood there: stony-faced and cynical? Disdainful of the long cultural heritage of Europe.

Give him a mustang that bit! That talked to him in horse-language!

Alonso very nearly gave him up.

The wail of the baby interrupted his thoughts. The bundle of lace, protesting feebly, was passed from the Bishop's hands, held up, sprinkled and sung over in Latin. Another generation, another duke to perpetuate the long line from El Cid. Then Alonso was conscious of a stillness at his side. Ten seconds ago he had felt Frank Dibbler fidget . . . he peered into his face, following his narrowed eyes.

He was staring directly across the nave at the six Estremadu-

30

ran sons. Why should he. . . ? And then Alonso corrected his glance. It was Maria, the Duke's daughter, he was watching; she had been temporarily hidden by Esteban, her brother. Alonso studied her, too. Tall. That slightly molten mixture of olive skin and black eyes and unnaturally sleek golden hair. A throwback to some ancestral Goth from the Rhine. The face spoiled by the arch of the brows and the sulkiness of the mouth. It seemed to Alonso to be permanently pursed to spit. Her fan restlessly active. She was watching the baby impassively. Time she had a couple herself. And then her attention strayed. She caught Frank Dibbler's stare—strangely and vulgarly intent— over the heads of the crowd.

Alonso thought: he must control the frankness of his expression. It is not proper to study a lady with such brutal candor. She thinned her eyes to a glare. Then muttered to herself. Up went the fan. She shut him out of existence. But his stare didn't waver by a degree . . . he waited for the fan to dip. Her eyes wandered back. She reddened. The lovely sullen mouth tightened.

Alonso saw her whisper offendedly to her brother Tomás. She directed his glance. He looked across. His face grew angry. He whispered back. He is telling her who the *Americano* is, Alonso thought. Her face, for the briefest moment, was startled. Then enraged. Oh, Mother of Heaven . . . not in church. He was afraid of a disturbance. Her glance was pure malevolence now.

"Francisco, my friend," Alonso murmured to him, "I beg of you. Look away."

"Why?"

"It is embarrassing to . . ."

"Who is she?"

"The Condesa de Rojas."

"What's she doing with that crowd?"

"She belongs to it. The Duke is her father."

"Ah." Chuckling? Alonso tried to nudge him out of sight behind the pillar. He was as unbudgeable as a rock.

31

"Francisco, for the last time, will you avert your glance? You are annoying her."

"Nobody ever got bitten by a look."

"You are examining her like a heifer."

Laughing again. Softly. "Yes." The service was almost over. The baby was blessed; the Duke lifted it high, exhibiting it like a candidate for sainthood; suitably exalted, they all began to pour out of the Cathedral into the glare of the sun. The prelates, the vivid mantillas, the high officers of Spain. Alonso elbowed Miguel and his guest through them, and stood blinking on the steps. He had the feeling that he was about to be hideously embarrassed in front of his friends. He glanced at Frank Dibbler. As imperturbable as an iceberg. "Miguel," he muttered. "Hurry. Find Emilio with the carriage . . ." Too late. Maria had emerged with her brother Tomás. He was the youngest of them, and therefore the most arrogant. Alonso looked at his elegant clothes, thinking: when you have paid your tailor, you can afford to stick your nose into the air. But Maria was sweeping forward.

"Miguel." She smiled at him faintly.

He was a delicately brought up boy. He bowed. "I hope you are well, Doña Maria?"

"Never better." Not a glance for Frank Dibbler. He might have been thin air; Alonso wished he was. "Don Alonso." She dipped her mantilla to him. There was nothing demure about her. She touched her lips to his cheek, whispering as she did so, "Get the animal out of my sight."

"Maria, I forbid you to . . ."

"Can you not see? He is undressing me with his eyes."

Alonso sweated. "He is my guest."

"I would have expected you to show better taste." She is off, he thought. It is going to be quite sickening. She let herself look at Frank Dibbler. She no longer cared who heard. "Is this the land-robber?"

"You forget yourself, Maria. You are talking like a slut."

"I have to suit myself to your company." Everybody was listening. The Cathedral bells had stopped. The silence was awful; it seemed to Alonso that his ears were plugged with cottonwool. She raked Frank Dibbler with her eyes. "So this is the *vaquero* who thinks he has the right to squat on our estates."

He was something more than a mere *vaquero*, a cowherdsman. Anybody who owned the two-million-acre spread mentioned in Jaquindo's letter was a feudal baron in his own right.

She called out to him, "Thief! When are you going to pay my father the rents you owe him?"

He will surely strike her. But Alonso heard a soft sound; it surprised him. Frank Dibbler was watching her appraisingly. He *is* undressing her with his eyes, Alonso thought. He heard him say mildly, "Let him come and collect them. Do better than that. Come and collect them yourself."

"Fetch them round to our tradesmen's entrance. We will set the dogs on your tail."

"Little old for those tantrums, aren't you?"

God, Alonso thought agonizedly, let me sink into the ground. It startled her. She hissed, "You dare to . . ."

"Something wrong with you, is there? Or isn't your husband man enough to keep you in line?"

She whipped him across the face with her fan. The blades splintered. It left no more than a faint white mark; the weathered skin had suffered worse from the dust blasts of the prairie. He did nothing. Alonso trembled with shock. He muttered, "Come away from her, I beg of you," but Tomás was about to intervene. That eighteen-year-old *hidalgo*. He was furious. His honor had been touched. He raised his hand to . . .

It was tweaked suddenly in Frank Dibbler's large hand. Alonso had never seen anything move so fast. "Not from you, boy," he heard him murmur. "Get some hair on your face first. Don't twist or I'll crack a bone." Tomás cried out with pain. "Your neck, too, if I have to," and Alonso knew with the deadliest certainty that, somewhere and sometime, Frank Dibbler

33

had cracked a neck. He grew limp with relief to see Esteban issue from the Cathedral, carrying his firstborn, followed by the Duke.

The civilized old face stiffened. He stared distressfully at the stub of the fan blades in his daughter's hand. "Maria. Have you shamed yourself?"

"He is insufferable."

"And you? With that scorpion's tongue? Into the coach."

She bridled; but nobody defied a Duke of Estremadura. She flounced with a swirl of her wide embroidered skirt and descended to the family coach.

"No skin broken. Nothing to make a fuss over," Frank Dibbler said.

The Duke stared at him. It seemed that a ghost had come out of the past to haunt him. He said tiredly, "Señor, I beg of you, relieve us of your company."

"Don't mind."

"If you have been affronted . . ."

"I haven't."

"So much the better. Don Alonso, oblige me by departing with your guest."

They drove off. Alonso couldn't bring himself to speak. It was Frank Dibbler who triggered off the conversation. Totally unmoved.

"Who's her husband?"

"What husband?"

Sidelong glance. "Why isn't there one? A little overripe for spinsterhood in Spain, wouldn't you think?"

"You have just had an exhibition of her tongue. What man could endure it?"

"Oh, that," Frank Dibbler said casually. "Nothing that a hard brush on her butt wouldn't cure."

"She would tear your heart out."

But he must have iron ribs to protect it. And he would probably break her wrist, as—Alonso was sure of it—he would have

34

broken Tomás's without compunction a few moments ago.

"Rich, are they?" Would he never let go?

"The family? Poor as church mice."

"Keep their noses pretty high in the air for paupers."

"It is where their noses have been for six hundred years."

And that ended the conversation.

Alonso was too shaken to enjoy his siesta. He was roused, as before, by a commotion of hoofs and voices in the stable yard. He went fretfully to the window to peer out. Frank Dibbler was cantering one of the horses about the cobbles. He sat hunched in the saddle: loose as a bag of corn, without dignity, but relaxed as if set to ride effortlessly all day. It was a spirited Arab barb, unaccustomed to a strange hand, eyes rolling and saliva dripping from its mouth. But he gentled it about the yard, letting it feel the bit. It accepted him tremulously. Miguel watched with awe. Frank Dibbler got down and heaved him into the saddle.

Alonso lay back on his couch. This is a strange and disconcerting animal, he thought. We do not know his kind. All has grown settled in Europe; there is no more pioneering to be done. But this breed of *Americano* has skipped back two centuries. They have peeled off the veneer of civilization like an onion skin; it has left them rough, much brutalized, but wondrously vital. They still have a few more voids to fill up. Deserts. Mountains. God knows what. And only God knows what they will do with them. We are lucky to be separated from them by three thousand miles of ocean, he thought.

He tried to doze. He couldn't. He was beginning to relent. I like him. Why? *Santo Dios!* He is a rather inhibiting creature, his manners lamentable. But who can blame him? He has had nobody to teach him but illiterate Kentuckians and Mexican *vaqueros.* I still like him. I will take him firmly in hand, he thought.

There is a cousin of mine in Pamplona. Nice girl, small dowry, but acquiescent. We will make a match of it!

He watched him over dinner. That gargantuan appetite! He ate as if stocking up against seven lean years of famine. Presently he said to his son, "Miguel, if you will . . ."

"You wish to talk business, Father?"

A kind of business. Of a delicate nature. Miguel left the table. Alonso offered his guest a noble Havana cigar. "I like my own," he said, offering in return a black Mexican cheroot. Both lit up. It hissed like tinder; as the ember curled round the potent leaf it made a spitting sound. A light sweat broke out on Alonso's face. He put it down.

"Francisco," he began, "you must let me apologize for the fracas outside the Cathedral. You are not the first to have suffered from her. No matter. I have given your affairs more thought. There is a tender girl in Pamplona . . ."

"Kind of you to bother. But I've seen what I want."

"She has a nice little . . ." and then Frank Dibbler's words caught up with him. "You *have?* Where?"

"You were there."

"Francisco, I am mystified . . ." and finally he understood. He was too choked to speak. "The Doña Maria? You must be out of your mind."

"Why so?"

"She is unattainable."

"To me?"

"Of course to you." Alonso felt himself growing both agitated and confused. Impossible! However painful, he had to voice the truth. "Do not be offended. But you are flying too high. She is far above you . . ."

"No one's above me." His voice quite rough.

"Her family is amongst the noblest in Spain . . ."

And Frank Dibbler interrupted him coarsely, "But Spain isn't all that much. It's a new world. Going to be a new nobility." *This* is the new nobility? Alonso stared at him. "Fifty years from now you won't know where to look for the Dukes of Estremadura in their musty tombs."

36

Alonso thought: mad, mad, mad. His arrogance is monumental. He didn't want to hurt him. "Francisco, my friend, you must forgive me, but she will spit at you."

"I know." He was grinning. "She can have the first spit. I'll duck the second. Third time—I'll let her have it back."

Alonso had to fortify himself with a whole glass of manzanilla. He was so confused that he absently relit Frank Dibbler's black cheroot. The sulphurous leaf hissed at him; and like a woman—just like Maria—it too spat.

II

HE WOKE in the morning thinking: suddenly I am tickled. It was an ungracious thought to have before going to Mass, but he'd fallen asleep chuckling. He woke with the same sly anticipation. I would like to see the end of this affair, he thought. Somebody—and he knew who it would be—would soon be wiping saliva off his face.

My poor Francisco! Well, he would recover from the rebuff. The world was filled with available women as the sea was filled with fish.

Before leaving for chapel with Miguel he said to Frank Dibbler—already eating breakfast, the heretic—"Francisco, I shall be visiting my nephew's bull farm after Mass. He breeds some of the best animals for the ring. It may turn out to be an interesting experience." In more ways than one. He knew that the Estremaduran family, who were fervent *aficionados*, would be there; the *fiesta nacional*, the season of the great bullfights, would open next week. "Would it please you, do you think? Or would you rather visit our fine old churches . . ."

"Sooner see the steers."

38

Alonso recoiled fastidiously. "They are not steers. They are fighting bulls."

"Cows or steers. Come visit Texas. You'll see how our long-horns fight."

Alonso had an almost religious feeling for the mystique of the bull. The cult obsessed him. The archaic spectacle of the *corrida de toros* moved him more violently than the act of sex; the bullring was the bed in which—as for most Spaniards—his manhood was sublimated. He was a rich man. It was his pleasure to sponsor a couple of promising young fighters—as in distant years to come his son, Miguel, would sponsor a baseball team in Kansas. But that astonishing prospect was hidden from him in the seeds of time.

Bullfighting, as Alonso knew deep in his bones, was not a sport, and therefore could not be regarded as cruel. It was an act of dedication. A ritual. Barbarous perhaps; but religious in origin, springing from the gladiatorial contests the Romans had bequeathed to Spain. The killing of the bull, to him, was not a sadistic thing, but a swelling of pride and passion: the passion of virility, and respect for a not ignoble death. The Spaniard had a strong stomach. He looked down in a transport of spiritual ecstasy at the traditional parade of the matadors in their dazzling capes, followed by the mule-team that would presently drag *Señor Toro*, dripping blood sacrificially, across the sand. The opening act of the drama caught at the throat.

That was when Alonso, normally the most civilized of men, suffered the *furia español*.

He was back early from Mass. He took his time over dressing; it would be both an important and festive occasion. The best Castilian blood would be there to give *cachet* to the bulls. He surveyed himself in the mirror: flat black hat, embroidered coat, tailored for him in Cádiz, slitted behind for the saddle, the softest leather high-heeled boots. And silver spurs. His cravat was impeccable. He went in to look Miguel over. A credit to him. And then they went downstairs.

39

Frank Dibbler was already there. He lounged sleepily outside the horse boxes. He wore a loose woolen shirt, bleached to no recognizable color, and heavy cord pants. His spurs were metallic implements, no more. A highly practical form of dress, no doubt familiar in Amarillo, but painfully without style. Alonso wished he'd warned him; but I cannot insult him by offering him the pick of my wardrobe, which wouldn't fit him anyway, he thought. He had already saddled a mare, the least decorative of the stable. What had made him choose it? A hard, rawboned beast, disconcertingly hairy, a pinto. She would go to the glue factory next year.

"Francisco," he said kindly, "I am sure you would prefer a nice Arab gelding . . ."

"She'll do."

"She is not very pretty."

"I'm not very pretty, either." He heaved himself into the saddle. He was instantly at home. He used his knees absently to guide the mare. He rode as if he could slip into a nap without falling off. He will arouse much derisive comment. I will have to think of some discreet explanation for my friends, Alonso thought.

It was growing hot. Cactus grew like pulpy green cardboard at the roadside. They trotted along, giving the farm carts a wide berth. Why, Alonso wondered, does Spain raise the most evil-smelling mules in the world? But the oranges looked inviting. He saw Frank Dibbler reach up, almost without waking, to pick one off. Now the road was thickening up with the fashionable carriages making for the bull-breeding ranch.

During winter the great herds wandered loose on the plain—fattening up for the dramatic death that awaited them in the hallowed sand. This was the country of that most noble animal, the Andalusian bull. A violent, jet-black blast of rage, all head and horns. Alonso's blood began to stir. They cantered into the corral. Already it was crowded with mounted spectators. For those who wished to observe the beasts in comparative safety there were slitted stone walls, furnished with wooden seats. Behind these protective palisades the breeders studied them like butchers.

"*Me gusta el negro!*" That's a fine piece of meat. A killer!

But the *toreros,* some of them famous, almost unrecognizable without the theatrical costume, stared at them with dark anxiety. Which of them might gore them this season? Kill them, even? Fearsome profession! But it isn't a profession; it's a priesthood, Alonso thought.

The bulls had been turned loose. They stood in sleepy groups in the grassy arena, watching the few jumpy heifers. The female of the species had been sent amongst them to stimulate them. No sex happened. Much too hot. The *garrochistas,* the herdsmen, wearing floppy sombreros, had to go galloping amongst them with wooden lances to stir them up.

They were the ones who had gone out with Cortés to stock Mexico with cows. They were the forerunners of the Western cowboy. Alonso saw Frank Dibbler watching them intently; he recognized the ancestry, of course.

And the *hidalgos* sat their horses in the shade of the trees like Roman senators watching the games. They discussed the bulls with the freedom of the knacker's yard. Bad lot this year! No *cojones.* No majesty in the hairy prick of sex. Where are the iron horns that can impale a horse?

The bull that had the hardihood to go for them would spill the bluest of Sevillian blood.

More of it had just arrived. Maria and her six brothers swept into the corral, a right royal entrance. Esteban, Pedro, Bernardo . . . but Alonso couldn't be bothered to identify them. The old Duke had given his wife, now relieved of his ardor in heaven, a busy sexual life. They rode good horses. The stable ate up the dregs of their estate. Tailors could wait for their money . . . but horses had to be fed. Maria reined up with a snort of foam. She rode her mare, as she rode everybody, hard.

"Don Alonso."

"You look well, Maria."

As she did. The wind had fanned her face pink. Full-breasted. Somebody, for her own sake, mused Alonso, should give her a busy sexual life. The black eyes sparkled. But the heavy red mouth was pursed.

She looked through Frank Dibbler. He was empty air, no, earth. She wrinkled her nose as if he smelled.

She said gaily, "Do the bulls please you, Don Alonso?"

"Second-rate lot, I fear. I fancy none of them."

"Nor I your friend." She was off again. She cocked her bold eyes at Frank Dibbler. "So you are still here, *hombre?*"

Hombre. Alonso sighed. She was getting ready to insult him. Frank Dibbler watched her sleepily. "Still here," he said. He had better wake up.

"But you will not delay your departure too long, I trust?"

He sat his ungainly piebald nag; it was hard to tell which of them was more impassive. "I will be gone when I have secured what I have come for," he said.

She was curious. She gave him a sharp look. "And what is that?"

"Woman, be patient." Woman. He could answer back. "Time will answer your questions."

What was he staring at? Her jacket was too tight for her bosom. Alonso followed his eyes. He wished he wouldn't.

She bit her lip. She was losing her composure. "Have you come to steal our bulls as you stole our land?"

"I see nothing worth stealing. Your bulls are feebler than our Texan cows."

"Watch your manners, *peón.*"

Peasant. Alonso felt faint. The dialogue was getting to be sultry. "And you your tongue." Frank Dibbler slipped into the Castilian *gracia* that didn't sound particularly gracious in his mouth. "God grant your father a quick release from it. It must be a sore trial to him," he said.

Was he laughing? Alonso was sure of it. He heard Tomás make a choked sound. He and Bernardo spurred forward an-

42

grily, but Esteban—who was now a father, with some sense of responsibility—shoved his horse between them and muttered, "Get back." Maria, less controllable, was trying to do what Alonso had told Frank Dibbler to expect. Her mouth was too dry to spit into his face.

"Francisco," he begged, "do not let her . . ." but he was still staring. Alonso fidgeted. He *must* stop looking at her breasts! He was suddenly startled to see him shift his glance reflectively to Esteban, then to Bernardo, then Pedro . . . one by one, as if numbering them off. Was that why he was interested in her? All those brothers? And the breasts! The fertility symbol?

He wants many, many sons, Jaquindo's letter had said.

The Duke, heaven be thanked, came cantering across. He called out sternly, "Maria. Esteban. Over into the trees, boys." He had seen enough. Maria whirled her horse about with a frustrated gasp and made for the aristocratic assembly in the shade of the trees.

Tomás said in a furious voice, "He is offensive, Father."

"He is an *Americano.*" As if that excused it. Tomás and his brothers rode off. The Duke said in an exhausted voice, "Señor, I wish I could find you welcome." He was angry with him; he was angry with Maria, too. How had he borne her so long? He trotted off after his family. Alonso felt sorry for him.

"Francisco," he said reproachfully, "you must watch your tongue."

"Never have. Never will."

"This is Spain. We are an inflammable race. Easily affronted. Our great old families . . ."

"Old doesn't make them great." Frank Dibbler suddenly grinned. Irreverently. He was eying the retreating Duke. "My father told me he came lording it over our land. Long, long time ago. My old man could have put a bullet between his eyes, easier than spitting." Only spitting wasn't the word he used. "He just shot his hat off. Fancy big beaver. I wonder if he still has it. He never came back."

I have brought a half-tamed bear into our midst, Alonso

43

thought. He glanced about. The bulls were dozing. A poor bunch this season, a fine spread of horns, but no fire seething in the balls. He doubted if they were worth putting into the ring. Miguel had gone to join his friends. He could see the Duke sitting on his horse solitarily under the trees. He looked stricken. He had removed himself from his family. Alonso guessed that he had had words with Maria. He felt that he must apologize to him. "Francisco," he said, "if you can amuse yourself for a few moments . . ." and he spurred across the field.

He was turning something rather dangerous over in his mind. It might resolve two problems. Why not? He would have to be terribly delicate about it. "Luis," he said to the Duke as he came up, "do not be too sad . . ."

"How many daughters have you?"

"Eh?" None, for which he never ceased to thank God.

"Or one like Maria? What have I done to deserve such a cross?"

"She is a spirited girl."

"She is a monster of self-will. Nothing bends her. Where is the humility a woman should have? I sometimes think I am doing penance for some crime I cannot recall."

"When she marries . . ."

"Alonso, do not pour salt into my wounds. Who will marry her? The cadets of the great families look for money. I have none for her. You are aware of our condition. She is not ill-favored; but they all know her temper . . ."

"She needs a man."

The Duke glanced sidelong at Alonso. "In bed?" He was a practical Spaniard. "Of course." He grinned wryly. "It would be a battlefield, my friend."

With one of them wounded. Or maybe dead. "The bulls are very sleepy today." To change the subject.

"Everything in Spain has gone bad."

"We have transferred our vitality to the Americas," Alonso said. Now he was edging the subject toward the objective he had in mind. He saw the Duke frown sternly across at Frank

44

Dibbler; he seemed to have fallen asleep on his ungainly nag at the far end of the field. He looked lonely. Nobody approached him. He had no friends in this noble assembly.

"You did me no service, Alonso, when you brought this man to Seville."

"I did not bring him. Jaquindo, my cousin, sent him."

"He has opened up a scar I thought long-healed." The Mexican estates, of course. But Texas was no longer Mexican. It was a law unto itself. The Duke lowered his voice. "He is something of a boor, is he not, Alonso?"

"It is a raw country. It has its own kind of magnate."

"*Magnate*, you said?"

"He is a colossal landowner."

"No doubt," the Duke said. His mouth twisted. "With my hundred thousand acres . . ."

"The smallest part of it. Jaquindo tells me that he has a spread of two million."

The Duke's head moved slowly about. It was so hard to absorb. "Did I hear you say two million?"

"More perhaps. There are no fences on the range."

The Duke's voice was oddly awed. "But it is almost a province in itself."

"You know how long it takes to ride round his domain? On a good horse? Three days."

"*Por Dios!*"

"You have been there. It is a vast land. And empty. A man, if he can hold it, takes what he needs." And Frank Dibbler, Alonso thought, could hold it.

The Duke was watching him with different eyes. How small Spain was! And how huge the Americas. What a prize to have lost!

"He is a boor," Alonso admitted. "Of course." But so was Tomás. So was Pedro. High-handed boors. Maria was a fishwife; one could imagine her screeching abuse across the wharf at Cádiz. "Señor Dibbler is probably the product of four generations of raw pioneers. Emigrants leave the soft arts of

45

culture behind them. I would guess that his father could neither read nor write." But he could shoot! Alonso's mouth twitched. He didn't want the Duke to see. He could imagine the shock of that bullet drilling a neat hole through the crown of his hat. No wonder he never went back.

"But times have changed, Luis," he went on persuasively. "One has to yield socially where important alliances are concerned."

The Duke still didn't understand what he was talking about. He shrugged.

Very well, then. To the point. "The fortunes of your family were founded six hundred years ago when one of your women married the Count of El Tarif."

"Alonso," the Duke sighed, "I am aware of the history of my house . . ."

"He was nothing but an Algerian pirate. No better than Señor Dibbler." And probably much worse. "He is interested in Maria."

"What are you trying to tell me?"

"Señor Dibbler is prepared to have her."

And Alonso was startled to see the Duke's face grow quite white. "Are you out of your mind?" He hissed, "Do you think I would permit a daughter of Estremadura to ally herself to a vulgar *Yanqui peón* . . ."

"Luis, there is nothing vulgar about great wealth."

"An illiterate oaf . . ."

"I said it was his father who could probably neither read nor write."

The Duke glared at him. "I once saw him. Some kind of hairy animal. A peasant."

"Forgive me for . . ."

"He shot at me!"

"He did?" Alonso shrugged blandly. "I am sorry to hear that. I find his son very much of a man."

"It would sully our house. Brutalized, all of them, unrefined . . ."

46

rich, Luis." He must be. Unbelievably rich, with all those acres.

"No matter."

"He is from a land of vast opportunity. It is like a giant about to wake up. One day it will be the powerhouse of the world. I think Maria would like it. It is a country made for a girl of her explosive spirit."

Better than the Convent of St. Teresa at Valladolid!

"Do not strain our friendship, Alonso."

"As you wish."

And he turned his horse about. Then he stiffened, reining it in. They were all laughing, the *hidalgos*, watching the sons and daughter of the house of Estremadura goading the bulls across the field. It puzzled Alonso. It seemed to be a game without purpose; if the *novillos*, the young and often vicious bulls, turned on them there could be a little blue blood on the grass . . . then Alonso understood the purpose. The *hidalgos* had already seen it. That was why they were laughing. There was the solitary figure of the *Americano* on his rawboned horse at the end of the field, and that was where the bulls were being driven. Alonso wanted to call out, "Into the fence, Francisco," but nobody would hear above the bellowing of the bulls. He half made to spur across.

He pulled back in time. There was nothing heroic about him, he was afraid of getting in the way of the horned flesh.

He just watched Maria gingering the beasts on, listening to the pounding of hoofs at the grass, saying to himself: run, run. That lethargic painted bag of a horse! Both it and its rider slept. Alonso turned furiously on the Duke, "You should have strangled her at birth," and then muttered, "*Madre de* . . ." but it was too late to pray.

The pinto woke up. Dreamy horse. Frank Dibbler had roused it. It pranced on. It could see the thick cluster of bulls approaching, but it went forward to meet them like a medieval steed. Could one call a horse idiotic? It was totally without

48

fear; more likely without sense. Perhaps it was the prick of its rider's spurs that was galling it on.

It suddenly occurred to Alonso that the creature was more imaginative than he had guessed. He saw the powerful hindquarters tense; it gave a galvanic leap. It curved off-course, and went racing fast about the herd. For an instant a horn sought to hook it, but it flowed by, sidestepping neatly. Alonso would not have dreamed that the ungainly beast was capable of so delicate a ballet. Another horn seeking out a vulnerable rib—it would be sliced! *Dios, Dios!* It would be ready for the glue factory sooner than he had thought. But it was past, sprinting in a tight circle about the confused bulls that came skidding to a stop.

Where was it? Alonso could hear them snorting frustratedly above the hiss of his breath.

And where were Maria and her brothers who had unleashed the whirlwind? They had fallen back curiously to watch.

Again the pinto leaped. A clown! And coming round fast this time, so close to the herd that the dust raised by horse and bulls mingled. Frank Dibbler rode it, loose bag-of-corn fashion. It seemed to Alonso that the next prance would unseat him; but he was rooted as firmly in the saddle as Burgos Cathedral in the ground. It struck Alonso then that there was some kind of tacit sympathy between rider and horse. The pinto suddenly swerved in, banging the rumps of the bewildered herd. Thump, thump! Alonso could hear the fleshy buffets. The wicked horns jabbed, but the pinto seemed to melt and all the spikes tore was air. The bulls were being driven round and round, in an ever-tightening circle, panting, gasping dust, red eyes aglare.

And as the pinto wove about them Frank Dibbler leaned down from the saddle and thwacked his hat ludicrously on their rumps.

He was turning it into a circus. Only those who knew the Spaniard's death-veneration of the bull, the religious awe of *Señor Toro* that ran like fire in his blood, could understand his

49

sense of shock. Thwack-thwack went the hat on the rumps, and the breeders got up on the fences and began to yell. A shudder of rage ran through the *hidalgos*.

Alonso licked his lips. He found himself watching Frank Dibbler with revulsion, as if he had caught him spitting in church. It was an act of desecration. The herd was being shoved in disorder over to the fringe of the field. And now the pinto drove in; it was cutting out the leader like a delinquent steer. Every herd had its acknowledged leader; this one was a *jabonera*, a creamy-yellow bullock with heavy sex organs. It felt itself being driven lonelily off from its mates.

Swish went the curved horns; would the pinto never be there to be impaled? The great neck muscle swelled. The small red eyes grew glazed with twisting. But now the pinto was coming in close; it could get at it . . . a vicious hook, and it wasn't the tear of horseflesh it felt, but a heavy thump. Frank Dibbler had bent from the saddle to slip onto its back.

It shook him convulsively. How long could he sit it? It was insufferable to both man and beast. And then he was over its side, digging heels into the ground, twisting hard at the horns. He was enormously strong. The bull leaned over tiredly. It fell with a thud that brought a murmur of sorrow from the crowd. It lay in the grass, like a carcass on the butcher's block, horns locked in Frank Dibbler's hands.

He got up. He stood watching the bull. It found its hoofs and rose. It glared at him. He walked steadily toward it, picking up a handful of dust and tossing it disdainfully into its eyes. Alonso distinctly heard—he was sure of it—the bull's sigh. It turned and trotted off.

Frank Dibbler mounted the pinto and came round the field. He was caked with dust. Alonso recoiled from him as he passed by; he is beyond pardon, he thought. But he didn't look amused. He was very angry. He jerked the pinto forward suddenly, making for Maria and the brothers watching by the trees. They had no time to scatter. The pinto's heavy flanks struck the nervous Arab horses and Tomás fell with a shout into the grass. Maria reeled in the saddle; she lost balance, her hat flying. Alonso heard her cry out with fear and rage.

Frank Dibbler rode on to the gate.

It was over. He had made a shambles of the archaic mystery of the bull. It would never be the same again. Alonso wiped his face. May God forgive him; I cannot, he thought.

"Francisco, I am wholly lost for words . . ."

"Then why use them?"

"You can look me in the eye and say that? What possessed you to . . . ?"

"Oh, come on now, Alonso. I couldn't let them intimidate me with a hysterical little bull."

Alonso said heatedly, "It was the pick of the *novillos*. It will be ready for the ring next year. The Valencia authorities have bought it."

"Tell them they haven't got themselves a bargain."

Alonso heard his son chuckle. "Miguel, has the source of amusement escaped me?"

"No, no, Father."

"Then keep your eyes on the plate. Small donkeys have long ears. They are made to be pulled."

They sat at lunch. It was a deliciously cooked *paella,* the chicken quite exquisite. It sat heavily on Alonso's stomach. The wine was the best Alicante in his cellar. He found no pleasure in it. His glance was drawn magnetically toward Frank Dibbler's hard weathered paws. They could break my neck as easily as cracking a twig, he thought. Alonso was a small dapper man, and great physical strength awed him. "Francisco," he said curiously, "what made you assault Maria and her brothers?"

"The men asked for it. The woman had to be warned."

Alonso's face grew prim. "That is not the way to refer to her. She is the Doña Maria de los Estremaduras, Condesa de Rojas . . ."

"When we're married she'll be my woman."

And Alonso peered at him with disbelief. Was he still pursuing that intractable pipe dream? He was either pathologically stubborn—or mad. Probably both. "Francisco," he said almost exhaustedly, "it's not to be thought of. Put her out of your mind."

"I'm leaving in three days. I intend to take her with me."

Alonso broke into a light sweat. "She has an allergy for you."

"She hate me that much?"

"Her family will never accept you."

"And you think that'd deter me? She's the one who has to be asked."

"Francisco," Alonso said with alarm, "you must not do that. It would be most improper. In Spain it is the father who has the right to bestow the daughter's hand in marriage."

"Then I'll ask him."

"He will set the dogs on you."

Frank Dibbler wiped his plate clean. His appetite was indestructible. "And you'd call that Spanish hospitality? I'd have to stamp them into the ground," he said.

A hand touched him. Alonso woke. For the third day in succession his siesta had been disturbed and he thought wearily: there is a conspiracy to destroy my rest. His aged majordomo peered down at him. He removed a cigar from the coverlet; Alonso had taken it to bed with him and it had fallen out of his mouth and burned a neat brown hole.

"Señor, if you will forgive me. The Duke of Estremadura has called."

He sat up. "Here? At my house?" Impossible. The Duke was used to granting audiences in semiroyal fashion; the lower orders were expected to attend on him.

"He awaits your pleasure, señor."

"Give him a glass of sherry."

"I have already gratified his grace."

Alonso grunted. "And tell him I will be down." He slipped on a robe and went below. He found the Duke in the tiled conservatory, surrounded by tall green plants like the peacock fans of a pasha's court. He sat in a heavy carved chair. He occupied it like a throne.

He waved a condescending arm. "Did I wake you, Alonso?"

What usually happened when one's siesta was broken? "No," Alonso lied with a sour twitch, "I was awake."

"I have been watching your boy, Miguel. He should grow into a quite excellent young man."

A little better than your haughty brood. Who does he think he is? Patronizing me. Alonso gave him a bleak look. He was getting a little tired of the ducal role. I wonder how many people know that he is up to his neck in hock with me—to put it crudely—with first and second mortgages on his estates?

He poured out a glass of sherry for himself. What has he come for? Another loan? I am not the royal mint. I am getting a little tired of his family, too. The furious blood-conscious sons, the turbulent Maria . . . Bitch. What a thing to do. She could have had Francisco impaled on a bull.

He was beginning to sympathize with his abused guest. "Why have you put yourself out for me, Luis?"

"This morning was a distressing experience for us all, Alonso. I fear I am obliged to . . ."

But voices broke in on them. Alonso went to the window to look out. They were forever in the stable yard. Miguel and Frank Dibbler: his son exercising that startling rawboned pinto, Frank Dibbler stripped to the waist—I wish he wouldn't, it incites the sexuality of the female servants—wet from the pump. He steamed in the heat.

The Duke was peering over his shoulder. "That is a very remarkable beast. I will buy it from you."

Its exhibition had saved it from the glue factory. "I would not sell it for anything you could afford," Alonso said.

"Your guest, too, is remarkable. In a coarse and somewhat fearful way."

53

Alonso stole a last glance at Frank Dibbler. "Yes."

"But what he did at the bull farm was execrable. The Marquis of Avila says he will kill him if he shows his face in town."

"He had better check with his funeral director. It is he who will need the coffin," Alonso said.

"It was a barbarous business."

Alonso gave him a sharp look. "Have you come to censure my friend, Luis?"

The Duke said stiffly, "I thought it necessary to offer an apology. However revolting his performance, what Maria and my sons did to him was unspeakable. It was dangerous. The bulls could have run him down."

"After what he showed us," Alonso said dryly, "I judge the risk small."

"Nevertheless, hospitality is an obligation. He is your guest, Alonso, and I have come to express my personal regrets."

"Why not to him?"

"I find his company discomfiting."

"He is a human being. He laughs. His ancestry is not illustrious. But he is not without wit." He was trying not to lose his temper. "He is violent? So is Maria. You find him arrogant? What are your sons, Luis? Why should we expect a stranger from a raw continent to conform to the rigid customs of Seville?"

The Duke said stormily, "Alonso, I am surprised by your tone . . ."

"I like him." The Duke had risen. Alonso stared at him grimly. "Luis, do not go."

It had made him very angry. He paced about. That frozen condescension! Holy Mother. The apology must have cost him a hemorrhage. It was time to put him in his place. The Estremadurans no longer had the ear of kings; not that the king mattered much, anyway. Nothing mattered today but money. And Alonso had plenty of that.

He said almost without thinking, "He is leaving in three days. I intend to give him a farewell party." He blinked. What had put the idea on his tongue? "It will be very nice." It would, indeed. A very pleasant revenge. "The day after tomorrow, Luis." Everything was suddenly taking shape in Alonso's mind. Time to send out the invitations by hand. He would invite the best of the crusted nobility. It would ravage them to meet the unspeakable *Americano,* but every one of them would come. Let them think of the mortgages he held. He was the major stockholder in Seville's two main banks.

He said dreamily, "I will arrange some good *flamenco.* A discreet little orchestra from Madrid." Long time since he'd given a party. He would actually enjoy it. "You will come, of course, Luis."

"I fear not . . ."

"I would think it fitting. Your children did not think it necessary to express their regrets personally to my guest. You will wish to fetch them."

The Duke stared at him. He recognized a threat. "I will send them."

"No, *fetch* them, Luis." Let him remember who held his personal notes. He could foreclose on them inside twenty-four hours.

"Very well." The Duke bowed ponderously. He looked old.

Alonso said with the faintest irony, "Or do you think they will not obey you?"

The old man flashed. For a moment, even without the doublet and ruff, he again looked like the Velasquez portrait of his ancestor at the court of Philip II. It didn't last long. "They will do as I tell them," he said.

Alonso spent two hours with his secretary and majordomo making plans. He drew up a list of guests. Thirty-eight. Were there that many marquises in Seville? Counts were as thick as acorns on the ground. Too many of them would come just for the food. He pruned down the list. Thirty-two. He was quite excited. Now the only one who had to be told was the guest of honor, and it was time to do that.

"Francisco," he called into the yard, "a glass of manzanilla?"

"Baby's milk," he shouted back. "No brandy?"

Alonso chuckled. "Come inside."

He brought a whiff of the stables with him. It wasn't a bad smell.

"Francisco, my friend," Alonso said, "your visit has given me much pleasure. I could not let you leave without honoring you with a small farewell party."

Frank Dibbler gave him a shrewd look. "Party means guests. Am I that popular?"

"You are popular with me, Francisco."

He continued to stare at Alonso. "Will she be there?"

"I have seen to it."

"You're a clever man. You must pull a lot of strings."

"It is money that pulls strings. That is what it is for."

It wouldn't be too expensive a party. But it would be different. *Flamenco* was a passion with Alonso. Its throat-racked emotionalism stirred something primitive in his soul. He knew *cante flamenco* expertly from *muy flamenco,* which was wild and Moorish and sexual. Both belonged to the gypsy. There was rather a good troupe that he'd seen in a *cantina* in the scrubby slums of Seville. They would smell, of course; it would offend their dignity if he asked them to wash. It would be a hot afternoon, but if he held the party in the garden, with spicy odorous food and much feminine, as well as masculine, perfume he hoped it wouldn't be noticed.

"Francisco, in the matter of Maria," Alonso said impulsively, "I am wholly on your side." It tumbled out of him. It was very foolish. He should be disengaging himself from the affair. But he knew what made him say it. He was tickled. He wanted to see how it turned out. He had seen Francisco play the bull without being impaled: now he wanted to see him play the woman.

This time he wouldn't be so lucky!

"But you must approach it with more subtlety. You are now a suitor," he said.

Frank Dibbler's eyes crinkled. "What do you want me to do? Sing under her window with a guitar?"

"*Can* you sing?"

"Like a crow."

"Then no serenade. But you must dress to impress." Alonso gave him a frank stare. "Your clothes are not fitted for a romantic occasion. You could cut quite a commanding figure, Francisco." If only he took that stern expression off his face. And if he hid those huge brown plebeian hands. So different from the Spanish gentry, who tended to be fragile and languid. Some Spanish women might find that brawny masculinity exciting. But not Maria. When he comes to propose to her I do not even want to be in the same house, Alonso thought.

He was surprised to find Frank Dibbler amenable. "All right." He laughed. "Make me pretty."

"Less impossible than you think. My tailor will fit you out in twenty-four hours," Alonso said.

His tailor was a bright-eyed, hunchbacked Basque. He sat cross-legged on his table, half-deafened by the chatter of his needle boys. Twenty-four hours! He spat out a mouthful of pins. It was asking for a miracle; but aided by heaven—and his apprentices, who would work all night—he would try to achieve one. He walked about Frank Dibbler like a horse fancier, patting his limbs. "Big, big," he muttered. He had replenished his mouth with pins. It would be a pleasure to fit him. "Señor, you are all authentic man. We will not have to pad you out."

The fashion had gone right back to the frills and foppishness of earlier days. Tight trouser-line, buckled under the heel, shirts daintily ruffled. "The señor can wear them. Those huge shoulders discount any suggestion of effeminacy." Silk facings on the frock coat. And a little embroidery. No, no, not much! And, naturally, silver buttons. They were all the rage.

"We will make the señor enticing," the tailor grinned. He had already suspected a woman. "Will we not, Don Alonso?"

"But gold buttons."

"Gold, of course!"

Alonso sat amusedly in the welter of cottons, watching Frank Dibbler being measured. He was still tickled. Then he found himself staring at the bland square-jawed face. The gray eyes were dreamily narrowed; but Alonso had seen them go flat like burnished steel, and that was when it came over him with a cold feeling of anxiety: I have made a terrible mistake! He is all resolution. Nothing will deter him. What persuaded me to poke my nose into the business? When he drove back with Frank Dibbler he was too uneasy to utter a single word.

But a golden morning reassured him. There was a slight haze; it promised a flaming afternoon. He was glad he had made it a garden party. They would trample all over his cherished rose bushes; there was nothing like the disdain of impoverished aristocracy for other people's property. But he was sacrificing them in a good cause. He went out early to survey the terrace with its fountains and cherubs. The marquee was already up. He inspected the buffet. That should keep the noble jaws working! He tasted a tidbit himself. There was Andalusian *gazpacho,* that traditional cold soup of cucumbers and peppers. Thin slivers of tender breast of chicken. Small honey-colored squid, done with a touch of paprika: luscious!

Champagne for the upper crust. He was careful to warn the wine waiters to dispense it only to marquises and dukes. He had the feeling that this party would be remembered. It should be worth the money it had cost.

The orchestra he had brought from Madrid was scraping industriously as he welcomed his guests. He was determined to receive them with Frank Dibbler at his side. Let them freeze him if they dared! Everyone he had invited would be here. Haunted by those notes in the bank, no doubt. A few old aristocratic mouths twisted at the sight of Frank Dibbler, as if it cost a pang to take his hand. But the women—young and old—studied his shoulders with lustrous eyes. The virility that must reside in those loins. "Señor," they said delicately, clicking fans. *Madre mia!* Mantillas reared. He must be a veritable Titan in bed.

Alonso noticed it. Hussies, he grinned.

He looks almost distinguished, he thought. His Basque tailor had worked wonders with him. A touch of the swashbuckler; very nice. Almost a Regency buck! All he needed was a Malacca cane and a snuffbox. And yet—in some curious way—his worn riding jacket and saddle-glazed pants suited him better. What was he really thinking? His eyes were very ironic as he bent over the señoritas' hands.

"You see, Francisco," Alonso whispered, "you have made quite a hit."

"Who are we fooling, Alonso?"

"That was the Marquis of Avila. He said he would shoot you if you showed your face in town. And yet he has just shaken your hand."

"Only because it's too hard to bite."

"Francisco, you are too brutal with people. Try to believe the best of them."

"Oh, I do. So long as I never turn my back on them. That's when you have to expect the worst."

Was that how men survived on the great plains? But the Duke of Estremadura had just arrived, like a half-pensioned general leading his army of six sons. He stopped three paces short of Frank Dibbler. He intended to make honorable amends. He wanted everybody to hear. "Señor Dibbler," he said in a clear voice, "for what my family did to you at the bull farm they wish to express their regrets." He turned to his firstborn. "Esteban!"

Esteban bowed. "Señor Dibbler, my profound regrets."

"Pedro!"

"Señor Dibbler . . ." and so on, right down to Jesús and Tomás. Frank Dibbler nodded absently. He was barely listening. He was searching for Maria. So was the Duke; his eyes roved angrily about. And there she was! She had just swept across the terrace on the arm of Colonel Manuel de Las Casas. A *caballero*. A gilded cavalry officer. He had had his yearning eye on Maria for a long time, but his family was as penniless as hers. There was no profit to either side in uniting poverty to poverty. He was a fiery young man with a wispy moustache.

"Maria." The Duke's voice rang across the garden.

"Father?" She turned to look at him coolly. She made no move to approach.

"Maria!!"

Her eyes hooded. She murmured something to Manuel de Las Casas that seemed to amuse him and came forward on his arm.

"Go away, Manuel," the Duke said to him irascibly. "This is not for your ears." But everybody could hear. He scowled and stepped back a few paces.

"Maria, I wish to hear you apologize to Señor Dibbler—and penitently—for what you engineered."

"What is there to worry about, Father?" she said with a shrug. Alonso saw her glance at Frank Dibbler's clothes with derision. "Nothing happened to the señor." Which was rather unfortunate, her tone said.

"Maria." He was losing his temper.

"As you wish." Her mantilla dipped. But the twitch of her full red lips made a mockery of the bow. "Señor Dibbler," she said, her clear voice rising for the benefit of her frozen audience, "I am required to express my regrets. I kow-tow three times. I knock my head on the ground with sorrow and humility in my heart. I don sackcloth and ashes." It wasn't quite a full-blown insult, but it wasn't much of an apology, either.

"Will that," she said to him demurely, "suffice?"

The Duke's mouth fell open. He didn't know what to make of it.

Now I would hit her, Alonso thought. No, I am too much of a

60

gentleman. But Francisco is no gentleman. He was watching her calmly. Not studying her décolletage again? "It'll do for the moment," he said.

Her fan stopped fluttering. "Only the moment?"

"Patience," he murmured, "works miracles with time." He was quoting somebody. Who? Alonso's eyebrows shot up. Don Quixote, of course! So he'd had time to read books when he was out of the saddle? He will never cease to surprise me, Alonso thought.

She was a little—what was the word?—foxed. Her mouth tightened. She covered her décolletage with the drape of her mantilla. There was still much to see.

"You will excuse me, Father?" She curtsied to him. You would think her so well-behaved! Alonso watched her retire on the arm of Manuel de Las Casas. Between the pair of them there wasn't enough money to pay for the champagne they would soon drink.

"Señor," the Duke said to Frank Dibbler defeatedly. "You see?" He lifted his arms.

"You've ridden her too long with a loose rein."

The Duke froze. "Señor, I cannot permit you to . . ."

"You've left her husband the job of breaking her in."

Their eyes met. It was the Duke who turned away with a shrug. He led off his six sons. All his ardor went on procreation, Alonso thought; there was no strength left in him to control a recalcitrant girl.

"Francisco, you are the guest of honor. Mingle with my friends."

A husky chuckle. "I'll mingle."

"There is going to be some marvelous *flamenco*. I will soon be back."

Alonso wanted to talk to Maria. It was very serious for her. She was being foolish. She seemed to have no notion of the dilemma she faced. Sooner or later—it was commonplace with the great houses of Spain—the convent swallowed their unmarriageable women. Better to be a bride of Christ than to demean the blood! Alonso had a great-aunt who had ended up in the cloisters. He had visited her as a boy. Already, barely forty, she had grown pallid, her eyes curiously lost; all he could remember of her now were the sounds of the chapel bell tolling away matins and vespers and the shuffle of shoes on worn stones. Anything but that for Maria! He caught her up and said peremptorily to Colonel de Las Casas, "Manuel, if you go to the buffet the wine waiter will give you an excellent bottle of Veuve Clicquot. You like champagne, don't you? I have something to say to Maria."

His face flamed. "Don Alonso, I am not to be bribed . . ."

Merciful heaven. How touchy he was! "It is an intimate matter. I am old enough to be her uncle."

"Ten minutes, then." Look at him. So haughty. He touched Maria's hand with his lips, glancing up at her meltingly, and went to the buffet. His family still owe the money for his commission, Alonso thought.

"Well, Don old-enough-to-be-my-uncle Alonso," Maria said coolly, "what is it you wish to say?"

"What are you drinking?"

"Why?"

"I want it to be something potent. I think you are going to suffer something of a shock."

She said sharply, "I am not a lily." That she wasn't. "I can take bad news as well as any man."

"Good. So come out of earshot. Maria, do not be so eager to antagonize my guest. He is a most unusual man."

"The wild beast from the prairie?"

"Maria, you have no right to refer to him like that . . ."

"I have lost interest in him."

"His interest in you has only begun."

It brought her head round with a small jerk. "What was that you said?"

"He would have approached you himself. He is—I admit it—

62

a little gauche. I have made him understand that it is your father he must ask for your hand in marriage."

She was so still that he was sure she hadn't heard. But when she put down her glass he saw it crack and crunch on the stone bench. Now he was afraid to look at her. She had reddened violently. And even as he recoiled from her—dear God, when will I learn to mind my own business?—all the color drained from her face.

He saw her shudder. "Animal," she hissed. "To even think of . . ."

"Maria, don't make things worse. Be careful what you say."

"*Bastardo.*" Perhaps he was. But Maria couldn't possibly know. She suddenly came out with a stream of profanity that made him put his hands to his ears.

"Maria, where did you learn such things?"

"In the gutter. The one he came from."

"Bite your tongue. We are not on the moon. There are people about."

"The insolence. I am an Estremaduran. I will kill him if he dares to . . ."

"It is your father he has to ask, not you."

"Then let my father kill him!"

"Maria," Alonso said wearily, "if there is any killing to be done, he is the one most likely to do it. Think it over."

"Are you mad?"

I must be. Never again will I be a matchmaker, he swore to himself. "He is at least a fine figure of a man. Not a dressed-up effigy like . . ." and Alonso glanced at Manuel de Las Casas. He was watching them jealously from the buffet.

More profanity streamed out of her. She must pick it up from the stableboys, he thought.

"He is quite a catch, Maria. Rich. Unimaginably rich. He owns an acreage as large as a king's. Any woman would want to be his queen."

"I am not 'any woman.' I am the Condesa de Rojas."

63

And up to her ears in debt. "Get out of my sight," she said. Now she wasn't talking like the Condesa de Rojas; more like Queen Isabella. He was saved the embarrassment of backing out of her presence by the first quavering cry of the *flamenco*. Poor Maria! Alonso took a last look at her. Her eyes glistened, but not with tears of self-pity; they were tears of rage.

The crowd had gathered about the gypsies. They have not been cheap; and I am not going to miss them, Alonso thought. It was a family of five, the daughters wild-looking, swarthy and arrogant, flaunting carnations in their raven hair. They swirled their wide skirts as they stamped. They smelled, of course; Alonso caught the first whiff at six paces. But the passion of their voices, trembling in hoarse semitones, gripped his heart. The strumming of the mother's guitar was mesmeric. "Ay-ay," Alonso murmured to himself as the tortured voices, straining at the throat, rose. They seemed to be searching for some soaring note like a swallow. The guests began to mutter excitedly, *"Olé, olé."*

Wonderful. And Alonso, glancing back, saw Maria leave the terrace and go into the house. To repair her face, no doubt. He searched the crowd for Frank Dibbler. What was he doing? He, too, had seen her. He was crossing the terrace. Following her into the house . . .

No, no, Alonso thought aghast, he must keep away. Give her time to adjust herself to the situation. How obdurate he is! This is *Spain*, not Amarillo, Alonso wanted to cry out; a woman's honor has to be handled like fragile glass.

He tore himself away from the *flamenco*. No one else, heaven be thanked, had seen. He went across to the house. He could hear their voices echoing in the dark hall; he couldn't immediately see them. His eyes were still dazzled by the glare of the sun. Maria's voice was the first he caught. Scathing and violent. "Bastard," she said. Alonso trembled. Not that word again!

He was eavesdropping. He would have gone away, but he was afraid of what might happen. He heard Frank Dibbler say softly, "That I'm not. Born in wedlock." And he was chuckling. "But I wouldn't be too sure about you."

"Be very careful, peasant . . ."

"Stop it. It isn't ladylike. When we're married first thing we'll do is wash your mouth out with soap."

"Even suggest marriage to my father and he will shoot you down."

He said in a calculating voice, "If I were you I wouldn't put my money on that."

"He will vomit. You? A vulgar . . ."

"And you? An unbridled bitch. We could be an interesting match."

She gasped. "I would see you dead first."

"Life's better. It's meant to be lived. Stop talking about shooting and being dead. What a furious woman you are."

"I find you detestable."

"You prefer that popinjay outside?"

Manuel de Las Casas? Alonso strained his ears. He heard Maria say, "His family . . ."

"Hell with his family." It was beginning to annoy him. "Everybody has a family. All started with Adam. We're flesh and spirit and damn all else. You'd like Amarillo."

"Get out of here."

"I'm taking you with me in two days."

"Never, never . . ."

"I wouldn't put my money on that, either."

And then the profanity started again. Hers. Her voice broke. It was time for Alonso to go away.

Too late. He'd been observed. Manuel de Las Casas had come up behind him. He said fiercely, "Where is she?"

"Manuel, in God's name, be quiet . . ."

"She is in there? With the *Yanqui?*"

"Must you raise your voice?"

Heads were turning at the commotion. The *flamenco* trailed off. The Duke caught Alonso's eye. He looked suddenly anxious and came hurrying across. The gypsies glared; the interruption had come at the very peak of a lyrical crescendo; the mother banged angrily on her guitar and the daughters threw down their castanets.

Maria came out of the house. Her eyes glittered.

"Maria?" It was the Duke who spoke.

Frank Dibbler appeared in the doorway. He was quite calm. It suddenly occurred to Alonso that he knew exactly what to expect.

"He used an obscenity on me," Maria said.

Manuel gasped. "What?"

"He called me a whore."

Lying slut. And she called herself a lady!

Alonso found himself stammering, "It is not true. He used no such expression."

"How would you know?"

He almost said in his fury: I listened to every word. But he couldn't betray himself. He gave her a malevolent look. "I know my friend. He is incapable of such a thing."

It was an exaggeration. He was capable of worse than that. But she was making trouble on a suicidal scale. Francisco is right; she is an unbridled bitch, Alonso thought. He looked uneasily at Manuel de Las Casas. He was plucking at his wispy moustache.

"Maria," the Duke said to her softly, "if you are . . ."

"Would I lie?"

"It is conceivable," the Duke said. He was studying Frank Dibbler's face intently. What he saw satisfied him. He exchanged a bitter stare with Alonso. "Do not look so horrified, Manuel. You are only wasting your rage."

Manuel said chokingly, "To insult her so and not to . . ."

"Do not argue with me, boy. You should know her. Go away."

The Duke breathed heavily. "Forgive me, Alonso," he said in an exhausted voice. "I will deal with her later. I beg of you, take the heat out of the situation. Attend to your guests."

"She is a veritable devil."

"I bear the marks of her cloven hoofs," the Duke said. Manuel de Las Casas let himself be tugged away by Esteban. Tomás began to mutter earnestly with Maria and drew her off. It had been terrible. It was the mercy of God that so few of the guests had heard. Whore! What an invention. Alonso shivered. And she was laughing. What sort of victory was it?

He saw her glance mockingly over her shoulder at Frank Dibbler as she went off.

He would have asked the gypsies to resume; but they'd been cruelly offended and departed in a huff. All the gusto of his party was gone. The heat settled like a heavy blanket over the garden. He had to let the orchestra play for dancing on the terrace. It was one of Strauss's newer waltzes: "Tales from the Vienna Woods." They played it as leadenly as a pavane. The waltz was still considered a little scandalous in Spain. But it was gay and infectious and the guests crowded onto the terrace.

What now happened had the semblance of a dream sequence. Alonso felt himself helpless to intervene. He saw Frank Dibbler cross over to Maria. Oh, God, not again? It scared him irrationally. He moved close to stop him. He wasn't in time to hear what he said, but he saw Maria give him a queer stare and say sardonically, "I did not think *Americanos* were civilized enough to dance."

"Try me, Doña."

"Doña!" She laughed. "You will trample me to death." Perhaps she thought there was still some fun to be got out of him; she nodded disdainfully and let him lead her to the terrace. Alonso tried uneasily to seize hold of Frank Dibbler's arm.

"No, don't," he muttered. "She will only . . ." but Frank Dibbler dislodged his hand firmly as if to say to him: I am now in command of events.

In years to come Alonso would realize that what he was watching were the classic moves of a prairie roundup. Maria was being got ready for the branding. She was unaware of it. They waltzed austerely at arm's distance; there was a lot of air between them. He wasn't too bad; not awfully adept, but quick and light on his feet. I do not know what is brewing, Alonso thought, but my skin is goose-pimpled. . . . The whirling on the terrace was making him giddy. It seemed to him that Frank Dibbler was steering her remorselessly to the fringe of the terrace where Manuel de Las Casas was watching them, red-faced and sullen, sucking wine from his glass.

What *did* happen? There was too much crowd and movement to be sure. Maria seemed to be swung sharply so that her white-gloved elbow nudged Manuel's glass, spilling the wine over his uniform.

He reacted almost without thinking. He dashed the rest of the wine into Frank Dibbler's face.

The orchestra died as if a knife had been plunged into its combined heart.

Frank Dibbler wiped his face, licking his lips thoughtfully as if not sure if he liked the taste of the wine. The silence was glacial. The Duke hurried across.

"Maria," he said savagely, "what have you been up to now?"

She said, almost wildly, "Father, as God is my judge, I did not . . ."

"You are incorrigible." His voice thick; he could hardly speak for rage. "I will see to you later. Leave the terrace."

She stared about, disconcerted. Alonso thought her shock was genuine. She met Frank Dibbler's glance. Did she sense it? The roundup was over. She had been roped.

"Manuel," the Duke said, "you will apologize instantly to the señor."

"Never."

"You are an idiot." The Duke glared across at Maria. "Cannot you see? You have been used."

He was a tragicomical young man with a downy moustache and an overdecorated uniform, sodden with wine. Too late to retract. "My seconds will call on him tomorrow."

Frank Dibbler peered at him almost with compassion. He murmured to Alonso, "I didn't catch his name."

"Colonel de Las Casas."

"Colonel. He's only a boy. Wouldn't rate corporal in our army."

Manuel's arm snaked out, but before it could reach Frank Dibbler's face it was caught in midmotion and bent back. He was greatly shamed.

"Pistols, then?" he muttered.

Frank Dibbler continued to stare at him with pity and said nothing.

Alonso said to himself frozenly: this is your house! In the name of God, come out of your dream. "You are mad," he said to Manuel in a high voice. "You are a young man. You are just beginning your life. He will kill you."

"My honor has been touched."

"They will bury you with it. He was used to guns before you could walk. He will put a bullet between your eyes before you can even take aim."

Manuel looked ghastly. His chest seemed to cave in. Alonso could hear the pathetic hiss of his breath.

"Francisco," he half-wept, "you cannot go on with this. The stain would follow you to your grave." Would nobody say anything? He stared over at Maria, sitting forlornly on the terrace. We have both been used, he thought. "Wait!" His voice cracked. He ran into the hall. There was a mahogany case with a pair of dueling pistols in the escritoire; they had been his father's. He looked to see if they were primed and loaded. He kept them against the remote possibility of a robbery. He went back with the case and thrust it at Frank Dibbler. "Show him," he said. "For the sake of our friendship. This is my home. I deserve better of you. Do you understand?"

Frank Dibbler lifted out the pistols absently. He hefted them for balance, changing them over in his hands. He sniffed them. For some inexplicable reason. Alonso thought: he is not going to be so cruel as to . . . and then the blast and stink of powder

69

shocked him almost to death. Both pistols had gone off together. Frank Dibbler had barely swiveled from his hips. He had glanced over at Maria sitting solitarily in the distance; she had just filled a wine glass from a bottle, and both glass and bottle shattered. Alonso's stomach clenched; never have I seen anything so dangerous; he could have splashed her face with splinters. She shivered.

He can be cruel!

"Yankee guns," he said, blowing at the barrels. "Made in Connecticut." He put them back in the case.

Manuel sighed. He looked down. Alonso beckoned to Esteban to take him away; he went quietly. A blob of sweat had gathered ludicrously at the tip of his nose.

Dusk was creeping across the terrace. How quiet the garden was. The last guest had melted away. I will indeed remember my party; but with shock and trembling, Alonso thought. Maria had gone inside. The tables had been brutally turned on her. She, too, would remember it.

Now for the branding. Alonso knew what was soon going to happen. It had been fated from the moment Frank Dibbler had set eyes on her in the Cathedral, picking her as one picks a heifer in the market. "That's the one!"

There he sat, at the far end of the terrace, seeking the last gleam of the sun, relaxed and impassive, smoking one of his long black cheroots. The Duke watched him with repugnance, a civilized overbred man. He had been greatly shaken. He sat with Alonso, finishing the last bottle of Veuve Clicquot.

"It was the action of a savage," he whispered. "He is hardly a *caballero*, is he?"

No, he is not a *caballero*, Alonso thought.

"It was unspeakable."

"It was necessary in his eyes. Something had to be demonstrated. He has so little time. Luis," Alonso lowered his voice, "he will shortly ask you for Maria's hand."

"Tell him not to."

"You must think of it."

"I cannot bear to . . ."

"Luis, you must. How long can you continue to endure her?"

"As long as God gives me strength." But his strength had almost run out. He looked old and unwell.

"The mere thought of his family . . ." he muttered.

"Luis, it isn't all that bad. Good basic English stock," Alonso said. He was lying in his throat. "He is very proud of his descent." He didn't dare mention the dash of Lipan Apache. Indians! May God forgive me, he thought.

"One must consider the question of blood, Alonso . . ."

"Luis, we all bleed red. The rest is self-perpetuating pomp. We were lucky in a few of our ancestors. Mine had a nose for money, yours for castles." I still have the money, Alonso thought, but you have lost all the castles. "You think she needs a *caballero*? I think she needs a primitive. A harsher hand. She has too much spirit. Luis, she stifles here in Spain. It is small and old and effete. She could go to a new and excitingly open land."

The Duke said piteously, "Four thousand miles off? She is my only daughter. I would never see her again."

"Distance will lend her enchantment," Alonso said. "There is something else."

"What, Alonso?"

"It would be the means of recovering your lost American estates. They would be reunited to your family."

The Duke stared at him. It had sunk in. He twisted to give Frank Dibbler a last lingering look. "He understands that I have no dowry for her?"

"He needs none."

"She will come to him with nothing but her grandmother's jewels."

"They would not interest him." He just needs the vehicle of her body for sons, Alonso thought.

71

It was over. I have sold her, he thought. The Duke sighed. "Very well." He got up and went into the house.

It was very peaceful. The midges hummed. No hint of the eruption that would soon begin inside. Alonso moved across to Frank Dibbler. "It will not be long now," he muttered.

Frank Dibbler looked at him steadily through the smoke of his cheroot.

Alonso burst out—he couldn't help it: "She will give you nothing but trouble!"

"Trouble's the condition of life."

"What joy will she give you?"

A mild chuckle. I will never understand him, Alonso thought.

Now both listened to the rising voices from the house. The Duke's cold and inflexible: "He will ask formally for your hand . . ."

"I shall refuse him."

"Maria, that is not the way the women of our house address their father."

"I will die first."

"There are worse things than death." Still cold. Still adamant. "This time you have gone too far."

"Father, again I swear it, I do not know what happened with Manuel . . ."

"But it happened. For the last time. I am an old man, too indulgent to you perhaps, and somebody else must take up the burden."

"That animal?"

"Curb your tongue. And accept him."

"Never."

"Maria," the Duke said so softly that Alonso had to strain to hear, "you are penniless. You know the fate in our families of undowried girls. You will go to the Convent of St. Teresa at Valladolid."

"Father," her voice broke, "how can you . . ."

"Because I must. It will be final. Choose one or the other.

Marriage. Or the cold stones of a convent cell and the withdrawal from life. Maria, I swear before God, if you do not . . ."

"Father! Do not swear it!"

A mutter. Both were deeply moved.

Tears? From Maria? Impossible. Then her strained voice, still broken, "Very well . . ."

"So be it."

"But he will regret it."

"As your husband it will be his affair."

Alonso glanced at Frank Dibbler. Expressionless. He'd heard every word. Shouldn't he be moved, too?

Then Maria came out on to the terrace. She was distraught. She stared intensely at Frank Dibbler, calling to her father inside, but intending everybody to hear, "Never let him turn his back on me." She would knife him. "He will get no joy out of me," she said.

73

III

THEY WERE married in the Cathedral. It took a little longer than the two-day deadline Frank Dibbler had set. There had to be a special dispensation from the Archbishop. He wasn't a Catholic; something rather strange, a Presbyterian; or so he thought. He wasn't too particular about it. He shrugged. It was an unseemly way to marry off a daughter of the Duke of Estremadura. It took five days. There was a lot to be done.

The requirements of pomp to be set in motion. Attendance at the Cathedral determined; the order of precedence; pages and maids of honor selected. A bridal gown. But no banquet. The Duke had borrowed all he could. Alonso would have offered him another loan with no strings—*almost* no strings, say five years at two percent—but it would only have added offense to bruised pride.

He saw Maria the day before the wedding. There was the briefest rehearsal at the Cathedral. Frank Dibbler was calm and reserved. He listened intently to the canon explaining the order of the ceremony. He mingled graciously with the family, not as if associating with his betters. Alonso watched him with approval. Very proper behavior. The educative effects of contact with a noble Spanish house were at last beginning to rub off. The *caballero* in him was showing up. I am sure that *au fond* he has the instincts of a gentleman, Alonso thought.

But Maria's appearance troubled him. Chill outside: fire within. Her face deadly pale, her eyes luminous with strain. Something was consuming her. He hoped that it was no more than the natural effort to adjust herself to her new condition; but when he caught her in an unguarded moment he saw that it was something much more destructive.

And that was when he was seized by a pang of guilt. He had been too deeply involved. He hadn't merely helped the match along; he had pushed her like a condemned *aristo* to the block. But it will be good for her, he told himself; it will open up her life! She will be a *Norte-Americano* citizen almost before she knows it. That passionate soul will find relief in a great empty land!

He drew her aside in the nave. "Maria," he said, "I hope you bear me no ill will."

It was a frozen face that stared at him.

"Why should I, Don Alonso?"

"I don't know." He glanced uneasily across at her husband-to-be. "I was worried you might think I had pressed his suit a little ardently."

"I am sure you had only my good at heart."

Was she being cynical? "I am so relieved to hear you say it."

"Be sure I will never forget it," she said, and the little lash in her tongue hurt.

"Alonso!" It was the Duke beckoning to him. A tired old man. He will never recover from this, Alonso thought.

"Will you spare me a few moments of your time? We can talk privately in the canon's office."

Money? wondered Alonso. He can have it. Maria had upset him. It will be my personal penance.

75

"Alonso," the Duke said when they were alone, "I know I can look to you for aid." So it was money. "We are the oldest of friends. I seek your comfort." A very strange remark. It wasn't money, after all? "I am greatly shaken by Maria's condition," the Duke went on. "No matter what I have endured from her, I cannot cast her out of my heart. She is my child. What will become of her? She goes unprotected into a wilderness."

"She will thrive in it!"

"But I will never know. She will be as distant from me as the moon."

"Luis," Alonso cried exasperatedly, "she will have her husband to guard her."

The Duke looked at him steadily. "I wish I were as confident. I hope you are sure of it, Alonso. After all, you know him best."

"I?" Alonso was stung to cry out, "I know him hardly better than you. It is only a few days since I met him . . ."

"But you thought fit to fetch him to Maria's door."

I am being maligned, Alonso thought. His mouth puckered. "That is unkind of you, Luis."

"Alonso," the Duke said softly, "the Chinese believe that if you presume to give a man the benefit of your wisdom, you usurp the mantle of the gods. You make yourself responsible for his life."

What is he talking about? "You misjudge my intentions," Alonso said.

"It was you who pressed Señor Dibbler's case. If you had been his counselor-at-law you could not have defended him better. I would never have countenanced him for Maria if you had not advised me to accept him." The Duke didn't remove his eyes from Alonso's face for an instant. "You have made yourself responsible for Maria's life."

Alonso thought sullenly: I am not a Chinese. And I will not be responsible for anybody's life.

"Your heart is very large. Everybody knows your natural goodness." And flattery will get you nothing, Alonso thought.

76

"We are both conscious of the duties of our rank. *Noblesse oblige*. Alonso," the Duke said gently, "you are a very rich man. You live on your rents. There is nothing that will not permit you to be away a few months. I beg of you, in the name of our friendship, to go with Maria. Watch over her."

"*What?*"

"For six months. No more."

"Impossible."

"Alonso, your conscience will not permit you to refuse."

It is already up in arms, Alonso thought. "Luis," he cried, "one cannot chaperone a married woman. What would I tell her husband?"

"You are going to visit your cousin, Jaquindo."

"I do not care if I never set eyes on my cousin, Jaquindo."

"Three months, then."

"No, no. It is too much to ask."

"Alonso," the Duke said intensely, "you have never been there. I have. It will excite you. You do not know what it is like. A horizon that goes on forever under an eternal sky. Grass, grass, grass, beyond the limit of one's dreams." Alonso stared at him hypnotically. "Air like wine. A sun that warms . . ."

Alonso said crossly, "Do not write me a brochure. I have to think of my son, Miguel."

"He has not escaped my thoughts."

"I cannot leave him."

"It would be an education for him. Take him with you."

"You are truly serious?"

"It would set my heart at rest. See Maria settled in. She is only a woman . . ."

She is six times more man than I am, Alonso thought. How very strange. He was actually giving the prospect some thought. He found the challenge exciting. Life in Seville had become suffocating; the bullring, the daily drive, the social round, the archaic religious festivals . . . a man could go to his grave and never know that there were new and colorful

77

lands beyond the sea. But what a sea! And what a voyage? He
quailed a little. He stared uncertainly at the Duke; he couldn't
get his mouth to form the words.

"Alonso, must I abase myself?"

"Very well," he said. "For three months, no more." It would
be three years before he saw Spain again.

Were there such things as premonitions? Alonso had one the
moment he woke. It was the morning of the wedding. It hadn't
even been a dream; all he knew was that he was filled with an
indescribable anxiety, every dark instinct in him on edge. He
should never have let the Duke talk him into it. *Noblesse
oblige!* I am a small, fat, selfish man and I should oblige nobody
but myself, he thought.

It was too late to retract. Miguel was beyond himself with
excitement; it would shatter him if he drew back. He had already appointed an agent to look after his affairs for three
months. Much of the packing for the voyage was done. All he
had to do now was dress for the ceremony.

He got out of bed and rang for his valet. A curiously poignant
thought: he would have no valet in Texas! Well, he expected to
have to survive worse tests.

And he let his man fit him out, adjusting the flare of his
buckled pants, frilling out his cravat, spitting discreetly on his
silver buttons to make them shine. A long hard rub at his beaver hat. He studied himself critically in the mirror. I will do. I
am getting podgy. I last wore these pants for the Duchess of
Mafalda's wedding; they fitted me then, but they do not fit me
now. Perhaps the winelike air of the *Norte-Americano* prairies
will thin me down.

He would look in on the groom. It was a glitteringly radiant
morning. . . . Alonso's mind strayed to Maria: happy is the
bride the sun shines on. But Frank Dibbler's room was empty.
He poked his head into Miguel's room.

"Where is he?"

78

"He has taken the pinto out for a canter."

Alonso stared at him with stupefaction. "On his wedding morn?"

"He says he can look at his wife any morning after their marriage. But he will never see the pinto again."

A highly practical thought—but disconcerting. Not what you might call the romantic approach. He knew that Frank Dibbler was back when he saw the stableboy rubbing the horse down in the yard. He went into his room. He was dressed, but for his coat. He lay on the bed, smoking a cheroot. How well he looks, Alonso thought appraisingly, vigorous and tanned. Somewhere in the Bible he'd read a tag about the bridegroom coming forth rejoicing from his chamber, like a giant about to run his course. He seemed to be rejoicing very calmly. Perhaps he was hoarding his strength for the marriage bed.

"Francisco, you will smell of cigars at the altar. It will disconcert Maria."

He puffed dreamily. "That's sad."

"I have the ring."

"That's good."

"Francisco, forgive me, but shouldn't you be, well, a little overwrought?"

He grinned. "Makes a bad lover." It didn't sound as though it would be the first time he had entered a woman's bed.

He got up. He slipped his capacious chest into his coat. He gave Alonso an impish look. "You still mean to come along? To visit your cousin, Jaquindo?"

"Of course."

"And to maybe keep an eye on Maria for her father?"

Alonso said in an injured voice, "How can you even suspect it? Your domestic affairs will be strictly your own."

"Never fear. They will be." Still grinning. "If it'll make him happy I'll keep a daily diary for the Duke."

"Francisco, everything has happened so swiftly. I have had no time to think of a wedding present. What may I give you?"

79

"You've given me your friendship, Alonso. That's enough."

"I, too, am blessed with your friendship. May it last forever. But marriage is a once and for all time affair."

Frank Dibbler looked at him slantingly. "Then give me the pinto."

"What?" Alonso's mouth sagged. "But . . ."

"You were going to put her down, weren't you? I saw you look at her that first day in the yard. What were her hoofs going to be? Glue? Give her to me."

"Very well. Take her."

"Many, many thanks."

"And one other thing. We shall be leaving soon after dawn. My personal suite is yours and Maria's for the night . . ."

"No." He shook his head. "I just rode over to the inn. Fixed the room, bedbugs and all. Once a man's married it's his privilege and duty to provide the roof over his wife's head. No offense, Alonso?"

"I understand."

Frank Dibbler looked at him searchingly. He said in the softest voice, "Do you, Alonso, my friend?"

"Yes." He is prouder than any Spaniard. "I do indeed," Alonso said.

He went to Mass. He prayed for the success of the marriage during the sacrament. Mother of Heaven, let it turn out all right for them. He was sure it would. They were two eruptively vital people; it should make for a fertile bed. Time would soften their passion to a natural sexual ardor. He hoped these thoughts weren't too profane for the sacrament.

And now for the holy union! He could hear the Cathedral bells tolling. He drove up with Frank Dibbler and Miguel in his carriage. The square was thronged with sightseers. They wanted to get a glimpse of the Duke of Estremadura's *Yanqui*. Look at him. They gasped. *Vasto*. Huge. *Color de bronce*. So brown. Inside those pants there is no doubt a considerable quantity of man . . . and here comes the bride. See her move

80

in on her father's arm. A true grandee. Followed by the six sons. All of them magnificent. But how pale she is! Like marble. Should she not be blushing with maidenly anticipation?

The ceremony, though overlong, moved Alonso extraordinarily, perhaps because he had helped to bring it about. But the incense pots made his head swim. The candles reeked. The Cathedral grew hot. He stared up at the stone saints in their niches watching—surely not with cynicism?—the formalized ritual. It moved on in precise stages. He saw the Archbishop now and again glance uneasily at the groom. What was the wild heretic from the plains doing in this ancient house of God?

Alonso stole a look at him. Expressionless. He seemed to be less of a participant than a spectator. The only spark of emotion he showed was when the rings were blessed. Maria showed even less. It was almost done. She had drawn back her veil. Frank Dibbler leaned forward to kiss her. The Archbishop peered at her with consternation; he had seen her withdraw her cheek perceptibly from his lips.

They were wedded. The choir burst into the *Magnificat*. The Duke looked worn. He had gained an unpredictable son-in-law, and been relieved of a turbulent daughter. It was only the flicker of the candles that made St. Isidore's stone mouth twitch. Alonso pressed Frank Dibbler's hand fervently. He went forward to embrace Maria. He began, "May God bless . . ." but something in her expression chilled his tongue.

They put their signatures to it in the vestry. Nothing could undo it now. There was no divorce in the sight of God. The procession moved out of the Cathedral into spasms of cheering from the crowd. They were throwing rose petals. Lovely gesture! Maria stared ahead into infinity. She got into the coach with Frank Dibbler and they drove off.

Alonso sat up in the darkness. He couldn't sleep. It had been altogether too emotional a day. There had been a small reception at the Duke's house after the wedding, and he had probably drunk too much. Something else was disturbing his mind. He wished he could pinpoint it. He grew hot and fretful in his bed. He heard clocks all over Seville striking the hours; and still sleep eluded him. His thoughts went back to the reception at the Duke's. Was it that that was scratching at his mind?

There had been toasts to the happy couple; endless toasts. The elite of Seville, haughty and high-nosed, had begun to soften to the Duke's son-in-law. Nothing would make them accept him; but since he would soon be departing forever, taking the Condesa de Rojas with him, they would speed him graciously on his way. He accepted it all with equanimity. He could read their minds.

Catching a glimpse of his ironic expression, Alonso whispered in his ear, "Francisco, we are a hidebound class. It is a noble trade-union. You will never join it. But you have, at least, married an influential member."

"I didn't marry her for that."

"For love, Francisco?"

"I think so."

He *thought* so! Alonso gave him a rueful glance. "It will be a great success. I promise you. There is so much life in the pair of you. I prophesy you both great happiness," though Alonso felt compelled to qualify it, "in the end." He was drinking too much. "I see a houseful of children . . ."

"*That* I can promise you."

Alonso looked across at Maria. She was smiling. But she might have been carved out of alabaster. That was how statues smiled.

Presently she came across. "Well, Francisco," she said briskly. It was the first time Alonso had ever heard her use his name. "Are you happy?"

"Yes. Are you?"

"Inconceivably." The conversation rang falsely: like a cracked glass. Now Alonso just wanted to get away. "Why are you not drinking?"

"I've drunk enough."

82

"You have a good head, I hope?"

He said thoughtfully, looking at her wedding dress, which was startlingly revealing and had provoked some stuffy furor from the Duke, "Good enough, Maria."

She cocked back her head with the faintest coquetry. "What else are you good at, my husband?"

"We'll soon find out."

"Yes." Still smiling. She beckoned him across the great throng in the hall to the ancestral pictures hung on the walls. "This is the third Duchess of Estremadura. She was a king's mistress. Very lusty. You would call her a bitch."

He said nothing. Watching her.

"This one is her granddaughter. She should have been a soldier. She loved to fight." And still nothing from Frank Dibbler. She moved along the aged canvases. "This one was the worst of all. My great-great-grandmother. It was she who went through the family estates. Do you not think I have inherited some wonderful qualities?"

She left him with a laugh. Her shoulders so bare; the candlelight caught them. She carried herself well. Alonso saw Frank Dibbler stare after her. He thought for a revealing instant that his eyes were full of sexual hunger.

Perhaps *that* is what is scratching at my mind, Alonso thought.

He had been glad to get away. He had waited only to see the couple depart with the baggage for the inn.

"In the morning, Francisco." Alonso pressed his arm. "I will be at the inn at dawn. In the meantime be happy."

Why should Maria laugh?

Alonso felt himself nodding. His eyelids suddenly glued. He was exhausted . . . he must have fallen asleep askew. He was stiff. What was that commotion at the back of the house? He got up with a mutter of despair. He dragged on his dressing gown and went to the top of the stairs. The majordomo stood in his nightshirt in the porch, furiously upbraiding Emilio Natchez, the innkeeper.

"Go away. I cannot disturb him . . ." and Emilio cried over the majordomo's shoulder, catching sight of Alonso, "Don Alonso, forgive me. I did not know what to do."

"Do you know what time it is?"

"I would have waited for dawn. But . . ."

"What is it? Man, speak up."

"Don Alonso, your guest the *Americano*." Half-incoherent. "It is his wife, Doña Maria."

Alonso froze with fear. "What has he done to her?"

"It is what she has done to him."

"Come in," Alonso interrupted him. He was suddenly very cold. This is why I had a bad dream, he thought. The servants were peering down the stairs. He drew Emilio into the library and let him speak.

The bridal room, Emilio said, had been prepared. The sheets aired and scented with herbs. Flowers. A bottle of champagne, his own wedding gift, on ice. The *Americano* had expressed an inconceivable desire for a bath. For the edification of the bride? It *was* conceivable. They gave him buckets of hot water in the scullery. Presently he went upstairs to join his wife . . .

"Don Alonso, it was an hour of agony. I can recollect it only with shame."

"She locked the door on him?"

"Bolted it. Barred it. Señor, he was like a balked animal trying to break it down. And . . ."

"Come on, Emilio!"

"I heard her laugh."

It consumed the man from the other side of the world. "Don Alonso, I sweated in sympathy with his rage and despair." He went into a glandular mutter about the physical torment . . . but Alonso put a stop to it. Talk like that was for the farmyard! By then, Emilio said, every soul in the inn was awake.

He tried to intercede by shouting through the door, "Doña Maria, what is wrong?"

"Send him off."

84

"He is your husband, Doña . . ."

"Does he think it gives him the license to share my bed?"

And they heard it creak. The ultimate affront. Silence. The light under the door vanished. She had blown out the candle. Emilio heard the *Americano's* chest make a deflated sound. He went down to the stable. "Don Alonso, it was pathetic. He spent the last hours of the night with his horse."

Pathetic? Macabre. Alonso peered out with a shiver. The first tints of dawn were flushing the sky. He rode in Emilio's cart to the inn. He looked into the stable. Frank Dibbler slept heavily in the straw. He hesitated to wake him. He went upstairs and tapped on the bedroom door.

"Maria."

He heard her yawn. "So soon, Don Alonso? Are we ready to travel? It is hardly dawn."

"I haven't come to chat with you through a thick oak door."

She let him in. Her eyes were dim and sensuous from the bed. Shameless. She'd barely bothered to cover herself with a robe; he couldn't tear his glance from the cleavage of her breasts. She would have made anybody's bridal night memorable, he thought. "Now I am hungry," she said.

"Do you know where your husband slept?"

"Nor care. So long as he understands that he will never sleep with me."

"Your marriage vows . . ."

"It was not a marriage."

"In the sight of God? In holy church?"

"My body is mine, and holy to me. My bed is my church. There is no door to it for him."

Maria! Cover up your . . . but he was being gently pushed out. Was she laughing at him, too? "Don Alonso, you are intruding on my privacy. This is a bedroom. Please go." And the door closed in his face.

He returned to the stable. "Francisco?" He was already up and dressed. Alonso averted his eyes from his face.

85

He was hoisting the saddle onto the pinto. "Collect Miguel and the baggage, Alonso. We'll start riding for Cádiz."

"Am I to speak of what happened?"

"No." Two white folds about the trap of his mouth where the muscles were clenched. Eyes filmed over like a snake's.

"Francisco, it will wear off in time . . ."

"Not with me. It'll stick. She's flesh. In the end she'll want it. She'll cringe. I'll take her when I'm ready, but she'll sweat for it." He tightened the cinch about the pinto. It squealed. "It was a long night for me. For her it'll be the longest and darkest night any woman ever spent."

She came down. She was dressed for the journey. Frank Dibbler stared bleakly at her boots.

She said to him banteringly, "And how far is Texas?"

"Quite a step. Eaten?"

"Soon."

"Eat well. You will need all your strength."

I am being dehydrated, Alonso thought. The sun was a torment. Dust caked his mouth. For days he'd seen nothing but the heat-shimmer of the prairie and he thought tiredly: we must be making a second circuit of the world. He would never forget the voyage. The sea hadn't been kind to him. Nor to Maria. Both had been sick for a week. It was as if an awful siege had been lifted when they finally raised American territory through the port of New Orleans.

He strained his eyes for the first glimpse of land. There was the estuary of a vast river that was pouring the yellow flesh of the continent into the sea. Mississippi, the schooner's mate told him. "The Father of Waters." Colossal. It made Spain's spindly torrents look like gutter drips. They ascended the river in a colorful stern-paddle steamer. It was more like a theatrical edifice than a vessel. Even the passengers resembled actors. They passed the time in the saloon playing cards. The tall iron smokestacks belched sparks. The decks were piled with bales of cotton. There was banjo music. Whenever Alonso heard a banjo, from now on, he would think of snowy shreds of cotton drifting across the flowing water like Arctic flakes in the sun.

For the first time he set eyes on shining black faces, split by flashing white teeth. Chesty voices in the plantations singing spirituals. What a seething assortment of humanity this America was!

They disembarked at a place called Natchez. It reminded Alonso of Emilio, the innkeeper, of the same name. The Spaniards, of course, had been here first. Only it wasn't Spanish now. Greasy Houma Indians, smelling of rotgut whiskey, snored on the boardwalks. Lean brown men wearing coonskin hats lounged dreamily in every doorway, intruders from the northern forests. *Kaintucks,* they called them. "Long Knives." They had cold blue Anglo-Saxon eyes that abashed Alonso. He couldn't even understand their heavy drawl. They sprayed the landscape copiously with tobacco juice with every breath.

Here, he thought, we leave civilization behind.

Now along another river. The Arkansas? This time in a flat-bottomed boat, poled half the way. It was a distressing journey. They slept on deck. It was a foretaste of hardships to come. They left it when the river grew unmanageable. They were now in frowning timberlands. Frank Dibbler bought a dozen horses at a livery stable in some dusty, half-formed town. From then on they rode.

There was no Arab blood in the horses, just spiteful Mexican mustang. Alonso, used to his upholstered coach, soon suffered. His bottom became one raw blaze from the saddle. I will never last out, he thought.

And suddenly—out of the timberlands—and here the prairie began! There was really nothing there but cottonwoods and grass. Grass that went on forever, reaching out to a vanishing horizon, billowing with waves like an inland sea. Sooner or later, Alonso thought, it will come to a finish—and we will all fall over the edge of the world. But it never finished. It unnerved him. And its loneliness struck fear into his heart.

And the wind! It blew and blew. With its every breath the

prairie changed color from green to honey-gold. But when the rain clouds marched across the sky it grew ominously purple. It was a land for fierce and virile men; no other kind could survive it. I certainly cannot, Alonso thought.

Why did I leave Seville? As the days passed he watched Maria with pity. Her face white and strained, teeth set on edge. She, too, suffered. But she would never betray it.

Would it never end?

"Mañana," Frank Dibbler told them casually. Always tomorrow! Usually he rode ahead with Miguel. They chatted interminably. One was tireless, the other springy with youth.

It nagged strangely at Alonso's mind. "Where are all the people?"

"What people?"

"In God's name, is the whole land naked?"

"Damn near." Frank Dibbler chuckled. "We'll maybe see some by and by. I'll give you a call when we do."

I have walked out of the cultural heart of Europe into a fearsome vacuum, Alonso thought.

The bone-hard jog of the ponies. Blistered buttocks. That ever-retreating horizon. And rain squalls. Now and again a blustering norther fell on them and tried to rip the clothes off their backs. They lay at night on a ghastly prairie alive with birdcalls that kept him awake.

But imperceptibly the climate was changing. So was the landscape. One day the wind died; the sky softened to a lambent Mediterranean blue. And it grew quite hot. Suddenly there were fat spiny plants, twice as devilish as the cactus Alonso knew in Spain, flourishing in the rocks. But presently they wilted; the whole land was turning into dust. It hovered over the sagebrush, covering it with a desiccated film. The horses puffed it out of their nostrils. It penetrated even the secret crevices of the body; bowed despairingly over his pony, Alonso scratched and itched. The sight of Maria shocked him: a dried-up mummy in its grave cloths. Do I look like that?

The grass growing weaker and dying off. Everything bleached off the face of the earth by the stunning sunlight. A vista out of Dante's *Inferno*. What could live here? But lizards? And ghosts?

They rode through it for two days. Alonso choked on grit: I shall never slake it out of my mouth. Late afternoon he called out exhaustedly to Frank Dibbler, "When do we reach your land?"

And he answered over his shoulder, "You've been riding across it all day."

"What!"

Alonso stared across the silent valleys. Everything arid. Dazzling bone-white canyons, dry and bouldered, that hadn't known a flash-flood in years.

He said painfully, "Where are all the cattle?"

"You have eyes to see, Alonso."

And Alonso made them out. Small herds bedded down in the gulches. Now he could hear them lowing and protesting at the sun. So few of them! And not much different from the long-horns he knew in Spain; lean flanked and leathery, bony-ribbed like the skeletons of foundered ships. Probably as hard to eat. Miserable creatures! Something clutched at his heart. He looked at Maria. He didn't know what to say.

He muttered, "But, Francisco, you are supposed to be incredibly rich."

"Who said I was rich?" Frank Dibbler turned in the saddle. He pulled away his facecloth to spit out dust. He looked at them sardonically. He'd let them think what they wanted to think. Cruel! "Must have been your cousin, Jaquindo. He's a chatterbox. Can't even remember when he was last here."

What, heaven forgive me, am I to write and tell the Duke?

"Where are all your millions of acres?"

Frank Dibbler pointed to the quivering horizon. "Out there."

"All like this?"

"Some worse."

Alonso said with pathos, "Francisco, what has happened to you here?"

"Three years of drought. I've lost the best of my stock. Paid off most of my men." It didn't seem to perturb him. "Soon be selling off what's left of my herds."

Maria began to laugh on a high note. It was dreadful to hear. She cried out, "I have been cheated."

Frank Dibbler looked at her. "I think not." He spoke softly. It lasted only a second; but in it Alonso saw the flame of rage in his encrusted eyes. "I think I'm the one who can say that."

Then he grinned. He was too dry to shout. He just hawked at his throat. "Cheer up. Be at the bunkhouse by dusk." He spurred on the pinto. Ugly tireless beast. "Get you freshened up with a steak. You'll like a wash." Was he laughing? "If there's water. And you don't much mind a little green scum."

It took a hard afternoon's ride to reach the *ranchero*. Nothing in the landscape improved. They came first to the sprawl of outhouses—barns, corrals, stocks of wild hay—the shacklike bunkhouses that had once slept extra hands. They were now empty. A few Mexican *vaqueros* appeared. The welcoming mutter for the master was in mangled Spanish. "Señor!" Frank Dibbler got down. He stretched. He let out air like a punctured bag. He slapped the pinto's rump.

"All the way!" He chuckled to it intimately. "You'd never have left Alonso's stable if you'd known."

The ranch house was old—adobe walls, enormously thick. Alonso could guess why. Marauding Indians. He hoped that was an old story now. The windows had heavy battle shutters. There was nothing here that would burn. Frank Dibbler led the way in. Cool. Stone floors. Pleasantly furnished. Even an antique Dutch desk; there'd been money in the family at one time. There was a picture of a heavily moustached man on the wall, hard and aggressive of expression. Frank Dibbler had something of his mouth and eyes. Was this the father who had put a bullet through the Duke of Estremadura's hat?

Maria had the best bedroom. The sheets were clean. The bed was vast; but Frank Dibbler had no intention of claiming a share. He had his own over the kitchen. Alonso and Miguel shared the second-best room.

They ate dinner in silence. Maria trembled continuously. She stared glitteringly at Alonso, waiting for him to say something. What could he say?

The steak, heavily laden with beans, was uneatable. It seemed to Alonso that the comfort and cuisine of Seville were as remote as the empire of Rome. They lit candles. He was bone-racked and exhausted. He went to bed. He slept badly. Miguel, with a curious exultation, slept well.

He was down early, for he was filled with the darkest apprehension. He was afraid of Maria's impending eruption. His bedroom was separated from hers by an adobe wall, and all night he had heard her gasping and talking embitteredly to herself. She had been cheated! But she no longer had the paternal protection of the Duke, nor her six Estremaduran brothers to look to for help. She was on her husband's territory; in this wilderness of dubious legality, with its patriarchal tradition, he probably owned her. Body and all.

It was a man's world, and no doubt permitted him to enforce his marital right.

Miguel still slept. Frank Dibbler was already down. He was relaxed; the color had come back to his drained face. They had breakfast together. Two pork chops sizzled in their inedible fat. Alonso recoiled from them; they were abhorrent. Frank Dibbler ate as if stocking up his stomach after a two-month fast. It seemed an act of indulgence to leave the bone on the plate.

"Come for a ride with me, Alonso."

"Francisco, I think I should wait. Maria will have something to say to you."

"I don't have anything to say to her. I want to show you something."

91

"Far? Have pity. I am red and ragged underneath."

"Not too far. Six miles."

They rode off. The vast sky was still vivid with dawn; heat wouldn't come welling out of it for some hours. Alonso could hear a couple of *vaqueros* singing to a scattering of cattle, leading them down to a waterhole. He had set eyes on no Anglo-Saxon cowboys. He supposed Frank Dibbler employed Mexicans because they were cheap.

He watched him sidelong. How he'd changed. In Seville he'd been hard and militant, as if his defensive hackles had been roused. Here he was at ease. He rode his pinto like a loose bag of meal. Dressed differently, too. Strictly for use. A heavy sweat-stained sombrero, tipped over his eyes. A bandana. A coarse blue shirt and tight knee-stretched pants. His boots high-heeled; but for the stirrup, not for show. Looped to his saddle was a *reata*, lariat. A rifle shoved into a battered leather holster. It seemed as natural in his baggage as a parasol in a lady's hand.

They crossed a salt flat. It rang under the hoofs like an old Roman road. Presently they saw the shine of water in a creek. Not far off was a tall ramshackle wooden tower. It was the first time Alonso had set eyes on a primitive drilling rig. Frank Dibbler halted to let him look at it. There was the thudding gasp of a donkey-engine. Nearby was a large outhouse, with a living hut built into it. At the sound of the hoofs a man came running out.

He was short and moon-faced, with a corpulent belly bulging over his belt. The reddish bronze of his shiny pocked skin seemed to reflect the glow of the sunrise. It was its natural color. His greasy black hair was dressed in two plaits.

Frank Dibbler called down to him affably, "Hullo there, Pablo."

"Hullo there, Frank," the man shouted back. He grinned, showing broken brown teeth. "I hear you fetched one back."

"A wife? That I have."

"They tell me she's choice."

92

"That she is." Though Frank Dibbler's mouth twisted. "She's a Condesa." As if that made her specially choice.

"What's that, Frank?"

"Countess."

"Hi-yi! An aristocrat, eh? What'll your brood be? Countesses and counts?"

He had come across. He leaned familiarly on Frank Dibbler's stirrup. Alonso could detect his personal aroma at six paces.

"Now you be respectful to my good friend, Don Alonso," Frank Dibbler said. "He's a grandee of Spain."

Alonso saw the hooded black eyes suddenly sparkle. "A Catholic?"

It startled him. "Of course."

The man said companionably, "So am I."

Who could feel joined to this creature in the communion of the faith? Alonso looked away.

"This is Pablo O'Hagerty," Frank Dibbler said. "He's Irish." Monstrous. "Sired by old Michael O'Hagerty on a full-blooded Arapaho squaw." He looked slyly at Alonso. "Pablo's full of aristocratic blood, too. Who was your grandfather, Pablo?"

"Warbonnet Chief Owl-in-the-Sky."

This is a dream-conversation, Alonso thought; it cannot be real. "Pablo's my geologist and driller," Frank Dibbler said. He beckoned across to the wooden tower. "How's it going?"

"Won't be long now. I hear her bubbling down there."

"Keep at it. Don't let her get away."

"I won't," Pablo O'Hagerty said. Who was she? It confused Alonso. "Minute she shows up I'll tie her down."

"Come on over to the creek," Frank Dibbler said. He had stopped being humorous. They rode down to the reeds. The stench was suddenly acrid. It rose from the water. What was it? Bitumen? Frank Dibbler got off his horse. He stooped to the water, scooping up its greasy black scum. It clotted his fingers. He let it drip off slimily. He sniffed it, with pleasure almost. "Oil," he said.

"It stinks."

93

"Yes." And crouched there, his eyes luminous and abstracted, he said to Alonso, "There's a goddamned lake of it down there. I know it in my bones."

Alonso eased himself in the saddle. He had been brought out on a very uncomfortable ride for nothing. He shrugged.

"It's going to change the whole world," Frank Dibbler said. "Nothing's ever going to be the same again. Nor me, either." There was a puff of wind—what they called a dust-devil—it whirled a spout of grit into the air. He glanced back across the arid range, already simmering in the rising sun. "I'm finished with cattle. Going to sell off my stock. Everything. This is my beginning." Alonso was too startled to speak. The Indian had come across to listen. Frank Dibbler thrust his hands hard down into the black scum. "Here's where I start," he said, and Alonso stared into the wolfish resolute face. He had no gift of foresight; but he knew for certain that he would one day remember that scene. The whinny of an impatient horse; a plump odorous Indian; a hot empty land. And Frank Dibbler's dreamy obsessed voice, barely heard, "I'm going to make myself an empire out of it."

For his unborn sons? The ones Maria would never give him? He had better drop his seed in more receptive loins. Alonso was too petrified to say a word to him as they rode back.

TWO:

The Roots of Violence

IV

AND THEN he was gone. The master had been away too long; it was presumably time to start checking over his domain. There was a quick clatter of hoofs that drew Alonso to the window; he caught a glimpse through the dust of Frank Dibbler riding hard over the skyline with a couple of his *vaqueros*.

He asked the Mexican cook what had happened. He found he could communicate with him better in Spanish than in English.

The man let his tongue loll out to express insufferable thirst. "Cattle die off like flies," he said. He looked sorrowfully up at the burning sky. Would it never rain?

"When will he be back?"

"*Mañana*," the Mexican said.

Tomorrow; maybe Friday week. There was no measure of time in this arid waste. He was the color of a well-roasted coffee bean. A fat benign man with a staggeringly confusing squint. One eye fixed on the cooking fire, the other studying Alonso, and both of them cheerfully alert. The lower half of his face

97

might have been Andalusian peasant; but the slitted eyes and bulging cheekbones were pure Aztec. Some long-moldered Spanish trooper of Cortés's army had lain in the grass with an Indian woman—the stream of sex had finally produced this.

Heaven, I fear, has a wry sense of humor, Alonso thought.

He went outside. Again with that sense of being totally alien, he stared beyond the adobe ranch house, beyond the corral in which a few vicious-looking ponies huddled for shade—and there was nothing in the affrighting scenery but dust, dry bone-white gulches and yellowing grass. An emptiness and a silence that gave him a brief shudder. He wished Frank Dibbler hadn't gone. He felt terribly vulnerable without his comforting presence.

He idled about the ranch house, learning its geography. It had been built to withstand fire-lance and siege. The walls were fortress-thick, the shutters massive with rifle slits. He wondered uneasily if they had ever been used. The kitchen was a kind of inner keep; all rooms led off it, every one penetrated by the Mexican's wicked culinary smell. There was the loft in which Frank Dibbler slept. It contained nothing but a primitive iron stove and a buffalo robe on his bunk. It was strung with rawhide. He slept hard.

Alonso now grew worried about Maria. She hadn't been down to breakfast, and she hadn't swallowed a thing at dinner last night. He tapped at her door. No reply. He'd expected to find it locked—but there was no key. He wondered if Frank Dibbler intended to make sure that there would be no repetition of the scene at the inn.

She sat by the window, staring poignantly across the windswept range. Her expression gave Alonso a pang. What was she picturing so nostalgically in the swirling dust? Seville?

He said anxiously, "Maria, you must try to eat something."

"I want nothing."

"You cannot starve . . ."

"I can and will. Ten times over," she told him bleakly. "I will not let a morsel of his food pass my lips."

98

Her face was hollow. Had she been crying? Impossible. The Condesa de Rojas couldn't cry. Her eyes were wild. She reminded Alonso of those vicious-looking ponies outside.

"Maria," he sighed, "it is foolish. What good can it do? You are here. Four thousand miles away from home. It is a fact of life. Francisco is your husband. He is not a bad man. He is a fact of life, too. You will learn to bear your misfortune with patience . . ."

"When one of us is dead," she said.

Obdurate. If it went on it was very possible that one of them would be dead—almost certainly not Frank Dibbler.

Some kind of screeching commotion was going on in the corral; he could see the stockhands roping the ponies. His son, Miguel, watched them excitedly, squatting on the fence. How rapidly he was acclimatizing himself to this fierce environment! The young were so flexible. But I am not; I will never get used to it; it is too late for me to be anything but a highly civilized Spanish nobleman, Alonso thought.

And he went out to join his son.

The Mexican stood watching the business with a steaming skillet in his hand. A group of men sprawled laughing and burping on the porch. For the first time Alonso set eyes on Anglo-Saxon faces. Thick saddle-bandy men with bleached moustaches and lusterless gray eyes. He could hardly make out a word they said. Their accent murdered the English tongue, which he found hard enough to understand. Their manners were execrable. Never had he heard such endless spitting and hawking at the throat. They went by such curious names as Alfalfa and Lofty and Nueces Joe.

He addressed them courteously. They looked at him as if a totem pole had opened its mouth. They got up with a jingle of spurs and went off.

Somewhat surprised, Alonso asked the Mexican, "Why are they so unapproachable?"

"They are barbarians, *amigo*," the Mexican said. The familiarity made Alonso frown. "What can one expect of a *gringo*?

They do not have our Spanish delicacy of feeling, nor our innate sense of breeding," and Alonso could only stare with stupefaction at the Aztec-brown face and the divergent slitted eyes. He went across to the corral fence where his son sat.

"Father, how expert they are with horses!"

"I would be ashamed to call them horses. They look more like unbroken wild beasts."

Wild, indeed. He drew unnervedly back from the fence. One of the ponies screamed and kicked at it so violently that it shook. They were obviously too primitive to be ridden, except by equally primitive specimens like Alfalfa and Lofty and Nueces Joe. One of the stockmen tossed his lariat about the neck of the screaming colt; it reared, writhing its lips. Forehoofs up to trample him into the ground, but he was out of range; so it snapped with its teeth to take off his arm. That wasn't there, either. Alonso sensed that the animal was slowly going mad. But it had always been half-mad; it was a descendant of the old Spanish stock, abandoned in this harsh continent. Running wild for maybe two centuries, beset by wolves, toughened by cruel winters and drought.

Fit only for barbarians. But how they could ride! Who was it tossing in the saddle? Nueces Joe? I am watching a naked suicidal attempt, Alonso thought. He was sure the enraged beast would buck him off, before taking the corral apart.

And then—stealing over his numbed senses—he was aware of a curious musky scent like nothing he had ever smelled before. Yes, he had: and not long ago, either. The buffalo robe in Frank Dibbler's room. But there were no buffaloes . . . and suddenly he felt Miguel's fingers tighten convulsively on his arm. He was staring over his shoulder.

Alonso turned. He thought he wouldn't survive the shock. An Indian sat an indescribably decayed nag less than two paces from his neck. They had come up so quietly that he hadn't heard a sound. Nothing moved in the coppery face, not even the lizard eyes that were absorbing his features one by one. Alonso had seen whiskey-sodden Houma Indians in Natchez, but this was the noble savage in his raw environment! And he stank. There was the shine of grease in his face. Two lank braids of hair hung over his shoulders. The flat muddy eyes were bloodshot by wind and grit. He carried a lance that seemed to belong to the times of the Crusaders.

Sweat sprang into Alonso's armpit; he felt a weakening tremor that left him loose at the knees. None of the cowmen took any notice of the Indian. Then the Mexican cook came across.

They spoke. But could one really call it speech? It was a business of hand signs, embroidered by guttural sounds. Stone-age men must have begun like that. Finally the Mexican beckoned to the storehouse and the Indian walked his horse across.

The Mexican came out with a beef carcass. The Indian slung it over his horse's crupper, glancing sardonically at Alonso with his lizard eyes, then ambled off. He took the buffalo smell with him.

"You are worried, *amigo?*" the Mexican said. "He is only a savage."

"Perhaps that is why I worry. My son is still young."

"I am not frightened, Father," Miguel said.

I am; and will remain so, deep in my stomach, until I set foot in civilized Seville, Alonso thought. "What did he want?" he asked the Mexican cook.

"Food. They are Señor Dibbler's orders that no Indian who comes to the door is to be sent away empty-handed."

"Why?"

"The señor has a soft heart."

Alonso touched his handkerchief to his face. What a bad morning it had been. First with Maria; then the mad pony and the malodorous Indian. The colt was still screaming, but tiring, and so was Nueces Joe. He crashed to the ground, and the pony made stiff-legged jumps to break him up. Alonso averted his eyes from his death. But Nueces Joe had leaped safely over the rail.

101

The Mexican squinted kindly into his face. "A little tequila, *amigo?*"

"No, no." Alonso caught his breath. "I am all right . . ."

"Call me Joachim."

Alonso stared at him soundlessly. It was too much. I am finished for the day, he thought; and went straight into the house.

Now lunch. And still no Maria. She didn't miss much; something called cornbread and sowbelly, concocted by the Mexican cook. Nobody assaulted him for it. The hired hands evidently had iron stomachs. And now the siesta; God be thanked for the mercy of sleep. But the bellowing of thirsty cattle in a nearby gulch wouldn't let him rest. He dressed with a sigh and went out into the baking sun.

One of the cowmen—the man called Alfalfa—snored on the boards of the porch. His moustache twitched with his throaty puffs. Everything somnolent, even the mad ponies sagged feebly in the heat. It was the wind that Alonso detested most. It sent hoops of tumbleweed skipping across the mesa. A hard, oven-blast, eroding the land, lifting it up to deposit it—where? Down in Mexico? They already had enough dust.

He still felt guilty about Maria. I am *in loco parentis,* he thought; the Duke would reproach me bitterly for permitting his daughter to starve. He sent the Mexican to her room with a plate of sowbelly. He returned, less the plate, his crossed eyes ashine.

He whispered confidentially, "The Condesa is a lady of noble parts. Language of surpassing feeling." He was greatly impressed. "It is a pleasure to serve her."

"She ate it?"

"No, *amigo.* She threw it outside."

No sound of life but the anvil-hammer from the blacksmith's shop. He swigged water by the bucketful in the Stygian gloom, and it reappeared in floods of sweat. He was forging branding irons, testing them with a gush of smoke on sacks of corn. Block-

D he called the design, Frank Dibbler's private seal. It would decorate the calves at the roundup.

Alonso thought: I am going to be here some time. I might as well look around. His buttocks were almost healed. The blacksmith saddled a mare for him and he trotted off.

He wouldn't go far, not in this unprotected wilderness. He had the keenest memory of the Indian with the lizard eyes and the Crusader's lance. He found himself cantering down the valley he had followed with Frank Dibbler. Then across the salt flat. He felt as lonely as Columbus in an uncharted sea. And then suddenly—just as he was growing nervous—the shine of water in the creek. And over there, protruding like a phallic symbol, the wooden drilling rig.

He could hear it thumping. No phallic symbol had ever been so busy. He trotted across.

The man with the Warbonnet Chief for a grandfather—what was his name?—Pablo O'Hagerty, came out of the hut. He was foul with sweat and dirt. Barrow loads of earth, banged or drilled or scooped out of the creek, whatever the process was, surrounded the rig like freshly opened graves. He peered at Alonso, then recognized him as a brother Catholic. "Hi there, Count," he cried.

"You are busy."

"Christ Jesus, yes." Not language for a Catholic. "You've come at a hell of a fine time." He seemed very excited. "Get down. Come into the hut for a swig. I think I'm on to something."

"What, for instance?"

"What do you think we're doing here? Tunneling into Mexico? I can smell the oil."

Alonso went with him into the hut. The stench was asphyxiating. He thought for a moment of revulsion that he had entered an anteroom of hell. Something was banging like Thor's hammer at the earth. The wooden rig shook with it. Enough light came through the slats to see what was going on.

103

He was in a twelve-foot-square chamber, occupied by a kind of oscillating beam: like a huge jerky grasshopper it was jabbing industriously at the earth. Up and down, up and down. Alonso, drawing back fastidiously, realized how very simply it worked. It seemed as primitive as early man's first tools. There was a hissing donkey engine that just lifted and dropped a heavy punching bit into the hole. He peered down at it. He thought he could smell the effluvia of Hades. The endless percussion was giving him a headache. He looked nervously up at the tall wooden tower that seemed ready to fall about his ears.

"How far down have you gone?" he asked.

"Two hundred and ten feet. One hell of a hole," Pablo O'Hagerty said proudly. He took a drink from an unlabeled bottle, handing it to Alonso. He drank. It almost erupted in his throat. He had never tasted anything so volcanic.

"Is it not dangerous?"

"God almighty, friend, ain't nothing in this scenery that isn't dangerous. Spice of life. Who wants to live forever?" Alonso did. "Another drink?"

Dear heaven, no.

"Used up most of our pipe," Pablo O'Hagerty said. He peered down the rope that was letting the thudding bit go probing into the earth. Bang, bang, bang. I just want to get out before it all comes down on me, Alonso thought. Pablo O'Hagerty said, "This here's the bull wheel." The axle about which the rope was wound. "This here's the socket." But it was all too technical for Alonso. "And down there's the bit. Wear 'em out like bad teeth. Cost money, too. Nothing on this planet's for free. And we're sure running out of pipe. And today I hit it."

"Hit what?"

"That's the awful miracle of it. Nothing. Just went with a jerk into an open crevice two hundred feet below. Fished out the bit," Pablo O'Hagerty said, trembling now, returning to the bottle for support. How he sweated! "Feel the sand that came up with it. Smell it!"

Alonso stared at the handfuls of greasy soil he was thrusting under his nose. It didn't look like sand—more like slime. But smell it did. It oozed a little, like black pus from a wound. "Oil," Pablo O'Hagerty said. "We're almost there."

"I cannot breathe here. May we go outside?"

"Friend, you're present at an earth-shaking event. The world's turning over in delirium and all you want is fresh air."

But they went outside. The sun blazed, the prairie shimmered; even the birds were too slumberous to sing in the willows of the creek. There was nothing dramatic in the scene to suggest a miracle. The man is mad, Alonso thought.

It debased nature to go probing into the mysteries of the earth's bowels. He wondered heavily what had directed Frank Dibbler to drill just here. Some divine signal?

And he was sure Pablo O'Hagerty could read his sarcastic mind. He grinned. "Come with me, friend." He went down to the creek. "Take this."

"What is it?"

"Hazel twig. Hold it. So. Gently, brother. As if you were clutching your baby's throat. Now walk. Just walk."

Alonso felt foolish, holding the hazel wand, tips up, as he walked. Something vaguely sacrilegious about it, like a pagan rite. He was hardly aware at first of the wand tugging lightly in his sweaty fingers. Then it grew quite perceptible. He wanted to stop at once. "Move," Pablo O'Hagerty said. "You're warm." Suddenly the forked twig fluttered as if it were alive. I am doing nothing, Alonso thought wildly; I swear it; it is like a bird in my hands.

As they neared the rig, the wand thrust tentatively forward like a blind man's stick, it jumped. The sensation was dreadful: it dipped and struggled to tear itself out of his hands, and he was so appalled by the spasm that he threw it down. He was shaken beyond words.

"We're damn near the epicenter," Pablo O'Hagerty said. "I got a theory. You know what I think? There's stuff down there,

105

under the layers, made when the earth was young. Been lying there, waiting for Frank Dibbler and me to let it come up. And come up it will. Got to!" A hysterical half-breed. "We're nearly out of pipe and money. I'll tell you something else."

Alonso wished he wouldn't. It had scared him indescribably. It is against God's will, he thought.

"I'm going to put a few quarts of nitroglycerine down there and crack the crust. Like lancing a boil. That'll start her off."

Alonso stared at the bronzed pocked face, shiny with sweat; at the plaited black hair; I am listening to the crazy talk of an aborigine, he thought. The grandson of Warbonnet Chief Owl-in-the-Sky. *Madre de Dios,* let me soon get back to the sanity of Spain.

He got onto his horse. He could hear Pablo O'Hagerty chuckling. He rode off without a word and, unlike Lot's wife, didn't look back.

The heat was going out of the sky. An hour to dusk. He spurred his horse. Who knew who was watching him from some distant *arroyo?* Lizard-eyes? He came on his hoof trail across the salt flat. Better than a compass.

And so home to the ranch, not exactly sweating, but damp with relief. There was a great commotion. The *vaqueros* were unsaddling their horses. Someone was rubbing down the pinto. Frank Dibbler was back.

He was dog-tired. Gray. But with something worse than dust. His appearance startled Alonso. His eyes were wild with shock. He was over at the trough by the corral, stark naked, sluicing himself down. He saw Alonso dismount and said over his wet shoulder, "Saved me sending someone to look for you. Don't roam after dark."

He shouted for a towel. The man called Nueces Joe hurried forward to him with a jingle of spurs. They are nervous of him; he commands their respect, Alonso thought. He wouldn't have thought it possible with such villainous types.

"I am glad to see you safely back, Francisco."

He grinned. But it was an effort. "Didn't you think I would?"

Something has happened, Alonso told himself. Something terrible. What can it be? "It is not the most peaceful of lands, Francisco," he said.

"Been looking around?"

"Just to see the prairie."

"It's beautiful."

It is the devil's playground, Alonso thought. "Have you ridden far?"

"Far enough." He dropped the towel into the dirt. He gave Alonso a grim look. "Enough to see what had to be seen." He dragged his pants over his still damp buttocks. Alonso saw Maria watching him through the window. He caught sight of her, too; his eyes narrowed sharply as if he had forgotten for the moment who she was. Then he went into the house, beckoning Alonso to follow.

He sat at the desk, his hair spilling drops. His feet were bare. He didn't belong to a desk.

He said in a quenched voice, so that he could hardly be heard, "I'm damn near ruined, Alonso."

"How so?"

"Drought. I've watched my cattle dropping in their tracks. I counted three hundred dead with my own eyes. Treble it, quadruple it maybe, over the whole range. If it goes on I won't have a cow left inside a month."

Alonso whispered, "May God forgive us."

"For what? Something I did?" He was suddenly angry. Then his bloodshot eyes half closed, and Alonso thought he had fallen asleep. But his voice came like an echo out of a grave. "You a great Bible reader, Alonso?"

"No, no." What was he trying to say?

"Talk about the valley of dry bones. I've seen gulches littered with bleached skulls that'd make old Ezekiel sit up. Buzzards are busy down there; sky's black with them. Smell it a mile off. Drives the horses mad."

107

You, too, Alonso thought. You have very nearly been driven mad. "What is to be done, Francisco?"

"Pray." He drew on his boots. His mouth was still full of dust and he went to the window to eject it. "Wait for rain. Or get the rest to pasture before they feed the buzzards, too."

He stretched himself awake. He walked stiffly. He'd ridden farther than Alonso guessed. He shouted into the kitchen, "Food, Joachim," as if he'd blotted all his troubles out of his mind. Miguel joined them. He was very chastened; he was usually the chatterbox at the table. The Mexican had set three places for dinner. He came hurrying in with a tureen of stew.

Frank Dibbler stared at him. "You been using your fat thumbs to count, Joachim?"

The Mexican's squint roamed to avoid his glance. Don't look at me, Alonso thought.

"Why three places?" Frank Dibbler asked.

"Señor, the Condesa . . ."

"Mrs. Dibbler." It had angered him. "Say it."

"Mrs. Dibbler." It grated oddly on Alonso's ears; six hundred years of nobility had suddenly been peeled off her. The Duke would have been outraged. The Mexican sweated. "Señor, she does not eat."

"Why not?"

Alonso sighed. My compassion will get me into trouble. But I must say something, he thought.

"Francisco," he murmured pacifyingly, "it is a question of pride. She is very well-born and therefore highly strung . . ."

"I've been strung as high as Haman these last few hours." He looked as if he still had the noose about his neck. "Lay a place for Mrs. Dibbler, Joachim."

"Si, señor." He ran out.

"Do not let her starve," Alonso muttered. "She must be ravenous. Not a morsel for almost two days."

"And what sort of tomfoolery's that?"

"Francisco, if you were to be a little patient." There was no

108

need to tell him about the sowbelly she threw out. "If you were to take her a tray of food . . ."

"She's my wife. My wife sits at my table. What do you think my hands would say if this got about?" Alonso thought he might have relented if he'd been less exhausted. But he'd suffered a numbing disaster; there was still no color in his face; his eyes were red-veined from the glare of the sun and the rasp of dust. He went along the corridor to her room. Mother of Mercy, Alonso prayed, do not let him raise a hand to her. He hurried outside to listen. The door was wide open. He could hear every word.

". . . nothing. I want nothing. It would choke me. I will starve rather than eat under your roof." This was Maria.

And his flat intractable voice, "That's for you to choose. But you take your seat at my table. You don't make a spectacle of me before my servants."

"Leave my room."

"With you. Walk or be carried. We start right now as we mean to go on." As *he* meant to go on. "I'll manhandle you if need be."

"You would not dare."

"Try me."

"Lay one finger on me . . ." then a high-pitched gasp. What was he about to do to her? Alonso cringed. Then Maria again, agonized with loathing, "Do not touch me. Do you hear?"

"Take your seat."

"I can walk by myself."

"Walk, then. And fast."

"You are vile."

"Unsavory." He didn't sound as if he liked her much, either. "Forgive me. I've had a hard sweaty ride."

Alonso returned to his chair. Miguel's horror-stricken eyes were fixed on him. "Pretend," he whispered to his son. "These matters are beyond your understanding. Do not embarrass her." They were eating as Maria walked in and sat. She stared emptily across the table; but her face was deathly pale. Frank Dibbler took his seat. He nodded to the Mexican hovering uneasily in the doorway, and he heaped Maria's plate with stew. Its aroma was fearfully attractive. She didn't glance at it. And everybody pretended that it wasn't there.

I will remember this conversation to the end of my days, Alonso thought. It was as unreal as a dream. He said to Frank Dibbler, "I visited your friend Pablo O'Hagerty this afternoon," trying to keep his fascinated eyes off Maria. She sat, head erect, averted from the plate. He would have bet every peso he had in the world she wouldn't eat. He knew the glacial pride of the Estremadurans; it would never break.

"So I figured, Alonso," Frank Dibbler said politely. As usual he was bolting his food. It was merely something to fill up his bottomless belly. As a matter of fact, by some miracle, the Mexican had managed to knock up a most appetizing stew. Accidents happened to everybody. "What did you think of Pablo?" he asked.

"He is either insane or a divinely inspired man."

"He could be both." Frank Dibbler grinned. As far as he was concerned, his wife Maria didn't exist. "He put you through the hazel-twig act, did he?"

"Yes. I don't believe it happened. Pure hallucination. It was some kind of Indian rope-vanishing trick." Though it was a different race of Indians who practiced that. "What does that primitive know about oil?"

"My father was a timberwolf. What did he know about cattle? But he built up the biggest herds this end of the Panhandle."

"What do *you* know about oil?"

"Less than Pablo. But I'm twice as mad. Four times as strong, and ten times as dedicated. It's a weapon I'm going to use. You don't have to know how a Winchester works to shoot."

Miguel was watching Maria frozenly. She looked ill. Alonso kicked his leg under the table to distract his attention.

110

"Your mad friend O'Hagerty is going to put a few quarts of nitroglycerine down the hole. He says it will start something off."

Frank Dibbler said pensively, "He'd better be careful. It's been known to start off more than you can stop. Joachim," he suddenly shouted, "more stew."

"Si, señor," the Mexican said. The scent of the opened tureen welled across the table.

Alonso saw Maria tremble. Her face was ghastly. Her empty stomach must be tearing her nerves to shreds.

Say something! He couldn't bear to look at her. "Where will you get the money to continue the drilling?" he asked.

"*Inshallah*," Frank Dibbler said. Where did he pick up such expressions? "It rests with God."

"Father," Miguel said in a high upset voice, "I cannot stay . . ."

He couldn't bear it, either. But Frank Dibbler put his hand firmly on his wrist. It had happened quite suddenly, at the very moment he'd said, "It rests with God." She had picked up her spoon tragically. The tears rolled down her face. She ate. She was famished. It almost broke Alonso's heart.

They ignored her. When she had finished, Frank Dibbler went to his den for his Cuban cheroots; but it was only to give her time to retire from the table with grace. And when he returned she had gone back to her room.

All that shouting? What was it? Did no one ever sleep in this territory? Alonso crept out of bed. It was barely dawn. A steely pink flush in the sky, as cold as the floorboards to his feet. A thin horned moon, and long ghastly shadows on the silent prairie. The commotion was over by the corral, where a horse was keening.

Another bad dream? He rubbed his eyes. Mother of . . . what *was* going on? Maria sat the horse. Frank Dibbler had it

111

by the bridle. It reared. Half the cowmen had been dragged bewilderedly out of bed.

Then Frank Dibbler's chill voice to Maria, "Where, goddamn it, do you think you are going?"

He was only half-dressed—shirt, long woolen underpants and bare feet. Clownish. There was nothing there to make Alonso laugh.

And Maria, trying to tear the horse loose, "I am leaving. I am going home."

She was beside herself. Alonso thought she would bring her whip down on Frank Dibbler's face.

"This is your home."

"My prison. I will suffer it no longer. I am not your slave."

But he was staring furiously about. "Who saddled this horse for her?"

The *vaqueros* shrank from him. The Anglo-Saxons called Alfalfa and Nueces Joe were as scantily dressed, but one of them, the man Lofty, wore boots. They were all looking at him. He began guiltily, "Now, then, Frank . . ."

"You?"

"Lady asked me. Seemed a polite thing to do," and yelped as Frank Dibbler lashed the back of his hand across his face.

"What did she give you for it?"

"Frank, nothing . . ."

"What did she let you do to her?" and Maria hit him hard with her whip.

"Get off that horse."

"Never. I am going to El Paso."

"And then?"

"There are people who will help me. I have my grandmother's jewels." She hardly knew what she was saying, or doing. She had a small velvet bag. She tore it open and there was a tiny red and white winking as the dawn light caught the stones. Alonso heard the *vaqueros* gasp. "They will pay to take me home to Spain."

112

"You'd never see El Paso."

"Take your hand off my horse."

"Mine," he corrected her brutally. "You're my wife. You don't have a thing that isn't mine." Spoken like a Turkish pasha; this is not a land that is kind to women, Alonso thought.

He saw Frank Dibbler's mouth loosen to a grim sardonic smile. He suddenly released the horse. "*Vaya usted con Dios*," he said. Go with God.

She reined the horse about. Alonso couldn't believe his ears. He was *letting* her go?

He called out to her, "But you won't get there with your hair intact." It held her for a few moments. "You'll meet Comanche hostiles who'd treasure that scalp of yours on a lance. There'll be wandering saddlebums who'd flatten you, soon as look at you, in the grass. Buffalo hunters who'd do it maybe sooner. You go flashing those jewels of yours and you're signing a warrant for a quick death." He gave the horse a hard slap to send it on its way. "You won't live out three days alone on the range."

She gave him a wild look and spurred her horse up the brow of the slope, and stopped. Alonso could see her still silhouette on the ridge. He knew what deterred her. The cold sky glittered. He'd looked out there himself and been similarly appalled.

The moan of the dawn wind. The dust already rising, a thin livid base of rainless cloud scurrying over the range. Vast, empty and malevolent. A bird crying out mournfully, the shadows creeping stealthily across boundless grass and gulch—a prison to all but the hardiest of men. It could chill the sturdiest heart.

Silence. Nothing happening. And suddenly a small distant flash. It came from the valley. A shock-puff striking Alonso's face a second or so later. Still no sound. Then, rising above the ridge, a soot-black pillar of smoke, all mixed up with yellow flame like a badly made sulphur match, and he heard Frank Dibbler say in a wry voice, "Pablo."

113

He had put those few quarts of nitroglycerine down the hole. No wonder God sometimes laughs at us, Alonso thought.

And then they were gone. As if a giant hand had swept them off like leaves. There was a rush for the horses, the pouring of hoofs over the ridge, the ludicrous sight of Frank Dibbler in long underpants astride an unsaddled horse, barefooted and unspurred. And the thunder of them receded and they were lost to sight in their dust. Alonso was left with Miguel stammering, "Father, what has happened?"

Alonso said grimly, "What would you expect to happen when you mix an Irish-Indian with the most dynamic explosive known to man." Trouble. He dressed hastily. He wanted to see for himself.

Nobody was left to saddle his horse for him but the Mexican cook. Miguel was already mounted, and impatient to be off. Alonso gave him a dubious look; how he has changed! If I am not careful he will turn into a veritable *gringo,* which, when we return to fastidious Seville society, will simply not do.

He was surprised to find Maria still sitting her horse, as frozen as a statue, on the brow of the slope. "Maria?" Her eyes were wet. Pale; how it tweaked his heart!

"I am trapped," she said. "It is a prison without bars," and he would never have thought she could cry so distressfully. The convent cell wouldn't have been so penal. She turned her horse back to the house.

They could see the earth spitting smoke and flame as they approached. Still half a mile off they could hear its roar. A filthy billowing gush, streaked with orange tongues. They couldn't get too near because of the heat. The stockhands had gathered in an awed circle about it, shielding their faces. They looked queerly helpless; there wasn't much they could do. The smell was revolting. The grass had been widely sprayed with oil, and it caught here and there, burning with little private fires until a cowman stamped them out. But nobody would stamp out that roaring jet. Nobody—even if he had the boot to do it—could get near enough.

Alonso caught sight of Frank Dibbler a quarter way round the inferno, shouting to Nueces Joe and Alfalfa. A little wild, he looked brisk and businesslike, and still ludicrous in his now-stained underpants. The two cowmen rode off fast. Pablo, the Prometheus who had started it all off, sat on a hillock some distance off, his hooded eyes drunk with elation. It was hard to get him to talk coherently.

"I told you," he said, "half a crock of nitro'd start her off . . ."

"How much is half a crock?"

"Two gallons."

Mad. And start her off—was she feminine?—it had. He said, "She just shook a little. Nothing much happened. I could hear the pop." He had dropped the can of nitro down and detonated it with a blasting stick. It just shuddered. "And then burst. Up like the hounds of hell."

He had to run for his life. He was lucky; he'd caught the first spray of oil, but he was well away before it ignited. All he'd suffered was a singed braid of hair. A burned Indian. This could happen nowhere but in a raw continent, Alonso thought.

"Muck and oil," Pablo said, gazing dimly about. "Must be burning God-knows-how-many dollars away." Alonso guessed that the gusher had crested a hundred and fifty feet. A fountain of stench and disruption. The *vaqueros*, sensitive as animals, were watching it uneasily. They knew that the old prairie would never be the same again.

The drilling rig? The hut? All gone. "Blown to hell-and-Oklahoma," Pablo said.

"You cannot let it burn forever."

"Frank's sent the boys off to the *rancheros* around. They'll pick up all the stump-blasting powder they can lay hands on. We'll snuff it out."

No, you won't; anyway, not as easily as you started it off,

Alonso thought. There will be much pain and misery, with the devil maybe welcoming a couple of newly scorched faces, before you snuff that roaring candle out.

Nothing was going to happen for a long time. It wasn't a situation that was agreeable to a delicately bred man. He decided to ride back before he became hungry. But Miguel said stubbornly, "Father, I wish to remain here."

"Why?"

"It excites me."

"How can that be so?" Alonso could no longer understand his son. "Everything smells. You may catch fire. These people are capable of unpredictable acts of violence and wildness."

"Yes, Father. That is why I wish to stay."

Presently the cook, Joachim, drove up with a chuck wagon, so there was no need to go back. He had slabs of congealed beef and coffee that suggested the hot mud of the gusher. It wasn't worth his journey. As the afternoon drew on it grew very hot. The pall of smoke that blanketed the creek made Alonso feel faint. He rode a little way up into the hills and nestled down in the grass. Here it was quite pleasant. A meadowlark sang; insects hummed . . . and he fell asleep.

A far-off yell woke him. He remembered where he was. He stared down at the creek; the flames were, if anything, fiercer than before, the smoke, dragged by the wind, like a fat oily finger pointing south. To some Biblical watcher up on the Judean heights, the end of Sodom and Gomorrah must have looked like that. He could see tiny figures running about. What were they up to? He had tied his horse to a cottonwood and he rode back.

Everything was heightened: heat, drama and stench. It was like a bad theatrical production that had got out of hand. There were many new faces in the crowd. Burly leathery men with drooping moustaches; Alonso guessed them to be neighboring ranchers, come to see what was happening to the range. He didn't think they liked it. The cattle wouldn't like it, either. The

116

oil spray had saturated the entire hillside so that not a blade of grass would grow there for years.

Nueces Joe and Alfalfa had returned like blockade-runners. They drove a wagon piled with wooden boxes. Alonso, with a slightly breathless feeling, could guess what they contained. A grizzled man sat dustily on the tailboard, smoking a cigar. Was it not dangerous? He drew back. He found himself near Pablo and asked him who the man was.

"That's Sam. From the old silver mine workings. Got us a nice load of blasting powder. Now we'll get the business done."

Alonso stared hard at the Irish-Indian. Surely he was frightened? But the hooded sultry eyes were exultant. Insensitive. He didn't know what fear was.

Frank Dibbler was conferring with the man, Sam, over by the wagon. Pablo went across to join them. Nueces Joe and Alfalfa were breaking open those ominous-looking boxes. Alonso went near enough to listen: no nearer.

He heard the grizzled man say, "Here's the stuff for you, Frank. You got a right royal fire. Now you snuff it out. I brought you the seed-corn. You plant it. It's as far as I'll go."

"You're a great help," Frank Dibbler said.

The man, Sam, chuckled throatily. "Be less help to my widow if I stuck my nose into a blaze like that."

"What'd blow it out?"

"Ask God to spit on it. Don't figure anything else will."

"Pablo," Frank Dibbler said wearily, "this is old man pessimist Job. Let's show him, shall we?"

Pablo said, bright-eyed, "A box at a time. Go in fast, over on the windward side, and toss it in."

"Drench the horses first."

"That's right."

"I hear Indians don't burn."

"Now's the time to find out."

How could they be laughing? And *were* Indians noninflam-

117

mable? Alonso thought: this is the kind of conversation that drives a rational man mad.

He no longer wanted to watch. But he couldn't take his eyes off the two horses trotting down to the creek. They entered the water, both riders dousing their bodies well. That poor pinto, it will soon regret leaving my comfortable stable in Seville. He was shocked to hear one of the leathery ranchers mutter to a companion, "Fifty dollars says the mad Indian won't make it," the other primitive nodding: "Fifty. Done." Humanity wasn't a flower that flourished on the range.

Alonso was suddenly aware of a solitary mounted figure on the hillside. Could it be Maria? Come to watch herself be widowed? For her, perhaps, a merciful release.

There should have been a dramatic silence: but the roar of burning gas dinned in his ears. The wind took the spray of bursting oil and dropped it on the heads of the watching crowd like a befouled veil. A black slimy lake was collecting in the hollow. When it ignited . . .

Ah, God! The riders were hurrying back. "Miguel," Alonso said agitatedly, approaching his son, "this is not for you to see."

"Father, I shall never see anything like it again."

"So I should hope."

"They are not afraid. Why should I be?"

But they should be afraid!

"Do not worry, Father. They are indestructible."

"Nobody is indestructible." As the two riders, splashing back to the wagon, were about to demonstrate. "Miguel, they will burn. The sight will mark you for life . . ." but it was too late. They had each hoisted up a wooden box.

Frank Dibbler was the first to plunge forward, sluicing water. The pinto's hoofs threw off a spray of flying drops. Horse and rider vanished into the fringe of the smoke. Alonso blinked: I cannot bear to watch. Would they never emerge? Suddenly a dull thud, as if a paper bag had been burst. The smoke swirled momentarily, the flames slanting. And that was all. They came

118

pelting out of the haze like stung ghosts as Pablo raced in past them with his load. Alonso could hear them hooting with laughter. It was what distressed him most of all.

And another detonation. Another shudder inside the black curtain: the fire fluffed. And still burned. Back to the creek to souse themselves, trailing rivulets of scummy water, and in again. Passing and repassing each other, hurling the wooden boxes into the inferno, like medieval javelin-men assaulting a besieged fort.

And all the time those ululating howls. Insensate! Demented hooligans! What was there to howl about?

"Miguel . . . ," he begged.

"Father, be still." His son had never spoken to him so peremptorily. He was rapt with excitement. What was this maniacal country doing to him?

Frank Dibbler panting back to the wagon for another load, but stiffening. Pablo's horse, less its rider, had just emerged. The rancher was about to make his fifty dollars. Back into the smoke, no longer hooting; he reappeared with Pablo running alongside, clinging to his stirrup.

The conversation—I am sure I am dreaming it, Alonso thought—wasn't credible. He heard Frank Dibbler say to Pablo, "You singed?"

"Roasted on one side. Michael O'Hagerty's side. I discovered something. Warbonnet Chief Owl-in-the-Sky's side doesn't burn."

And again both laughing. Alonso couldn't see Maria very clearly; his eyelashes were beaded with sweat. It was a bitter business getting her widowed.

"Wasting our breath," he heard Frank Dibbler say. "It's like spitting into a brazier." That grizzled cynic, Sam, had been right. Only God could spit it out.

"Let's shove the lot in," Frank Dibbler said. "One trick. All or nothing."

"Whole wagon?"

119

"Take her up top." He scanned the slope. It was a rough grassy descent to the inferno. "Let's run her in."

"Whatever you say, Frank."

"Scared?"

"It's Michael O'Hagerty in me that's scared."

"Then get Warbonnet Chief Owl-in-the-Sky aboard. I'll stay with the wagon. You take the mules."

He climbed into the driving seat. Pablo mounted the leading mule of the pair. Their eyes rolled; they scented danger. You have every reason to, Alonso thought. He watched Pablo spur them up the slope. The wagon trundled heavily. There were still a lot of those wooden boxes left. It reached the crest, and waited, outlined starkly against the sky. It was interminable. What were they doing up there? Fiddling with the harness?

Alonso stared wildly across at Maria. He didn't think she'd moved a muscle all this time.

The leathery one said softly, "Two hundred dollars say they'll blow themselves to hell," and the other rancher contemplated the run of the grassy slope, judging the value of each tussock, and said, "You have yourself a bet."

"Something you gambling gentlemen might care to consider," the man Sam said. He was chewing a straw. "We're right in the line of the run. If that wagon misses the fire we're all liable to meet in hell."

Alonso had never seen such unanimity of decision. There was a quick rush to a safer knoll over at the edge of the valley. Still no movement of the wagon. Frank Dibbler standing up in it, a small figure on the skyline. Alonso saw him suddenly wave.

"Knew his father," the grizzled man said. He was at Alonso's side. "Don't know which of them is madder. Ain't the only thing that makes them alike. One of them's dead. Inside half a minute, if I'm not mistaken, t'other's going to be dead too."

And Pablo screeching from the back of the mule. The wagon was on the move. The whip cracked. The mules stretched, showing their teeth, gravity shoving the wagon hard behind. It rocked violently, gathering speed. I cannot breathe, Alonso

120

thought. He had his hand on Miguel's shoulder and felt the sweat on his neck. They were halfway down, and still racing, the wooden boxes jolting, the . . . and suddenly a yell that echoed through the roar of the burning gas. A space appeared between the wagon and mules. Frank Dibbler had slashed away the traces and the shaft pole was free. The mules veered off at an angle, the wagon continuing on its way.

It was off course; and so little distance to go. Suicidal, Alonso thought. It had dried the saliva in his mouth. He saw Frank Dibbler leap and bury himself in the grass, arms hooded to protect his head. A heave of the grass took the wagon and corrected its course.

Miracles sometimes happen, Alonso thought; it plunged straight into the heart of the fire. His knees wouldn't bend. His mind said: get down. It was the shock of the explosion that threw him to the ground. Hideously fascinated, he peered through the cage of his fingers. The smoke gave a vast fluff. The flames streaked sideways and vanished. Debris soared into the sky, a fountain of unmelted bits of the engine and the drilling rig, raining down with a patter like hail. The whole force of the gas was directed upward. It ignited for the last time in a thin yellow jet, and what Alonso now saw belonged only to the imagination of hell. It was as if some frustrated demon had launched a variation of the Indian rope trick: the pipe came writhing out of the hole, shooting aloft through the pall of smoke, section after section, twisting into fantastic hairpin shapes, hot and red, sinking back into the smoke like spent rockets.

And then nothing but the hiss of steam issuing from the bowels of the earth. It was the demon's last gasp. The debris continued to fall for a little while. But the fire was out.

Alonso got up. He searched about for Maria. Still disappointingly unwidowed. She was gone.

He saw Frank Dibbler come slithering down the slope. Nobody seemed to think it peculiar that he wore nothing but a shirt and long woolen underpants.

Alonso suddenly remembered him in his shabby Mexican

121

suit, getting out of the coach at Seville, big and reserved, murmuring delicately, "Dusty, don't you think?" It wasn't the same man! "We're different animals, Alonso," Frank Dibbler had said. I don't want to be that kind of animal, Alonso thought.

He unlocked his jaw. His shirt was wet. "What happens now?" he asked.

The grizzled man was picking himself up at his side. "Now? He'll cap it. Hole's probably caved in, anyway. Seal it off with a few tons of earth and manure. It'll keep. He's got himself an oil well. He's in business," he said.

The frenetic activity that ensued passed over Alonso's head. He could take no part in it. It lasted three days. There was a steady coming and going of men with mattocks to seal off the well. Everybody was recruited: stockmen, horse wranglers and blacksmith. Even the Mexican cook was drawn in. Alonso had to subsist on what they called "cold vittles." Lead in his stomach.

Then, late afternoon of the third day, Frank Dibbler returned. It was done. "Alonso," he said gravely. Dusty, worn and exhausted: but serene. Alonso hardly recognized him. He found himself staring into the hard, entranced eyes of a supremely confident man.

He washed himself down at the corral trough. He was toweling his naked body when Pablo rode in with a quite remarkably attired man. Everything about him was white: the broadbrimmed hat, the swallow-tailed coat and the beautifully tooled Mexican boots. Even the trimmed Vandyke beard. The only touch of color lay in the shrewd pink face and the ornate cravat with its improbable diamond pin. Alonso asked whisperingly who he was.

"Money." He *looks* money, Alonso thought. He saw Frank Dibbler smile faintly. "Colonel M'Guffy. Oilman from Oklahoma. Come to muscle in on me," he said.

Alonso was by now sufficiently familiar with American custom to know that "Colonel" wasn't necessarily a military rank, but an honorary title accorded to a theatrical character. In Natchez he'd seen a "Judge" behind a roulette wheel. The Colonel called down from his horse, "How are you, Frank? You remember me, don't you?"

"I remember you, Colonel."

"I knew your father."

Frank Dibbler's eyes slanted sardonically as if to say: He knew you, too. He nodded. "Come on in. You're just in time for supper."

It was an astonishing meeting: a kind of white-clothed medicine-fakir and a totally naked man. Neither seemed disconcerted.

"Drink will do me kindly," the Colonel said, descending from his horse. He was smaller, and less dramatic on the ground. They went inside. Frank Dibbler dressed. He introduced Alonso, but the Colonel seemed to be a man of large vision and barely listened; he bowed absently. Pablo followed and stood watching amusedly, leaning on the door.

The Colonel glanced at the portrait of Frank Dibbler's father on the wall as if hoping he wouldn't enter the conversation. "Frank," he said, "I been looking at your hole in the ground . . ."

"It isn't a hole, Colonel. It's a well." Frank Dibbler's voice was very soft.

"Could be so. And again not." The Colonel was vaguely skeptical. "Most likely *not*. I have a nose for dry wells. Frank, son," he said sorrowfully, "I've drilled more sterile holes in this earth of ours . . ."

"Tequila?"

"Yes, son." The Colonel frowned at the interruption. "Tequila will do." They drank.

"I been looking at the two-hundred-feet sands your bit brought up. This Indian of yours . . ."

"He's half-Irish, Colonel."

123

"This breed," the Colonel corrected himself. "Stuff *smells* oil. Only the Almighty knows how much . . ."

"Colonel, I have the biggest gusher this continent has ever seen."

"Mighty big inference to draw out of a handful of sand."

"Out of a burst that's blown a hundred thousand dollars into the sky."

The Colonel stared at him. "You're a very confident man, Frank."

"I'm an arrogant man."

These people are like *condottiere,* Alonso thought. Robber barons. I don't know which of them is the hardest and shrewdest.

"All right, son. We'll stop playing words," the Colonel said. "You'll need money. Your rig's gone. Drilling gear. All your pipe's twisted tin. You're betting on a gusher, but it could be a quick spray, up and out, and nothing left but mud and smell. That's the risk of the game. Can you afford it?" The Colonel thawed and lit a cigar. "I've reached the age of foolishness when a man finds joy in a gamble. I'd grubstake you," he said, searching Frank Dibbler's face, "to say, a hundred thousand dollars as a starter . . ."

"Colonel, I thank you. But no."

The Colonel's eyes narrowed. He heard Pablo chuckle. He was faintly put out. "Frank, you won't get far, without me. I'm oil. I have the banks in my pocket. It'd be a fair split. Say, sixty-forty . . ."

"I share with nobody."

"Don't seem a reasonable business attitude, son. We could say seventy-thirty . . ."

"There's only cold beef, Colonel. Cook's been out at the well."

"No, thanking you kindly." A sharper, slightly fretful note in his voice. "Frank, let's talk plain. Say you have an eighty thousand barrel a day flow. There'll be storage tanks, pipeline to

124

tidewater, refinery deals to be made. Needs cash. And Frank, I happen to know—no offense, son?—you don't have ten dollars to clink one against the other at the bank."

"I have access to all the funds I need," Frank Dibbler said. "This is Don Alonso de los Sanchez, Count of Fuende. He's the largest and richest landowner in Spain."

Alonso felt a sharp, quite violent tremor. Never! And I am not the largest, certainly not the richest, landowner in Spain.

He was aware of the Colonel staring at him intently for the first time. "You in this business, sir?"

Alonso said with hauteur, "I am in no business, sir." He saw Frank Dibbler watching him blandly. He walked out.

He found Maria on the porch, sitting by the open window. Listening, of course. They could hear the continuing murmur of dry voices, the Colonel argumentative, Frank Dibbler cool and bone-hard. It seemed to Alonso that he'd been presented with a golden opportunity. Why hadn't he seized it? Presently, adamant as ever, Frank Dibbler saying, "No partners, Colonel. Sorry. You've had a long ride for nothing. I stand on my own feet."

And then the scraping of chairs, the Colonel coming out, nonplussed; he looked like a medicine man whose pills had unexpectedly failed. He gave Alonso a curiously antagonistic stare. He mounted his horse and rode off.

They heard Pablo say unsurely, "Frank, it was money."

"It was a rope round my neck. I don't take kindly to bridles. I keep what's mine."

"That Dibbler," Maria muttered scornfully to Alonso. Dibbler! What a way to refer to her husband. "King oil. You really think there is oil in his hole?"

"Ask the Indian. He is the diviner."

"You are going to give him money?"

"I? Are you mad? It was playacting. To impress the Colonel. Not a peso," Alonso said.

Supper began on a subdued note. Frank Dibbler at one end

125

of the table, Maria at the other, facing each other like antagonists kept safely out of physical reach, Alonso and Miguel like unwilling referees in between. Alonso was on pins to get the matter cleared.

"Francisco," he said with some urgency, "forgive me. It was something you said to the Colonel . . ."

"Forget it. I don't want your money, Alonso. It was just to spread the message that I have backing. Sooner or later I'm going to need the banks."

"You understand? It is no reflection on your prospects . . ."

"Day'll come when you'll be glad to go in with me. It'll make your son the wealthiest man in Spain."

Alonso glanced at Maria. Her dark eyes were mirrorless pools. She said nothing: saw nothing: heard nothing. She was a caged animal that wasn't interested in what went on inside the bars of her cage.

"But, Francisco, you have lost everything. The rig. Driller. Pipe and all. That man was right. You will need money to start again. Where will you get it?"

"I told you. I'm going to sell off what's left of my cows. Should be able to round up three thousand that can travel on the hoof." Three thousand! It seemed a gigantic operation. Alonso would learn that it was a small-to-moderate herd. Herds of ten thousand had been known. "Trail them north to the railhead. Wichita, maybe. Or Baxter Springs." They sounded dubiously dangerous places. "Might even fatten them a little on the way." Alonso watched Frank Dibbler's eyes narrow calculatingly: and suddenly he had a vision of countless hoofs treading north, dust unbelievable, the bellowing of thirsty cattle rumbling like thunder. "We'll lose a few stragglers. Hope to pick up a few stray calves. There's always wastage. There'll be Indian *wo-haw*," and he saw Alonso blink. "Indian tax. We'll be crossing their territory. We may have to pay what's due. But with God's luck we should be able to get twenty-eight hundred through. I've done better. A four-dollar cow'll get me thirty dol-

126

lars clear. Say, eighty thousand dollars." He was satisfied. "It'll do."

The balance sheet staggered Alonso. All he could do was blink.

"And then watch me," Frank Dibbler said. He was once more entranced. "Won't be anything to stop me. You'll live to look across that valley and see rigs growing like trees, pumping stations and tanks. It's just the start."

Maria spoke. It was unexpected. "How long will you be away?"

"Four, five weeks."

Her eyes glittered. When he gets back she will be gone, Alonso thought.

He saw Frank Dibbler glance at her fleetingly. He knew it, too.

Joachim, the cook, came in with supper. Cold beef as Frank Dibbler had threatened. If the longhorns were this muscular here, how unchewable would they be when they had walked six hundred miles north? The hardy *Americanos* must have specially sharp teeth.

Then Frank Dibbler surprised them. He bent his head to say grace. "Lord, for this meal set before us we give thanks . . ." but he wasn't really thanking God for the food. He was thanking Him for the oil.

V

ALONSO NOW STOOD back to watch the mechanics of a trail drive. He was astounded. He had thought that one merely collected together three thousand cows—it *was* three thousand, wasn't it?—and said to them: "Walk." And submissively they walked. He was wrong in the very first particular. The longhorn wasn't a submissive creature. It was the psychopath of the animal kingdom—a sullen, unpredictable neurotic that could roam with mindless apathy through storm and drought, and explode with mob rage at the creak of a tree. It had arrived from Spain with an ancestral ill-temper; in America it had acquired the unlovable disposition of an Arapaho savage. It was hard to lead, and if possible harder to eat.

But an expanding nation was clamoring for beef; if ever a statue was raised to the benefactor of early Texas it would portray a trudging four-legged ferocity with vast horns twisted meaningfully into the dollar sign.

The operation began with dust, the din of an Andalusian cattle-market and the awful stench of branded hide. Alonso shrank fastidiously from the bedlam. He felt lost. Frank Dibbler vanished overnight and returned leading a small posse of hired hands. Eleven bleak-eyed rednecks who said little and spat a great deal. They wore grimy bandana neckerchiefs and frayed hats that seemed to have been used for every conceivable hygienic purpose. Some of them had a curious faceless quality—blurred, perhaps intentionally, by a heavy moustache. It gave Alonso the uneasy suspicion that there might be lawmen about who could pin faces to them. It is a profession for bandits, he thought.

It disturbed him to see his son associating with them freely. "Miguel," he said with heavy paternalism, "you will one day be a grandee of Spain. One must choose one's company . . ."

"Father, how can you not find them exciting?"

How? Alonso peered at him incredulously. One had only to use one's nose. They stank. "Miguel, they are rather dubious characters . . ."

"I have met worse in Spain."

So had Alonso. With sonorous titles, too. He gave his rebellious son a sharp look. Someone had fitted him out with a small pony and leather pants and a coarse working shirt. Hardly proper for the heir to the Count of Fuende! "Miguel," he said testily, "you are getting to be very argumentative . . ."

"It is this country, Father. It stirs the blood. I have never felt so free."

Free! Trapped in a camp of whiskered primitives. All it did was chill Alonso's blood. He came out with Maria to watch the new arrivals, and they raised their disreputable hats to her politely, saying one by one, "Howdy, ma'am," studying her appraisingly from breasts to hips as they trotted by. Alonso heard her grit her teeth. "*Peons*," she said.

"Maria," he sighed, "it is the kind of humanity you will have to live with. Try to . . ."

"Did you see their eyes?"

He wasn't blind. "Eyes don't break bones."

"My brothers would break their backs for them if they were

129

here." But they weren't, and maybe it was just as well. Alonso had eyes, too. He had observed that these cattle-*bandidos* were belted with guns. To them the noble family of Estremadura was nothing but a fairytale sham.

He saw Maria's glance wander venomously to Frank Dibbler, getting down from his horse, as if hoping that he would at least slip and break a bone; but he wasn't the kind of man to oblige. He heard her swear softly. She went inside.

And then, unexpectedly, the whole brawling business of getting an army of mentally deranged cattle to walk six hundred miles suddenly fascinated Alonso. He didn't know how it began. Maybe with the startling discovery that a great trail drive didn't just happen: it was put together like a military operation. Efficiently, too—despite the bedlam of bleating longhorns and the obscene yelling of cowmen that curdled his blood. He got himself a pony out of the livery stable and, in his silk-faced frock coat and tall beaver hat, trotted interestedly about to watch. The cowmen ignored him; there was too much to be done. He was just something odd on the landscape. (They called him privately "Don Quixote" and "the Spanish duke," knowing that he was under the special protection of Frank Dibbler, being very careful not to let him hear.) And while he was contentedly roaming the corrals the ground began queerly to shake; he felt his pony shiver. What was it? It grew into the drumming of countless hoofs; the winter-wild stock of horses was being brought in from the range. The maniacal howling of the outriders hustled them on. They came swooping into the corrals, raising a haze like a northern fog.

Alonso hung back, watching the barbarians making usable mounts out of mustangs that had never felt a rope. It appalled him. He couldn't understand men who made a profession out of battling with such murderous hoofs. They were all gaunt hairy geldings, descended like the longhorns from abandoned stock, and very nearly as mad. In Seville he would have had them exterminated as vermin. "Breaking-in" they called it. He expected it to end up more ominously with men being broken-up.

He left hurriedly. Already there was one rider less for the trail: he lay in the dirt with a cracked arm. The shrieking pony had been shot.

In those ten minutes of horrified observation he had learned that the guns the rednecks carried weren't just theatrical adornment. Only a quick bullet had saved the sprawling man from being kicked to death.

He found a haven of peace in the Mexican cook's kitchen. Out of it came the suffocating odor of beans boiling and salt pork being fried—the provisioning of a regiment of migrating cowmen was going on. Joachim steamed in the heat; peering in on him, Alonso shuddered to discover that he was flavoring every barrel of beans with a pint of sweat. Thank God I will not have to eat it. He said insincerely, "It smells good." It smelled rank.

"Help yourself, my friend."

"Thank you." Alonso recoiled. "I have already eaten." He wished he could shut out the battering of horses' hoofs on the corral fence and the yells of men running for their lives. "You will no doubt be relieved to see them go."

"But, Señor Alonso," Joachim said, squinting at him curiously, "I am going with them."

You are? Heaven help you, Alonso thought. "And you are not frightened?"

"Of course I am frightened. It is a terrible journey. I have made it four times. Once to Dodge City, which is a sink of iniquity, and three times to Abilene, which is not much better. *Por Dios.*" Joachim shrugged fatalistically. "Our lives are in the hands of God."

"There are great dangers, are there? Indians and the like?"

"Wherever there are *gringos* there are great dangers. They are worse than the Indians. They are all mad, as you have doubtless observed."

Alonso thought it a little harsh. "Reckless, I admit. But wonderfully self-sufficient."

131

"*Caballeros* of quality like us," Joachim said loftily, "are above such vulgar considerations," and went back to sweat-flavoring his beans.

And Frank Dibbler? Alonso caught only fleeting glimpses of him—into the ranch house for a snatched meal, wolfed down as if a thunderstorm might burst outside, then back to the saddle, riding the range like a medieval baron who didn't dare take his eyes off his fief. Alonso guessed that he was out with his hands, rounding up the steers from remote gulches, running them into bunches that would finally be thrown into one huge herd. Alonso could hear them bawling unmusically over the horizon, as if already they suspected the grinding journey they were about to make. Six hundred miles of daunting prairie to cross. With raiding Comanches. Storms unspeakable. And a pitiless wind. What a walk!

And the end of it? The butcher's yard.

Terrible to be a Texan cow, Alonso thought.

One afternoon he saw a motionless rider on the crest of a hill, knew that it was Frank Dibbler, and joined him. Silently they stared down at the bleached valley. Strings of cattle were being driven up. The cowboys, for some reason that escaped Alonso, were singing to them. It seemed to give the irascible beasts peace.

Frank Dibbler glanced at him with a sidelong chuckle. "You'll sweat to death in that outfit, Alonso."

Alonso thought rather stiffly: even in the jungle one owes it to oneself to dress like a gentleman. He eased the wet brim of his furry hat. He was sure he would melt.

"Will you never rest, Francisco?"

Another soft chuckle. "Plenty of rest in the grave. Lots to do between now and then."

An eruptive man. Alonso peered at him sadly; the grave was the only place in which he would ever rest.

They were very high up, and he could see far across the shimmering range, flowing with heat, the dried-up *arroyos* like

132

lime-white gashes, the bleak hills . . . and then distance. Nothing but distance. He felt as he'd felt once before: a man could go on and on until he fell over the edge of the earth. It was as if Satan had brought him up here to show him the king-doms of the world to tempt him—and it didn't. It only fright-ened him. That burning sun! And worst of all, harsher than any other affliction, that harassing wind! It swept up the crest, bear-ing all the topsoil of the dry valley, tearing at his face like the edge of a saw. He looked again at Frank Dibbler; there he sat, boneless, always like that squashed sack of corn, squinting calmly across the maltreated land as if he knew all its tricks and exactly how to trump them. Squatting relaxed in the saddle, burned to the color of bronze; the blown earth fringed his eye-lashes, settling on his hooded lids like dust on a shelf.

"The wind, Francisco," Alonso sighed. "It blows everything away."

"That's what the wind's for."

"How can men stand it? Such a cruel country. How can you even love it?"

"Didn't say I love it, Alonso. Just aim to tame it. That's what men are for."

Let him tame it. Heavenly Mother, work me a small miracle; let me go to sleep and wake up tomorrow in my kindly home in Seville.

He watched the cattle laboring up the slope—they had found themselves a leader. Another Frank Dibbler! A hard muscular steer that shoved on, never looking back to see if it was being followed, taking its authority for granted.

"Francisco." He touched his arm, wondering if perhaps he felt a sentimental pang . . . but he wasn't even looking at them. He was finished with them. All he wanted was the dollar-worth of their carcasses to bail him out.

He was staring like an obsessed lover down at the creek. He'd twisted his head to get a glimpse of the mountain of earth they'd thrown over his gusher. Alonso knew suddenly that he

133

came here every day to look at it. It wasn't a perfect seal; already the soil was saturated with leaking oil. Inside a month, at its rate of escape, the broken-backed rig would poke like the funnel of a foundered ship out of a slimy lake.

And then a smell so offensive that Alonso reeled. His pony uttered a whinny of pure fear; even Frank Dibbler's pinto, that stolid beast, went tap-tapping fastidiously back. A forest of horns came shoving up the defile. *Madre mía.* The stench of the brethren. Humped shoulders. Legs like steel picks. Cunning little hair-shrouded eyes. Alonso retreated without dignity from the malignancy of their stare. He thought: a five-week pilgrimage with them across the prairie would age me fifty years.

He said, handkerchief to nose, "How much longer, Francisco?"

Frank Dibbler ran a professional eye over the rabble. "To get them in? Brand them? Four days."

"And *then* you rest?"

"Then we start to walk."

I will be thinking of you. Alonso shrugged. *Vaya usted con Dios.* Walk with God. But not with me.

Now something had to be said. It lay on his conscience. "Francisco," he began uneasily, "about Maria . . ."

"I know about Maria."

"Then you know, too, that she will not be here when you return?"

He grinned. "I'm a sensitive animal. Doesn't take much to figure out what's in her mind."

Alonso said with pity, "Let her go, Francisco. You will never be able to keep her. It is against nature. A man cannot hold a wife who hates him . . ." and then his tongue froze: Frank Dibbler was staring at him with surprise as if he'd said something foul in church.

"*Amigo,*" he murmured, "this is the sovereign state of Texas. We don't permit our wives to hate us."

Alonso blinked at him. "You don't?"

134

"Nor leave us." He took off his hat to wave it about. It was ledged with grit and the wind blew it back into his mouth. He expectorated it in a solid glob. How his manners had suffered since he left Spain. He said calmly, "I own this land, far as you can see. You think it's mine just because it's there? It's mine because I *hold* it. Maria is my woman. I hold her, too."

Like a Biblical patriarch. Listen to him. Thinks he owns her like his horses and his cows.

"That's right," Frank Dibbler said dryly, as if he could read Alonso's mind through glass. "You heard her take her vows, didn't you?"

How holy he was! "Francisco," Alonso begged, "be a little considerate . . ."

"We made a bargain. I never went back on one in my life. I expect her to keep to hers." He gave Alonso a sardonic look. "I didn't exactly drag her by her hair to the altar."

No. He'd just put his big shoulder behind her and shoved her in that general direction. And I helped him, Alonso thought. Somebody up there will judge me for that.

The heat. He thought he would burst out of his silk-faced frock coat like a snake out of its skin. "What is it you want of her, Francisco?"

"Sons."

In plural? He might as well put her out to stud. "She will never . . ."

Frank Dibbler said implacably, "She will. In time."

Three centuries, perhaps. One last try. Poor Maria! "Francisco, I beg of you . . ."

"That's enough, Alonso."

"You cannot treat her like that. She is an Estremaduran . . ."

"She's a Dibbler," he said flatly. "*Amigo,* shut up."

It wouldn't make any difference. Alonso bit his tongue. Before the cow-army was six miles along the trail she would be off.

He still had himself and Miguel to think of. He watched

Frank Dibbler jerk his pinto about. "Who will look after us while you are gone?"

"Be a smattering of *vaqueros* left to watch shop."

Alonso suddenly remembered the fortress-thick walls and heavy battle-shutters of the ranch house. They weren't for nothing. There were always roving hostiles about. Kiowa. What, in the name of horror, would I do if a painted war-party came knocking at the door? He cried out nervously, "Is that all?"

"Should be enough." He heard Frank Dibbler laugh, "Might be safer if you came along."

Does he think I am mad? "Never."

"Be good for Miguel's education. Open him up."

Alonso thought tartly: he has already been opened up enough. The herd was straggling out into a disorganized mob and Frank Dibbler went spurring after them, shouting over his shoulder, "*Dios le guarde.*" Trust in God.

Easy to say. It was a terribly big prairie, and God had other places to watch. It had given Alonso another anxiety. He took off his stylish beaver to wipe his damp brow, and followed Frank Dibbler down.

He found the ranch house silent. They were all out at the branding. No sign of Miguel; Alonso thought exasperatedly, he will stink of those unsavory beasts. He could hear them bleating as if they were being burned alive. The Mexican cook had deserted the kitchen to stock up the chuck wagon: the traveling commissariat. Alonso wandered aimlessly about the empty house, his footsteps echoing eerily on the stone floor. He thought he heard a creak in Maria's room.

He knocked at the door. No answer. He looked in.

She turned on him sharply. What was she up to? "Don Alonso, it is customary to knock."

"Didn't you hear?"

"No." She had been too busy packing a valise with her

136

clothes. She couldn't even wait. But it was what was strewn glitteringly across the table that mesmerized his eyes. Her grandmother's jewels.

"You should keep them locked up, Maria."

She said in an arid voice, "Do you think I would trust them with *him?*"

"What are you doing?" As if he needed to ask.

"They will be gone in four days. Thirty minutes later I will be off, too."

But not in the same direction. He went close to look at the jewels. A few antique trinkets, most of them gold. The dead duchess who had bequeathed them had hung on to the heirlooms even when bread was short. Rubies. Pearls. A bracelet that had been hammered by a silversmith in Queen Isabella's day. Not too valuable intrinsically; but in them lay the history of a great noble house.

"Maria, you cannot be thinking of . . ."

She took up a heavy gold ring. It was encrusted with seed pearls. "This will pay to get me to the coast." She slipped on a couple of bracelets. "These will pay for the voyage back to Spain."

"And who pays for your husband's passage?"

She said something rather vile that suggested she would sacrifice another trinket to pay for his passage to hell.

"You are still his wife."

"But not for long. My father still has some influence with the church. It will not take long to get it annulled."

She was very excited, almost triumphant. Already she could sense the familiar smell of dead leaves in the courtyard of the Duke's house in Seville. It was a long, long way off. Her eyes glowed; her cheeks flushed. She would have less to glow about by the time she got to New Orleans. She would be a lot less flushed, a lot sicker, after the fearful crossing in a bucket of a ship to Spain. He studied her intently. A very handsome woman, if you liked them mad with arrogance. Dusky, red-

137

lipped and full-figured. She *was* equipped to bear sons. In plural. Pity. She and that implacable husband of hers could start a small Texan dynasty.

"Think about it carefully, Maria."

"For weeks I have thought of nothing else."

"Has he ever . . . ?"

She stiffened. "Tried to use me? Force me?"

"He has *some* marital rights, Maria."

"He would not survive the night with his eyes in his head."

"This will be a great country one day. Much greater than Spain. Richer by far. Your children would inherit a . . ."

She said scathingly, "As *Americanos?*" As if she could wish nothing worse on them, not even death.

"You will never make it alone."

She seized his arm. "Then come with me. My father left me in your charge." Well, hardly. As a male chaperone, perhaps. It was her husband who had her in his charge.

He stared at her begrudgingly. It was a terrible temptation. Poor Francisco. He felt sorry for him. But to be back home, where civilization lay like a fine old patina on a gracious life; how he yearned to hear the boom of ancient church bells, the murmur of pigeons in the squares. And the thought of rescuing his son, Miguel, from this raw and dangerous land . . . he licked his lips.

"Maria," he muttered, "he is my friend. It would be a kind of betrayal."

She cried out, "Better to betray me? What do you think my father would say?"

Alonso had a shewd suspicion that the Duke, who had threatened her with the convent, would receive them with very mixed feelings. But they would meet that problem when they were back in Seville. "Very well." He had made up his mind. "We will need a guide, of course."

"In El Paso," she said. "I have relations there."

"If Francisco so much as suspects . . ."

138

"Let him. He cannot keep me in chains."

"Say nothing to Miguel. He is terribly smitten with this land."

She said curiously, "Is he out of his mind?"

"And put away those jewels. Hide your valise. For the last few days, at least, behave with decorum."

She laughed. She was exultant. "There is only one thing I regret." He knew what it was. "I would like to see his face when he gets back."

But Alonso didn't feel very exultant. There was a guilt complex somewhere; he felt rather sad.

Now the operation gathered pace. Everything that had happened so far, the din and the bedlam, had been merely a curtain-raiser. Just before dawn Alonso was awakened by a long, sighing grumble. It seemed to come from every part of the prairie. It dragged him out of bed. The red and saffron streaks that glittered in the sky bathed the landscape with an unearthly light. He peered out. His skin crept. The prairie was *moving*. Hillocks of it rippling like dark waves . . . but they were only huge blobs of cattle. The herds were coming in.

Something took him hurriedly into Miguel's room. As he suspected he was out. He thought with despair: What am I to do with him? He is getting out of control. He put on his robe and went outside. A hard cold wind whisked under his nightgown.

It was as if he were watching Attila's Hun army on the move: bawling brutes, those awful horns rattling like spears. Miguel was somewhere out there and he would get himself pierced. The spur-jingling cowmen bustling them on didn't seem very perturbed. "Monsters," Alonso muttered with distaste, and a voice behind him said, "Friend, they are lovely. There's thirty dollars on every set of hoofs."

Pablo O'Hagerty. Alonso looked round. How had he managed to come up so silently on his horse?

He said with a chuckle, "Up bright and early, Duke."

139

Was the man teasing him? Alonso said coldly, "I am not a duke. I am the Count of . . ."

"There I go again. My protocol's all shot to hell," Pablo said.

Alonso stared suspiciously at the fat, coppery moonface. He couldn't get used to the greasy plaits of hair. Something else he couldn't get used to: who was it grinning at him out of those hooded black eyes? Irish Michael O'Hagerty or Indian Warbonnet Chief Owl-in-the-Sky? He had lost his eyebrows in the fire. It gave him a Chinese look. It only added to the confusion.

"My son is out there," Alonso said anxiously. "He will be hurt."

"Bump or two. Won't matter. Come to no harm."

"You must lose a lot of men with these dangerous beasts?"

Pablo screwed his eyes as if counting them off. "I've helped plant a few in the prairie. Nobody lives forever," he said.

"You are going with them?"

"That I am." And chuckled. "But when the trumpet sounds for Pablo O'Hagerty, it ain't going to be over cows. It's going to be over drink and wild women."

Hooligan. The trumpet had very nearly sounded for him during the oil inferno. It must take a special kind of unfeeling desperado to do what he did, Alonso thought.

Suddenly the sun flashed up. Pablo stared at it mystically, as if in the act of worship. It gave Alonso goosepimples; he is nothing but an Arapaho pagan, he thought. The cows were now spilling in from the range. Pablo uttered a shrill whoop and went charging off.

The branding that went on all day was an offense to the ear and the nose. There was no way Alonso could escape it; the fumes of burning hide permeated the house. They had built chutes for the beasts to run through, but not fast enough to avoid being stamped on both sides by cherry-red irons, while those two Anglo-Saxon roughs, Nueces Joe and Alfalfa, skillfully slit a dangling strip of skin on each ear. Butcher's business. They had a name for everything: a jingle, they called it. I have a name for them too, Alonso thought; but I would not dream of using it in the presence of those gun-belted *bandidos*.

"Miguel," he said to his son irascibly at dinner, "there is blood on your hands."

"Cow's blood, Father. I helped mark their ears."

"I utterly forbid you to . . ."

"It is very valuable experience, Father."

For what? The dignified life of an *hidalgo*? They are turning him into a bumpkin. He felt Maria touch his hand. Their eyes met in silent understanding. Not much longer.

Then all branding done. What now? Did someone say to the restless beasts: march? The Mexican's chuck wagon was all stocked up. Alonso looked it over. Not a very inspiring diet; it would kill me in three days, he thought. Corn meal, molasses, sowbelly and beans. A stack of salted hams. *Madre mía*, I would rather eat grass.

The riding stock, which they called the *remuda* (you see, Alonso thought proudly, the language of our great Conquistadores still lives on), was ready. The hired hands had selected their mounts. There was a perceptible tension about the ranch, almost a desire to see the leading herds shoved off. Alonso began to feel a sympathetic nervous tension, too.

He had packed. Miguel knew nothing. It was like waiting for the blade of the guillotine to drop.

Dawn. Today? Surely. Alonso had hardly slept a wink. He stared at Maria over breakfast. She was icily calm and collected. Only her dark eyes had a glint of anticipatory fire. The cattle knew the omens. It was today. The uneasy moaning and bellowing. Frank Dibbler must have eaten in darkness. He was already out on the range. Who gave the signal?

Suddenly a broad, slow-moving belt of horned beasts was trudging into the distance, stretching within the hour as far as the eye could reach. Far ahead rode the leading point-rider at a

141

walk. Pablo O'Hagerty. Good-bye, oil-diviner and sun-worshipper, Alonso thought. Then the rebellious rabble of cattle; then the chuck wagon, hooped with canvas, dragged by six insanitary mules. Joachim screamed down to Alonso, "*Adiós, amigo,*" and the frantic squint was gone. After them came the saddle stock, the loose ponies loafing along at their own speed. And finally Frank Dibbler. He had suddenly appeared behind.

He had held back the bed wagon for some purpose. Alonso looked up at him, topping a heavy saddle; that big craggy body, thick legs wrapped in bullhide leggings, and something gave him an anxious tremor. The shell-gray eyes were watching him amusedly. Alonso wanted to mutter frozenly to Maria: "He knows!"

"You're ready?" Frank Dibbler said to her pleasantly.

She barely glanced at him. "Good-bye."

"Hardly. You're coming along."

Alonso heard her gasp, "I will not . . ."

"You're packed. Got your jewels safe? Then get aboard."

"You dare not . . ."

He said coolly, "You think I'd leave you behind for some saddle tramp to bed while I'm gone? You're safer under my eyes."

She screamed, "Don Alonso . . . ," and Alonso, shaken beyond comprehension, cried, "Francisco, you cannot. It is not for a woman. It is a terrible journey."

"No worse than the one you had in mind," Frank Dibbler said. So he *knew.* "My mother did it. My wife can do it, too." Suddenly Maria ran; but there was nowhere for the rabbit to run. The pinto moved spasmodically at the touch of a spur; Alonso, as if out of a dream, saw Frank Dibbler bend from the saddle as the horse came alongside and scoop her up. Then she was bundled in a blanket so that her suffocated screams could hardly be heard, dumped like a writhing sack into the back of the wagon. One of the *vaqueros* had run into the house and reappeared with her valise. It was tossed in, too.

"*Adiós,* Alonso," Frank Dibbler said. He bent down to press Miguel's hand. "*Muchacho!*" The boy's eyes filled with tears.

The wagon jolted on. Frank Dibbler trotted alongside, and the dust raised by the disappearing cattle swallowed them and muffled Maria's cries.

"Father," Miguel said.

I will not listen. All life had departed from the house. No sound but the whinny of a few lonely ponies in the corral. The *vaqueros* mooned about, like the wives of a ship's crew that had just sailed. There would be a long enforced wait for the master to return; they would spend the time mending saddles and repairing fences.

"Father," Miguel said again.

"Miguel," Alonso said, "I must ask you not to look at me as if I . . ."

"To let her go like that."

"She did not go. She was taken."

"And you stood by."

Alonso said wildly, "It was a dreadful predicament. There was nothing I could do. You are too young to understand the situation. Husbands have rights. This is a half-barbarous country. They are very cruel to women." No crueller than they were in Spain, where an outraged husband could shoot his adulterous wife, together with her lover, and leave the court, if he *even* entered one, without a stain. "I am heartbroken . . ."

"And Maria is not?"

How dare he reproach me? He is tormenting me. I never looked at my father like that.

"Father," Miguel insisted wryly, "she is alone. She needs our comfort."

"Her husband is there to provide it."

"You cannot be serious."

Well, I am. "They have gone. I want to hear no more of it." Alonso made the gesture of washing his hands of it; he felt a little like Pilate. "Miguel, I order you to be quiet."

The morning dragged. He would have taken a pony out for a

143

canter, but he was nervous of roving Kiowa on the unprotected range. What am I to do here for five landlocked weeks? I will go out of my mind. The afternoon was a penance. Supper even worse. He and his son sat at opposite ends of the big table, separated not by eight feet, but by a gulf of sorrow and guilt.

"Father," Miguel said.

He is starting again!

"Miguel, you are to stop worrying about it . . ."

"It is you I am worried about." *Me?* Alonso stared at him. "You are a man of good conscience. It will knock at your heart."

"In God's name, let me be . . ."

"She was left in your charge." Listen to him. Talking like Maria! "It was a solemn responsibility."

"I will explain everything to the Duke . . ."

"But not the stain on our honor."

Alonso said bitterly, "Kindly leave the honor of our house in my hands." His appetite was ruined. He slept badly. He dreamed of a trail of mournful beasts vanishing into the wilderness, Frank Dibbler leading them to hell like a jailer: and from the back of the bed wagon Maria's sorrowful cries. He came down to breakfast very tired.

Where was Miguel?

The *vaquero* who had served him the inedible mess called breakfast said obtusely, "Señor, he is selecting a horse."

A *what?*

"He did not tell you? He is leaving to join Señor Dibbler."

Alonso's heart twitched. He hurried outside. He had slept late; the morning was already half gone and the sun struck cruelly at his bare head. The wind that never ceased trundled a hoop of tumbleweed by him and he kicked it aside. Through the haze that permanently engulfed the ranch he made out the small figure of his son saddling a horse.

"Miguel!"

"Yes, Father." He mounted and came trotting across.

"Where are you going?"

144

"To join Maria."

"You must be insane. You are only a boy. It is not your business," and Miguel looked at him, steadily and gravely, and said, "Father, it is."

"I forbid you to . . ."

"Father, someone must be with her. We will never rest again if we do not go."

We? Alonso sighed. He is wearing me down. "Miguel, how obdurate you are."

"Your saddlebags will hold all we need. Fill your canteens with water."

"They are a day and a half ahead. We will not find them."

"Father, the cows have left a trail a blind man could follow."

I am defeated. Alonso stared at him exhaustedly. I have a monster for a son. "Very well. We will go," he said.

He filled the canteens with water; packed some cold beef; selected the sturdiest horse he could find. As they rode off together he caught a sidelong glimpse of Miguel's face. He was smiling smugly. He had always wanted to join the drive. Hypocrite! He has done it by trampling on my conscience. What a clever boy he is.

And the wind met them with redoubled fury over the crest, filling his mouth with dust; below them lay the loneliest of valleys and silent gulches. They will find our bleached bones out there, Alonso thought.

Miguel had been right. It wasn't hard to follow the trail. It had been used by herds for a generation, stamped like a highway on the map. A quarter-mile-wide band of torn earth, all grass grazed off, actually crushed below the level of the prairie by countless steel hoofs. Not all of them had walked to the final ignominy of the butcher's knife. A horned skull grinned at them like a milestone on the track.

They passed the ashes of a fire. A litter of condensed milk

145

cans. Cowboys weren't the tidiest of travelers. Then a bloated horse with a broken leg; it had been shot. The sun was working on it horrifically. Alonso averted his eyes.

He ran with sweat. This hat is no pleasure; and there are better outfits for the prairie than a frock coat, he thought. Miguel, taking pity on him, gave him his neckerchief to bind over his mouth. He could now breathe air instead of dust. They pushed on steadily, resting only for the midday meal. The afternoon slipped away. How much longer to catch them up?

"Six hours, Father."

Alonso grimaced. "How do you know?"

"I felt the ashes of the fire. It was still warm."

Listen to this experienced prairie navigator! I can teach him something, too. Alonso looked uneasily at his watch, then up at the sun. In three hours it will be dusk.

The dry treeless plain was lifting to a range of dim hills. The sun, much lower, now slanted straight into their eyes. They came into canyon country, pink ridges of rock on which the hoofs of their ponies rang. They turned a sharp bluff, never leaving the trail of the herd. There was no fear of losing it. The air was electric with their droppings.

And suddenly, as the first star glimmered in the sky, there was no longer a single track, but two. Alonso's heart froze. Many herds had passed this way; there was a trampled trail that went due north, and another that slanted in an easterly direction up into the hills. Both seemed fresh.

"Which one, Miguel?"

Miguel stared at them. Smelled them. He was an honest boy. "Father, I do not know."

"But you must . . ."

"I would guess the one going east. You must not be frightened, Father. Sooner or later we will catch it up."

We had better. And I *am* frightened. I do not want my skull for a milestone on this trail.

They began the slow climb. It grew colder. The basin of the

146

sky was scarlet; sunset very near. And suddenly long unnerving shadows, cliffs shutting out what little light there was. Miguel reined in his horse. He peered into the shelter of a fold in the rocks. "This is where we will camp for the night, Father."

"Very well."

"It is really quite exciting. I will make some coffee. Everything will look better in the morning."

But first a very cold night. And rocks for a bed. They tethered the horses to a stump and made a fire of dry twigs. The coffee simmered. Alonso lay watching the flicker of the flames on the stony slopes. Presently the fire went out; Miguel was asleep. He found himself listening intently to the hiss of the wind, the whine of some restless bird . . . and then he, too, was asleep.

What woke him? A curious rattle like dried peas in a can. A long way off. Shouting, too? But nothing was quite clear in the grumble of the wind. It went on spasmodically. He woke Miguel. What could it be? Both lay listening. Alonso thought he heard a shrill ululating howl; but *that* could have been the bird. Then silence.

"One hears many strange things at night on the prairie," Miguel said. He didn't seem perturbed.

"It sounded human."

"Father, you are stretching your imagination. We will have a long ride tomorrow. Try to sleep."

Now every nerve in Alonso was agog. The wind was as eerie as a distraught ghost. He couldn't find a comfortable spot on the hard ground. He began hypnotically to count stars, as one counts sheep; and then the moon rose, huge and cold, laying a silvery carpet on the rocks. He nodded tiredly . . .

That sudden drumming. Horses racing? It certainly wasn't a bird. The sound came nearer and nearer, echoing up the defile. He didn't have to touch Miguel. It had roused him, too. "Father, hush." He was on edge. They crept up the slope, crouching behind the rocks to look down on the track.

Indians. They came in a long, breathless, thrusting column up the defile. They weren't twenty paces distant, and Alonso held his breath. The moon shone full on them. He could see every face. Something wild and panicky about them. He could hear the ponies' nostrils whistling. Men and squaws, children hooked behind the saddles. A few horseless braves ran with them. They had a ghostly look in the silvery shine; it might have been a dream but for the dust they raised and the cough of exhausted horses. They were very corpulent, not lean and hard as he expected Indians to be. He had heard that Comanches were fat and bowlegged; he never wanted to get near enough to them to find out. They looked mad with rage. They carried lances with fluttering pennons of soft fur that he would learn in time were scalps. A few odd painted shields, with rifles poking behind. Were those bodies slung over the necks of the horses?

Then the hammer of hoofs faded; there was nothing left but haze in the moonlight, and they were gone.

"Miguel, what could have happened? They look as if the devil is behind them."

"Or more Indians. There has been fighting."

Violence. Nothing but violence. Even amongst aborigines. It is a tormented land. They crept back to the fire. Alonso poked the pale ashes; the coffee was cold. Miguel said thoughtfully, "It might be better if one of us stayed awake."

"Go to sleep. I could not close my eyes if I tried," Alonso said. He settled himself against the rocks with a sigh, thinking: how peaceful it was at the ranch . . . and then a hand on his shoulder almost lifted him out of his skin. Miguel was shaking him. There was a brilliant blue sky.

"Did I . . . ?"

"Yes, Father. You were very tired."

"But nothing happened?"

"You snored."

They made coffee, chewed a little cold beef, and resumed their journey along the valley. They were following a stream

148

that had been churned into a quagmire by the massive trampling of the herd. Their droppings decorated the landscape. No animal, *en masse,* can be so objectionable, Alonso thought. Suddenly they smelled smoke. It eddied foully along the ravines. The ponies hung back, snorting uneasily. They didn't want to go on. Neither did Alonso. "No," he said in a loud reluctant voice, but it was too late; they were round the bend of the valley and into the clearing. Saw what was left of the Indian village before they could stop.

"May God forgive us." He shivered. He had never seen death—couldn't possibly imagine it—in so casual and wholesale a form. Butchery. He stared at the loose coppery bodies, half bare, wrapped in breechclouts, lying in the ditches as if taking a rest. But there was too much blood about. Buffalo robes scattered. The grass gashed like a plowed field by tearing hoofs. A few half-mad mustangs trotted tremblingly between the burned-out tepees. And dogs. Yapping curs, sniffing at the bodies, turning with a snarl on the ponies as if denying them a share.

"Miguel," Alonso said faintly—I am going to be sick—"turn back."

"Father, there is no other road. Let us get through it quickly. Compose yourself."

How? The reek of smoldering tepees was suffocating. The village lay on a slope descending to the stream, and everything seemed to have been shoved down it by the violence of the attack. Or whatever it was that had happened. Twenty or thirty lodges, with the scratch marks of fleeing travois. Lances stuck like burial markers in the reeds. I cannot go on! Alonso's pony shied; he hadn't seen what lay in its path. A wooden-looking squaw, watching him with hard metallic eyes. He wondered why—feeling so ill—he could still gaze intently at the priest's cross, that he was sure was Spanish, dangling about the fat brown neck. The relic of some ancient raid on a Mexican settlement.

He had to stop.

149

"Father, we must . . ."

"Miguel, give me a moment. I feel unwell."

And Miguel, that gritty boy—where did he get his resolution? he didn't inherit it from his mother or me—dragged at his rein and said harshly, "Father, get hold of yourself. We dare not stop."

But they did. And froze. There was the soft jingle of harness behind them, the pad of hoofs, and Alonso's body arched instinctively, expecting a lance in his back.

Two of them. But not Indians. Troopers. Tight-buttoned cavalry uniform, brass tarnished, with heavy broad-brimmed hats. Rifles thrust into saddle holsters. Both of them grizzled. Both foul with dirt and sweat. Alonso's eyes shifted with a twitch of horror to the blotches of blood on the troopers' cuffs. They were staring at him with crinkled amazement, as if they had never seen anything so ludicrous in their lives.

"Jesus God," one of them said softly, "if I couldn't reach out and touch it I wouldn't believe it."

It is this hat, Alonso mumbled to himself; I must get rid of it. It makes everybody laugh. He was very frightened. He took it off to wipe his face.

"What are you doing here, friend?"

"We are following the . . ."

"Mex?"

Mexican? "No, no." Alonso frowned offendedly. He let Miguel tell them calmly, "My father is the Count of Fuende. We are looking for Señor Dibbler's herd."

A heavy disconcerting silence. Cold Anglo-Saxon eyes, Alonso thought. They would use those rifles on us as soon as spit. Which one of them did. "And you shoved your nose into an adder's nest."

"Yes." Alonso stared furtively at the graceless sprawl of brown bodies in the ditch. "It is terrible . . ."

"Passel of murdering savages. Be a long while 'fore they come raiding and looting this way again."

150

"They passed us in the night."

"What's left of 'em. Don't you wet your nose with no tears for them." They were still dark with suspicion; but the one who had spat was queerly intrigued by Alonso's clothes.

"That's a right rare coat, mister."

Alonso looked at Miguel. He shrugged.

"Who in hell did you say you were?"

Alonso said nothing. Still frightened. Better not to open one's mouth.

Then there was a jingle of metal, a heavier thud of hoofs, and the rest of the troop came wheeling round the bend. It was led by a black-whiskered sergeant. He said irritably, "Goddamn it, McCleary, what you got hold of now?"

"Some kind of fancy Spanish, sergeant. Boy says they're looking for a Dibbler outfit."

"There's a herd down at the neck of the valley." The sergeant stared curiously at Alonso. Scratched his whiskers. Relieved himself of phlegm. It was as habitual as drawing breath. "Mister, you sure are dressed up for a ball. Take 'em down to the camp. See what the major says."

Then: "Move!" The troop shoved forward; the man McCleary grabbed at Alonso's rein, yanked hard, and the pony leaped forward with the troop.

They forded the stream, rode down the narrowing valley, passed the outlying vedette of the cavalry camp, where the dismounted sentry yelled them on in the direction of the wagon park. Alonso stared at the lines of tethered horses, the squatting blood-weary troopers resting and chewing in the sun. He could hear the lowing of the herd in the far tunnel of the valley; could smell them before he saw their enveloping cloud of dust. He felt a surge of almost hysterical relief. Frank Dibbler would be there.

And then they pulled up at the commanding officer's tent, flaps wide open to sun and breeze, and in the shadow of the tent he saw three things in this order: the shaggy fatigued major, bearded like Abe Lincoln, blood-smeared like his men, sitting

151

frozenly at his trestle table; Maria sheltering breathlessly behind him, face white, eyes enormously enlarged; and Frank Dibbler, with Pablo for company, both with shotguns leveled at the major's belly.

A squad of troopers suddenly lining up tensely at the major's back, rifles cocked, as if waiting for the order that would start a war. Alonso felt his bowels loosen. Now he was beyond shock and despair. I will just have to get used to the country; it is always going to be like this, he thought.

VI

He would get the story in time. A little of it from Frank Dibbler; a few bleak sentences thrown off, brows knitted, as if surprised to find qualities in Maria as savage and ruthless as his own. What a way to describe a marriage! Savage. Ruthless. Pablo would tell him something, but carefully veiled. He was unswervingly loyal to Frank Dibbler. A lot more from Maria, poured out in impassioned Spanish. Much of it unprintably obscene.

He thought he got the truth from Joachim, the cook—as near to the truth, perhaps, as a Mexican with an exotic imagination and crossed eyes could get. He was the Boswell of the cattle drive. Every incident raptly recorded. "Señor Alonso," he said, "I had a dark instinct before the herd was out of sight of the ranch . . ."

"Joachim, no embroidery. The facts."

"She was in the bed wagon, you know, and crying out. Tragic! It upset everybody on the trail. The prairie is no place for a woman. The *vaqueros* didn't like it. They are very superstitious. The others"—he always referred to the Anglo-Saxon

153

cowboys as "the others"—"started to mutter, but Señor Dibbler rode back to look at them and they shut up. He has that kind of look. I heard what Pablo O'Hagerty, the mad Irish-Indian, said to him when we made camp."

"You heard? Or guessed?"

"All right. So both. It was plain on their faces. Such a terribly disruptive influence! Cowboys are very deprived creatures." Alonso had heard that somewhere before; ah, yes, from Francisco himself, that evening in Seville. Joachim's disjointed eyes glittered. "You know what I mean?" Alonso knew. "And a woman on the drive . . ."

"Sex?"

"You took the word out of my mouth. What do you think they look forward to in Dodge City? That sink of abomination? A dance-hall girl, and quick into bed," Joachim said coldly. As if no such thought ever entered his mind.

"Joachim, Señor Dibbler would kill the first who let his eyes stray in his wife's direction . . ."

And Joachim interrupted him slyly, "She is so? In truth?"

"What? His wife? Of course."

"They do not sleep together."

"Joachim, just mention it to him and he will . . ."

"Señor, I mind my own business. I heard what Pablo O'Hagerty said."

What Pablo said to Frank Dibbler, Alonso got direct from the horse's mouth. Pablo himself. "Sure. I told him. Christ, it's so *bad*. Women are hell enough in a cowtown; on the trail they're plain murder. Five weeks out in all weather, herding a bunch of maniac cows; man gets a little edgy. Little vicious. Puts strange thoughts into his mind." The kind of sexual thoughts Joachim presumably didn't have. "I said to Frank, you must be plumb crazy . . ."

And Frank Dibbler said, "Pablo, you watch your tongue."

"She was safe enough back in the ranch."

"Safer still under my eye."

"It's asking for trouble."

154

"I don't mind trouble."

"You're the boss. She's your woman."

"That's settled then." Frank Dibbler grinned. "*Now* will you shut up?"

But nothing was settled. The first day out was always the worst. Alonso could picture the gaunt mass of pugnacious, dirt-caked longhorns, plodding over the curvature of the earth, complaining with a mass grumble that could be heard in the adjoining state. It would take a few days for the bovine mob to find themselves a leader and settle down. Sooner or later some punchy old steer would assert his authority as monarch of the drive. There was no water (Pablo said) that first day out. The longhorns ate each other's dust. It got to be rather terrible; the cowboys, lips frosted with windborne dirt, eyes getting blood-shot and tempers fretted, found it hard to keep the thirst-mad rabble intact. Frank Dibbler riding ahead, peering out for the gleam of a waterhole from every crest, then back to curse on the stragglers. "Exhausted his goddamned dictionary of oaths," Pablo said.

And Maria? The bed wagon at the tail end was the worst of places. She ate *everybody's* dust.

They halted at a scummy mud-wallow. The frantic hoofs trampled it into a mire. The herd was now sprawled out in rough alignment, a mutinous army three miles long. Insubordinate squads of them taking off for lone walks into the gulches. The men flogging after them got no rest. The sun very high, mercilessly baking bodies and tempers alike. And at that rather electric moment, Pablo thought it necessary to canter across to Frank Dibbler, perched on his pinto like Columbus watching his Atlantic armada, and put a small ruby-crusted ring into his hand.

Frank Dibbler said softly, "Where'd you get it?"

"*Vaquero.*"

"And he got it from—?"

"Your wife. Scared the living daylights out of him. She said to him; just get me a horse."

155

"Tell him *gracias*. I'm obliged."

"Oblige me, Frank. Send her back."

"She stays."

"Frank, you'll . . ."

"Pablo, will you never learn to bite your tongue? She stays."

And Pablo, looking into the intractable face, the cold dust-tormented eyes, knew that there was some hurt involved, and that she was paying for it. What it was he would never be told. He said with a sad wry smile, "I've bitten it." His tongue.

Alonso now had to rely on Frank Dibbler's and Maria's rather biased accounts. The truth lay somewhere between them. One thing was certain: he rode back to the bed wagon and talked to her. Something else was certain. It was a short bitter conversation, and from that moment on everything was changed.

According to Frank Dibbler he tossed the ring back into her lap and said, "Here's the price of your horse. Stuff your jewels in your wallet." Probably something cruder. "Don't try to bribe my men again."

And Maria—if her words were to be trusted—looked at him and said calmly, "There will always be something. I will do it again and again."

"You know what'll happen."

"You will kill me?"

"There are other ways. They'll be painful."

"For you, too." She continued to stare at him. It was she who told Alonso that at that moment everything was changed.

"No more tears," she said. "No more despair. All that was finished. He was suddenly uncertain. I could see it in his face. I am an Estremaduran, and it is a family that knows how to fight. I would fight him back and trample him into the ground." Big, big words. But she was a redoubtable woman. And out on that windswept prairie, her hair blown wild, her voluptuous bosom tensed, Alonso wondered if Frank Dibbler shouldn't be warned to take care. There'd been a duchess of the family in the twelfth century who'd ridden out in coat-armor to fight the Moors.

"Maria, what can come of it?"

"Misery. For him. Either that, or he must let me go."

"You are his wife."

And the rabble of cattle began a rowdy bleating; it seemed to Alonso that even they had to laugh.

Joachim supplied the rest. During the worst of the afternoon, with the sun roasting them in a stew of dust, he saw Maria leave the bed wagon and begin to walk. Everybody was suddenly conscious of her. The swing riders, working in from the flanks of the herd, watched her uneasily. The *vaqueros* avoided her as if she were infected. She caught up with Joachim's chuck wagon, the traveling kitchen, and climbed in coolly at his side.

"Joachim," she said, "I will not bite you. Move up."

"Señora, everybody is watching . . ."

"Let them. How much further to go today?"

"Until Señor Dibbler tells us to stop."

She gave him a dry sidelong smile. "He is God to you, is he?"

He had never really thought of it like that. He considered it. "Yes. He is," he said.

"He has feet of clay."

"Señora, I beg of you . . ."

"Why are you frightened of him?"

He didn't have to consider that. He could answer it instantly. "Because he is a fearsome man," he said. He saw Frank Dibbler turn in the saddle to watch them stonily. "Señora, it would be better if you kept to yourself until we get to Baxter Springs . . ."

"You will never get there," she said.

He looked at her with shock. "What are you saying?"

"I am telling you. Not a man, not a solitary cow, will make it."

He averted his head from her. It was like listening to the prophetess of doom. He had to relieve his feelings by cracking his whip across the backs of the mules.

"Señor," he told Alonso, "she was all rage and fire. I could feel

157

the heat of her. If she had not got down I would have left the wagon myself."

There was little to graze, and nothing to drink, and they pushed the herd on cruelly, tongues hanging out, ribs beginning to show. They were now plodding along the arid canyon, tightly bunched, and as the shadows lengthened they felt the first cool breeze. The cattle suddenly smelled water. There was a wild bawling, the mad scrape of hoofs; the cowmen stopped them bolting just in time. They came down to the narrow neck of the valley, catching the red glint of the sinking sun on the stream. The cattle plunged straight in. It had been an awful day; but there was the satisfaction of knowing that it was behind. Joachim had pulled ahead to make camp. It was a pleasant bedding ground, good grass, skirted by silent blue hills.

Joachim said: "They came suddenly out of the shadows. A lieutenant and six troopers. As silently as ghosts. They stood staring at us, rifles half out of holsters, and then the lieutenant trotted forward and was met by Señor Dibbler. And Pablo, of course. Wherever Señor Dibbler went, Pablo went too."

The lieutenant said, "Mister, you keep your cows quiet."

They were all very tired; and Frank Dibbler said caustically, "*Mister*, it's natural for cows to holler. You expect me to stick my fists in their mouths?"

"You'd oblige me by moving your herd back."

"This herd is drier than tinder. First watering for twenty-four hours. No law against letting them drink." But it was a very young lieutenant, overtense and unshaven, and Joachim's skin suddenly tingled. He could see Frank Dibbler watching him intently.

Heard him say softly to the lieutenant, "More of you behind?"

"Enough. We're bivouacked in the neck of the valley."

"Some good reason?"

"Are Pawnees a good reason?"

Sufficient to make Joachim's stomach slip. Pawnees, he told

Alonso, shaved the head, leaving a vermilion-dyed scalp lock for the taking. A man would have to be in love with death to attempt to take it. He peered up at the darkling hills. Were their scouts out watching? He very nearly fouled his pants.

"You're going to flush them out?"

"Before moon-up."

And Joachim saw the corners of Frank Dibbler's mouth turn down. He had that curious feeling for Indians. He called them the dispossessed.

The lieutenant said harshly, "You want ten more reasons? There's a wagon with ten bodies in the camp. Four of them women. Fetch something to stuff in your nostrils, unless you like the smell of burned flesh. And don't look for their hair." He stared with naked hatred at the skyline. "It's up there on their lances." He used one word of quivering obscenity to describe them, and prepared to ride off.

Then he wheeled about from the narrowing valley, in which the camp lay unseen in the gloaming, to stare sternly at the restless mass of the herd. "Those beasts look damn edgy to me. Mister, you keep 'em well penned in. If something starts them running they'll flatten us into the earth." His saber jingled; and this time he rode off. If it hadn't been too dark for a war-party to sight them, Joachim was sure he would have had an arrow in his back.

Pablo said: "We debated ten minutes. Whether to pull the herd back. We were walking beef, not looking for trouble. But it would have taken an hour to shift them—*if* we could tear 'em away from the water—and by that time it'd be too late. Moon'd be up."

Who could sleep? "How quiet it was," Joachim said. "No moon yet and the hills so black." He ate nothing. It would have stuck in his throat. "Even the herd sensed anxiety. They would not lie down. They grumbled as if the devil had come down to haunt them." Frank Dibbler put out full night watches, each of three hours; he himself would spend the hours of darkness rid-

159

ing tirelessly about. "Señor," Joachim said simply, "one has to have iron loins to spend a whole day and night in the saddle. It can ruin a man's private parts." He was bathed in a light sweat.

Those melting shadows on the moonless slopes: the faint slither of rocks. Pawnees, were they? It was like listening out for the tick of a bomb; the first shrill howl that would explode the herd into panic so that out of the bedlam they could run a few off.

For the mental instability of the neurotic longhorn was the major hazard of the trail. There was hardly a drive that didn't have to cope with a stampede—the cry of a coyote, a spatter of rain, even the spark of a cowboy's cigarette in the night could electrify that basic hysteria: and they were off. Horns down, with the thunderous rush of hoofs, killing and maiming as they went. Joachim had experienced it twice and on both occasions he had wanted to die.

"Señor, they are the distillation of evil. God must have had a lot of brutishness left over, and He sewed it all into one terrible horned sack. When you hear it rumble—run."

And still no moon; the cowboys circling the herd watchfully, soothing them with song. Soulful ballads like "Bury Me Not on the Lone Prairie," mixed with the vilest of operatic insults. There wasn't much affection between cowboy and steer. The first alarm came before midnight. There was a lot of sheet lightning about, the faint bump of thunder—and a few touchy old bulls struggled up and glared about. "Get down, old nasty," the cowboys crooned to them, and they sullenly settled down. Now everybody was on edge. A silver gleam had shown above the hills. How soon would it happen?

It was as if the thought had triggered it off. Joachim would never forget the screams that echoed down from the ravines—rifles volleying, horses whinnying; and the herd was up, snorting dangerously, ready to run. "I believe in miracles," he said. "They were penned so hard together that they could escape only by trampling one another down. It was still a shambles."

160

He thought he could hear the hoof-hammer of the Indian ponies that got away. A few scattered shots reverberating in the hills as the "flushing-out" went on. Joachim never knew when he dozed off; only that the sun was glittering in his eyes when he woke. The cavalry was returning, blooded and tired. It was the same lieutenant who led his troop back to camp, pausing again to stare at the still-trembling herd. He wasn't a cow-lover. "You watch them, mister," he told Frank Dibbler coldly. "Like I said."

And then? Joachim was incoherent. She had mounted a horse; Maria, of course. She was off in a rush, straight past the startled lieutenant and his troop, vanishing into the valley toward the camp. Frank Dibbler after her. Embroiled with the scattered troopers, getting past them, Pablo pounding close behind. When they caught up with her she was pleading with the major in his tent. He was an exhausted man; he'd led the first attack on the village, and he was yelling at the sentries struggling to shove Frank Dibbler and Pablo away from the tent. He'd had enough shooting. And that was when Alonso arrived.

He couldn't quite make out Maria's expression. Triumph shining in her enlarged eyes; she had something to be exultant about. She was crying pitifully, "In God's name, help me. I have been taken by force." That was true. "I have lain in the wagon trussed like a hog." That was stretching the truth a little. The major was shouting, "For Christ's sake," staring disbelievingly at the shotguns pointed at his belly.

Frank Dibbler saying, "Put her outside, Major."

"And who the hell are you?"

"I'll tell you who *she* is. She's my wife."

The major said wearily to the sentries, "Get back to your posts. I can sort this mess out." Alonso doubted it.

You do not know how hard and unsuccessfully I have tried, he thought.

"Madam, sit down." She preferred to stand trembling. How

marvelously she acts, Alonso thought. The major had caught her accent. "Mexican, are you?"

Alonso had to speak for her. She was too near to tears. If they were real. "Spanish," he said. "She is the Condesa de Rojas."

The major stared at him. "And who are you?"

"The Conde de Fuende . . ."

"Holy God," he said unendurably, "I'm up to my knees in blue blood." The Indian blood that marked his pants was red.

He rubbed his tired eyes. "Mister," he said to Frank Dibbler, "is she, or is she not, your wife?"

"You heard me say so."

"Will you put that goddamned gun down? And tell the breed behind you to do the same."

"Put it down, Pablo. The man makes sense."

"Madam, you *are* married to this man?"

"I hate him . . ."

"But he's still your husband?"

She said nothing. She let tears come into her eyes.

The major turned with a sigh to Alonso. "Is she, for God's sake?"

"His wife?"

"If you can put it in plainer language."

She could hardly expect him to lie. Alonso nodded. "They were married in church." But there was more to be said. "Francisco," he begged, "why try to hold her? Sooner or later she will . . ."

"Not sooner and not later. Wife's a wife. Church makes it so," and Alonso thought: like scratching granite with your fingers. All you get is broken nails. "Major," Frank Dibbler said, "I want my woman back." Alonso shrugged. Why say woman? Say property and be done.

The major tugged at his beard. He *did* look like Abe Lincoln. But he had more problems. A wagonload of corpses, and some dreadful mementoes brought back from the Indian village. A few scalps less identifiable than the dead. "Madam, I'm no

162

knight-errant. There isn't a thing I can do for you," he said. He was beginning to have doubts about her. She was very beautiful, if you liked them violent and full-busted. "I'm army. Not in the Lancelot business. You're his wife, and he has his sacred rights. This is a man's world. You're his: much the same as his horse and gunbelt. He can bundle you off under his arm"—and he's big enough to do it, the major thought, stealing a look at him—"and I can't stop him. Not without bumping into the laws of this sovereign state." He saw her eyes widen with a fearful shine and he thought with a shiver: if I slept with her I'd feel safer with a gun in bed.

"It is barbarous."

"For women. Not for men."

The slow tears slid down her face. "I beg of you . . ."

He just looked at her. He wished they would go. It had been a sickening battle; there'd been an old squaw who'd shoved an ancient flintlock into his face and he'd had to . . . he just wanted to sleep and get it out of his mind.

Alonso sighed. Touched Maria's arm. She didn't look at him; she was staring at her husband, and as she went through the tent-flaps her head swiveled so that her chilled eyes didn't leave his face. She was still looking at him as she got onto her horse.

"Mister," the major suggested, "I'd take care. You could find yourself in heaven"—or hell—"with a surprised look on your face and a knife in your back. Not my business, of course."

Frank Dibbler chuckled. "And that's a fact. When are you shoving off, Major? I need the valley clear."

"Inside the hour. Hold on to that herd. My lieutenant tells me it's touchy."

"Like me. I'll hold it."

He went out with his hair-plaited Indian and the major watched him mount his horse. Size of the man. Must need it to hold down a woman like that. Those eyes! Liquid murder. He wondered dreamily: would he have used that shotgun if I'd placed her under guard? Glad I didn't have to put it to the test.

163

And he shouted to his lieutenant to break camp, listening to the squeal of the bugles, the snort of horses being saddled, thinking: if that's marriage, give me war.

Maria had ridden hard back as if she could tolerate nobody's company. Alonso and Miguel followed. The herd was already astir. Still nervous, red-eyed, as humans would be from lack of sleep. The morning's watering. It didn't improve their temper. The coarse bellowing got on Alonso's nerves; he regarded them as one huge animal that could only be improved by the butcher's block. The cowmen who had been up most of the night crawled achingly out of their bedrolls. A mouthful of cold bacon; then a quick cigarette before saddling up. Joachim gave Alonso a cup of coffee. Hot and petrifying. It drew his teeth.

"Señor," he said in a low voice, "do you not think it ominous?"

"Think what ominous?"

"Hardly two days out and nothing has gone right."

Superstitious *peón*. "Joachim, all you have to do is walk cows. And make better coffee. I have had a shattering night and if you give me any heartrending premonitions I will ride straight back."

They could hear the bugles sounding distantly in the camp. They, too, were off. The herd was pushed out of its bed. The grumbling never ceased. It took a long time to pacify them. The cowboy's ballads seemed only to aggravate them; but slowly they were turned into the valley, a long sullen procession, horns rattling, dropping dung. Frank Dibbler had ridden across to the stream to water his pinto. Maria back in the bed wagon. Alonso felt Miguel touch his arm. "Father, encourage her a little."

"How?"

"Tell her to have faith. She will learn in time what it is to be married to a truly remarkable man."

Alonso stared at him. My son is out of his mind. But he was still haunted by Maria's face. He would ride behind to keep her company. The herd was now shoving ahead. He turned his pony. She wasn't in the wagon. She was leaning on the tail-board, steadying herself. He couldn't at first see what she was doing, only her face, calm and resolute. Then he saw the shotgun leveled at Frank Dibbler; and while his mouth was still dry the shotgun blasted off. Frank Dibbler clutched his shoulder with a shout; but it was the pinto's buttocks that got most of the scattering of pellets. It screamed. The bang echoed thunderously back from the hills, mixed with the shout and the scream, and the herd stiffened: a few thousand horns reared, and they were off.

In his senile years Alonso would say with horror, not with boastfulness, "I saw two things nobody would believe if he didn't see them with his own eyes. I saw Frank Dibbler throw a fighting bull in the grass at Seville, and I saw the Battle of Dibbler's Cows."

That was how the U.S. Cavalry would record that classic engagement. Not with pride. Nobody came out of it with any pride—not the cavalry, not Frank Dibbler, certainly not Maria, least of all that maniacal herd.

It was fortunate for Alonso that he saw it from behind. If he'd been a forward spectator he wouldn't have survived. All he saw at first was an acreage of dust from which emerged the Niagara-drumming of hoofs. Through it he made out the rumps of the herd, rushing into the neck of the valley like a fat cork into a bottle. Pablo was trying to seize the rearing pinto, but Frank Dibbler yelled to him violently to get ahead and stop the herd. It seemed to be asking a great deal.

Alonso didn't think anything could stop them. He could feel the gritty tremor of the earth; as if a mountain were slipping. It was a mile-long mass of animal hysteria that was on the move. He heard a pony shriek. Two of the forward riders—madmen! —were racing across the leading bunch, firing their pistols point-blank into their faces. It had no more effect on them than a firecracker. The pony he heard vanished into the dust. Mira-

165

cles seemed to be normal on the prairie. Alonso saw the man emerge on the backs of the cattle, walking them like a heaving bridge, jumping off them into the verge and rolling out of the way of the hoofs. He would have something to tell his grandchildren. The other pony showed more sense. It leapt for the rocky slopes, scuttling up them like a goat.

The swing riders were bellowing alongside, trying to turn them off: try to divert an avalanche, Alonso thought. And then it was all gone: haze and yelling, the stampeding cattle disappearing into the valley. The drumming faded. Nobody was left but Maria, white and glacial. Frank Dibbler blaspheming, stiff with pain. He gave her a stark look. Then he, too, was gone.

Where was Miguel? Alonso was frightened for him. Tiredly, as if he had been physically pounded by the experience, he went too.

But he was a late spectator at the Battle of Dibbler's Cows. It was Trooper McCleary, the one who had picked him up in the Indian village, who gave him the picture of the opening skirmish. He'd heard cattle. Smelled them. Saw them coming.

"Mother of Grace." An Irishman. A fellow Catholic. He was still incoherent. "We'd just struck camp. Half of us still saddling up. Mules watered. Wagons lined up to roll. And then, by Jesus, fifty thousand cattle coming up the canyon." There were less than three thousand: but enough. Alonso would have been incoherent, too. "Nowhere to move. We were the plug in the canyon and them crazy steers were going to shove us out."

"Why did you not run?"

"Cavalry don't run. Major's an old Indian fighter; never feared a Comanche, and he took one look at that stampeding herd and shouted us to defense quarters. Believe it or not. Cows! Repel the attack. What the hell could you do? Be mowed down? We pumped a few shots into them, but they came on over the dead steers, madder than a saloon full of drunks. Then we *did* start dropping them. Had to. It was us or them.

"Butchered them like a knacker's yard. And still coming. We

had some sharpshooters. I figure I dropped thirty—more maybe—with my Remington. And still coming! Crazy cows."

The air full of drifting dust, the cowboys yelling in the distance, and cattle dropping in bunches. Then the avalanche was almost on them and the troop made a battle-square, horses in the middle, well behind the wagons. And that slowed them just a little. The great hooped wagons took the brunt of the shove. Canvas swaying, then the splintering of timber, and all tramped into matchwood. That awful hysterical bleating . . .

"Scattered us like chaff." It wasn't the same thing as running. The major cursing the air blue. Rifles smashing out, picking off the steers remorselessly: and then finally they stopped. "All burned out. Ran themselves to a standstill. Suddenly they were just a great mess of horns and red eyes and worn-out legs, trying to get over the heaps of their dead. You know how many we killed? *Had* to kill?"

"Señor Dibbler says nearly half his herd."

"Damn near right. Twelve hundred. Friend, come tomorrow's heat that canyon will stink to high heaven. Good for the buzzards. We could see them up in the sky collecting for the feast."

So ended the Battle of Dibbler's Cows. There was a terrible row at the scene of the slaughter between the major and Frank Dibbler. Nobody won that battle, either.

What was it Joachim had said? "Hardly two days out and nothing has gone right. Do you not think it ominous?" That superstitious *peón* had second sight. They had started with three thousand cattle, and only eighteen hundred left. Alonso, worn and enfeebled, hoped Joachim's dark premonitions would now dry up.

"Maria."

"I warned him. Did I not?"

"Are you insane? To try to kill your own . . ."

"He is my husband in name only. Nothing else. And if it is necessary to kill him I will."

167

"Do you know what you have done? How many cattle lost?"

"Then tell him to let me go."

"He will not. Less than ever now. He is a terribly stubborn man."

Alonso saw her eyes shine. Not a trace of remorse. "I am a terribly stubborn woman. Before this drive is over he will have no cattle at all."

The cavalry had departed. The wounded steers had been shot. The rest wandered dazedly about, all hysteria gone. It had been a shattering ordeal for both horses and cattle, and there began the distressing business of soothing wild-eyed ponies and bunching the remnants of the herd to move off. It had never occurred to Alonso that the hired hands might also have been affected. In a different way. The pandemonium of the last hour had drained him and he climbed into the chuck wagon, settling himself against a pile of sacks for a nap. He'd hardly closed his eyes when he felt the wagon creak. He peered behind. Frank Dibbler lay face down across the tailboard, stripped to the waist. Pablo was delicately picking shotgun pellets out of his back.

Fearful thing she'd done! But for the leather jerkin he wore she might have stripped his spine.

Pablo muttering, "Frank, you better hear what I got to say . . ."

What was he so agitated about? Alonso didn't want to eavesdrop; but he was too tired to move.

Frank Dibbler saying in a muffled voice, "Easy with that knife. What are you digging for? Gold?"

"Don't you *ever* listen?"

"No." Alonso could have told Pablo not to waste his breath. He has his own voices, his own will; he listens to nothing else.

"Goddamn it, Frank, the men are all shook up. They don't like what they see . . ."

"I pay them to like it."

"They can kiss your pay good-bye. Any time they like. Prairie's one large hell of a lonely place. Nothing but wind and cold and cows. Puts crazy ideas into a man's head." Hesitation. As if Pablo were carefully weighing his words. He went on dangerously, "Such as a woman being a kind of hoodoo . . ."

A throaty sound like a dog worrying a bone. Some of the pellets must have gone deep. "It isn't a woman. It's my wife."

"Who're you fooling, Frank?" and Alonso froze. He would never have dared to say that.

He felt the tailboard jerk. "Pablo, I told you before to bite your tongue. Say that again and *I'll* bite it off."

"Lie still. I'm holding a knife. You can lose a liver like that. Frank, the men'll take off . . ."

"Let them try."

"They will. And they have. You're down four *vaqueros*. They took off in the last hour. Now will you listen!"

Frank Dibbler suddenly very still. It must have come as a shock. "Finished?"

"I'm finished." A curious smell; Pablo was rubbing some kind of balsam into Frank Dibbler's back. "You're all patched up. You *stubborn* man." He was very angry. Peeping through the canvas, Alonso saw him fling the knife with an exasperated sound at the side of the wagon, leaving it quivering in the timber. He stalked off.

Frank Dibbler lifted himself up. He called out, "Heard enough, Alonso?"

Alonso got down sheepishly. "Forgive me. I did not wish to listen."

"It's all right. I meant you to hear."

"Francisco, how long can you go on making her pay? It will not break her. What will it get you? Sex? She will never let you . . ." and Frank Dibbler looked at him with a grim smile. Alonso's mouth sagged. He would never dare to . . . ? "Wouldn't I, though," Frank Dibbler said. "When I'm ripe for it. When it suits my turn." He dragged up his pants. "Tell you something, *amigo*. I've heard it said that in marriage there's one

169

that loves, and one that lets himself be loved. I go a little further than that. There's one that serves, and one that lets himself be served." Terrible philosophy! "When we get *that* settled," he said, "she can bed down to making my family."

He pulled on his shirt. He winced. His back must have been copiously peppered. "There's a lot of bad blood in her," he said. Alonso stared at him with amazement. The best blood in Spain! "Too much spleen in her," Frank Dibbler said. "I'm an arrogant man, Alonso, and there's no place under my roof for two arrogant people." Alonso was evidently meant to tell her. But she'd been told. Like trying to tell a fire not to scorch. "If one of us has to break, it isn't going to be me."

He waved his hat across to Pablo. "Move, now. The day's a-wearing. Shove off." And the bleating grew to a crescendo, the dust rose, and the herd began to crawl past the heaps of their fallen comrades. Twelve hundred of them. Alonso looked up at the buzzards circling in the sky. By this time tomorrow they would be mounds of picked bones.

And now five days that seemed to Alonso to merge into one stupefying grunt. A sea of waving, unsavory rumps. A haze through which the sun struggled to shine like a lamp in a fog. His thighs grew saddle-raw. I shall walk splay-legged like a duck for the rest of my life, he thought.

Uneatable grit in unspeakable food; he wondered why Joachim hadn't been shot. He traveled for a while with Maria, but she was queerly silent. She was all dark-hooded eyes and scornful red mouth. He thought she despised him. He tried riding with Joachim in the chuck wagon, but the Mexican had become a veritable Cassandra. It wasn't possible to suffer his forebodings without being steeped in gloom.

Better the saddle that was torturing his loins! He returned to his bone-jarring pony, tall hat perched on his sweaty brow to keep the sun out of his eyes. One day just like another; hard cold earth for a bed, a harder and colder breakfast, then the unending company of a beastly army that never ceased to complain to God.

Pablo, for some reason, took a sudden fancy to him. They rode together. Very democratic. In Seville, Alonso thought, I would have shrunk from letting that hair-plaited Indian shine my shoes.

"Pablo," he said—how familiar we are getting!—"is this a vocation for civilized men?"

A husky chuckle. "You see any civilized men about?"

"No." But it was leading up to the dangerous question he wanted to ask. It had been worrying him for days. "I will tell you what I *do* see. There are four men less than started out."

Pablo said carelessly, "Lot of cows less, too." He gave Alonso a sidelong look. "So you had your ears flapping in the wagon."

"How did you know?"

"Smelled you." That sensitive Indian nose! "Stop counting them. It'll only give you bad dreams."

"You think more will go?"

"Could be there won't be a man left by the time we get to Baxter Springs if somebody doesn't tie that madam of yours down."

Alonso recoiled. "She is not my . . ."

"You fetched her."

"I did not marry her. She is a highly bred woman. She comes of a race of Spanish warriors . . ."

"I come of a race of scalp-hunting braves. There'd be hell in the tepee if we let a squaw get out of line."

Alonso said haughtily, "There's a difference." It was absurd to compare the daughter of a great duke with a bear-greased squaw. Just the same, it was rather distressing. A lot of money had gone down under the rifles of the cavalry. She had cost Francisco very nearly half his herd. Alonso watched him sympathetically, riding at the flank, hands in his pockets, reins swinging from the horn, guiding the pinto sleepily with his knees and undetectable shifts of his weight. The moment the

171

herd sprawled loosely he was hard across, shoving the stragglers back into compact line.

Well, it was the very last drive he would ever make. He was now in oil! Whatever that meant. Alonso shrugged cynically. A potential tycoon.

"Hit her," Pablo said. "Or shoot her. You get an unbroken horse that won't take a saddle, you shoot it." He couldn't be serious? Alonso drew away from him offendedly and rode on.

Three more days. And how the country changed! But it was a whole assortment of countries. Dry canyons far behind, the wind cooler, the grass richer. The hills still dark and empty. Alonso found them oppressive. In Spain there would be white-washed villages perched on the slopes, painted wine-carts trundling down from . . . but there *was* something up there! Alonso focused his eyes. The sun was falling, silhouetting a mounted figure on the skyline, pacing them slowly, disappearing for seconds below the ridge, reappearing like an interested spectator.

Alonso spurred across to Pablo. "There is a man up there!"

"He's been there all afternoon."

"Who is he?" Alonso squinted up again. He could see a rifle. "A soldier?"

"Dog soldier," Pablo said laconically.

An Indian. Why should the mere suggestion crinkle Alonso's skin? "Why is he following us?"

"He's assessing us." *What?* "He's counting the herd." He would need hawk's eyes to do that. "We're coming up to their territory. If we cross it they expect us to pay them tax."

"I thought it was a free country? Why should anyone have to pay . . ."

"Because Indians have to eat. Same as you and me. They like prime beef, too. You kill off their buffaloes, you have to pay them back in cows."

The half of Pablo that sprang from Warbonnet Chief Owl-in-the-Sky would think it no more than fair. Alonso wondered

172

whether some painted, lance-bearing tax-inspector would come trotting down on his pony . . . it was a country of bewildering extremes! But they were already bedding the herd. And the figure still up there. Night came quickly. A descending flash on the skyline: then dusk. A chill. Some bird (was it *only* a bird?) whooping. The supper fires were lit.

Presently Frank Dibbler and Pablo removed themselves from the fringe of the fire; there was to be a concentrated discussion. Alonso wanted to hear. He moved close, hidden in the darkness by a knoll. A lot of the muttering was unintelligible. They were talking about "wo-haw" and "chuck-away" which he took to be the Indian toll; evidently a legal and unavoidable right. But again and again he heard Frank Dibbler say obdurately, "Can't pay it. I've lost too many." What Maria had done to him! "It'll be a solid chunk of the herd," with Pablo still muttering uneasily.

"Have to bypass them," Frank Dibbler said.

"Long way round, Frank."

"But cheaper. We'll swing east over the hills, down to the Cimarron. Valley should be ridable . . ."

"Supposing the river's in flood?"

"Supposing the moon's all green cheese? We've crossed it before. You making me problems, Pablo?"

"No." Pablo chuckling. "You like me to scout ahead tonight?"

"I'll do it. Watch the men. I want no more of them taking off."

Watch Maria, Alonso thought.

Frank Dibbler trod by him in the blackness, calling down courteously, "Join us whenever you want, Alonso. Don't lie out there in the cold."

Alonso watched him saddle his horse. He said suddenly, "May I come with you?" startled by his own recklessness. He regretted it instantly.

"Surely, Alonso," Frank Dibbler said gravely. "Be glad of your company."

173

"Not too far? Not too dangerous?"

"Not far at all. And nothing more dangerous than gopher holes in the dark."

The moon had risen. It was a relief to Alonso; the hills were less eerie, silvery-lit. They traveled broken ridges that made the horses gasp. Then down into a shadowed sea of grass. A ghost-haunted valley: a distant yammering raised the hairs on Alonso's spine. Coyotes, Frank Dibbler said. If that shelterless valley had a presiding ghost it was the bitter blustery wind. Not too far, Frank Dibbler had said; so what was near? Thirty miles? Then—suddenly—they were almost over a bluff and Frank Dibbler seized Alonso's reins and held him back.

They were looking down on the moonlit river, running fast and creamy. Wide; so wide! Was this what they meant to cross? Somebody must be joking . . . and Alonso stared inquiringly at Frank Dibbler. "Not from here, Alonso. Lower down."

"No bridges?"

A hoarse chuckle. They trotted down to the edge of the river. So herds *had* crossed it! It was a vast trodden arena: the staging-post from which they had taken off. Stretching far back into the valley was their dungy, hoof-mashed trail.

"How fast it is, Francisco."

"Seen it worse." Half a tree, borne on the tossing water, vanished into the night, spiky branches waving like the arms of a drowning man. Could it be worse? Frank Dibbler studied it for a long time: looking for sinkholes and quicksand. Judging the strength of the current, Alonso guessed, and the rise of the opposite bank. He seemed content. "Make it from here. Not to worry, Alonso. It's been done. *I've* done it twice. And never lost a cow."

So long as he does not lose *me*, Alonso thought. I shall cross it blindfold. Praying to the Blessed Virgin. They rode back. They had been out four hours. The camp slept, but for the night watch circling the snoring herd.

The morning was fine. Alonso rose stiffly. His first thought was for the Indian tax-assessors on the skyline; two of them watching. The herd swung away from their territory, laboring into the broken hills. No tax. By midmorning they were down into the valley where the coyotes had howled. Nothing but birdsong now. They grazed steadily until they reached the river, massing in the jumpoff area, watering belly-deep.

The current seemed more violent in the bright sun. Frigid, too; Alonso tried the icy freshets lapping the bank and recoiled.

It began like an amphibious operation. He thought begrudgingly: they know what they are at. Nueces Joe stripped naked, ignoring Maria's bleak eye, and swam testingly across. Alonso was sure he'd seen the last of the sodden blond head; but he was over on the far bank, yelling gaspingly to Frank Dibbler: no rocks. He'd trodden no quicksand. Pushes hard in the middle, he cried; keep them slanted well upstream.

Pablo was having the chuck wagon rafted. It would be hauled across by ropes. Alonso would ride in it; pray God it does not become my funeral hearse, he thought. The mules would be skinned across brutally and fast, being allergic to water. The cowboys, half-stripped, lashed meal bags and coffee to their saddles and took to the river. The herd followed in grumbling bunches, a few fearless old steers in the lead, the rest plashing dubiously into the shallows—and then off! Breasting the current. The rushing foamy water was spiky with tossing horns; it seemed to Alonso, still landlocked, waiting to ride with Maria and Miguel in the wagon, that the river was one seething mass of disembodied heads, starting eyes and flaring nostrils.

Clump by clump—for not all were courageous—they were shoved across, yelled on by half-naked swimming cowboys. The sun gleamed on bare torsos that seemed to sprout from the backs of half-seen horses. Something mythological about them; they reminded Alonso of the Greek centaurs of old. He didn't envy them their job, which was to keep the fat snake of the milling herd, already bent into a U-curve by the hard shove of the water midstream, in line. They would otherwise go lazily with the current. Moronic beasts. There was a lot of gasping. It is miraculous, Alonso supposed, that cows *can* swim.

It was now his turn. He, of course, would float.

Frank Dibbler came trotting across. He'd been watching the operation from up on the bluff. "In with you, Alonso. Miguel." They got aboard. Maria stood ankle-deep in the shallows where Joachim was tying their horses to the wagon. "You, too, madam," he said.

"Must I?"

He looked at her. Eyes bloodshot; he was gaunt. He'd had no sleep; perhaps worried by Joachim's premonitions he'd kept watch on the herd all night. "Unless you want to stay this side. It's only a six-day trot back."

"I am not afraid of water," she said.

She is afraid of nothing, Alonso thought, not even of the wrath of God. One day He will punish her for that terrible arrogance. She wasn't a particularly lovely sight—hair coated with a layer of grit, shirt torn. He thought she smelled. She hadn't washed since they'd left. He wondered what Frank Dibbler could still see in her. Perhaps that was what she had in mind.

His voice cracked. He was tired. "Don't hold us up." He turned and rode back to the top of the bluff.

"Come, Maria," Alonso said. He felt the wagon swirl as it took to the water, hauled by the ropes. The mules had already gone. Where was she? She called out to him, "If cows can swim, so can I." And laughed. In that moment he hated her. She'd mounted her horse to splash across. "Maria," he shouted, his voice lost in the bleating of the herd.

"Maria!"

VII

But there was nothing he could do. He was the worst kind of spectator; totally divorced from events and caught up in their backwash. He hated the way they were sliding. A tilt, almost half a turnabout . . . and still nowhere near the full flood of the river. He could feel the wagon dragging hard at the ropes. If they were to break . . . "Father, it cannot sink," and Alonso said with a kind of anguish, "Miguel, do not tell me what it cannot do." He knew what *he* couldn't do: he couldn't swim.

They were coming into the mass of the milling herd, his ears stunned by the plaintive bleating; he was sure the saberlike horns tossing all about would puncture their ark. The wind cut the spray off the choppy water, lashing it against the canvas. And Maria . . . ?

Riding her submerged horse over by the tangle of steers in the flank. The wind whipping her hair horizontal; eyes aglow. Exulting in it. Madwoman. A jerk, and a sack of coffee bruised his back. He wanted to hide his face from everything until the wagon bumped the opposite bank.

177

"Miguel, what is she doing?" He could no longer distinguish her from the swimming cowboys.

"Riding, Father. We will all be across in ten minutes."

Ten minutes that would feel like ten years. "She listens to nobody . . ."

"Father, sit still."

"What is it?"

"I do not know. She has . . ."

"*What?*" Agony.

But the wagon was midstream and twisting in the flood. Everything rotated; the sea of bovine faces, snorting and straining, the cowboys packing them hard into a compact belt . . . the current had now curved it into a great loop. The foremost steers were very near the opposite bank, a few actually scrambling ashore, but the huge tail had a long way to go. And then Alonso saw Maria's riderless horse; something had whirled to the surface, a drowned calf shawled across the saddle, the pony rearing to be free of it, as it had freed itself of Maria. And there was her sodden hair. Hands holding on to the pony's cinch. It dipped sideways, rolling her off. She was gone.

Alonso muttered to himself, "I will never be able to face the Duke . . ." and the wagon was now placed so that he could see—fantastic sight!—the bluff from which Frank Dibbler was watching. He thought: my eyes are deceiving me . . . for the pinto was treading air. His mouth opened and no sound came out. Horse and Frank Dibbler had rocketed straight off the bluff, twenty feet up, hoofs reaching for the river as they splashed into it. Never, but *never*, would I have thought it possible. Pegasus, the flying horse! The explosion of the water as they hit it just short of Maria's horse was stunning. A churn of foam and they were up again, Frank Dibbler dislodged from the saddle, but holding on, the pinto surging to the surface . . . I hope he is a religious man, Alonso thought, for he has just felt the preserving hand of God.

He is even madder than she is. He wondered rather cruelly

178

what had made him do it. I would have thought he would be glad to see her go.

The shock explosion of the water had burst the cordon. Everything was suddenly chaos: the cowboys holding in the herd had gone plunging across to help, and the herd, feeling the release, turned in a loose straggle to drift with the current. Then more following. More and more! And then it was a milling surge of horns sweeping downstream. They butted against the wagon. They will take us with them, Alonso thought. The yelling of the cowboys!

"Father, see . . ."

I have seen enough. "Be quiet, Miguel. I am ill."

"She is all right."

She is? She doesn't deserve to be. Alonso peered along the strewn river. Ludicrous! Hair floating like a black cloud, she was making fast for the bank; what a strong swimmer she was. Frank Dibbler—tragicomic hero—lumbered by his *chaparreras*, the heavy bull-hide leggings, weighed down by his gunbelt, wallowed, vomiting cattle-fouled water. *He* wouldn't make it. Pablo got to him first. He reached down from the saddle to grab him by the scruff of the neck, hauling him to the bank.

And there he lay, pants gushing like burst buckets, still vomiting. What a way to end a spectacular rescue! Exit a clown. Maria watched him, wringing out her hair. Alonso trembled. Not laughing, I hope.

For it was no longer tragicomic; it was purely tragic. Where the belt of the herd had broken a great mass of stragglers was being swept off downstream. The hired hands were racing their ponies along the bank to head them off; the *vaqueros* still in the river trying desperately to bunch the rest together, pointing their noses to the land.

The wagon bumped. Alonso got out. He was glad to plant his feet on swampy earth. Pablo bent over Frank Dibbler, working his chest like a pump. Water spilled out of his mouth. The land-borne herd trod by them in an indifferent rush. Nueces Joe couldn't take his frozen eyes off Maria. He muttered to Alonso, "Woman's mad . . ."

Pablo heard him. "Hold your tongue."

"She's witch-bait."

"Get him to his feet." They stood Frank Dibbler up. He was earth-smeared, still spilling water. "Get the hell off me . . ." It was all he could say. Choking. He was staring cloudily at the swirling horns of his cattle receding down the river.

He moved across to Maria. His eyes a little mad; but, then, he'd been seven-eighths drowned. She watched him warily, tossing back her wet hair so that it whipped his face. Alonso wondered what he would say to her; something vilely and deservedly abusive, he hoped. He wasn't prepared for what happened. He hardly saw it; it was so fast. A hard upchopping movement of the fist, the sound of wood on wood. It was bone on bone, her head rocking back, and it seemed to Alonso that he was looking at her out of a dream, lying there senseless, skirt sprawled immodestly above her knees. Barbarous. He trembled violently. He didn't know that she wore red drawers.

The herd, the stunted remnant, grazed offshore. It was like the aftermath of a battle; the sodden survivors lowed miserably. It would take hours to discover how many mothers had lost calves: how many calves were motherless. Frank Dibbler had gone downriver with Pablo and the *vaqueros* to see how many could be retrieved. Fearful price to pay for a woman's wilfulness. If it wasn't something a little more calculated than that. She sat, jaw swollen, in the chuck wagon, staring emptily at the sky. She wouldn't speak. Alonso didn't think she could. Miguel told him softly, "She has lost a tooth."

"She very nearly lost Francisco his life."

"Are all women like that?" Miguel asked with the latent curiosity of the adolescent male.

God forbid. The race of men would never have survived.

(But to strike a wife. Alonso's chivalrous instincts shuddered. Unforgivable . . . Francisco, of what cold flesh are Texans made?)

The search party was a long time gone. Alonso trotted downriver to see what was going on. He found them sprawled along the bank many miles on. The lost herd had been carried downstream into a narrowing channel, pent in by tall bluffs, where the racing water trapped them; there was no way to turn back. No foothold. Nothing to do but drown. The shallows farther down were packed with a drift-mess of dead cattle, more than Alonso could possibly count.

This is scriptural punishment, he thought. It would break ordinary men.

A couple of steers—miraculous beasts—bleated up in the hills. How had they made it? They deserved to be remembered in song.

Pablo had the grim reckoning. He wasn't singing. "Seven-fifty," he said.

Alonso gasped. "Seven *hundred* and fifty?" *Madre de . . .*

"Give or take twenty." Pablo spat. He was watching Frank Dibbler's curiously desolate face.

Two drowned horses in the tally; but no men. They were lucky. Many a rider had disappeared into such a churning frenzy and never been seen again.

They rode back. It was a funeral cortege. Alonso kept timidly to the rear. It put him in the close company of Nueces Joe and a bunch of the hired Anglo-Saxons, and he heard Nueces Joe say softly, "Ain't staying."

It froze him. He caught Alfalfa's careful murmur, "You aim to pull out?"

"Right now. No man's safe with that female devil about."

"Hellion, ain't she?"

Somebody dubiously scratching his whiskers. "Figure I deserve my pay . . ."

"They'll bury you with it. Let's go."

181

Alonso wanted to cry out to Pablo, but the bleak aggressive faces scared him. There was a communal mutter that was lost in the clatter and jingle of the horses: and suddenly a sharp whirling movement and the whole bunch of them was tearing off into the hills.

Pablo, well ahead, turned. He yelled. Frank Dibbler, with his reduced squad of *vaqueros,* stopped. He didn't move. It was Pablo who went racing after them, cursing as he belted his heels into his horse's flanks; he went by Alonso in a whisk. Alonso thought with a feeling of abysmal guilt: what could I do? The absconding hands were dust on the skyline and receding fast. Pablo stopped his horse frustratedly on the crest. They could hear him howling into the wind. Then he came back.

Still cursing. He said to Frank Dibbler, "Could still cut them off ahead of the canyon."

"Let them go."

"Frank, they signed on."

"Now they've signed off."

"You could hang them. It's the law . . ."

"I know the law. Law won't move my cattle. I don't want anybody hanged."

Could that be Francisco speaking? Alonso was surprised. He wouldn't have expected such compassion. Perhaps the gray pained eyes were a little confused; he was learning a few bitter lessons. Pray God he wouldn't have to learn any more.

"Let's get back," he said, and now Alonso found himself watching the *vaqueros.* The brown faces were very still, the oblique eyes expressionless. He was sensitive to the Spanish strain in them and he thought: they will be the next to go.

He got into the chuck wagon with Maria and Miguel. What a diminished herd! He stared at them with shock. He could actually *count* them. Over two thirds of them lost, half the men gone. The beasts resumed the journey with direful misgivings, grumbling like a dying volcano. Frank Dibbler rode up.

"I'm short of men." That he was. "I need Joachim to ride drag." Joachim groaned dismally. The dragman rode in the rear

182

of the herd and ate its dust. Considering the food he'd given the men to eat, it seemed only fair. He got down. "Would you drive the wagon, Alonso?"

Alonso sighed. What could he say? In Seville he'd driven his high-stepping Arab horses, but these cross-grained mules un-nerved him. Even worse, they stank. "Very well." He got onto the driving board and took the reins.

"Move!" Frank Dibbler waved his hat.

Alonso twitched the reins. He was surprised by the docility of the mules. They trundled off.

They were back on the well-mashed trail, still littered with memorials to long-gone herds. The bleached horned skulls grinned ominously at Alonso, saying to him: do we not all come to this? He wished he could cover his eyes with his bandana, as he had to cover his mouth. The haze clogged his lungs so that he wheezed like a pump. It was certainly necessary to cover his nose; he couldn't understand how the mules, whose rumps immediately faced him, weren't overcome by their personal stench. The sun burned. The wind blew. Nothing much happened. It might have been uncannily silent on the prairie but for the massed snort and the cracking of ankle-joints of the plodding herd.

How many more weeks? I shall go out of my mind, Alonso thought.

He glanced forlornly back into the wagon, and Miguel gave him a cheerful grin. Foolish boy! And then from him to Maria's dark brooding eyes. Her whole face had been made lopsided by the puffed jaw. Awful! There would be blood on the grass if her father, the Duke, were here to see it. It wrenched at his heart.

Somebody had to say something. "Maria . . ." he began.

"Don Alonso," she said in a muffled voice, "conversation will be a little difficult." So she had lost a tooth.

"Do you blame me?"

"For this?" She touched her face with a crooked smile. "No. Only him."

Alonso peered through the driving haze; he could just make

183

out Francisco riding far ahead, rolling loosely on his pinto, apparently half-asleep. If he could see his wife's haunted eyes he would be instantly awake.

"Maria, let it come to an end."

"There will be an end," she said.

"There will?" It sounded hopeful. "When?"

"When I am his widow."

He cried out, "Maria, has he not already paid enough? See what you have done to him . . ."

"It is not enough." She was quiet for a while, seeming very sad. Then she said in a low voice, "I shall leave him at the next town."

He looked at her. "It is best. I think this time he will let you go."

If only he'd done it earlier. What he could have been spared!

"He will not be asked." She pressed hard against his back. "You will come with me? I have my grandmother's jewels. They will pay our way."

He was seized by a terrible wave of homesickness; all he could think of was his fine comfortable bedroom, the great four-poster in which his ancestors had slept for three hundred years, the cup of steaming chocolate with which his valet woke him every morning. Tonight he would sleep on the prairie, to be awakened by the toe of somebody's boot.

"We will come, Maria," he said.

"But first . . ."

"But nothing else. Do you hear? You have done him harm enough." What did she want? His head on a plate? Like John the Baptist? That Spanish Salome! He was having trouble with the mules, too. He seemed to have no control over them; they strayed obstinately all over the trail, ignoring his reins.

"Father," Miguel said calmly in his ear, "I shall not go with you."

"What do you mean?" He almost dropped the reins. "You will do as you are told . . ."

"No. I like it here. I have tasted freedom and it is very good.

184

You are an old man, Father" (*what?* not so old!) "and you belong to Spain. It is a worn and effete country, not for the young. Here I can fill my lungs and grow. And here I shall stay."

What had come over this rebellious generation? The wagon gave a lurch; they were mounting a slope. Mad mules! Miguel slid forward and took hold of the reins. "I shall drive, Father. You are not very capable. Sit back and leave it to me."

So another day gone. Then two more, equally bad. This is my Odyssey, Alonso thought; I am sure the mad Greek never had to suffer like this. He had long since lost the helmet of his top hat. Joachim had given him a smelly sombrero in which he knew he looked grotesque. Cooped behind with Maria. He was in a cage; its bars were the awful emptiness of the land. Grass succeeding grass. Every lonely clump of cottonwoods just like the last. They seemed to be navigating a vast sea without compass or chart. Alonso wondered if God had lost them, if He could even put His finger on a map and say: this is where you are.

He sought a little relief in the saddle. How it chafed! Pablo called out to him blandly, "Be glad to rub a little bear-grease into your ass." Was he laughing? He rode with one leg hooked over his horse's neck so that he could sweep the herd with his eye. "Least a man can do to oblige a friend."

So back to the wagon. It jarred his spine. Another week behind them. Maria rarely uttering a word. Miguel clucking contentedly to the mules, singing the only verse he knew of a curiously dramatic dirge:

> Pore young dying cowboy,

> Never more he'll roam,
> Shot right through the chest five times,
> He ain't never coming home . . .

Neither are we. Nobody will ever find us, Alonso thought. We shall go on and on until we have eaten every cow; then we shall all be bleached bones.

The weather suddenly changing. A blustery wind ripping by

185

them to shake the buffalo-hide lodges back in Indian territory. How it moaned! Then a mat of black clouds that bore no rain, just scurrying over the land, so that afternoon became as dim as twilight; morning bleak and sunless. No blanket could keep Alonso warm. I shall be a rheumaticky old man when I get back to Seville, he sighed.

What had got into him? He couldn't put a finger on it; it must be psychic. The feeling that something ominous impended. They were passing through chains of low timbered hills. The wind they emitted had a hostile sound. Something *is* going to happen; I know it; I feel it with every twinge of my gouty bones.

Miguel no longer singing. (Thank God.) Maria also on edge? Her eyes sharpened to watch the overcast prairie. We are not Spanish for nothing. We smell trouble before it comes.

They bedded the herd late afternoon. The camping ground was a narrow arena inside the hills; a long darkling pass. There was grass and water. Fires were lit. An uninspired supper of cold pork and coffee sweetened with molasses. Alonso couldn't eat; it was nagging him again. That psychic instinct. He heard Pablo utter a low sound, and before he knew what he had seen, he thought: *this* is it.

A troop of men were cantering along the pass. While they were still distant Alonso counted twelve. There were others; again Pablo grunted, looking back, and Alonso saw a shadowy group halted at the other end of the pass. Just waiting. For what?

Frank Dibbler said softly, "Hold still, Pablo." He beckoned to the *vaqueros*, making a significant sign. They muttered, reaching quietly for their rifles. But they didn't get up.

As the troop approached, coming out of the twilight into the glow of the fires, Alonso's eyes fastened on the leader. He rode a sleazy nag that matched his dress. Patched pants and a floppy hat that half-hid a long lugubrious face. But his bright eyes, when Alonso finally saw them, were very sardonic. His drooping moustache gave him the look of a Chinese mandarin. The rest of the troop were *bandidos*. It was the only word Alonso could find for them. Coarse and unwashed. They halted with a rattle of harness, the horses neighing, and the lugubrious man looked at the *vaqueros*, then at Pablo, then at Frank Dibbler standing by the fire.

"Sir," he said in a mild twangy voice, "I bid you good evening." A nice courteous approach. He looked up at the driving clouds. "Going to be a cold rough night."

Frank Dibbler said gently, "Coffee might warm you."

And the lugubrious man replied, "Sir, you are very gracious. But we've supped."

A highly articulate man. He talked like a schoolteacher, though few parents would trust a class of children to so grubby and unshaven a tutor. Bizarre. He gave Alonso the shivers.

He said gravely, "Sir, that is a sad, sick-looking herd you have."

"Healthy as fleas," Frank Dibbler said.

"Not to these aging eyes. Tick fever if ever I saw it. Infected, mothers and calves. I recognize the signs."

The cattle grazed in the gloaming. Alonso could see nothing wrong with them. He was bewildered. He stared at the unwashed, rough-whiskered group; they didn't look like vets. If they had any medical knowledge it was discounted by their oafish grins.

Pablo wandered round the back of his horse, resting his rifle absently on the saddle. It seemed to point vaguely in the direction of the lugubrious man.

"All you see are fine clean cattle," Frank Dibbler said. "And your friends don't need guns to know it."

"Texas fever," the lugubrious man sighed. He was very obdurate about it. It occurred tensely to Alonso that he had rather a lot of rifles to back his diagnosis.

He muttered to Miguel, "Who are they?" and got the puzzling reply:

187

"Jayhawkers, Father."

Still confusing. "And what are *they*?"

Miguel nudged him to silence. "Rustlers." Cattle thieves? Where did he get that monstrous education? Alonso's education in outlawry was about to begin. He would learn that tick fever —some kind of fearsome bovine disease—was merely the pretext for poker-faced thugs to rob drovers of their herds. It could only happen in this gloomy desolate land of no-law. The grab could be very brutal; battles had been fought over bawling steers. If there were enough trailhands, armed and resolute, the thugs could be driven off. And usually were. But with a dozen despondent *vaqueros*, already robbed of their spirit . . . Alonso mumbled to himself: I would like to be up in the hills. Just watching. I am an uninhibited coward.

Now he knew why his goosepimples were crying out to him. He had never seen anybody killed.

He found himself listening to the lugubrious man with the rapt interest of a rabbit in a snake. "Sir," he heard him say to Frank Dibbler in his twangy tutorial voice, "we will take your herd into temporary custody. Fatten them up in the valley. Do them a power of good." But the Chinese moustache was twitching. He was laughing. Satanic! "Come back in, say, five years to collect them. There'll be a small nominal charge for the cure, of course."

"You'll take nothing," Frank Dibbler said.

"It's a point of view. But you won't push it, will you? Violence is repugnant to me," the lugubrious man said. He added carelessly, "I hope that Indian's hand is steady. His rifle is inconveniencing my stomach."

"Pablo."

"Only when you tell me, Frank."

The lugubrious man chuckled. "Then don't tell him, Frank." He suddenly leaned down from the saddle. "Something familiar about you, sir. Would I know your name?"

"Dibbler. If it's any business of yours."

"From Panhandle way? Ah!" He beamed. "I knew your father. He tried to hang me."

"I might still do that."

"You might try." Still laughing. Then his eyes narrowing; Maria had just walked across the grass past the fire. Alonso had been so intent that he hadn't heard her get down from the wagon.

She called out to the man in the saddle, "Where are you from?" He looked at her as if it were an indelicate question. She tried again, her voice rising, "What is the nearest town?"

"Jake's Creek, ma'am. Other side of the valley. If you can call it a town."

"But there is a stagecoach out of it? To anywhere?"

He said gravely, "To Ellsworthy, ma'am. Once a week." He was intrigued.

"Will you take me with you? I would pay you. Here," she cried, holding up her hand, "take my ring."

Alonso cried out in his mind: Maria, how *can* you? But he didn't open his mouth.

"Wedding ring, ma'am?"

"It means nothing to me."

Maria!!

"Sir," the lugubrious man said to Frank Dibbler, "who is the lady?"

He was sweating. "My wife."

"Curious kind of wifely devotion, wouldn't you think?" The lugubrious man gazed sternly at Maria. "Ma'am, I hold the bonds of matrimony sacred. No business of mine to interfere in a marriage." He waved; the horses reared. He laughed over his shoulder, "Seems to me somebody's forgotten how to use the whip," and they were gone.

The thudding of hoofs lost in the gloaming; it seemed a very tame end to a terrifying situation. Frank Dibbler stared strangely at Maria. She was crying. She walked unsteadily back to the wagon and climbed aboard.

189

"Maria," Alonso muttered, "it was unforgivable."

She said wretchedly, "There are things I, too, will not easily forgive," and lay down.

Nobody will sleep tonight, Alonso thought. He wouldn't anyway; his supper lay as indigestible as iron in his gut. Darkness settled slowly and inexorably over the hills. The moon would be up in half an hour. He wished he could hurry it up. The birds screamed their forebodings out of the sky. But the cattle were unnaturally still. They know something, he thought.

A hand suddenly touched his boot. He almost leaped out of it. It was Joachim.

"Señor," he whispered, "withdraw with me a little distance."

"What is it?"

"*Por favor,* a few words with you." Alonso went with him away from the wagon. What was the matter with him? The squint was petrifying. The ugly Mexican face worked.

"Don Alonso, is she not a frightful woman?"

Alonso said exasperatedly, "Joachim, it is not your business . . ."

"It is the business of us all. Out of her great hate she will drag us all down to damnation. That droll on the saddle was right. He said somebody had forgotten how to use the whip."

"Yes." Alonso sighed. It was too late to blame the Duke. Who had ever been able to control her? She was a force of nature, a great hot wind.

Joachim said very softly, "They will be back, of course. You know?" Alonso nodded. He knew it. The cattle knew it, too. "As soon as the moon is up . . ."

"Why the moon?" Cold fingers stroked Alonso's skin.

"There will be a killing. Do you think Señor Dibbler will willingly yield up his herd? Don Alonso, we *caballeros* must stand together. I have a great fondness for you. Permit me to give you a few words of advice. There are only three men at the other end of the pass."

"How do you know?"

"One of the *vaqueros* has talked to them. They say they will

190

stop nobody who wishes to leave. Señor, I beg of you, do not waste a moment. Go at once."

Alonso said huskily, "I could not. It would be a gross act of betrayal . . ."

"What can you do? Shoot? Chase cattle? You will be a useless spectator. A target for a bullet. For the sake of your son, señor, you must leave."

"And you?"

Joachim put on his sombrero so that Alonso could no longer see his face. He shrugged and walked away. Alonso peered at the *vaqueros* sitting silently about the fire. They looked curiously impassive. He felt the trickle of sweat down his neck. They are going to leave, he thought.

They will not wait too long. If it is going to happen it will be before the first glimmer of the moon. Frank Dibbler and Pablo were patrolling the herd; the horses passed him intermittently like the wheeling figures of a medieval clock: waiting for the hour to strike? The sky glistened . . . and one of the *vaqueros* rose casually from the fire with the preparatory motion of relieving himself. He was a long time gone. There was a nervous neighing where the saddle band was tethered. The fire was suddenly empty of human shadows. Pablo came peering forward . . . the rush of horses past him almost trampled him down. Somebody's sombrero went flying. Joachim's? And then they were gone, drumming hard for the neck of the pass, Pablo pursuing, abusing them heartbrokenly.

God forgive me, Alonso thought. Frank Dibbler's horse moved into the light of the fire. "Francisco, I knew. I should have warned you . . ."

"I knew it, too. No use trying to hold them. They wouldn't have been any good."

Pause. Then softly: "Alonso, why didn't you go?"

Tears came into Alonso's eyes. "I am not a very resolute man. I even vacillate about betrayal."

"Take Miguel. Go up into the hills. Take Maria, too."

"And you?"

191

"I have Pablo."

"Is the herd worth it?"

"Alonso, it's all I've got."

May the Mother of Heaven have mercy on . . . and Alonso trembled: it was so violent, happening so suddenly that his spine jarred. He was too frozen to get off the ground. They were coming in from all sides.

They went ruthlessly about the business; he guessed that they'd lifted enough herds to know the value of shock. Noise indescribable, the valley echoing with frenetic screams and pistol shots. The herd moaned. The moonlight making everything ghastly. Horses weaving all about. A wild hoof planted in the fire showered Alonso with sparks.

They knew what they were doing. They were split into three sections. The first bunch of raiders going straight for the herd, flapping blankets, firing behind their rumps. The second section waiting to run the beasts off into the hills. They needed no persuasion. They ran off into the darkness like a black undulating rug. The third section strung out in a thin line facing Alonso in case there might be *vaqueros* about. There aren't any; and you have nothing to fear from me, Alonso thought. Lugubrious Man calmly directing the operation from the saddle, like Napoleon at Marengo. He looked wolfish in the light of the moon.

A passing horse threw a clod into Alonso's face. It was enough. "Maria, get down." He was aware of her standing behind him, watching intently in the light of the fire. Madwoman. He grabbed Miguel close.

This is where it becomes tragedy, he thought. It can have no other end. He watched it happen. Frank Dibbler spurring into the melée, met by a sheer wall of horses that banged him to the ground. He rolled over twice, and somebody shot him on the second roll. It seemed to have been done without malice, as if he were a source of trouble that had to be stopped. The pinto was gone, swept off with the herd. Alonso knew he would never see it again.

192

He still had Miguel's face clutched to his breast. He thought the young lungs would burst. Be still. It is not our herd. You are only a boy. . . you still have a long life to live. He closed his eyes. He didn't want to look anymore. But he couldn't help listening. There was a high yammering cry that Warbonnet Chief Owl-in-the-Sky might have uttered; it could only be Pablo coming back. He rode in the most extraordinary fashion, hung horizontally over the side, one heel hooked on the saddle, supporting himself by the bit so that his rifle poked under the horse's neck. He never had the chance to fire it. Lugubrious Man shot him. It was as if a clown had come howling into a circus act to which he didn't belong. The act even ended ludicrously; Pablo's heel still hooked on the saddle so that as the horse ran about his braided hair dragged in the dirt.

Then the horse jerked him off. He lay a dozen yards from Frank Dibbler, and Alonso knew that he was dead.

Now there was only Frank Dibbler to watch. He had turned on his side, straining to look at Pablo, clutching his thigh. It was black between his fingers; but that was the fault of the moonlight; blood was red. He couldn't be weeping? By no stretch of imagination could Alonso connect Frank Dibbler with tears. There was a croak: it wasn't Miguel. It came from Frank Dibbler's chest. Now he was staring at Pablo's fallen rifle. He bedded his elbows in the grass and started dragging himself across. One of the raiders half-moved forward; Lugubrious Man beckoned him away. He leaned sardonically over his saddlehorn, watching. There was almost no sound; even the horses fascinated.

They are playing with him. Alonso sensed somebody walking past him: Maria. Then across the grass, over to the rifle. Frank Dibbler peered up at her. "Throw it to me." She looked at him. Again, "Throw it to . . ." and still nothing. And still dragging himself across. He reached out to it and she kicked it away from his hands.

Now I have seen everything. Alonso put his arms across Miguel's eyes. Let him grow up with a few illusions about women. He couldn't bear Frank Dibbler's upturned face: Christ must have looked like that on the . . .

And then the horses rushed forward. There was no need to wait; the herd was gone. There was a crack as they leaped past and Maria cried out with pain. Lugubrious Man stooping over her cynically as he passed. Somebody, in the end, had had to use the whip.

Dawn now very near. And hideously dank. The birds wept for Pablo. Nobody looked at him; it might have been a heap of castoffs left by one of the *vaqueros* on the grass. The bullet had entered the fleshy part of Frank Dibbler's thigh, leaving a raw, flowerlike aperture. It had missed the bone. But it must have scored or torn a nerve, for he couldn't stand without cringing. Alonso slit his pants to the crotch. What could he do with it? He flinched. There was a great jelly of half-clotted blood. His hands were soon red as a butcher's.

Miguel said with an impatient fidget, "You are too delicate, Father. If you have to be sick go where we cannot hear. Leave it to me."

He filled a bucket from the water-barrel and mopped the wound. Some whispering went on; Alonso strained to hear; Miguel looked at Frank Dibbler and sighed. He fetched a flask of brandy from the wagon, but neither of them drank. He doused the wound with it. He wasn't going to . . . ? Alonso retired hastily to the trees as Miguel ignited it, recoiling from the smell of scorching flesh. He returned shakenly, having lost the contents of his stomach. Miguel, much paler, was binding the leg with strips torn from one of his silk shirts. He'd used the cord of his robe to make a tourniquet.

Frank Dibbler lay watching him intently. He wishes he had a son like that, Alonso thought. He stared at the bristly face, the color of yellowing paper. He will never be the same again. Mountains can be worn down; men can be broken. The bone of

194

his skull seemed to be coming through his skin, his eyes sunk into black sockets.

And the ministering angel who should have seen to her husband—what are women for?—sat gray-faced in the wagon. She was shivering. It wasn't that cold.

"Miguel, chop me a stick to help me get about."

"Yes, señor . . ."

"Francisco."

"It is quite clean, Francisco." Miguel spat to cleanse his mouth of the fumes of the brandy. "I do not think you need worry. It will soon heal." Torn nerve-sheaths were less predictable; he may walk with a lurch for the rest of his life, Alonso thought.

He looked at Pablo. He couldn't just be abandoned. He muttered, "We must get him into the town and buried . . ."

Shocked to hear Frank Dibbler say cruelly, "He was an Indian. They wouldn't touch him." But he was a human being! "He wouldn't want to be boxed up and dropped in some gulch. This is his prairie. He'll breathe better here. This is where he'll lie."

They buried him shallowly, the earth layered only a few inches above his belly. They piled the grave with stones. With a kind of fussy propriety Alonso began to make a wooden cross, again starkly shocked when Frank Dibbler said impatiently, "What are you doing with that?"

"It is only decent. He was a Catholic . . ."

"He was Irish on Sunday. Monday to Saturday he was just plain Arapaho. You don't have to decorate him. Let them sort it out wherever he is."

Then hobbling a few steps, testing the staff Miguel had chopped. "Christ Jesus." He gritted his teeth with despair. "A cripple." He stared about. A chill mist was rolling down from the hills. Four steers, left like a consolation prize by the raiders, grazed on the slope. He moved across to them, yelling, "Git, now. Go on. Git!" and they ran.

Surely they were worth something? What sort of crazy ges-

195

ture was that? "Now I'm stripped clean," he said. "Way my father walked into this land. With nothing." It had a Biblical ring. "Naked came I out of my mother's womb, and naked shall I return . . ." But Job had added with humility, "The Lord gave, and the Lord hath taken away," and there was nothing humble about Frank Dibbler: one way or another he would get it all back.

They climbed into the chuck wagon and rolled off for the town. Jake's Creek. "If you can call it a town," Lugubrious Man had said. We started out like a conqueror's army, Alonso thought; three thousand cows and a regiment of men, and all we have left is a wagon and a span of sickeningly smelly mules.

"Maria," Frank Dibbler said with a gentleness that surprised him, "how you've blooded me." And grinned. Ghoulish kind of grin. He didn't have to look round; he knew that she was staring at the back of his neck. He drove, his bandaged leg thrust out like a gouty aristocrat in his coach. "But we won't let it get to be a habit, will we? There's so much more to marriage than ducking blows."

"I, at least, warned you."

He nodded fairly. "You surely did."

"And there is more to marriage than selecting a woman and saying, this is my cow. This is the one that will breed me my calves! I am nobody's cow! And if I were," she said passionately, "I would at least choose my own bull. I am the Condesa de Rojas . . ."

"I'm Dibbler de Amarillo." Baron in his own right. How could he joke with his leg on fire and every bone in him crying out?

"Barbarian."

He twisted to look at her. "I could be polished." He uttered only five more words. Alonso thought they were very meaningful. "And I'm still your bull."

The pass turned and twisted. It opened up into the valley. The chill wind fluttered the canvas. It carried something

196

vaguely familiar; Alonso's nose twitched. What was it? And why should it make him think of Pablo? It was as if his ghost were tapping him on the back. He suddenly remembered Pablo saying to him excitedly, back at that creek in Texas, "What do you think we're doing here? Tunneling into Mexico? I can smell the oil . . ." for it was what Alonso now smelled. It seemed to ooze heavily out of every fold of the hills. He saw Frank Dibbler glance strangely about. Even Miguel sniffed. They came on it with the last twist of the pass.

Oil town! A squalid sprawl of wooden derricks, sprouting like a mushroom growth of clothes pegs out of the greasy earth. Hideous. For a few moments they all stared at it in silence. Frank Dibbler jerked the wagon to a stop. His eyes gleamed. Alonso could sense his awakened excitement; he'd been granted a glimpse of a Promised Land that wasn't his. No matter. He had his own!

He was so moved that his voice actually shook. "What's it saying to you, Alonso? Or don't you believe in fate?"

Alonso shrugged. He believed in fate, but he didn't believe in oil. He thought candles had style. He preferred the great candelabra that for three centuries had dazzled the diamonds of beautiful women in his hall. Oil had no style. And it stank. *How* it stank. In the beginning God had said, "Let there be light," but there was no Biblical record that He had said, "Let it also smell."

Maria muttered, "It is not much of a place."

"No."

"What is its name again?"

"Jake's Creek."

The messy hovels of a temporary boom-town; it probably hadn't existed last year. Oklahoma fever had crept in. It seemed to vibrate with a fearful energy; there was a distant thudding that could be drilling bits or trees being felled. Cart tracks ran out to the towering derricks. The Indians had prettier totems. Something terribly potent was happening down there and it filled Alonso with a vague unease; he glanced at his son, think-

197

ing: out of this madness he will inherit a demonic kind of world.

He heard Maria sigh. All she was interested in was the stagecoach. He could almost sense her praying: Blessed Virgin, do not let me be deposited in this evil place.

They crawled down to it. It had a lurid fascination close to. People lived here? In civilized society? It was just a single street, a vile snarl of teamsters' wagons and lurching barrels, a welter of garbage that rivaled petroleum for sheer reek. And everything oily, even the hitching posts outside the saloons. A hodgepodge of stores, hurdy-gurdy halls: and brothels. It didn't need a sophisticated eye to recognize the soiled doves who leaned out of the windows of what they euphemistically called "boardinghouses." Maria, so delicately bred, froze with horror. Everywhere mud. The rutted street squelched with it. There were no boardwalks. God must be preparing something dreadful for this Sodom-and-Gomorrah excrescence, Alonso thought.

There was a creek that teemed with greasy flatboats. Barrels rolling about. The din of snorting mules and language that would have defiled a Spanish debtors' prison.

Frank Dibbler said laconically, "Watch your pockets."

It is my soul I must watch, Alonso thought. He glanced anxiously at Miguel. It was a bad, bad day when I brought my innocent son from Seville to this pestiferous resting place.

"Do we sleep in the wagon?"

"Hotel," Frank Dibbler said. The wagon had stopped. Hotel, he'd said? Alonso peered at it. A clapboard structure that reverberated with a hammering piano: the Paradise Palace. If this is the Paradise of Jake's Creek, I shudder to think of its comparable Hell. They went inside. Beyond the desk clerk, besieged by oily prospectors, was a thronged plushy hall. Gaming tables and a gaudy bar. It was there that the piano thumped. The "hostesses" were terribly in evidence. I will not stay here, Alonso thought; but Frank Dibbler had already fixed the rooms.

The desk clerk glanced impassively at his slit gory pants and said, "Mister, don't bleed in the bed."

"Won't. Where's the doctor?"

"Back of the stable."

Alonso accompanied him behind. Maria and Miguel had gone upstairs. A thick horny-handed man held a mule's mouth open while he peered at its teeth. "Doc?" Frank Dibbler asked.

"Friend, I have all the customers I can accommodate today," the man said. The stable, his waiting room, was crowded with teamsters' mules. But his eyes strayed to Frank Dibbler's blood-stained pants. "Barrel fell on you?"

"Bullet."

"That so?" It didn't seem to disconcert him. "Give me ten minutes and I'll probe for it . . ."

"It's out."

"Dress it for you soon as I've fixed this bastard's mouth." The mule spat.

"With those hands?"

"Kind of fastidious, aren't you?"

"Kind of don't want tetanus. Or whatever it is you sell. Thank you, *Doctor*," and Frank Dibbler hobbled out.

Alonso now retired like a hibernating animal to his room. The brass bed he would share with Miguel was commodious. Only heaven, if it kept a record of venal sin, knew what lusts had been consummated in it. He sat at the window, staring with awe and revulsion down into the seething street. Wagons creaked in the mud; oxen lowed. Men threshed about in thigh boots. A pile of barrels fell off a wagon and inspired a flood of profanity that burned his ears. I have come to the end of the world, he thought, Armageddon itself. They are all oil-mad, sucking that noxious black fluid out of the earth as if it is liquid gold.

And perhaps it is.

Dusk fell. Jake's Creek was like a horrid nocturnal flower that opened its petals at night. The street filled up with a different

199

kind of custom. Watching the sexual traffic, Alonso thought: I will not leave this room until we can get away. But hunger drove him down. He joined Frank Dibbler and Miguel in the dining room. A brawny waitress slapped thick steaks on the raw wood table. Permeated, as he anticipated, with mineral oil. Maria was wise not to appear before the stagecoach left. Back in that plushy gambling saloon they were lining up three deep at the bar as if fearful that the stock of whiskey might run out. The tables were as busy. Money seemed to be flowing through the hands of the faro and monte dealers as fast as the derricks could suck it out. There was a lot of low-keyed cursing. It sounded vicious. The piano had now been joined by a sawing fiddle, and the din, added to the alcoholic fumes, made Alonso feel faint.

He muttered apologetically to Frank Dibbler, who seemed totally unaffected—bandaged leg stuck out from the table, a danger to all who passed—and took Miguel upstairs.

They crept into bed. Heaven itself after so many nights on the prairie. He closed his eyes with exhaustion. But the room was at the head of the stairs; there was an endless procession of clumping boots and giggling women in the corridor, followed by hair-raising gasps and mattress creaks in the adjoining rooms. He wanted to stuff his fingers into Miguel's unsoiled ears. But either he was too young to understand — unlikely after a liberalizing association with randy cowboys—or he accepted it as a fact of life: for he sighed cozily and fell instantly asleep.

THREE:

All Passion Spent

VIII

THE RACKET of dawn woke Alonso. Not that it had been quiet for many moments during the night. But he'd slept better than he'd expected; *all this is part of a great education, even if it has overtaken me in middle age, so we mustn't complain too much,* he thought. *He would never see anything like it again. Where else could one meet men who drank rotgut whiskey for breakfast? Who addressed mules in terms of intimate blasphemy that would make Balaam's ass turn and spit back?*

There was a warm hollow in the bed; he hadn't felt Miguel go. *I hope he will be careful. This is such a violent place.* He went to the window in his nightgown. The wagons never stopped creaking. Everybody rushing about: teamsters, thigh-booted prospectors, all splashed with the same common mud. There'd been a time when Arapaho Indians had watered their ponies at that primeval creek; now it was a slimy mess of barrel-high flatboats. *Something terribly explosive is going on; these ferocious men,* Alonso thought, *are clawing the wealth out of the land. In fifty years they will make Spain, the great Conquistador, look like a village backwater.*

203

He sighed. He liked village backwaters. He dressed and went below.

The same brawny waitress served him a platter of ham and eggs. She said briskly, "Eat hearty, pop. In this town a man needs all his strength." He didn't doubt it. Women, too. He looked at her strong red arms. He wondered if she doubled up jobs, if in her off-hours she joined the nightly procession upstairs. The bar smelled stalely of cigars. They were spreading sawdust on the floor. The silent gaming-tables looked like the hangover of an orgy. There was a blear-eyed faro dealer counting chips.

A portly gentleman sat at the next table, contemplating a spread of handsomely engraved certificates. He looked like a banker who had brought his securities out of the vault to enjoy them. He leaned over to Alonso and said in a grave voice, "Sir, you look like a man who would be interested in buying himself a stake in a nice well."

I am interested in buying myself a ticket out of Jake's Creek. "Thank you, no," Alonso said.

"I have here a set of choice oil leases. Hundred dollars gets you your pick."

Alonso shook his head.

"Fifty dollars buys you a promising hole in the ground."

"I hope it makes you a rich man."

"I'm a thirsty man, sir. Half a dollar buys me a drink."

Alonso blinked at the waitress. She chuckled. He pushed half a dollar across. He hadn't seen Maria since they'd arrived and he said to the waitress, "If you will send up breakfast to the Condesa . . ."

"The *what?*"

He'd forgotten where he was. "The lady in room ten."

"Any ladies you find here is purely by chance. If she wants breakfast she comes down and yells for it," she said.

Hard to imagine Maria doing any such thing. He ate the eggs, abandoning the ham; it was redolent of petroleum. He was sure if he lighted it it would burn with a clear oily flame. He went outside. Miguel sat on the hotel porch, enraptured by the scene.

Mud. Oxen waded in it like water buffaloes. The wagons didn't so much roll through it as float on it. The teamsters cracked their whips, howling obscenities like cavalrymen urging their beasts into battle. Where were all those barrels going? To China?

"Miguel," he said in a low voice, "restrain yourself. This is not for us. Think of our history. We are gentlemen of coat armor."

Miguel looked up at him. "Father, we have been gentlemen of coat armor for four hundred years. History has never been interested in us."

It stung Alonso. "At least we have lived good and distinguished lives . . ."

"In obscurity. I do not want to be obscure. I want to be something. Wonderful things are happening here. The stuff in those barrels is going to change the world. Spain is growing old, and this country is growing up."

"Miguel, if I were to order you to go . . ."

"Father, I would kiss your hands and feet, as we say in Spain. I love you. And I would still not go. I am staying with Señor Dibbler. He is the one who is going to change my life."

I will not be flouted. Alonso seethed. I will have to assert myself . . . and was astonished to see Maria coming down the street. Skirts tucked up to avoid the slush. Head held high. A parasol carried in stately fashion, though the morning sun was still low. He thought she looked exalted. "Maria," he said with shock, "you should not have gone out alone."

"Nobody has molested me."

It wouldn't have surprised him if someone had. The whores outside the sporting-houses watched her coldly. The mule-skinners looked back from the wagons with a flow of sexual offer he hoped she hadn't heard. She was unaffected, her calm eyes disdaining everything about her, as only an Estremaduran's would. She was as incongruous in Jake's Creek as a Rembrandt in the bar of the Paradise Palace Hotel.

"You should have called me, Maria."

"I have no time to waste. You were asleep. Don Alonso," she burst out jubilantly, "there's a stagecoach to Wichita in three days."

"Where is Wichita?"

"I neither know nor care, except that it is on our way. From there to Memphis, then on to New Orleans. Then a ship to Spain and we are back in Seville."

"And then?"

"Freedom. The sanctity of my body. I will be shut of him. My life becomes once more my own."

Would it? The corners of Alonso's mouth went down. She would exchange the cage of the prairie for a convent cell, where she would be a prisoner of vespers and evensong, her life a sad monotony of chanted prayers. Pity. He felt a great sorrow for her. She was so alive! She searched his face. "You are coming with me, are you not?"

"How can I, Maria?" he muttered. "Francisco is crippled. I cannot leave him until he is safely set for home."

"He would not hesitate to leave you."

"He is still my friend . . ."

"He is no friend of mine. I am going, with or without you, Alonso. He cannot stop me. There is a sheriff's office here. I have seen it." She sounded triumphant. "He would never dare to manhandle me again."

Alonso stared at her. "Have you no sense of guilt?"

"Guilt?" Her eyes flashed. "Why should I feel guilty?"

"If it were not for you he would probably still have two sound legs. You have brought him down to the ground. You have left him nothing." Only millions of drought-ridden acres in Texas, and a dubious lake of oil beneath them. "I may even have to pay for his journey home."

206

"More fool you."

"Maria!"

And Miguel said with the cold logic of youth, "If I were your husband, Maria, I would not be sorry to wave your stagecoach good-bye. When I marry I shall expect my wife to stand by me in sickness and in health."

Be quiet, Alonso thought. This is not for adolescents. Maria gave him a bitter look. She said in a stricken whisper, so that only he could hear, "You cannot know how I feel. Sooner or later he will seek to touch me. The thought haunts me. I could never let him. Never," and, startlingly pale, she went into the hotel.

"Miguel," Alonso said sternly, "you are not old enough to understand . . ."

"What is there to understand?" Miguel shrugged. "He has the right to bed her. She will not let him. Everybody knows it. The cowboys talk of nothing else."

Listen to the prairie *boulevardier*. Alonso gasped. Stripling! My father would have flayed the skin off my bottom if I had spoken to him like that.

He is crippled, he'd said to Maria; he is still my friend . . . and he hadn't given Francisco a solitary thought. He was nowhere about. Nobody in the hotel had seen him. And as the day drew on, Alonso grew uneasy, then nervous. Could he have absconded? Leaving them like useless baggage in this frantic, harlot-ridden Gomorrah . . . Never! He would as soon have yielded up his faith in God. And late afternoon he appeared, stalking into the hotel on a crutch some barrel-cooper must have knocked up for him. He would need a little more practice, for he cracked every table leg with it as he passed. He sat by Alonso, nestling his chin on the heel of the crutch. His face very luminous. His mind so far away that Alonso spoke to him three times before he replied.

"Where have you been, Francisco?"

"Oh, nosing about. Looking over some oil lots."

Strange. What would he use for money? "I was offered a promising hole in the ground for fifty dollars," Alonso said.

"Land-shark. Don't bite."

I have no intention of biting or being bitten; Jake's Creek is nothing but a seething pool of assorted sharks, Alonso thought. He couldn't take his curious eyes off Frank Dibbler. Something was churning about in that hard exploratory mind. As if he were planning some . . . but he had nothing to plan with but the shirt on his back. And that patched!

He said peevishly, "What is wrong with you?"

Frank Dibbler looked at him gravely. "Who said anything's wrong, *amigo?*"

"You are all on heat. As if . . ."

"I'm no tomcat, Alonso."

"Something has happened. I can sense it . . ."

And Frank Dibbler laughed. Then raised his eyes casually from the crutch. Maria stood before them. She was pale, but collected. She stared at a point above her husband's head as if a direct look might have recognized his existence. With a dignity that impressed Alonso (now she is behaving like a duke's daughter!), she said, "I shall be leaving you in three days. I would not wish you to hear it from somebody else." Stiffening as if expecting a violent response. "There is nothing you can do to stop me."

And he said serenely, "Have yourself a nice journey." As if barely aware of her. His chin had nestled absently back on the heel of the crutch.

Did he actually *say* that? Alonso looked at him incredulously. It unsettled him. What is going on?

Maria frowned. "I do not think you could have heard me. I said I shall be leaving you in three . . ."

"I heard you, Maria. Stagecoach to Wichita?"

"Yes."

"Could be a cold trip this time of the year. See that they give you a hot brick wrapped in a blanket. Warm feet and a good conscience'll see you through."

Her eyes sought Alonso's. She was as baffled as he was. "You intend to make no trouble?"

"Been enough trouble, wouldn't you think? Don't see that it's done much good. I tried, didn't I? It just didn't work out." My ears must be deceiving me, Alonso thought. He heard Frank Dibbler say to her in the same pleasant, but disinterested tone, "Got enough money to make it back to Spain?"

"Enough."

"That's fine. Takes a load off my conscience. Not that I could help you. I'm all cleaned out." Alonso bent his head. I simply refuse to believe this conversation! *"Vaya usted con Dios,"* Frank Dibbler said to her simply. Go with God.

A last uncertain glance at Alonso. Finally she stared down at the ground. She looked deflated. She'd expected to meet a wall of unyielding granite, and she was beating her fists on empty air. The war was over; it had ended, not with a big matrimonial bang, but the ridiculous hiss of a punctured balloon.

"Very well, then." She froze. No longer quite so collected. "We may not be seeing each other again . . ."

"You'll get the marriage annulled, will you?"

"As quickly as possible. I will send you a message when it is done."

"No need to bother. Probably never reach me. Won't make much difference; next woman'll have to be content without a ring." He was done with her. His eyes had suddenly sharpened; he was staring across the hotel lobby at a swarthy little Slavic-looking man, wearing the kind of black broad-brimmed hat Middle Europeans wore, who had just come in. He struggled up on his crutch and beckoned to him. The man nodded. Odd little creature; he reminded Alonso of a kobold out of some Bohemian forest. Who was he? Frank Dibbler started to hobble off, then, as if remembering just in time, said with a fleeting smile over his shoulder, "Good-bye, Maria. I'll think of you." But not too often. He grinned, "I'll have a few scars to remind me of you," and he was halfway across the lobby, waving to a waiter to fetch a bottle. He joined his visitor at a corner table.

Maria watched him with knitted brows. "Do you understand him?"

"What is there so difficult to understand? It is very commendable. He is behaving like a gentleman," Alonso said.

"You are absurd."

"All right, then." He shrugged. "So he is having second thoughts. Do you blame him? You could hardly call it a marriage of undiluted joy." It could so easily have ended in undiluted blood. Just the same, he had never been so staggered in his life. Was this how it was to be wound up? It was as if a thunderous Wagnerian opera had faded off into a mouse-squeak; what a terribly tame and spiritless last act! "You should be pleased, Maria."

"More than pleased," she said emptily, and walked out.

Alonso watched them at the table. A queerly assorted couple. What could they have to talk about? He would have given a lot to know. The swarthy little creature with the Bohemian hat, making broken foreign gestures, sometimes speaking excitedly, peering forlornly into Frank Dibbler's face—probably the most unforlorn man on the face of the earth. He sat listening intently, his chin resting on the ledge of the crutch. He towered above his visitor. Presently he nodded; he leaned across to pat the little man's hand. He filled two glasses ceremoniously and both of them drank. What were they settling? Alonso simmered with curiosity. If I go across they will probably shut up, and then I will never find out. Perhaps Miguel . . . ?

His son sat outside on the porch. Alonso joined him. He twitched his head confidentially back toward the lobby and said, "You have long ears for a boy. Who is that strange man with Francisco?"

"What makes him strange, Father?"

Always evasive. "Answer a question," Alonso said testily. "Speak up."

"His name is Dlujeck."

"An alien."

"We too are aliens, Father."

210

"So?"

"They are talking business."

"How can that be so?" Absurd. "What money does Francisco have to make business? He has been stripped to the bone."

"But it is very strong bone. And money is not the first essential," Miguel said in a faintly supercilious tone. "Brains and power are."

"Stop lecturing your father." I was in high finance—well, mortgages *are* a kind of finance, aren't they?—before he cut his teeth. He gets to be more articulate every hour. His tongue will have to be clipped. "What is the man's business?"

"I cannot tell you, Father."

Can't? Or won't? It was too frustrating. He could see Maria sitting solitarily at the far end of the porch. How frustrating for her, too. To have been so summarily dismissed from her husband's life! It was the children of the Duke of Estremadura who were accustomed to dismissing people like serfs.

He saw her tense. There was the clop of wood on boards and her husband came hobbling out, accompanied by his guest. He hadn't removed that awful Bohemian hat since he'd arrived. He stood peering desolately up and down the street, shrinking from the obscenities of the mule-skinners wading through the mud, a sad little alien in a brawling madhouse. He was chunkier—and grubbier—than he'd seemed in the hotel. He wore hideously beslimed high boots into which his equally greasy pants were tucked. His coat was clotted with the same stains of oil. Alonso's mind pricked. *Oil.* Was it possible that Francisco . . . ? No. Who could do business with someone whose pockets barely rattled enough dollars to pay for his room?

He watched the man Dlujeck walk across to a rickety cart hitched to a dejected mule. Saw him wave as he got aboard. He shouted, "Tomorrow then, Mr. Dibbler. Early?"

"Be there sunup." Frank Dibbler waved to him with a grin. "Don't you linger, Stanislav. Drive straight home. Leave the women alone."

Stanislav. The little man chuckled. The sporting-girls would eat him. He clamped his boot on the rump of the mule and the cart rolled off.

Frank Dibbler came swinging back. Now I will find out, Alonso thought. "Francisco," he began in an inquisitive rush, "what is going on . . . ?" but the crutch snicked his ankle inadvertently as he passed.

"Forgive me, Alonso."

"It's all right." Alonso winced. "Who is that man?"

"Friend of my uncle Josiah."

"Do you have an uncle Josiah?"

"No. I'm hog-famished. Coming in to eat, Alonso?"

"No," Alonso said huffily. He rubbed his ankle. It hurt.

"Come on, Miguel, let's eat," Frank Dibbler said, and the pair of them went in.

Maria came slowly across. She hadn't removed her eyes from the receding cart. "Who is that man?"

Why ask me? "His name is Dlujeck," Alonso said.

"What is he doing here?"

"A matter of business."

She glanced ironically at her husband through the dining-room window. "How do you do business with a man who is in the gutter?"

Where she had put him. "Why don't you ask him, Maria?"

"I have exchanged my last word with him. Are you not curious?"

"No." And he burst out, "The less they tell me the better. I do not wish to be involved."

But it was a little more complex than that. He'd been sucked too deeply into their affairs. He had dinner alone. He stood watching one of the poker games until some whiskered primitive accused him rancidly of "puttin' a bad eye" on his cards and he went insultedly to bed. Miguel was already asleep. He said his prayers; would God listen to him from this sink of sin? And before he could close his eyes the traffic on the stairs began. The rowdy howls, the shameless thumping of adjacent

212

mattresses, kept him erotically on edge . . . he barely got a wink of sleep before dawn. He got up tiredly and poked his head through the curtains to look out.

He could hear the chirp of a bird. The light was gray. The oil wagons were parked over at the creek like war chariots silently awaiting battle. A cat sniffed selectively at the garbage dumped outside the hotel. And from behind the livery stable a mule came plodding slowly, its rider perched sidelong on its back so that one leg stuck out like a wounded warrior's. He carried a crutch over his shoulder lance-fashion.

Where could he be going? Alonso watched him lumber off down the quiet street. *I have come such a long way, suffering hardships that have prematurely aged me; I am entitled to know!* He dressed hurriedly and went round to the livery stable where Francisco's mules were kept. He threw a blanket over a drowsy female—less likely to be troublesome—and mounted it. Its femininity didn't save it from a stomach-turning stink. He rode down the hushed street, into the glitter of the rising sun, down into the dark valley thick with the ghostly forest of towering derricks. He caught sight of Frank Dibbler in the growing light, trundling sleepily along the trail.

He followed secretively, hugging the clumps of the trees. He felt a little guilty; it wasn't the way an *hidalgo* should behave. *But I only want to know what is going on,* he thought. He never let his eyes stray from Frank Dibbler, seemingly dozing on the sway-rumped mule, the lance of the crutch balanced awkwardly on his back. *Look at them. Don Quixote on Rocinante!* He saw them turn into a dried-up gully and hurried to catch up. . . .

"Nothing like a morning trot to work up an appetite, Alonso," Frank Dibbler said demurely. He was waiting for him round the bend.

"I was following you, Francisco." Alonso hung his head.

"I'd never have known if you hadn't hopped all over the skyline. If you hadn't crunched every twig you could lay hoof on.

If your beast didn't stink like a polecat in the wind. Alonso," he chuckled deprecatingly, "that mule's on heat."

"It is making me ill."

"Not far to go." Wherever they were going. "Always glad of your company, *amigo*. Ride this side of me, will you?" he said delicately. "No need for both of us to be asphyxiated," and together they trotted down into the valley.

The dawn breeze whistled. So cold, Alonso thought. And so lonely. How will they ever manage to fill up this empty land? All he could see was dark grass, rolling on into an infinity of grass . . . and a long streaky shadow as the sun suddenly flashed. Thrown by a solitary derrick. What was it doing here? All alone on the silent prairie? As if some wildcatter had planted it and forgotten to come back.

Alonso peered sharply into Francisco's face. Was it this deserted rig he had come to see? He must be mad. He sensed a sudden danger to his purse-strings and thought with alarm: I hope he doesn't expect *me* to put a peso into an abandoned hole in the ground . . . but a man had just come out of the living-shack and waved. Dlujeck. Still wearing the Bohemian hat. Did he sleep in it? His feet were bare. He wore a long woolen undergarment that encased him like a glove. That and the hat made him grotesque. They rode down to him. He shouted, "Breakfast on the stove. All ready," squinting into the sun to make out Alonso's face. He recognized him and grinned. He'd seen him yesterday on the hotel porch.

"Stan Dlujeck," Frank Dibbler said gravely to Alonso. As if he didn't know. "Stan, this is my good friend, Don Alonso. He's the Count of Fuende," and Dlujeck glanced at them slyly as if he were making a joke. "He is, though," Frank Dibbler said. "So treat him like God."

"You are welcome," Dlujeck said. He put out the oiliest, most broken-nailed hand Alonso had ever touched. "Come inside," and they followed him into the shack. It smelled like an animal's cage. No woman had ever lived here; it was a bachelor's comfortable mess. Grimy blankets flung across a wooden bunk. An antique iron stove. Caesar must have cooked on it. Ham and a huge litter of eggs sizzled in a skillet. The raw table was laid with cracked plates and tin mugs. Two places only. Alonso hadn't been expected. He saw Dlujeck hastily wipe a plate for him on his pants. Holy Mother. Does he expect me to eat?

Frank Dibbler and Dlujeck ate vastly, not uttering a word. Food was too serious a business with them to waste unnecessary breath. Alonso drank a little of the hot rancid coffee. He thought it capable of dissolving the taste buds of his tongue.

Presently they finished. Frank Dibbler said to Dlujeck, "Seems to be light enough. I think we can look round."

"Whenever you want, Mr. Dibbler."

Alonso rose. Frank Dibbler said to him kindly, "You've had a long ride, Alonso. Better rest awhile," pressing him back. It was a polite way of saying: This isn't for your ears. Stay where you are.

"How long will you be?"

"Long as it takes. Maybe ten minutes longer." He reached for his crutch and followed Dlujeck out.

Alonso watched them through the window. They walked about the towering derrick, peering into its depths. There was a vast store of iron pipe. Dlujeck had evidently expected to drill deep. Frank Dibbler looked it over. They disappeared into the engine-shack. Suddenly the ghost of Pablo was back, muttering excitedly into Alonso's ear, "Smell it, smell it. One hell of a lake down there," and Alonso, for a creepy moment, almost heard the spooky thud of the drilling bit, the bobble of the engine . . . but the derrick here was as silent as Pablo's grave. And at that moment it began to thud. Alonso's skin froze. They had started up the engine; he watched the great rocking beam jerk, the bull-wheel wind up the steel rope, the heavy punching-bit begin to drop. And as suddenly as it started it stopped. The two emerged from the shack. They shook hands. Something had been settled. Well, what?

"Ready, Alonso?" Frank Dibbler looked in.

Alonso said stiffly, "Yes." He thought offendedly: why am I being kept in the dark?

"Fix it tomorrow, Stan," Frank Dibbler said, and Dlujeck, his sweaty face aglow, said, "You will not regret it."

Regret what? They mounted the mules and rode off. Silence while they crossed the valley. The sun glittered on the dewy grass. "Francisco," Alonso said earnestly, looking into his preoccupied face, "I beg of you, do not risk a dollar in this man's well," and Frank Dibbler interrupted him surprisingly, "He doesn't have one. All he's got is a dry hole. It's broken his heart. He's finished with it. It's his gear I'm interested in. Engine, pipe, beams and punching drill. I'm buying him out."

"What for?"

"To take back. I have a prime well of my own."

In God's name. "All the way to Amarillo . . . ?"

"Damn near brought three thousand cows this far." And would have, but for Maria. "I can ride a wagonload of iron home."

"And pay for it how?" Coming to the crux of the business.

"Bank here'll see me through."

"For how much?"

"Five thousand dollars."

"*What?* Francisco . . ."

Frank Dibbler said reproachfully, "My credit's good, Alonso. My name's known."

Names weren't security. Alonso shook his head. Banks wanted collateral: and all he had was a million arid acres in Texas. Who would loan him money on that?

He was in a highly disturbed state when they got back to Jake's Creek; and grew somewhat more disturbed to find Maria and Miguel in his room. They'd seen the mules return.

She listened to him with freezing disdain. "Can he be quite mad?"

"He is cold-bloodedly determined. It is an insane venture. A cripple. A crutch and a wagon, all the way to Amarillo . . ."

216

"Good riddance."

"But he will do it," Miguel said.

Alonso sighed. "I am too old to believe in miracles."

"Men like Francisco know how to make them happen." He heard Miguel chuckle. "How I would like to go with him."

Not while I can lay a hand on you, Alonso thought. The mere prospect of trusting this suckling to so mad a trek across the prairie made him sweat.

He said tartly, "You rattle too much."

"Yes, Father."

"So cool your tongue. I intend to take you back to Seville alive." His mind had been made up for him. We leave with Maria in the stagecoach. And that is final. I have had enough of Jake's Creek, he thought.

He spent the next day preparing for the journey. There were spare seats in the stagecoach for Miguel and himself. He bought some blankets. It would be a cold, bone-jarring ride. There wasn't much to pack; no more than he'd carried on the saddle. He would ask Francisco to dispatch the rest of his baggage from Amarillo . . . but where was he?

He peeped in his room. He hadn't slept in the bed.

The blear-eyed faro dealer had substituted for the desk clerk, who was taking a rest. He answered Alonso's inquiry. "Him with the leg? Ain't set eyes on him."

"Where can he be?"

"Can think of six different possibilities," and he listed them absently. "Madam Fay's, Sadie's Academy of Pleasure . . ." all of them brothels.

"He is not that kind."

"Everybody's that kind."

"And you are not worried?"

"Only that he might skip without paying his bill."

But, of course, he must have spent the night at Dlujeck's shack. They would be busy dismantling the rig. It gave Alonso a pang; how can I leave without saying good-bye?

217

No sign of him in the morning. His bed still untouched. The stagecoach would leave at midday. Alonso hung about with a heavy heart. There was no more time to waste. He joined Maria and Miguel reluctantly outside the office where the passengers had assembled. It was an old Concord coach; a battered, solid-oak, iron-rimmed vehicle that had almost ridden out the half-million miles of its life. Its six wild-eyed horses were being fed. The driver dozed stertorously on his seat; he would no doubt sleep all the way to Wichita. Alonso stared anxiously up and down the street. An hour to go. The baggage had already been loaded on the boot. Miguel's face was tight. Alonso's heart twitched for him; he will cry if I so much as utter a sympathetic word. Maria, cool and uncommunicative, a little pale perhaps, her parasol shielding her face from the bitter sun. Alonso thought cynically: nothing like anticipating a situation. He saw that she had already removed her wedding ring.

And—suddenly—a sight that made his heart leap. He heard Miguel utter a cry. The largest wagon he had ever seen, drawn by eight lowing oxen, lumbered toward them. It creaked like an overburdened hearse. The canvas canopy couldn't cover the tall iron chimney of the steam engine roped on board. Beams, bull-wheels and dismantled derrick strapped in the waist. Pipe, in great quantities, protruded from the back. Frank Dibbler perched on the driver's seat. The teamsters had to shift their wagons to let it squelch by. Alonso gasped; how will he ever get that monstrous assembly to Amarillo?

The oxen stopped and Frank Dibbler leaned down. He has been up all night, Alonso thought; his face was hollow. "Had to say good-bye to you, *amigo*," he grinned.

"Thank God." Alonso's throat thickened. I am going to cry. "Shall we ever meet again, Francisco?"

"Oddest things happen. It isn't such a big world."

"I wish you a safe journey." And Alonso *did* cry. Why am I so fond of him? He pressed his arms. He has been a tonic to my life, he thought.

Miguel's face was wet with tears.

"See you again, *muchacho.*"

"I swear it," Miguel said.

Frank Dibbler glanced fleetingly at Maria. She sat statuesquely outside the stage office, stony face averted. Already they are strangers, Alonso thought.

The wagon moved on. The effort it needed was colossal; the oxen strained. Alonso watched it creak down the street, turn slowly into the valley, the iron chimney of the engine swaying and clanking with every roll: and it was gone. Something has also gone out of my life, Alonso thought.

He looked mistily at Maria. "It is finished."

"Do you expect me to cry?"

He muttered, "Maria, one day you will have to learn to cry." If she was ever to be a complete woman. He sat on the stage-office bench watching the horses being fed.

Half an hour to go. He wasn't looking forward to the journey. He glanced at his son's strained face. Do not blame me, Miguel; it had to end. And staring across the muddy street at the Wells-Fargo Bank he saw Dlujeck emerge. He was buttoning up his pocket. His face shone. So he has got his money!

Miraculous. I will never understand it. I thought *Yanqui* banks had hearts of stone.

He called out to him as he passed, "You have been paid, have you?"

"But of course. Mr. Dibbler is an honest man."

"Five thousand dollars is a lot of money for an oil rig."

"I could have sold it six times over," Dlujeck said in an injured voice. "Any prospector would have bought it. It had to be hauled here a long way."

"And you are finished with drilling for oil?"

"Forever. I shall buy myself a store. Wildcatting is for madmen."

Alonso nodded indulgently. I couldn't agree with you more. A question itched on his tongue; he had to ask it. "Mr. Dlujeck,

219

I am very curious. What personal magnetism did our friend Francisco exert on the bank to get so much credit?"

"What was so magnetic about it?" Dlujeck gave him a surprised look. "He pawned his mother's jewels."

"I see . . ." Alonso's mind suddenly numb. "He *what?*"

"The bank required security."

Alonso stared at him. He doubted if Francisco's mother, a rawboned pioneer from Kentucky, ever owned a trinket worth fifty cents. He knew whose jewels they were and his brain spun in ever-tightening circles, narrowing down to one awful point: does she know? He glanced at Maria.

Should I hold my tongue? I dare not. The Duke would never forgive me. He went across to her and muttered, "Maria, when did you last open your valise?"

"When I packed."

"Yes, but when?"

"Two days ago."

"Maria, look for your jewels."

Her face froze. She hurried across to the stage and called up to the driver. She was trembling. He muttered resentfully and tossed her baggage down. She fumbled under a mound of clothes for the little velvet valise. She opened it. Alonso didn't have to look over her shoulder. He heard her utter a distraught cry.

"He has stolen them."

"Maria, how can he steal them? A wife's property is her husband's in this lawless land." As naturally as it was in Spain.

"My jewels!"

"Yes, yes, Maria . . ."

"They were my grandmother's. And hers before her. They have been in our family for three hundred years."

Now they lay in the vault of the Wells-Fargo Bank in Jake's Creek. He glanced across at it significantly. She followed his eyes.

"There?" She made a husky sound. "What are they doing there?"

220

"They are in pawn."

"Thief," she said stridently, and was across the street before he could lay a hand on her arm.

He licked his lips. Why didn't I bite my tongue? I didn't *have* to ask Dlujeck. Now she will make a fearful scene. He knew just how violent she could be. He sighed and went across to the bank.

It was hardly more than a clapboard shack, as if Wells-Fargo expected to move out as soon as Jake's Creek's oil wells ran dry. The teller stood stiffly behind his barred cage, listening at the open door of the manager's office from which issued a loud exasperated voice, half-drowned by Maria's shrill abuse . . . "Ma'am," he heard the man cry, "matrimony ain't no business for a bank. Money is. You're a married woman. That makes your husband your keeper. You don't own a thing that the marriage settlement laws of this state don't put in his charge, from the joy of your body to the shift on your back. Could be a nice legal point whether you even have the right to spit without his consent . . ." and there was the sound of a smack and Maria came running out.

The bank manager emerged shakenly, holding his face. "There's a crazy woman. Goddamn it, she hit me. Should have bopped her . . ." but Alonso had already gone.

There was a small crowd outside the sheriff's office and he guessed that that was where she was. He had to stand on tiptoe to peer over the heads of the sporting-girls and the bullwhackers. The sheriff sat impassively at the table, eating his lunch: Maria stood over him, a torrent of Spanish and English vituperation issuing from her lips . . . She would not dare hit *him?* Alonso could see the rack of rifles on the wall. The sheriff went on knifing his steak, looking up at her woodenly now and again as if she were a fly buzzing about the room. She gave a cry of sheerest anguish and rushed out.

And now it was all over. There was nothing more she could do. She had run down the street, behind the hotel. Alonso met Miguel's astounded eyes. I must soothe her . . . as if any man

221

born of woman could do that. He followed her down the narrow alley. He could hear her breathless rage and the stamping of hoofs in the livery stable; and suddenly she was on him, pounding at a mule. She almost rode him down. He ran into the street. The packed wagons balked her and she went hammering along the wooden porch of the hotel, scattering the patrons sunning themselves. The last he saw of her—was to see of her for weeks—was her bent back and the rump of the galloping mule. Then she was a speck in the empty valley into which Francisco had vanished. It swallowed her. And she, too, was gone.

Ten minutes later the stagecoach went bucketing off for Wichita. He wasn't aboard. His baggage lay symbolically in the mud. Something evil is sniggering over my shoulder, Alonso thought; it will never let me get away from Jake's Creek. The mad-eyed horses spattered him with foam; the coach dwindled to a flea-hop in the boundless grass, and his last thread with home was snapped. He felt unutterably friendless. Miguel, my son, we are children lost in a haunted forest.

The barrel-laden wagons squelched past the hostesses decorating the porch of Sadie's Academy. That is all Jake's Creek is: oil and sex. Both hideously inflammable.

They trudged back to the hotel.

Miguel said crisply, "You have nothing to reproach yourself with, Father. Your conscience is good." Hypocrite. As if he had wanted to go. "There will be another coach in three days."

Alonso gave him a mournful look. "But not for Maria."

"She is no longer your worry. She is gone. She is off your back."

But not off my soul. "Miguel," Alonso muttered, "I am so frightened. She will kill him if she finds him."

"Oh, Father, it is a lot simpler than that."

"It is?" What could be simpler?

"He will kill her," Miguel said.

"Miguel, what are you saying?"

"I think he planned it. He wants her to himself. There are no witnesses on the prairie. Who will ever look for Pablo? He lies in an unmarked grave. Who will look for Maria?"

In God's name. He is chilling my blood. . . .

"She is a very headstrong woman. He has baited a trap for her. She has walked into it."

How did I come to beget this young monster? Alonso cried, "He could never be so cruel."

"Father, if you will forgive me, you are pathetically naïve. How do you think these people survive? By being meek? They are half-savage. Have you never seen Francisco act with cruelty?"

Too often. I do not want to hear anymore.

"But you can sleep well, Father. Nobody could do more. You can face God with a clear heart."

Tongue like a stiletto. He is twisting it in my wound. "Somebody will do something. There must be some semblance of compassion in this place."

"Let me know when you find it. I would like to be the first to see it," Miguel said.

He is right, Alonso thought. I can do no more. She is off my back. I shall write to the Duke and explain . . . no, better; I will book our seats on the next stage and tell him face to face. Where is she now? Half a day had gone. Perhaps she will never find him. The prairie is no place for a woman on a mule; it has broken the hearts of tougher pioneers. She may soon be back.

He sat for hours at the hotel window, peering across the lonely valley, hoping any moment to see the mule plodding home; but nothing moved on the slopes but the slimy wagons lumbering back from the derricks.

Then dusk. He didn't go down to dinner. She has either found him; or she is lost. Perhaps dead. This is a land of unimaginable barbarity, infested with Pawnees and saddle tramps. I shall not sleep tonight for worry, Alonso thought; as if Jake's

223

Creek would, anyway, let him sleep. Have they no shame? Those awful audible mattresses . . . He sat watching the cold moonlight shining into the bedroom. The same moon could be glimmering on a lonely body.

Miguel woke him. He had fallen asleep by the window and he was stiff and heartsick. "What is the bed for, Father? It is more comfortable than a chair."

"Are you not worried?"

"But of course. There is a waiting list of passengers for the stagecoach. We must book at once."

"You are callous." The young were without feeling. Alonso said tensely, "Our families have been close for two hundred years. Could you go back to Seville and look her father in the eye?"

Miguel said coolly, "It is a matter for your eye, Father, not mine. I made no promises. You did."

"Then show some sign of your delicate birth. You are an *hidalgo*." He heard Miguel chuckle. "You are a Sanchez of Fuende." How ludicrous it sounded in this bedlam. The muleskinners were yelling outside.

"I shall go and see the sheriff," Alonso said.

"Do that, Father."

"He must send out a search party. There is a spark of humanity somewhere in this town."

He dressed early and went down the street to the sheriff's office. The sheriff sat eating his breakfast; he seemed to do nothing but eat in that shabby sanctum, stacked with rifles as if at any moment there might be a riotous assembly and he would have to call out his deputies to shoot. The deputies were probably the most riotous villains of all.

"What can I do for you, mister?" He was slicing a steak. At that hour of the morning. He pushed across a tin mug of coffee, from which Alonso shrank. He had tasted that fearful brew.

"The Condesa de Rojas . . ."

"Say that again?"

"All right. Mrs. Dibbler. She was here yesterday in your office . . ."

"Oh, that one. Madwoman. She clobbered Jack Dennison in the Wells-Fargo Bank. Thought she was ripe to clobber me, too. I'd have clobbered her back."

"She has gone after her husband."

"Glad to hear it," he said approvingly. "Let her clobber him."

"You do not understand. He has pawned her jewels. He should never have . . ."

"You got some queer ideas of a husband's authority, mister. He can do what he wants."

"Something terrible will happen. They are enraged with each other. It is hardly describable. One of them will kill the other. If you can muster—what do you call it—a posse . . ."

And the sheriff wiped his mouth on his sleeve, went to the window to spit and lighted a cigar. "Mister," he said, staring at Alonso as if examining a particularly retarded child, "I stand enough from this sinful community without acting as matrimonial court. Had a shooting last night at the Applejack Bar. Coroner's busy right now laying him out. Rumor says there was a spat that led to assault and battery at Sadie's place, and I'm hoping it's just a rumor and they won't fetch it to me. You know what makes a successful sheriff? Calluses on his ass." He put his boots up on the table and demonstrated what he meant. "He has to learn to sit in the chair and let the ruffianly element rub itself out. That makes everybody happy. Church, community and lawgivers, though there ain't no church here, and it's a community that'd turn the stomach of hell, and I'm the only lawgiver about." He looked dreamily at Alonso through the fumes of the suffocating cigar. "What was that you were saying? Posse? After some overheated woman? Jesus, friend," he said with righteous emotion, "can't that man of hers cool her down in bed?"

Alonso thought: he has put his finger on the root of the matter. But where is the matrimonial bed that can hold her?

"So no posse," the sheriff said. He stirred in his chair to scratch the calluses. "What was it you said she was?"

"A Condesa. Of the noblest blood of Spain . . ."

"Bleed her a little. Does a woman a power of good. Little cold this morning, ain't it, mister? Shut the door behind you as you go out."

I can search this town till doomsday for a spark of humanity, Alonso thought. He studied the faces in the street: the aboriginal bullwhackers, the storekeepers standing guard by their windows, perpetually edgy because the boss-eyed mules tended to back into the shops. All of them indifferent. The women were of a pattern. Genial slatterns. With little feeling for their sisters in sin, what hope was there of pity for Maria?

God, it was simple goodness that brought me here, he thought, and if You are the spur of human compassion, show me a ray of light. He went back to the hotel. Miguel sat drinking a tankard of light beer in the bar.

"Miguel," he said testily, "how wanton can you be? That is a drink for a man."

"One becomes a man here at twelve."

"I shall remedy that situation rapidly. You will return to adolescence in Seville."

"Father," Miguel mused, "if it occurred to you to seek Maria yourself . . ."

"It has not. And never will."

"In case it should. There is a guide available. We should need one, of course. I have talked to the desk clerk." These are the present associates of my son, Alonso thought: faro dealers and procurers. He didn't imagine that amorous prospectors discovered the available women on their own. "He has a great sense of the country," Miguel said. "It is in his blood. He is an Indian."

Alonso said sarcastically, "That makes him enticing."

"He will not be expensive."

"I need a guide only to take me as far as the stage office when we leave."

226

"Father," Miguel said gently, "will you not find it difficult to live with yourself when we get home?"

Alonso's face suffused. "You are not the keeper of my conscience," he cried, and a poker game by his elbow was suspended while they listened. "I lived peacefully with myself before you were born, and I hope to sleep peacefully with my ancestors when you lay me in my tomb."

"Mister," one of the poker players said, "won't be long, either, if you don't soften your voice."

"May it be long deferred," Miguel said.

Amen to that. But the way events are pressing on me, Alonso thought, I have less and less hope.

Miguel drained his glass. "And what will you dream of in eternity, Father?" He was starting again. "The lost opportunities? Poor Maria? Eternity is such a long time to spend in useless regret."

Santo Dios. Who does he inherit that tongue from? Not from me. "Miguel, we are neither experienced nor fitted for such expeditions . . ."

"That is what the guide is for. The desk clerk thinks highly of him. He knows every kilometer of the land between here and Amarillo. He is a Kiowa-Apache. They can smell a man's trail six days after he has crossed the grass."

I have no doubt that he is highly scented himself, Alonso thought. He was tired and dispirited. He sat. It was an awful nettle; and it had to be grasped. Miguel had voiced it with his adder's tongue. How will you live with yourself, Alonso? You cannot abandon Maria to the loneliness of the prairie and a husband who has a long score to settle with her. This comes of an open heart and high moral principles, and next time I am asked a favor I will retire instantly behind locked doors.

"This Indian," he said to Miguel. "You have talked to him, too?"

"I would not dream of doing so without your permission."

Smug! "Where is he to be found?"

"The desk clerk will know."

227

It was a faro dealer who was now officiating at the desk. "Hell, you don't mean Charley?"

"You sound less than enthusiastic," Alonso said. "Is he not a guide?"

"Oh, sure. Far as that goes. And you can go a long way toward the madhouse with Charley, if you know what I mean." Alonso didn't; but it filled him with unease. "He's an educated Indian. Speaks three languages, English, Spanish and Kiowa-sign, and given half a chance he'll spout them at you all at once. Where do you want him to take you?"

"We would like him to pick up the trail of some friends we seek."

"He can do that all right. Pick the birds off the trees. Pick the fillings out of your teeth and the gold-dust out of your belt." Less encouraging still. "You'll find him in his tepee back of the hotel." Alonso stared at him. His what? "His hut," the faro dealer said. "You have to bother him now? He's in labor."

In *labor?* Did Miguel have to grin? "He has three wives simultaneously dropping papooses," the faro dealer said. "There's a lot of nice bets going on the race." He became a gambler again. "Woman Quehanna's well ahead. You like me to give you the odds?"

"No."

"I'll send him round to the front if you wait outside. Indians ain't allowed in the hotel."

They stood in the street, watching the blasphemous furor of the wagons. "Miguel," Alonso said, "I cannot contemplate it. The man sounds like an aberration."

"A character," Miguel said. "The country is full of them."

"He could lead us into disaster."

Miguel said gravely, "You may be right, Father. Maria is no weakling. I see no reason why she shouldn't survive."

Did he *have* to say that? Alonso sighed. He was suddenly aware of a smell behind him: he'd grown to associate it with bear grease and a different kind of flesh. He turned. It was a

228

bandy corpulent man. The round moonface was the color of
bronze gone old. Two very long, very greasy plaits dangled
below a floppy black hat with a high pointed crown. His eyes
had the shine of reddish marbles. He looked very good-hu-
mored.

He said in a deep gravel voice, "You ask Eddie? Say see me?
You have job?"

Alonso said with distaste, "You are Charley?"

"Charley Hoot-Owl."

"You are supposed to be an educated Indian."

And, chuckling, he said in an entirely different voice, "The
white men'd throw a fit if I didn't talk like that. One has to
conform. You gentlemen are Spanish?"

"Yes."

"*Como está usted?* Forgive me. I cannot ask you in for a
drink."

A character. The country *is* full of them, Alonso agreed.
Smells of them, too. That hat! And the plaits! I will have so
much to tell them when I get back to Seville. "You know the
country between here and Amarillo?"

"Every yard. I was born in Susquemenna. The Texans call it
Brazos. It's the man with the leg, is it?"

"What makes you say that?"

"My women work in the hotel. The wife doesn't cohabit with
her husband." He grinned. He suffered from no such trouble.
"Odd, wouldn't you think? I'd have said he was a highly sexed
man."

"It is no business of yours."

"The quirks of mankind are the business of us all. How much
do you want to pay me?"

"Whatever is reasonable . . ."

"Two dollars a day would be reasonable. But you have a generous face and I think you will pay me three. We will need
horses."

"If you will buy them for me."

229

"I can do no less. I will get a small commission on the deal. We can start off in four days."

Alonso gasped. "Four . . . ?"

"I expect a happy event in triplicate. I have some side bets on the issue," Charley said. "Not to worry. Your friend has slow oxen. He will not get too far. You are frightened for the woman?"

"We are, indeed."

"*Sea como Dios quiera.* Let us trust in God. Her man looks like a ferocity, but she may still be alive."

It was all so familiar. Dust in the face, the wind whistling at them from frontiers unknown. A bitter red sun parching them to tinder—leaving them to a cruelly cold night. They were out of the valley, three mounts and two packhorses; the oily smudge of the derricks already far behind. The prairie suddenly empty. This was the raw grass that the Pawnees knew.

Once they saw a black woolly stream on the horizon—the buffalo still roamed. Charley, his eyes closed, plodded somnolently ahead. Did he even know where he was going? Miguel said to him softly that same evening, "I see no sign of their trail."

"*Muchacho,*" Charley said, "you do not have an Indian's eye. You look at grass. I look beneath it. His wagon passed this way. She was not far behind him. About twelve hours I would say."

He is either a liar or . . . but Alonso felt a little reassured when they made camp for the night. "See?" The embers of a fire. Charley smelled the ashes. "I could tell you what he had for breakfast but you would not believe me. Why bother? Tomorrow we find them."

"The lady, too?"

"She slept the night in the hollow two miles back."

As they lay under the stars, Charley said thoughtfully, "Did she carry food?"

Alonso stared at him with shock. It hadn't occurred to him. "She was in such a hurry to be after him." He shook his head.

230

"A gun?"

"Dear heaven, no."

"Then she will be both hungry and frightened."

"Nothing frightens her."

Charley stared at him curiously. In sixty seconds he was fast asleep.

Off early. Barely time for the gulp of coffee. Charley pointed to a soggy dip. Alonso saw nothing. "Wagon wheels," Miguel said. He has sharper eyes than mine, Alonso thought. And later, "Father, her hoof tracks." That solitary splotch by a waterhole? Had she drunk here? Then into the stony bed of a canyon that threaded the pass.

They trotted on for a while, their ponies clattering hollowly on solid rock. The glowing reddish marbles of Charley's eyes flitted about. He looked suddenly perplexed. After an hour he stopped. Still deep in the canyon. He got down and drew a little circle about some crunched stone. "This is as far as the wagon came."

Puzzling. For no reason he could understand, Alonso felt nervous. Charley murmured, "I think the woman lost him back in the valley. Strange. He knew it and turned back."

"Why would he do that?"

Charley's eyes glistened. "Come. Hurry." It seemed that there was no time to be lost. They trotted back along the canyon, returning to the valley where Maria had presumably lost Francisco. They picked up her trail. She'd missed the canyon and gone along by the river. "Now it is all different," Charley said. "She is no longer following him. He is following her."

Alonso's heart thudded. "I see nothing to suggest . . ."

"Look. The wheels overlaying her hoof marks. Does *he* have a gun?"

I will be sick, Alonso thought. "Do not even hint at it . . . ," but Charley had cantered up the bluff to search the stretch of the river. He sat his horse like a fat red centaur. Then pointed. He raced below. They followed him to a soggy clearing by the river. Alonso stared about. Why was the place so familiar? Of course. Here Francisco's cattle had crossed in full flood. Here Maria had . . . but it was all too terrible to recall. Charley got down. "She is not such a fool, after all. She knew he was behind." Pointing to the mess of footmarks and wheelscrapes as if reading a crystal ball. They meant nothing to Alonso. "Here she waited for him. And here they fought."

IX

ALONSO WOULD GET a little of it from Maria, highly colored and emotional. A little of it from Frank Dibbler, coldly and surgically told. It would be like listening to contrary accounts of Waterloo from the lips of one of Wellington's troopers and a veteran of Napoleon's old guard; it mightn't have been the same battle. He would get something nearer the truth of what happened on that homicidal trek across the prairie from the few shocked witnesses and Charley the Indian, who looked at the silent evidence of the trail and knew what he saw.

Maria told Alonso, "If I had caught him in the street of Jake's Creek it would have ended there and then. I would have killed him." But she hadn't. And he might well have killed her. Her brain was aflame. She had come out of the bank and the sheriff's office with a feeling of insufferable frustration. There was no justice in this wilderness, and all she could think was: my grandmother's jewels. Her family had guarded them like holy relics for centuries, and a barbarian had raped them. He had pawned them for five thousand dollars.

233

Five thousand dollars! It was the ultimate affront. If Alonso had been able to stop her he might have said, "Maria, if you mean to kill him, at least take a gun," but she was divorced from reason. She was as much on heat as the mule she took. She had to go after him before it was too late.

She went down the valley, pounding the mule stupid. She left the derricks behind her, then into the silence of the grass, following the indentations of his wagon. He was only half an hour ahead. But the ground hardened and she lost them; the valley wove snakily, throwing off many subsidiary passes, and she took the wrong one. She had to go back to the point of false detour. Peering into the distance she saw the fresh dung of the oxen. She had him again; but it had cost her two hours.

Now she went at a more sedate trot: the headlong rush wasted valuable time. She searched the prairie carefully. He was beckoning her on with the scrapes of his wheels. The oxen droppings helped. One clump still steamed, and she thought vengefully: not far. But somehow he was never there. The horizon empty, just grass billowing off into the vacuum of the land. There was a lot of militant blood in her; duchesses had ridden with her ancestors to war, and they murmured in her ear, take care. He could be waiting for you in some gulch.

She, too, had seen Pablo's grave; how easy it was to disappear under a pile of stones! And a little cold reason crept into her brain. She regretted her impetuosity; this could take a long time, much longer than she'd anticipated, and she had neither food nor water. Four hours later she was still searching the empty prairie. Wheel tracks, yes; but no wagon.

Had he mounted the sky like Elijah in his chariot of fire?

Alonso said to her, "So you were frightened?"

"Frightened? Of him? When there is so much hate there is no room for fear," and Alonso thought: it is a terrible family. Estremadura will not be the same when the last of them is gone.

Then dusk. And hunger. She found a scummy waterhole, but she was too thirsty to be fastidious and she lay on her belly

234

drinking at the side of the mule. The first star. And getting cold. When it was too dark to go on she made a windbreak of branches in a hollow and tied up the mule. She woke at dawn as stiff as a board. And ravenously hungry. The mule cropped the grass. She envied it.

On again. And suddenly heartened; he *hadn't* been that far ahead. She found the embers of a fire, still warm, and she cursed herself. If she'd continued only an hour she'd have been on him.

"And if you had, Maria? What then?"

"Are you mad? Everything in that wagon was mine. Mine! Bought with my jewels."

"Possession is supposed to be nine tenths of the law."

She said coldly, "He could be dispossessed. Remember. He was alone. And crippled. He had to sleep sometime. I think I would have . . ."

"Maria, be quiet. You are not a murderess. I don't want to hear."

She was running out of time. Her belly clawing at her. She hadn't eaten for thirty-six hours; if she didn't sight him by sunset she would have to turn back.

It drove her mad. The sun dehydrated her. She had visions: she thought she saw mirages on the prairie, great streams of black heavy-shouldered beasts, but it hadn't been a mirage. She'd seen a buffalo herd. If I do not eat soon I will be too exhausted even to go back. She'd lost the wagon tracks for the last time. Where had he gone? She had to choose between a stony canyon and the trail alongside a river, and she chose the latter. Presently she came to that memorable clearing. She recognized it at once. The cattle had crossed here. He'd leaped off that bluff on his mad pinto straight into the river; almost drowned; and how she wished he had. Over there on the distant bank he'd struck her. . . . God may forgive you for that, she thought. But I never will.

And this is where I turn back. I am finished. But one last try.

235

She climbed the bluff from which Francisco had leaped, tearing her hands on thorn and twig, and from that height she searched the land. Empty. The mule had wandered off. Mother of Heaven, she thought, do not abandon me; show me something more than grass . . . and suddenly, her eyes sharpening, heart bounding, she saw the fat oxen-drawn wagon come crawling out of the distant canyon and thrust back along the river. He was waiting there, she thought; it is not I who am doing the stalking. He is stalking me!

She watched him. The wagon stopped at the clearing. He stared about, maybe perplexed; no, I am not too far off, she thought. Nearer than you think. He let the oxen water. He hobbled awkwardly across, letting the crutch drop while he lay flat drinking, washing the dust off his sweaty face, writhing suddenly as she fell on him. Screaming. That is what it is to be Spanish, Alonso thought; there is no race quite like us. *Gracias a Dios.* Thank God.

But she grabbed only water. He seemed to twist from under her. He'd known she was there. She hadn't had such a moment of terror since the ugly dreams of childhood. She would have cried out if her face hadn't been buried in the mud of the creek. There was a *Yanqui* expression for it: she'd put her head in a bear trap.

Now she only wanted to get it out. But he had her hair in his hand and was grinding her face on the gravel bottom. The feel of slime in her teeth. I am drowning . . .

As at Waterloo the belligerents saw it with different eyes. Frank Dibbler said with a careless shrug to Alonso, "It was a small thing. No need to exaggerate. She got a little wet."

Maria said shiveringly, "He enjoyed it. Animal. His callousness was indescribable. If I had not prayed to the Blessed Virgin I would have been dead." There was no other explanation; heaven gave her the strength to squirm out of his hand and lash her sodden hair into his face.

236

She heard him grunt. It had annoyed him? All right; she'd annoy him some more. Floundering knee-deep in the river her groping hand found the heel of the crutch. She jabbed it into his face. Then, escaping him for a moment, whirled it over her head and brought it down on his back. That hurt. She was sure of it. He tore it out of her hand. His face wasn't six inches from hers; and he was laughing. Cruelly. She'd said to Alonso, "Where there is so much hate there is no room for fear," and she discovered her mistake. She *could* be frightened. She was. "Bitch," he said to her as if she were a recalcitrant dog.

She spat at him. What else could she do? He'd framed her face in his hands and was pressing it down into the water. She could just see him through a veil of mud. She heard him say, "Wife," in a tone of disgust, and if she hadn't already been so wet she was sure he would have spat back. "You don't know a wifely duty from a cow's udder," and she tried to writhe from under him before she drowned. Holy Mother, make him pay for my life.

"I don't know why in hell you came," he said. "There's nothing for you here. I'm not your man." Now he had his knee in her groin. Wicked. "But since you're here we'll take that uplifted nose of yours down a notch. It hasn't stopped sniffing at ordinary flesh as if it stinks. It does, too. But so does yours." He got a better grip of her. To drown her. "You do 'this' and 'that' like the rest of us," he said, except that 'this' and 'that' weren't the words he used; they were the crudest lavatorial expressions. They would have brought a flush to Maria's face if there wasn't so much icy water about to cool her down.

"You're all bile and spleen. You're not a desired woman. You're old varnish and canvas. You haven't stopped acting the duchess out of your father's musty pictures," and all the time he was watching her retch. The slime was nauseous. The oxen watched impassively. Nobody to help.

"This isn't Estremadura," he said. "It isn't anything. Just grass. So holler your head off. There's nobody to hear."

237

And then he slapped her. Quite hard. She was afraid of them; those terrible peasant hands. "That's for my three thousand cows. All my sustenance, all my father built up." He slapped her again. "That's for my leg." It still hurt; she could tell. "And that's for Pablo." This time so violently that her face grew numb. He was angriest of all over Pablo.

She thought there were tears in his eyes. Suddenly, as if bored with her, or revolted, he picked her up like a sack, sodden as she was, and threw her off into the river. She was a mess of mud and humiliation; she'd never been so disdained.

Nor so scared out of her wits, Alonso thought.

"He was unhinged," she told him.

Queer word to use. "Maria," Alonso sighed, "you haven't been properly hinged since you were weaned. All that playacting. History has gone to your head. Duchesses are a joke in this cruel land."

She flared. "I would not expect to hear that from a grandee of Spain . . ."

"On the prairie," he corrected her ruefully, "I am just a comical animal called Don Alonso."

"He struck me."

Thrashed her would be more descriptive. And deservedly, he thought. It suddenly occurred to him that what might have unhinged Francisco wasn't so much his mind as his terribly deprived loins. By now they must be pretty explosive. But it was too delicate a subject to discuss with Maria. She might have spat at him, too.

And she lay shivering in the bitter river, bruised beyond feeling, watching her husband strip off his drenched shirt. Then his pants. It was a difficult maneuver, leaning on his crutch. He rubbed himself dry in the sun, as naked as Adam. More so. Adam had at least had a fig leaf. She found the exposure shameful. Then she shouldn't have looked, Alonso thought. He had rather a hairy body, she said. Curiously observant for a discomfited woman. He hung his wet clothes on the hooped canvas

238

and slipped on a fresh pair of pants from the wagon. Then went across to the driving seat and got aboard. She called out to him from the bed of the river, "Where do you think you are going with that?"

"Home."

"Everything in that wagon belongs to me. Paid for with my grandmother's jewels. Mine!"

He grinned at her ironically as if she'd made rather an unfortunate joke. And lying there, jaw chattering, like jetsam tossed out of some passing barge, perhaps she had. She waded out.

"Where is my mule?"

"Find it."

"It is gone."

He sighed. "How useless can you be? Mules have ears. Screech for it."

Her nerves were unbearably stretched. She screeched. The beast came plunging down the scrub of the bluff. She hadn't seen it up there.

"You learn hard," Frank Dibbler said. "But something's beginning to take." He pointed dismissively to the mule. "Now get on it and go back. I'd like not to see you again."

He prodded the oxen with the crutch, and the wagon trundled off. She watched it disappear round the bend of the river, the mass of protruding pipes bouncing, the tall iron chimney of the engine jangling like a calliope; it could be something out of a circus. With only the clowns missing. Standing there, muddied beyond recognition, hair plastered over her face, water puddling about her feet, she might have substituted for one. Now she could barely hear the distant creak of the wagon. She gritted her teeth. She would never yield it up to him. Mine! The mule recoiled from her as she climbed soddenly on its back. She went plodding after him. It was a hideous mistake.

Now Charley the Indian lost her. He still had the wagon; even Alonso couldn't lose the deep cuts of its wheels. He was

239

becoming quite an adequate scout. Already he had learned to distinguish the texture of the oxen's dung from Maria's mule's. They littered frequently. Every now and again he picked up the half-obliterated trace of the mule's hoof triumphantly and cried out. But eight miles on—which was four hours of slow tracking—the wheel marks vanished as if the wagon had taken off. A ponderous three-ton wagon couldn't fly. Where had it gone?

Charley got down to poke about the gravel. "Crossed the river," he said.

Alonso stared at it with consternation. Here the channel narrowed; it foamed and hammered in full flood from the hills. A mess of branches rushed by like feathers borne in the breeze. It must have been a very hazardous operation. "What for?"

Charley's moonface glowed. It was more than mere professionalism; he was growing quite intrigued. "I'd say he was trying to shake her off."

"And has he?"

Charley chuckled cryptically. "She didn't cross." He seemed to know why. But he didn't say. He got back on his horse. "So which do we follow? The man or the woman?"

"The woman, of course," Alonso cried. "How long can she last? She has no food," though there was plenty of water about. "No weapon. She is utterly defenseless. Hurry, hurry."

"Señor," Charley said calmly, "these tracks are three days old. If she is alive we will find her. If she isn't the buzzards are already picking her bones."

For half a mile they couldn't trace Maria's mule in the gravel. Then it dunged helpfully; the earth grew softer. They had picked her up.

The sun was a furnace. Alonso sweated with anxiety. Three days gone, and they didn't even know if she was alive. Mile after mile of slow progress, tracking the washed-out prints of the mule. He lagged behind. He wasn't a natural horseman. His rump ached. Late afternoon he heard Miguel cry out in the distance. Charley had dismounted and was staring curiously about.

Alonso trotted up. What had happened here? He couldn't begin to make it out. Bitten out of the grass, as if by battering hoofs, was a wide circle of still-raw earth. His first confused thought could only connect it with a circus: liberty horses racing about. He watched Charley hold up a stained dyed feather.

"Pawnees."

And he shivered. "Then she is dead."

"Children," Charley said.

Children!

"Small boys. Two of them, maybe three." Charley showed him the single red bar on the feather. "See? Novices. They still have to be initiated. Not even a scalp-lock between them. Nothing. Just small boys."

"Then she is all right!" Alonso gasped with relief. Children would help her. Heaven, always abundantly merciful, is guarding her, he thought.

Maria thought otherwise. Her heavenly guardian, she told Alonso grimly, must have been dozing that hot afternoon. She had followed the wagon along the river during the cool of the morning; never letting it out of her sight, not knowing what to do but hang on to her property. It was in the hands of a bailiff, who was also her husband. She was sick with hunger. As clammy and malodorous as a soiled rag. As the sun heaved up she began to steam. She thought: my poor father would not recognize me, beslimed and bedraggled. No Estremaduran has ever come to this.

Too late to go back. I would never make it. And I *would* not, if I could! But I must eat . . . I cannot . . . her head seemed to float and once she almost fell off the mule. As the sun reached its blazing zenith she saw the wagon stop. Saw Frank Dibbler descend: wave to her peremptorily and leave something on the ground. It rolled on. She caught up to see what he had

241

left. Some cuts of cold pork, a bag of biscuits and a canteen of water. So he had some vestige of coarse feeling. It was his way of saying good-bye. She thought with revulsion, I would die rather than touch his . . . and found herself squatting by the rushing eddies, wolfing down the cold greasy pork.

She watched the wagon turn into the river a hundred yards ahead—heard the wheels grind on the bouldered bottom, sinking axle-deep. The racing water battered the laboring oxen. Only the great weight of the top-heavy wagon kept it upright. There must have been a moment of anxiety for Frank Dibbler as it lurched into a submerged sinkhole; but it came out of it and dragged on. She could see his crutch slapping the rumps of the oxen. Finally the wagon reached the far bank, gushing water like a split bucket, and it went creaking off on solid earth.

No matter; I shall soon be with you, she thought.

She bundled the remnants of the food in her shawl and mounted the mule. Get in with you, she said. It went knee-deep, whinnying. The rush of the water frightened her, too. But she had to get across. The wagon was out of sight. Get on! She hammered her heels into the mule's flanks; it just stood shivering. Immovable. It would be swept off before it made midstream, and both she and the mule knew it. It uttered a piteous moan of fear and she had to yield to mulish obstinacy and let it go back. The conflict with the beast had exhausted her; she was uncontrollably near to the bitterest of tears. She stared about. Loneliness unimaginable. No sound but the roar of the river, and she rode along the bank thinking: Mother of God, I am in your hands.

Two hours on. Where was the wagon? Only the eye of heaven knew. She found herself rolling drunkenly on the mule. I must rest; I will die, anyway, but let me at least die without this fearful cramp in my seat. No mule ever had so rocky a spine. She dismounted. It was a wide grassy arena, with not even a meadowlark to break the eerie silence; and she lay in the grass, wondering how death would come. Perhaps as soft as a feather. Perhaps with the freezing clutch of approaching night. She watched the sun sink.

Out of it came two small figures mounted on ponies. She rubbed her eyes. It was a dream. Who lives in this inhuman land? She sat up. Indians. Boys! Quite small, as bronzed as old pennies, chests hairless, wearing loose moccasins and rubbed doeskin clouts. Each with a single dyed feather bound in the short greasy hair. They stared at her.

And she stared back. How do we communicate? They had no weapons. The ponies were rough and shaggy, smaller than anything she had ever seen; they were the original mustangs, half-mule, half-devil. She put out a pathetic hand to them. And suddenly both of them grinned and started trotting about.

They kept to a wide circle, faster and faster, so that the ground thudded with the beat of the unshod hoofs. What were they up to? It made her head swim. Round and round, so that she had to close her eyes: she was growing dizzy. She thought: it is some kind of game. They were still grinning, but whooping throatily, little boys enjoying the thrill of wild ponies, the rush of air, trying to demonstrate their manhood.

Thieves! Suddenly, with her head still reeling, they closed in, twitched at her mule and all three of them were gone; scampering over the skyline. Then silence. As if it had never happened. Perhaps it hadn't? But she had no mule; it was the end; and she put her face in the grass and let her heart break.

Dusk. She slept. It grew very cold. When something touched her she thought: this is the hand of death. But death was cold and the hand was warm. She lay shivering. Then something harder—prodding her side, and suddenly she smelled oxen and opened her eyes. The wagon lay ten yards off. Frank Dibbler stood over her, nudging her with the crutch as if she were a mess of abandoned clothes. He stared at her so emptily that she thought: he is measuring me for my grave.

He said with a gritty sigh, "You damned fool. They hopped your mule, did they?"

243

She croaked, "Boys . . ."

"Pawnee kids." Then again, with unutterable disdain, "You damned fool."

He is going to leave me here, she thought. Look at that cruel wooden face. But he said, "Get in," nodding over to the wagon. He wouldn't lift her. Perhaps couldn't; his crutch was a curse to him. She shrugged him off, crying, and he said, voice harshening impatiently, "Lie here and you'll be stiff by night." She crawled across to the wagon and rolled inside. She could hear him grumbling obscenely under his breath.

She lay on the hard boards as the oxen dragged off and the queerest thought came to her: at least, I have recovered what is mine. My wagon. All this mad monstrous equipment, jangling pipes and swaying engine. All smelling vilely of oil. The waste of my jewels! Her eyes burned. My ancestral grandmothers must be rolling in their graves.

She woke once in the night, frozen by a bad dream. The whisper of the prairie was petrifying. Wind hissing under the canvas canopy, the rattle of grit on the sides, and a sobbing cry that could have been the ghost of some ancient pioneer, but was probably a hungry coyote complaining to the moon.

Where was he? Gone? She climbed out, her heart thudding. He lay under the wagon, rolled in a blanket, watching her. Not a word exchanged. We are strangers, she thought; worse than that. He looks at me as if I were Lugubrious Man who had him shot. Perhaps I had something to do with it . . .

And she crept back into the wagon with a shudder of guilt, shrinking from the cold sardonic shine of his eyes. I dare not trust him. He will abandon me when it suits his convenience, letting the cruel prairie finish me off. How can I sleep under this mountain of terror . . . ?

And when she woke again, stiff as a board, the sun was red. She didn't know how far they'd traveled during the dawn. He was hunched over the crackle of a fire. He looked up at her calmly. "Get yourself some coffee," he said.

Madre! She winced. I cannot move. My rusty bones are locked. She crawled down from the wagon. He pushed across a tin plate of fried dough and cold meat as unchewable as hide. She couldn't penetrate it with her teeth. The coffee, at least, gave a little warmth. She peered about. They might have been lost in some unexplored corner of the world; does nothing sound here but the wind? Are there no birds to witness what he might do to her? He ate busily, as if replenishing a cupboard in his belly, still not uttering a word. He scrubbed the skillet clean with grass. Kicked out the fire. Then vanished into a hollow.

He wasn't gone long. He said carelessly, "Down there if you want to relieve the urge," and she looked away with a grimace. Who but a half-animal would address a woman like that?

Back into the wagon and off it rolled. She crouched behind, framed by the creaking mass of oily iron that threatened to crush her with every jolt of the wheels. She was foul; she could smell her own unsavory juices. There was a mirror hanging on the rib of the canopy and she looked at herself.

She shrank. It cannot be me. It cannot! She was unrecognizable—her face gaunt, dirt in the dark hollows of her eyes, hair as tangled as a bird's nest. She wanted to cry, but all tears had dried up. Who is there to succor me?

I must have been mad. I must go back. *He* will reach Amarillo: but without me. I will rot in the emptiness of this prairie. Came midday, and she muttered across to him, "I am hungry," but he took no notice, whistling softly, so that she had to repeat it.

"Chef's busy," he said.

"Is it to torment me?"

"We eat by the sun. Not by the clock. I'll wake you when dinner's on the table."

Traveling all day. The hammer of the wagon bottom on her spine. If there was only one comfortable spot. She slept in

245

numb spasms. Then woke with shock. Something was happening. The sun was low in the clouds. There was a thudding of myriads of hoofs, black beasts streaming across the sunset, guns banging, and she thought: I have blundered into another war.

She was seeing buffalo as the early Americans had seen them —shaggy hordes stretching uncountably to the dark horizon. Not as many as the Conquistadores had seen when they'd come pushing north of the Rio Grande. The guns were thinning them out. She listened to the heavy detonations and the wagon suddenly stopped. She unstiffened herself to look out, and Frank Dibbler, six feet ahead of her on the driving board, said softly, "Stay where you are."

"What is going on?"

"Didn't God give you eyes?"

He had, at least, given her a nose; it didn't have to strain to catch the reek of death. She could hear the firing squads: that steady thumping fusillade. She saw the bewildered buffalo scatter confusedly into easily destroyed groups. They weren't very intelligent animals. But where were the hunters? The sky suddenly flashed and she saw the camouflaged dugouts. Two of them. The buffalo guns ruthlessly dividing up the herds and picking them off. She saw them stumble, heard them grunt. Butcher's business. Why didn't they run? It was as if they possessed a death-wish. Even the sunset suited the occasion; it flooded the prairie blood-red. But in the end the smell of doom penetrated even those thick skulls and they gathered into a fleeing mass, blackening the horizon like migrating birds.

She turned away with a shudder. She couldn't count the carcasses that littered the grass.

Something drew her eyes to a solitary willow. There was another spectator. The most ancient Indian she had ever seen. So still that he might have been a ghost. Perhaps a contemporary of Columbus. He sat his emaciated nag, watching the needless slaughter with lusterless eyes, his creased face set with despair. It wasn't only the buffalo that had the death-wish. She turned

246

only for a moment to watch the vanishing herds, and when she looked back the sad old Indian had gone.

This land is all heartbreak. "It is enough," she muttered to Frank Dibbler. "Let us go."

"Oxen have to be watered." There was the glisten of a pool by the willows. He got down.

"Then hurry," she said impatiently, and he gave her a slanted look as if one of the oxen had talked back. All right; so hit me, she thought. He grinned. He unyoked them. Arduous business. He was beginning to hate the crutch. She could hear him abusing it. He looked up at her narrowly as if she might help. In my condition? I am not your serf, she thought.

The shooting from the dugouts had stopped. She saw the two hunters get up and stretch. They caught sight of the wagon for the first time. It seemed to amaze them. It would have amazed anyone; the tall iron funnel poked high above the canvas canopy as if it were a steam engine, not oxen, that was dragging the wagon across the grass. They came across.

As shaggy as wolves. They wore fur hats and rough hide coats that presumably swarmed with lice; the way they scratched. Small bright inquisitive eyes peered out of a month's growth of whisker. She could smell them at ten paces. It was the stench of the knacker's yard. She looked at the skinner's knives in their belts and thought: these are not people my father would wish to know.

"Mister," the first of them said as he came up, "for a minute you had us seeing dreams." He wore a black patch over one eye. It gave him a faintly piratical look. He patted a wheel. "Real, is it?"

"It's real."

"Curiousest contraption I ever saw." He chuckled, walking round the wagon to prod the iron pipes. He hadn't seen Maria inside. The solitary eye sharpened. "Ma'am," he said politely, touching his fur hat. He walked off a few steps to peer incredulously at the strapped-down engine. "What in hell is it?"

"Oil rig."

"That so? You got a well?"

Frank Dibbler said coolly, "I have a hole in the ground." Not according to him, Maria thought; he thinks he has an ocean of oil.

She saw him sniff fastidiously. He wasn't exactly odorless himself.

Black Patch's partner had come up. "Where you from, friend?"

"Jake's Creek."

"Heading where?" It was only to maintain talk; Maria saw Black Patch murmur in his ear and he walked round the wagon to look at her himself.

"Home."

"And where'd that be?"

"Where home usually is."

They grinned. "You figure to drag this crazy outfit a long way?" Black Patch asked. Would he never leave his lice alone?

"Far enough," Frank Dibbler said. They were beginning to bother him; he'd half got the oxen unyoked, propped insecurely on the crutch.

"Sound to me like a Texan, friend."

"*Friend,*" Frank Dibbler said with the faintest exasperation, "I'll write my genealogy up for you when I get time. When you think up a few more questions. And you ask a hell of a lot."

They weren't offended. "We're clean out of liquor. You got a spare bottle handy?"

"Don't drink."

Not true, Maria thought. There was a full bottle behind.

"Hell," Black Patch sighed, "buffalo butcherin' gives a man a raging thirst. Like to chew some chaw?" He offered Frank Dibbler a greasy plug of tobacco.

"Don't chew."

"What do you do, mister, when you ain't hopping on one leg?" The crutch fascinated them. "Bullet?"

"Lice bite."

"That so?" Both guffawed. "Some lice."

248

And they went. Maria could hear them guffawing all the way back to the dugouts. Frank Dibbler mounted the leading ox and rode the span of them down to the pool.

She was stiffening up. She hadn't really dried off. She sighed: I will never dare look in a mirror again. I am destroyed. She peered across the darkling prairie; the grass shivered; nothing lives here but the wind. Nothing would want to! And every mile farther I go into it, that much deeper am I trapped. How lonely she felt. She had only to close her eyes and the warm orange groves of Andalusia came back; the brown friendly faces of her father's peasants; a melancholy guitar, a voice singing *"Como se pasa la vida . . . ,"* meaning: How soon life passes. Her eyes stung with tears. Has mine almost passed?

One of the buffalo hunters had brought over a team of mules from around the slope. They dragged in the carcasses. She caught the sour tang as they began the business of skinning: a knife slitting the hide along the belly and legs, twitching it off as one peeled an orange. No orange ever smelled like that. Presently the mules came by the wagon, hauling a sled-full of hides across to the pool. The two hunters stopped. The small bright eyes looked her over.

"Ma'am," Black Patch said with a compassion she wouldn't have thought him capable of, "don't like to butt into another man's affairs. Just seems like you been through one hell of a rough time."

She said nothing. She couldn't. It was the first considerate voice she'd heard for a long time.

"Just common decency," he said. "Figure you need some help."

Who could help? She didn't want them to see her tears.

"No offense, ma'am, but you sure all messed up. Somebody hit you?"

"No." Dear God.

Black Patch glanced down at Frank Dibbler by the pool. "That your man?"

She shook her head.

"Ain't your husband, that's for sure." The single eye had looked to see that she wore no wedding ring. He said primly, "Man's proper duty's to stand by a lady in trouble. All you have to do is yell."

She stared at them. Something stirred in her mind. They seemed kind men, unbelievably coarse, but kind. Almost before she knew what she was doing she said, "Would you take me back to Jake's Creek?"

"Don't quite catch on."

"With my wagon? I beg of you. Everything you see here is mine . . ."

"We still got a week's huntin' ahead."

"You would be well paid. Anything you ask. I have friends who will reward you." She saw Frank Dibbler turn. He was watching. She said desperately, "I am in his hands." She might have remembered that if she hadn't followed him from Jake's Creek she wouldn't be in them. But she was too distressed. "He has stolen all I have in the world."

Black Patch ejected a stream of tobacco juice sympathetically. "That's bad."

He looked at his partner. Both stared again at Frank Dibbler. He was gathering the oxen together to return. He said softly, "With or without him?"

She hesitated. She licked her lips. She'd gone too far. "Without."

"Ma'am, not to worry. We'll fix him for you."

"But no violence . . ."

"If he don't offer none." She didn't think there would be any. They were very thick men. "He'll give us no trouble." She sighed. "Cripple. Two 'gainst one." She felt a slight queasiness; she wished she hadn't spoken. Too late. "Just one thing," Black Patch murmured. "He has a gun?"

Her mouth opened soundlessly.

"Ma'am?"

"A rifle in the back."

"Rest easy, ma'am. Be a pleasure to combine chivalry with

250

pay." She thought they were looking at her a little more bla-
tantly than gentlemen should; but who met gentlemen on the
prairie? "Mexican, are you?"

"I am Spanish." She felt insulted.

"Lady of quality. Of course." He went round the wagon. She
heard him poking and rattling behind. He came back with the
rifle and dropped it under the hides in the sled. They sat on it,
very calm, quite assured, the one without the patch pleasurably
cracking his knuckles. What large hands they had. Frank Dibbler came leading the oxen across the grass. He watched the
hunters slantingly. He said nothing. But he was rather pale. He
yoked up the oxen, turning on the pivot of the crutch so that his
back wasn't to them. Maria looked into his stony eyes and
thought: He knows about the rifle. He has seen.

Nothing said for a while. It seemed as if the world hung in
suspense. Her mouth was dry. The plain slanted steeply and the
wagon had no brakes; she watched Frank Dibbler begin to lock
a chain about a front wheel.

"Mister, don't hurry," Black Patch said.

"Nobody's hurrying." Frank Dibbler looked strangely at
Maria. He will spit.

"You ain't going anywhere with that wagon."

"I'm not?" He leaned across the wheel, watching them both
through the spokes.

"Man like you needs a little discipline. One cracked leg's
enough, ain't it? Two'd put you in bad shape," and Maria
wasn't sure which of them moved first: Black Patch or Frank
Dibbler. The wagon seemed to heave and legs whirled across
the driving board. Two things would always remain in her
mind—the utter indifference of the oxen and the haste with
which she fled into the back of the wagon. She had opened Pandora's Box and only God knew what dreadful things would now
come out.

Alonso would never really know what came out of it. Violence, of course, quite sickening savagery. It was as much a part

251

of the cruel prairie as the wind and the endless sky. He and Miguel and Charley the Indian had left the circus-ring of the Indian boys, following the track of the wagon. No sign of the mule, and they assumed that Maria and Frank Dibbler had finally joined up. Unholy alliance. Surely we are close to their wheels? We must almost be on them. But nothing in sight. Nothing but . . . *Dios!* The smell!

They'd come on a vista of skinned buffaloes. Every buzzard in the prairie had gathered there for the feast. Alonso muffled his nose and said with a grimace, "Let us get on . . ."

But Charley the Indian said, "Something to be seen."

"What? Bones?"

"Come look." There *was* something the buffaloes hadn't caused. Grass clawed and trampled as if dinosaurs had fought. Then—it froze Alonso's stomach—a smashed crutch. No need to ask whose it was. Something else: how peculiar. A great splotch of axle grease and the remains of a burst keg. And even *that* wasn't all. A spattering of dusky drops. Blood? Too terrible. What human eyes had watched?

They came on them two hours later. Only three eyes, all three of them hideously bloated. A pair of whiskered buffalo-hunters. They were bathing their bruises in a creek. One of them, who could only speak in shuddering obscenities, wore a black patch. Alonso had never seen such maltreated men. They were so incoherent that he scarcely understood a word they said. But one outraged expression made him prick up his ears. "Goddamned demon bitch . . ."

"Who?"

"The woman."

Maria? It was all too confused. And when he came to hear the story from her own lips it only confused him more. She was holding something back. Guilt; he could read it in her eyes. She'd behaved badly. As she usually did.

He thought he got the truth from Francisco. They'd come to him—the buffalo men—as casually as one chops down a tree.

Who expected the tree to hit back? A cripple, too. They had him pinned on the driving board; he should have understood the hopeless odds against him. Two whiskered faces grinning over him confidently. Black Patch, a saloon brawler, going straight for the throat. And the tree, with its good leg, jabbed him brutally and inexplicably in his tenderest private parts.

He took it badly. He was out of action for a few moments, moaning his complaint. "Goddamn near unmanned me," Black Patch said. Indeed, when he walked away from the creek, Alonso saw that he moved with a queer sideways lurch like a crab. Now everything grew cruel. Elbows and fists thumping, the mule team whimpering. The oxen drawing off, lowing softly, as if used to the idiocy of human beings. Maria shivering in the wagon. Alonso thought she had every reason to shiver; it was she who'd opened up Pandora's Box.

The wagon heaved. She couldn't get off. The iron funnel jangled. If it came down on her . . . she told Alonso that she knew what it was to be a Roman wife watching gladiators tearing at each other in the arena; at least they'd been able to modestly avert their eyes. She couldn't. They were spitting and gasping an arm's stretch from her knees.

She said that he fought like a trapped beast: Francisco, she meant. And trapped he was. Restricted by his bad leg. They'd dragged him off the wagon; Black Patch, testicles sore, had come back into the battle. Pounding. They propped him stiffly against a wheel to demolish him.

And she saw blood on his face. An eye suddenly suffuse. She watched him, Francisco, twist anguishedly to avoid them. Another eye hideously puffed. But still savaging them back.

She said faintly, "It was when . . ."

"When what, Maria?"

"I saw him spit out a tooth. Dear God."

"A little late for contrition, wouldn't you think?"

"You are not very charitable, Don Alonso. I did what I could."

253

Yes, what? This was where it grew confused. Frank Dibbler told him that his eyes were so swollen that he could hardly see. He had to feel for his persecutors; fists jarring on bone. He didn't know how long he could take it. He could hear the mules going mad. They had him in the posture of the crucifixion against the wheel, arms spread, Black Patch holding him while his partner worked on him. And Maria—according to Black Patch—reached maliciously for the first thing that came to her hand: a keg of axle grease. She thrust it hard on his head as one snuffs out a candle.

She said she did it without thought. He groped blindly about, grease streaming from under the keg; he looked like a medieval knight in a pot helmet, and Francisco brought the crutch down on it with a thud.

She said with reminiscent horror, "He fell under the mules."

"If you would rather not tell me . . ."

"They trampled him." She heard him scream like an assaulted girl.

The rest was all sound and fury under the wagon. Obscenity, panting, then the rattle of the brake chain from the wheel. She could only guess what Francisco was doing with it. Somebody was being throttled. Presently he crept out, his eyes so bloated that he had to feel his way along the side of the wagon. She looked at him. His nose was changed, not for the better. Blood from his slit mouth. And his eyes awful. She cringed from the sight.

Black Patch was crawling brokenly from under the terrified mules. His partner lay soundlessly under the axles.

Francisco looked at her—no, he turned his destroyed eyes in her direction: he couldn't look. "What was it they expected?"

"Money," she said in a dim voice. "I thought Don Alonso would reward them . . ."

"It wasn't the reward they expected."

"What then?"

"You." He was angry. "They'd have flattened you between

254

them. Poked you stiff in the grass," and then he was sick behind the wagon. He came back. "You're a foolish woman." She trembled. He searched for his rifle under the hides. He fumbled about blearily in the dugouts for the buffalo guns. He stumbled down to the pool and threw them into the water. He didn't wait for the hunters to stir; he got up on the driving board and muttered to the oxen and they creaked off.

X

CHARLEY THE INDIAN said thoughtfully to Alonso and Miguel, "He wouldn't waste much time getting away." They were cantering hard after the wagon. He'd listened to the buffalo men with glittering eyes. Savagery fascinated him. That Kiowa-Apache! "He'd taken a lot from them. They could go after him and give him some more."

But he'd evened up the odds. He had his rifle. Alonso didn't doubt that he would use it if he had to. Maria, when he mentioned it to her later, thought so too. "Violence," she said with a shudder. As if she were the meekest of women. "They are saturated with it." She thought it was something that grew out of the landscape.

For the wagon was crawling across the bleakest of plains, under the coldest of stars. Hardly a sound but the lowing of disgruntled oxen and the rusty creak of the wheels. A few ghostly trees. Some maverick bird screeching out of the darkness, warning them not to go on. But on they went. A hard northering wind sprang up. It flapped the canvas canopy. Would he never stop? She was afraid to speak to him. And suddenly they jerked to a halt; he'd gone far enough. But not for supper. The oxen had sounded off at the smell of a waterhole, and he got down to fill a bucket before they could reach it and dung.

He took off his shirt to bathe his wounds.

She inched forward and lighted a lamp so that he could see what he was doing. She saw enough herself. Hardly a hand's breadth of his chest and back wasn't blotched. She muttered, "Let me . . ."

"I can cope."

"Your back." He couldn't cope with that. He let her sponge off the crust of rawly formed scabs. She said it was only common humanity. The icy water bit into the open wounds. He gasped. She felt queer too; outside her brothers she'd never touched masculine flesh so intimately. Certainly never a man's belly. He was black down there under the navel where they'd kneed him. He had a strange smile on his face as if wondering if she'd go further . . . and she recoiled with a flush.

No ribs broken. He felt them all. There was nothing else she could do about his eyes, puffed like birds' eggs. He could barely see out of the slits. She thought uneasily: somebody will have to see where we are traveling. I will have to be his eyes.

All finished. He dressed. "Get some sleep," he said, and rolled himself in a blanket under the wheels.

"It will be insufferable down there."

"It is at that." He turned his sightless face up at her and grinned. He crawled into the wagon. He curled up under the driving wheel of the engine and before she had taken six breaths was fast asleep.

As insensitive as a log. I will not close my eyes all night . . . but it was he who woke her at dawn.

He'd hobbled out to yoke up the oxen. He climbed back breathlessly. "No coffee in this." The wind had risen. It cracked the canvas like a whip. She unlocked her joints to peer out. A mat of black clouds rushed across the grim sky. The few trees leaned like stalks in the gale. He was a sight to behold. She was afraid to look at him. He talked thickly as if his cheeks were packed with wadding; but there was nothing there but abused flesh. A tooth missing.

He chuckled, "Be a long time before I'm lovely again."

If ever. Never in her eyes. They made breakfast out of cold sowbelly; she chewed it like a dog with an unappetizing bone. A hard biscuit spread with molasses. Then a swig of murky water from the canteen and off they rolled. The wagon seemed to reel with every thump of the wind. The canvas billowed. There was a scratching outside the wagon as if cats were trying to get in, but it was just flying grit. Suddenly a blinding flurry. "Rain," he said.

And here it came. Sheets of it. She cowered deeper into the wagon. It belted down on the canopy. In an instant the oxen, most miserable of beasts, were sluicing water. They squelched on. The wheels slithered in the rivulets tearing down the gullies. They were leaving the plain behind them, climbing a low chain of black hills. She watched the gray mist skidding across the heights. It looked terribly inhospitable up by the topmost timber.

"Must we?"

"What?"

"Go up there?"

He shrugged. "Have to cross them or go back." He wouldn't do that, not if Lucifer himself were waiting to trap them in those dark canyons. "Shouldn't last too long," he said. An hour? A day? She couldn't get deep enough into the wagon. She'd always had a nervous aversion to rain.

By midday they were toiling into the mist. Hideous. The pass closing in. The sparse timber poked wetly out of the shreddy clouds. Everything in the wagon damp to the touch; the condensation ran down her back pressed against the cold iron of the engine. I will be arthritic for life, she thought. They couldn't stop to eat. Just toil on, waiting for the sky to lift, but it grew darker and more ominous. How the wind moaned.

Afternoon. Now they were up in the towering buttes, and nothing visible beyond the sodden heads of the oxen. The wind

258

going mad. The track went coiling about the precipitous slope; if there was any compensation it was that she couldn't see what lay far below. Wouldn't see it anyway for the mist. This must be the roof of the world: this is where the wind is born. The rain sheeted solidly. If the oxen were lowing nobody could hear them above its roar.

The wagon sliding in the stream of mud. It lurched into the stony side of the butte, which wasn't too fearful; it was when it skidded close to the naked edge of the track that she grew scared. It must be a long, long drop through the mist . . . she looked at Frank Dibbler, and he said, "Sounds worse than it is. Good for the crops."

Madman.

"Lie back in there." But it was wet everywhere. The pipes streaming, water flooding down through the engine funnel, emerging urinally from its iron crevices.

"Can we not shelter?"

"Where?"

Where, God help us? And then—she would remember that moment to her last day—the wind gathered its strength. It flew at them like a cat. It must have been waiting patiently for them at the top. There was a bang of air; her face rasped by driving drops, her hair whipped by the gust; the canopy bubbled like an overblown ballon, and there came an even harder gust and it burst. The canvas flew up in shreds, leaving them naked to the open sky. And she was drowning in the rain.

The oxen stopped. She heard Frank Dibbler cursing them. Nothing would get them to move. They were terrified like her. He shoved the reins into her hand and flopped out into the deluge to drag at their muzzles. Still cursing. It was like heaving at rock. She could see the beasts cringing. He fell about; he couldn't get a purchase in the mud with his damaged leg. He peered up at her from his knees with a queer expression of helplessness. She thought: I cannot be wetter. We dare not stay here. And she climbed down.

Mad, too. It was only then, she told Alonso—still shuddering

259

in recollection—that she realized where the wagon stood. It was no more than a thin shelf cut out of the stony side of the bluff. Is this what we have been traveling along? Her brain almost screamed. No wonder the oxen shrank from it. "We cannot," she gasped to Frank Dibbler . . . but they had to. He couldn't even see where they were going out of his engorged eyes. We will die, she thought: either washed down into the ravines or blown over the edge. The oxen looked at her piteously. She grabbed the muzzles of the leaders and howled into their ears.

"Move. Move."

Half-choked by the sodden mass of her hair flattened across her mouth, ankle deep in rushing water. Nothing left of her dress but a dripping rag. The oxen yielded to her and went snuffling on. The wheels slithering. The edge of the track disintegrating, rocks vanishing into the abyss of the mist. She knew she would never hear them fall and thought: so don't look! She was curiously enraged with Frank Dibbler and she cried to him, "Get back." He was useless; half-blind and crippled. Worse than Samson.

He got back into the wagon. He was in pain. She told Alonso that she literally dragged the oxen four miles. An exaggeration. They'd already topped the slope and were sliding down into the shelter of the lower buttes. Still purgatory for a delicate woman. The oxen felt the wagon pushing at them encouragingly and hurried on. She crept like a bundle of saturated hay into the wagon. She couldn't speak. Her lungs were filled with rain.

He said nothing to her. By dusk they were moving through thicker timber that protected them from the blast, and when darkness closed in the wind suddenly stopped. It had done its worst and hadn't stopped them.

Her mind was going out like a guttering candle. Her last flicker of thought was: he owes our inheritance to me. It was the first time she'd ever used the word "our" in his connection and it confused her. Mine! She looked at him, squinting dimly into the darkness, nursing his useless leg. He is only half a husband . . . she must have been in a very bad way, she told Alonso, to merely allow the word "husband" to enter her brain.

He could at least thank her. Nothing. Not a sound. She felt deflated. Water ran out of every crevice of her body; she suffered the torment of the disintegrating track all over again, the fear of that misty abyss, the blasting horror of the rain, and she curled up, near to tears, and slept her misery away.

Madre. I am stiff. Why wasn't the wagon jolting? She got up from the hard boards and looked out. No sun; a gray dawn. Very cold. But windless. They were back into rolling grass as if the nightmare of the buttes had been something she'd suffered in sleep. He had a small fire burning. She wondered where he'd got dry wood to make it and crept out. If he looks at me and laughs I will kill him; she knew that she was a fearful sight. But so was he. Mother of Sorrows. We will laugh at each other. He said mildly, "Fried dough. Best I can do. Coffee's at least hot."

"Thank you."

Again a curious twinge . . . it wasn't the kind of courtesy they usually exchanged.

She eased herself down into the damp grass. She heard her bones grind. "How is your leg?"

"Which one?"

"Then it cannot be so bad. I thought I would die last night."

"You're a tough woman." He laughed softly. "Take more than a bucket of rain and a bit of a blow to kill you."

"Is that all it was?"

"No. You want me to say thank you."

"A word of gratitude wouldn't come amiss."

"*Gracias*, Doña Maria."

Like getting blood out of a stone. "How much longer to go?"

"Week and a half."

She sniffed. There was a sour odor. It came from her soiled body. "I would like to bathe. I am unsavory. Is there enough water?"

261

"Plenty in that creek. Take the bucket." Turning his back on her ostentatiously like the *caballero* he wasn't. "I won't look."

"Pray God they came through it," Alonso said anxiously to Charley the Indian, remembering only as he spoke that this Kiowa-Apache's God probably didn't resemble his. Something on a totem pole. Horrific. They had had to lie up in a homesteader's barn to shelter from the blast. It had lost them a day and a half. He was damp, bone-sore and flea-ridden. The straw had crawled with them. He was afraid he had become their permanent host. Their ponies were now mounting the same dark hills up to the buttes. "I hope he didn't let her suffer too much discomfort . . ."

"A drop of rain never drowned anybody," Charley the Indian said.

A drop? Was he mad? The sky had actually opened up. He sagged sleepily in the saddle like a red Buddha studying his navel. Alonso wondered how he could follow the trail.

He said stiffly, "You would not understand. We are speaking of a lady of the most distinguished armorial bearings . . ."

"Me, too," Charley the Indian said. "My father never had less than ten scalps on his lance."

Aborigine. I am wasting my breath. By late afternoon the ponies had reached the topmost bluff, treading precariously along the narrow ledge the wagon had crossed. Alonso stared at it with shock. It must have been awful up here. A flash flood had half-washed it away. He could look down from the rubbled edge and see what Maria hadn't seen because of the mist; his stomach failed him and he drew back, closing his eyes. "What made them do it?"

"Simple question demands a simple answer," Charley the Indian said. "Because wagons don't fly."

"It could have killed her."

"Something will have to kill her in the end. Old age. Pneumonia. Too much sex . . ."

262

"That will do. Did they get across?"

Charley the Indian pointed reassuringly to the receding wheel-tracks. "They got across," he said.

Presently they, too, were over the top. It was like looking down from an eagle's eyrie; Alonso found himself searching the hazed vastness of the prairie on the other side. More grass. America seemed to be all unoccupied grass. He strained his eyes for a speck that might be a wagon. Nothing. Shall we ever catch up with them? I wonder where they are now?

They were a two-and-a-half-day stretch ahead, a flea-crawl on the expanse of the range. Watched by silent thickets of pin-scrub oak; they had seen nothing like the gaunt, canvas-ripped wagon that creaked by, bent under its load of exposed iron, a swaying smokeless chimney protruding from the jangling cargo. It signaled its approach like a factory alarm at half a mile. The oxen making their own unhurried pace, lowing and dunging—easy over the slopes, catching up on the downgrades, doing their steady stint of eighteen miles between dawn and sunset.

The air very cold. Curiously cold. The sun bright. The wind sunk to a whisper—welcome change! But it had frosty fingers.

Maria felt oddly naked in the belly of the wagon with the shredded canopy gone. The dust clouded down on her. It was as if her house had lost its roof. Creak, creak, creak. I shall dream of rusted wheels when this is done. She and Frank Dibbler had begun to talk. You couldn't just listen to the lowing of the oxen all day! Human beings had to communicate. What were tongues for?

She had to bait him a little, anyway. She gave him a sly look and said, "What a fearful land."

"You'll like it in time."

"Not in ten thousand years. Look at it. Raw. A desert of grass. You will never civilize it. Who would want to live here?"

"Try it and find out."

263

"Thank you for nothing. It would break my heart."

He might have been listening to a child. "Never broke mine."

She couldn't resist another dig. "You have one?"

He ignored it. Calling out to the oxen, "Hup, hup, hup," as if he made more sense out of them than he could out of her. She heard him say softly above the groan of the wheels, "It's clean. It's new. You lie the night on the prairie, you're lying in the bosom of God. Feel the grass pushing. You see stars you never saw in Spain. Goddamn it," he said blasphemously, "it's a different heaven up here."

H'm. Poetic, too. As if he even believed a word of it. She tried again.

"It is very cruel."

"Men make it cruel."

"Like you?"

And he said quite seriously—cynic!—"I'm not the best of men. I'm not the worst. I just try to get by with the talents I've got." She could only peer at him. That overweening ambition? His ruthless assertiveness? God help anyone who got in his way. She found herself listening to him reluctantly. "It's a hard land," he said. "It tests you. Makes you or breaks you," looking her over slantingly. "It hasn't broken you."

And never would—as he'd discovered to his cost. But she was still listening; it would have surprised her father, who'd never been able to get her to listen since he'd pricked his finger on her first tooth.

She muttered, "You will be rich one day, will you?"

"We will."

The collective "we" didn't pass unnoticed. She shrugged. The swaying mass of iron back in the wagon had begun to intimidate her, and she now sat by him on the driving board. It made her aware of his animal smell. She bathed more frequently but probably smelled, too. He'd sprouted a thick beard; he hadn't shaved since Jake's Creek, for there was nobody to be fastidious for but her. Suffused slitted eyes. Hardly an Adonis. The gap in his teeth visible when he grinned. If he looks like that, what must I look like? A wreck. He was watching her humorously. If he so much as utters a word of derision . . . but he just said mildly, "Call out when you're hungry, Maria."

Maria. How personal we are getting.

"I am hungry, *hombre*."

"Set the table, woman."

And so the days passed. Three of them without incident, jolting endlessly, eating the oxen's dust. She would remember the fourth. It began with a sharp chill that bit beneath her ravaged dress. She'd pinned it up where a naked shoulder might incite her husband to unhealthy thoughts. If there was any lust in him it didn't show. He slouched on the board, his leg propped on a cushion of canvas, hat tipped forward like a blind to keep the sun out of his battered eyes. When he wasn't murmuring he was yawning. Or spitting out dust. She'd seen healthier men. She felt safe. The sun was brilliant, but it had no warmth. She saw him glance up at it pensively as if the weather might change. There was a white edge low on the horizon as if the dawn were rolling back a wall of mist. Perhaps it was a wall of mist rolling in.

But for two miles back something else had been occupying his attention. It stiffened him like a pointing dog. He climbed off the wagon and hunkered down. She watched him brushing his fingers absently in the dust—like an Indian *shaman,* she told Alonso, reading signs. She called out to him, "What is it?" But he didn't reply. She got down to see what he was looking at in the dirt.

She thought she knew what the double-pole scrapes were: travois marks. A great many of them, crisscrossing, smudged by countless ponies' hoofs. A rather large party had traveled this way. She even thought she caught the musky scent of buffalo robe—purely imagination. But it gave her stomach a cold turn. She had an irrational fear of Indians; she'd felt it less on the drive only because of the armed *vaqueros* about. She looked at

265

Frank Dibbler dabbling in the dust. She doubted if he could see along a rifle barrel out of those bloated eyes. Her first anxious thought was: are they very close?

He squinted up at her reassuringly. "No cause to worry. These are two days old."

"But a lot of them?"

"Dozen or so lodges." He struggled up. She almost put out her hand to help him. "Hurrying south to winter quarters."

"Why hurrying?"

He looked up at the sky. The wind was busy shredding the mist. We haven't suffered enough, she thought.

She said, "Then let them go, Francisco," trying impulsively to grab back his name; but it was off her tongue.

He climbed back. Why was he grinning? On they rolled. It was four miles before they caught the next sign of the migrating Indians. They smelled it before they saw it. The flies were at it. A butchered pony; meat hacked off; the rest left for the scavengers. Comanches, maybe. Horses were cheap, Frank Dibbler said. He could have spared her the education. "They ride them to death. Eat them. Get two kinds of service out of one set of hoofs." He didn't seem to find it unnatural. They were well behind, and moving slower than the departing Indians. There was that relief.

They came suddenly on one of the abandoned villages; they would have avoided it if they could. It was as if rootless vagrants had lived here a season and decamped without cleaning up. Maria muffled her nose. Even the oxen sniffed. Utterest desolation. A couple of decayed tepees flapped in the breeze. The ashes of old fires. And garbage unmentionable; night-soil and gnawed bones littered the silent street. They creaked by. But was it totally silent? Maria thought she heard a strange tuneless drone . . . it wasn't the wheels. Frank Dibbler stopped the wagon. Two aged crones sat keening in a tent flap. That quavering dirge! She thought: it's a death song, her skin crawling, and she tugged at Frank Dibbler's arm to get on. Did he *have* to stop?

"Move."

He looked at her. She said querulously, "What is it?"

"They've been left to die."

So? They were almost as decayed as the rotting tepee. The misty eyes watching them impassively, the dark skin crinkled like folded dry paper. They moldered there and stank. She put her handkerchief delicately again to her nose. "Leave them some food."

"No teeth."

Oh, God. He sat for a while, watching them. Then he nodded to her. "Fetch them aboard."

"Are you mad?"

"They're old."

"I am not blind. I can also smell . . ."

He said brusquely, "You're not too fragrant yourself." Then again, "Fetch them aboard."

"Fetch them yourself."

"Maria."

She flared, "I will not suffer them behind . . ." and he looked at her as he'd looked at her once before: when he'd hit her. She touched her jaw reminiscently. He hobbled down. She wouldn't move. She watched him go over and speak to them; except that it wasn't speech as she knew it: twisting movements of his fingers, emphasized by soft grunts. He lifted up the bundles of rags and trundled them across. *Dios.* They are awful. He hoisted them up, muttering as the effort strained his leg, and propped them behind. Does he think I am going to *sleep* in their noxious stench? She shivered with revulsion. Indians did something queer to her, anyway.

He spooned a little water into their mouths. They seemed neither grateful nor resentful.

"Feed them, Maria."

She licked her lips. If I refuse he will . . . and he said again, cruelly, "Feed them." She chopped up some biscuits and mixed it with molasses. An unappetizing mess. She pushed the tin plate across to him and he just stared at her. Me? I will not

267

. . . but she crawled back, spooning it into the toothless gums. She avoided the lusterless eyes. The odor she couldn't avoid.

Then they slept. The wagon rolled on. She looked back at the soiled bundles of unsavory flesh and winced.

"Christian charity, Maria," he said. He sounded stern. Like her father. "They didn't raise you too well."

"I do not need you to teach me . . ."

He said vulgarly, "You've needed teaching since they lifted your ass out of your cot." Oaf.

The brief honeymoon was over. They no longer talked. She flounced. Any one of my brothers would have horsewhipped him for so shaming his sister . . . and she had the sudden startling vision of the whip being broken in her brother's hand. And his face pushed in. She glanced at her husband's big hands. Bastard. Oh, Mother. I am beginning to talk like him.

She felt a knuckle prod her back. The crones were mumbling. They wanted feeding again. What am I? A wet-nurse? She heard him chuckle. She crawled behind and made up the revolting hash of biscuits and molasses. They sucked it like babies. She thought there was a spark of gratitude in the aged eyes.

Water? Drink, then. But worst of all . . . much, much worse . . . she had to help them into the bushes at nature's call. Wait for them. Help them back. Would my father believe it? Never. And I shall never tell.

One of them croaked like a raven to Frank Dibbler. A black claw fluttered. He answered back. He said with a straight face, "Grandmother asks how many ponies I paid for you."

"Tell her you paid none."

"Puts you in rather a bad light. Suggests a defective squaw. Ill-tempered. Insubordinate. I told her I paid ten."

"A fair price?"

"She sees your loins bursting with much papoose. She says I got you cheap."

268

The day might come when he would demand value for his ten ponies . . . it was hard to tell where sour comedy ended and savagery began. But he'd had his joke. He was peering up at the darkling sky. The wind was whisking that approaching veil of mist into mare's tails. She couldn't hear it; it was high up in the atmosphere. But the cold it brought was fierce. Then the mist was on them, a clammy cloud, as sudden and disconcerting as one of Pharaoh's plagues. Suddenly a white flurry. Snow? The merest whisper of it, touching her face like icy gnats.

The oxen twisted plaintively to peer back at them; the wagon didn't stop. She guessed that Frank Dibbler was looking for a sheltered gulch, a patch of buckbrush that might break the wind she was sure would come. And come it did. Abruptly, as if it had been waiting to pounce. A moan in the sky. A feathery puff and the snow flew horizontally, driving deep into her dress, so that her shocked face was crusted before she could brush it off. She glanced back at the crones sitting impassively under the driving wheel of the engine. All she could see was the shine of patient eyes.

Presently they blundered down into a gully, patched with willow; it broke the wind and the oxen settled here. Both they and Frank Dibbler knew they would find nothing better. He unyoked them and made ready to camp.

They ate nothing. No fire was possible. She watched the whispering curtain of snow; it was beginning to pile. She stared numbly at Frank Dibbler. He motioned her behind. She crouched deep under the iron feet of the engine. She remembered the crones. They waited politely to be invited into her shelter. She beckoned to them to join her, and they bundled together for warmth, wet rags and smell and ancient bones. And so night fell. She wouldn't sleep, of course; but when she opened her eyes there was the first glimmer of gray light, the dazzle of snow drifted mountainously about the wagon. Frank Dibbler hunched stiffly on the driving board. She wondered if he'd watched all night. His face was gaunt. Whiskers white

269

with rime. She thought nervously: he isn't made of iron and if he isn't careful he will die.

Charley the Indian smelled snow as a coyote smelled carrion. He woke suddenly out of his normal trance and hurried the ponies on. "Fort Trent," he said. No need to ask why; there was a petrifying bite in the air that spoke for itself. A steel-gray fringe on the horizon was melting into a bitter mist. Alonso had never ridden so fast in his life. Nor been so scared. He could barely credit the first flurry that crusted his face. Within twenty minutes there was no more green grass, nothing but whitening slopes. They reached Fort Trent at a gasp, snow piled on their shoulders like epaulettes. And there they holed up for the night.

They would be blockaded by the blizzard for three days. Not even a cavalry troop would stir out in that fearsome fall. Alonso looked out in the morning and saw a bleak white world: they might have been in the highest Sierras of Spain. There was the silence of the grave. It was the grave in which Francisco and Maria—nobody could doubt it—now lay.

He talked to the shaggy adjutant who spat brown tobacco juice into the snow of the stockade. "Ain't that bad. Texan, is he?"

"He is."

"Then he'll know what to do. Woman's tough?"

"She is a lady of quality . . ."

"Only quality she'll have when this melts is cold bones. Mister," he waved dismissively, "this is just *weather.*"

Weather to silence the birds. To freeze the goddamned testicles off a brass monkey, so one of the profane troopers said.

How *had* they survived? Out of Francisco, Alonso would get nothing but a bleak shrug; it was something he preferred to forget. What had happened in that lonely drift? Maria—allowing for natural Spanish *bravura*—was more forthcoming. First a sense of serene relief. It lasted only long enough to take stock of

270

the situation and begin to take steps to remain alive. She would have died before morning, she said; she wouldn't have known what to do but bury her face in the drift and hope the end would come quick. They parked the oxen into a huddle about the wagon. Then backed up against the soft hides so that animals and humans shared a common warmth. Francisco—she was beginning to use his name with familiarity—got footwrappings on the oxen: the hoofs might freeze where they stood. They planted the two crones under the bellies. They shared a common stench.

Next? He built snow into a kind of parapet above the gully. The drift gathered against it and sheltered them from the wind. Not that it was exactly cozy; they lay, intermixed with the lowing oxen, on a chilly tarpaulin. Breathing. But buried alive.

A fire? Willow sprigs too sodden. He chopped up the great hickory bows of the wagon that had supported the vanished canopy. He got the fire going. They took turns on watch to see that it never went out.

"Maria, you make it sound almost interesting . . ."

"As a deathwatch is interesting. Don Alonso, you must be mad."

Now food. Snow melted in a pan. Biscuits mashed up for the shivering crones, laced with molasses and brandy. It was Maria's business to force it into the puckered toothless mouths. They had become her babies; a kind of passion had overtaken her to see that they came through it alive.

The first day grim. The snow never ceasing. She thought the oxen would starve. Frank Dibbler drove them out of the gully and let them chew the bark off every tree in sight. They themselves ate lumps of congealed sowbelly boiled in water. She spat out the first sickening mouthful; he made her force it down.

Second day frightful. Maria was stiffening up. Her skin cracked, lips blistered. She no longer cared whether she lived or died. "He became violent." She didn't want to remember this

271

part of the ordeal. He got her up, shoving her in a tramped circle about the wagon to get her blood moving. Made her stamp her feet like a soldier on parade. Then got her to rub the oxen's legs, who had no room to stamp.

Something had happened. She said sullenly to Alonso, "Peculiar man."

"Maria, is that the best expression you can find? Heroic sounds more descriptive . . ."

"I let the fire go out."

"He hit you?"

"He ill-used me." She didn't say how. "He had no right to blame me. You do not know what it was like."

Third day not describable. She thought the end was near. "It couldn't go on." The tarpaulin was ice-hard. He wouldn't let her rest for more than an hour, forcing her awake and tramping her about. She fed the crones. They could barely open their rigid mouths. It made her want to cry. She gathered them, like infants, very close to her body, endlessly rubbing their bony wrists. She was afraid they would break like sticks. She fell asleep with them still in her embrace . . . and woke at dawn: he was nudging her. Did he never sleep?

The sun shone. It was a Christmas scene. Unbelievable. The snow had stopped. It gushed in melting rivulets. He bent over her compassionately, the stubble of his beard white like splintered bone, and said, "Get up."

"It is over? Thank God." She blinked her crusted eyes open. She still had the crones wrapped in her arms and he said in a curious voice, "Let them loose."

"They are so cold . . ."

"They're dead."

"No, no. They cannot be . . ."

"They died in the night. Didn't want to wake you. You needed the sleep."

The reaction was uncontrollable. She wept. She watched him lay the stiff corpses in a niche in the gully; the ground was too hard to chop up. How tiny they were. He got the oxen yoked and the wagon hauled up into the drift. They looked at each other: bloodshot eyes and cracked blackened lips. The wagon crawled off. By midday they were over the Texas state line. Descending that familiar canyon Alonso knew. Maria said to him bitterly, "But it wasn't enough. They were waiting for us."

"Who?"

"The Indians."

What Indians?

Eight of them. No more. They looked like the remnants of a defeated war party. They were gathered in a sorry bunch at the head of the canyon as if barring their passage. They looked less fearsome as the wagon approached. Maria's first tremor of fear vanished: they were pathetic. Old, old men. A stage-crowd of antiques, all befeathered and painted up like operatic clowns working out their last jobs. She heard them chanting feebly. The nags frozen. Half-dead on their hoofs. One of the ancients wore the great eagle-feather bonnet of a war chief, but it no longer fitted. It fell loosely over his bony brow.

He waved a lance. It wasn't very intimidating. Frank Dibbler had reined the oxen to a halt. She said to him irritably, "Do they think they can stop us? Get on."

He just sat watching; mouth wry as if he'd tasted something bad.

"You have a gun. They are ridiculous. Why are you waiting?"

Still nothing. Didn't he have a tongue?

"What is it they want?" But she'd already guessed the answer before she opened her mouth. Old men, like old squaws left in rotted tent-flaps, were encumbrances to tribes moving fast after meat. Buffalo waited for no man.

"They're hungry, Maria."

She was in a terribly edgy condition. She thought she'd borne enough. "We cannot feed them. Get on."

"Maria," he said.

And it angered her. It was his expression, she told Alonso. Like her father's. Full of stern, sorrowful reproof.

"We have hardly enough for ourselves."

"I know. Cut the two forward oxen loose and let them have them."

She gasped. "Are you mad? We have a long way to go."

"Five days. Downgrade all the way. God willing, we'll make it. So cut the beasts loose and take them across."

To have endured so much, and lose everything now! She stared hysterically back at the colossal, rusting oil rig as if she'd hauled every pound of it sufferingly on her back.

"No."

"Maria, it's the price of our redemption. Take them."

He was going Biblical on her. It drove her mad. "Take them yourself."

He wouldn't even lift his hurt leg off the yoke. Perhaps he thought her education wasn't complete. "Maria," he said for the last time, and she sighed. He'd broken her. She would never forgive him for it; it would haunt her till the day she died. He pushed the axe across to her. She climbed down and chopped the leather traces of the two leading oxen free of the span. She led them slowly up the canyon. Poor beasts. She got within ten feet of the painted old men. Decrepit. She pointed soundlessly to the oxen. She saw the dim eyes brighten; the one with the eagle bonnet nodded and gestured with his lance. She turned and ran back half-expecting to feel it in her spine. But before she reached the wagon she heard a thin yammering cry, and when she looked round they were galloping off, driving the sacrificial oxen ahead.

She said to Frank Dibbler in a suffocated voice, "Never force me again. I will not stand it."

"I have to keep trying, Maria."

"You must despise me."

"Didn't think you cared a damn. Get aboard, Maria. Only five days to go." And downhill all the way. Bastard. She hoped they met mountains. The reduced span of oxen dragged off.

274

Suddenly back in familiar Texas country. Getting nearer and nearer to home. Home? The word confused her. Where was home? An awful tearless nostalgia assailed her. I am lost, she thought. A drought-ridden land, all dried up by a pitiless sun. Three days to go. There was so much to remind her of the way they'd come. The whitening bones of dead cattle marking the trail of some long-forgotten drive. Two days left. The wind lifted the land and blew it into her face.

Nothing more can happen, she thought. But it could. There was a puff of dust far behind in the mesa. They let it catch up. It turned into a troop of Rangers. She'd never set eyes on their kind before: Alonso had. A kind of loose, carelessly disciplined militia, not even properly uniformed. He thought them rather oafish. Dangerously free with the gun.

They circled the wagon slowly, staring at it with bewilderment—if those hard faces could register anything as human as bewilderment—and the weathered officer with them called out, "Mister, haul up."

Frank Dibbler drew the wagon to a stop.

"Name wouldn't be Dibbler, would it?"

"It could be."

"Wondered if we'd ever pick you up." He hadn't taken his eyes off Maria. Yes, she thought distressfully; I know I am a sight. He was a beefy man with a brown dust-blasted face. He leaned absently on his saddle horn to spit a little of it out. "Had word from Fort Trent to watch out for a wagon out of Jake's Creek. Some complaint from the sheriff about abducting a woman," and Maria thought with a shiver: you have taken your time!

XI

So THE SHERIFF had discovered a twinge of compassion in the end. I hope he chokes on it. She felt like crying. Jake's Creek had reached out a hand to rescue her, and she couldn't screw any more emotion out of it . . . not hope, not gratitude. Not even relief. How quiet it was. The wind hissed. It rolled a hoop of tumbleweed across the mesa, and one of the ponies reared. No sound but the jangle of harness. She stared emptily at the knights of the prairie who had come trotting out of the dust, the bleak battle-worn eyes looking her over as if she were something that had strayed out of a cage.

I have been in one, she thought. She gave her husband a stealthy glance. The things I have endured at his hands. Humiliation, disparagement and pain—everything short of outright rape. If I am left with him a little longer I will no doubt suffer that, too. The Ranger officer was still watching her intently. She put her hand up to her face. There was nothing she could do with it. All right, then: so I am foul.

He said, "Captain Sol Clemp, ma'am," touching his hat. She inclined her head, which was the nearest the Condesa de Rojas

276

could come to a bow. She was so stiff that she almost creaked like a rusty hinge.

"Figured we'd catch up with you," he said. He glanced narrowly at the chopped traces at the head of the span. "Picked up a bunch of crazy old Kiowa Injuns two days back. Gorged belly-full on your oxen . . ."

"We gave them to them," she said.

He peered incredulously at the wagon, measuring its colossal load. "With all that to haul? Why in hell would you do that, ma'am?"

"They were hungry."

She was beginning to bewilder him. "Ma'am, you just don't *feed* Injuns." The Rangers shifted disapprovingly in their saddles. He shrugged. "This here complaint of the sheriff's . . ."

"I did not complain to him." She thought faintly: now what made me say that?

The captain thought: something queer and mixed up here. Stories don't tally. Sheriff's complaint talked of abduction. He watched her face. This woman is one unholy mess. Never seen anything like it. Scared, is she? Don't seem to know her own mind.

He said truculently, "This man your husband?"

And Frank Dibbler interrupted him softly, "Captain, interrogate me. Not my wife."

"I'll come to you presently, mister." Captain Clemp gave him a hostile look. Big bastard, but beaten up. Bunged-up eyes. Something wrong with the leg? What in glory's name happened to these people? "Ma'am," he said with awful gallantry, "if you'll forgive me, you look like you been through one hell of a bad time."

"Something like it." And heard her sigh.

"This man roughed you up?"

She stared at him. Licked her lips. Figured so, the captain thought. Jesus God. What did he do to her? Drag her through the cactus? And what in hell do they have there in the wagon?

277

"It has been a hard journey," she said. And sighed again.

"But you been forced?"

Yes, she thought; it is a fair description. She stole another look at Frank Dibbler. Not a muscle moved in his face. "No," she said.

Lie. Can smell it at two yards, Captain Sol Clemp thought. He said grimly, "No cause to fear. Don't be scared of this man. Nothing here we can't handle," staring hard at Frank Dibbler.

"He is my husband."

He'd looked at her hand. He wasn't blind. And getting impatient. "Wedding ring ain't too plain."

"It was stolen from me," Maria said. She thought: what is happening to my tongue? It is running away with me. She felt a nervous desire to giggle. They will think I am mad.

Captain Sol Clemp rasped his unshaven cheek. Another lie. Sticks out like a sore thumb. Who, for God's sake, does she think she's fooling? Something queer as old Mick is going on here. And getting queerer by the minute.

He muttered dubiously, "You still look awful messed up."

"You are not very polite."

"Story we got says this man lifted your jewels."

"My dowry," Maria heard herself say. Is it *me* talking? "Who else would they belong to but him?"

Glib, goddamn it. Who started this thing? Captain Clemp was beginning to be rattled. The Rangers were taking an amused interest in the proceedings.

"Ma'am, you got one last chance to speak up . . ."

"Captain," Frank Dibbler said, "you doubt the lady's word?"

"You butt in when I talk to you. Not before." He glowered at him. "You bear out what this woman says?"

"You call my wife 'this woman' and I'll come down there and tear off your head."

One of the Rangers guffawed. The captain turned testily and said, "Next man who opens his mouth gets my boot in it." He stared gloomily at the man on the driving board. I could take

278

him, big as he is; particularly with both eyes clobbered and only one sound leg. But it wouldn't look good.

"Where you heading, mister?"

"Long way from you."

"Answer my question."

"Make it polite and I might give it some thought."

"What you got in that wagon?"

"Indian stone axes. Contraband rifles. Old iron."

I'll hit him. Goddamn it, I will. One of the Rangers made a husky sound and Captain Clemp thought: I'll hit him, too. He stared for the last time at the woman. Kind of heavy accent. Mexican, is she? Spanish? Clean her up, comb that awful mess of hair, and she wouldn't look too bad. Pair of liars, both of them. And I'll never know why.

He was defeated. The hell with the sheriff of Jake's Creek. He said wearily, "On your way, mister."

"See you again, captain."

"Not if I see you first." The captain waved to the troop, "Hup," and they trotted off. He couldn't get them out of his mind. One memory stayed with him most of the day. That bruise on her cheek. The entranced look—kind of lost and frozen—when she stared at her husband. If that was what he was. Woman *ought* to show her wedding ring. As dusk fell they came on another party, almost as queer as the one they had left.

A plump sore-buttocked man with a worn doleful look. Boy of twelve. And an Indian guide with a ludicrous high-pointed hat clapped like a snuffer on his greasy plaits.

He waved the troop to a halt. "You people lost?"

The plump man sighed, "We have been lost for weeks." Accent curiously reminiscent. Spanish, too?

"This is lonely country. What's brought you here?"

"We are searching for some friends." The man's soft brown eyes gazed at him like a hurt dog's. "You would not have seen a wagon with . . ."

279

"Dibbler? Man and wife?"

The man shivered as if he'd been stung. "Then you *have* seen them?"

"What're they to you?"

"I am *in loco parentis.*" The captain looked insulted. "The lady is my ward. If she needs help . . ."

"Mister, what that lady needs is a priest to teach her to talk truth. A hospital nurse. And a bath. Straight down the valley. Half a day ahead."

Goddamn it, Captain Clemp thought, this country is filling up with the queerest types. Don't know what our civilization is coming to. His troop jangled on. Anyone mentions Jake's Creek to me again I'll just spit.

Alonso said urgently to Charley the Indian, "You heard what he said?"

"Very agitated man. I wonder what upset him?"

"Only half a day ahead." Alonso stared up. A thin moon had risen above the mesa. He began to tremble: they had never been so close. "If we ride all night we may catch them up by morning."

"Señor, your ass is sore."

"She must be in despair."

"As you wish. I am at your command. After all, it is you who are paying me four dollars a day." Alonso thought they had made it three. "Tighten your cinch, señor," Charley the Indian said, "or you will fall off your horse." He closed his eyes. He would sleep in the saddle. They pushed on.

It was an endless night. Alonso regretted it before he was three hours out. The sky blazed with the iciest of stars. The spines of huge cactus tore viciously at his pants in the dark. And his loins! A nest of fire. He saw Miguel reel tiredly in the saddle; his pony stumbled in a gopher hole and almost tossed him off. Charley the Indian, fast asleep, barely swayed. Alonso wondered what magic equilibrium kept him erect. Would dawn never come?

It flushed the sky with a chilly pink. Alonso searched the

desolate mesa—nothing but sparse grass and dust-devils spinning in the bitter breeze. A jackrabbit, bolting out of its hole, very nearly unhorsed him. It was the final tribulation. The sun was now high and scorching his head. His tongue thick with dust. Dizzy. I am finished. He said faintly to Charley the Indian, "Stop. I am done."

There was a log farmhouse down in a copse. They turned off toward it. He thought he would die if he didn't rest.

A skinny scarecrow of an old man peered at them out of the barn. He was hoisting a forkful of manure; he reeked of it. He had a bony nose that jutted like a beak, and milky, wickedly sparkling eyes. A hellion. He called out, "You folks crossed the desert?"

The desert of despair, Alonso thought. He dropped off his pony. He said feebly, "If we might rest. Perhaps some food . . ."

"Set yourself down inside. Name's Witherspoon. Call me Jake." He screamed out in a thin falsetto, "Maw, we got guests," and a burly woman issued from the house. She was more masculine than her husband. One of his tattered hats was crammed on a wiry tangle of gray hair. Both were villainously unwashed. A jovial old slattern. She grinned, "Fried pork do you?"

"Please."

"Injun'll have to eat outside."

Charley the Indian said with dignity, "Do not let me embarrass you," and sat on a pile of logs in the yard.

Fate is laughing at us, Alonso thought. I have no more hope. We shall never find them. Charley the Indian was beckoning to him. His eyes twinkled. Alonso saw him point to something in the mud outside the barn.

He went across. "I think they must be dead."

"I think they are very much alive. They were here less than four hours ago," and with a tremor that ran right through him Alonso saw the deep imprints of the wheels in the mud.

He stared at the aged hellion leaning on his fork. He said in an unsteady voice, "Did a wagon stop by . . . ?"

"Sure did. Left few hours back. Folks stayed the night. Goddamn it. Ain't going to forget that night as long as I live." Something set him laughing. "You know 'em?"

"Yes, yes."

"Maw! These people know the two Dibblers stayed here last night!"

She came out with a skillet in her hand. She cackled. She looked at her husband. It seemed to Alonso that a witch and a warlock were sharing some lecherous joke. "They do? Goldarn it, Jake, wasn't that something? Busted up our second-best bed."

They are mad. Or perhaps it is I who am mad: what brought me to this impossible land? The Witherspoon couple were still shaking wickedly, the old scarecrow heh-hehing out of his bony nose, the woman guffawing, and Alonso sat by Charley the Indian on the pile of logs. He was astonished to see his hands tremble. It had taken too much out of him. But he was very near the end now, and he waited to be told how Francisco and Maria had busted up their second-best bed.

The end product of the story was appalling. Very nearly beyond belief. It was disjointed. It had to be. He would get a dark hint or two from Maria to substantiate it. A few words dropped ambiguously by Frank Dibbler with a curious glitter in his eye. He had to depend for most of it on Jake and Maw Witherspoon. That scandalous old couple. Eavesdroppers. Without shame. Everything exaggerated into one glorious cackle. But it had the ring of naked truth.

And pretty naked it was. The wagon had rolled up to the farm after dark. "Came a-clanking up," Jake said. He sat in the kitchen with them as they ate. The fragrance of manure was nauseous. "Goddamnedest craziest wagon I ever seen. Ingine in it! Saw it myself. Like something out of a carnival. Man gets down, hopping like a crow with a broken leg, and asks if he and his wife could stay the night."

Maw was waiting on edge to get in her share. The story was

282

told between them in spasmodic jerks. "Dibbler, he said, was his name. Nice feller, big as a house, but all beat-up. Couldn't hardly see the door to come in. Jake, I said to my man, that feller didn't get battered hitting his wife. Kind of funny idea I had. Way she looked at him. All shaken. Foreign woman. One minute doing the duchess, the next shivering like she had the plague."

"Wife she said," old Jake chuckled ironically. "Where's the wedding ring? I said to Maw."

"Damnedest couple I ever did see"—this was Maw. Her old man couldn't compete with her for the attention of their audience. Charley the Indian was listening intently with hooded amused eyes outside the door. "Gave 'em what I give you. Fried pork. Beans. They ate like they ain't seen good food in two years."

Maw had made up their room. The shanty cabin had two bedrooms, one with the second-best bed. This was the one she prepared. She was very curious. "Kind of inquisitive. I got an inquisitive nose." It was as prominent as her husband's who made everybody's business his own. Loneliness perhaps; Alonso didn't know. "Mister," Maw said to him, planting her elbows by his plate, "for a lovin' married couple that pair didn't have a word to say to each other. Got me wondering. Woman's accent. Not Mexican. Too high-class. Him—I figured *him*. Raw Texan. Nothing but. Well, they was all ate up and time to go to bed."

And then the two Witherspoons started giggling and Alonso —with some nervous anticipation—sent Miguel off to bed. He had the feeling that something was coming that unsoiled adolescent ears shouldn't hear.

"Gave 'em a candle and saw them next door," old Jake said. "Fine big bed. Sleep well, I said. I figured if I was with the woman in that bed I wouldn't have strength nor time to sleep a solitary wink."

"Spunky old buster," Maw reproved him. "Watch your tongue."

283

"Fine woman."

"You already got a fine woman for your wife."

The old scandalmongers turned in themselves. They were separated from the bedroom only by the log wall, and through the rough crevices they could see the candle gleaming next door.

Could hear a tense muttering. It didn't sound natural. It was a sharp night and Maw remembered that she had some spare blankets and went with them hospitably next door. As good an excuse as any for an inveterate nosey-parker, Alonso thought. "Mister," Maw said to him, "you could have dropped me with a feather. The husband was rolled up in a blanket on the hard floor and the wife curled up in bed."

She said nothing to them, casting her inquisitive lecherous eyes about. She went back to the warmth of Jake and whispered to him. Nothing now could keep their pricked ears from the log wall.

They heard Maria's voice, strangely brittle, "You there, on the floor. Is it necessary to shame me?"

And he answered from under the blankets on the floor, "Shame you how?"

"The woman saw."

"Maria, that woman would see what she wanted to see through six brick walls. Go to sleep."

"When shall we be home?"

Strange word to use, Alonso thought. When was Amarillo ever home?

"Late tomorrow," Frank Dibbler said.

"And then?"

"Fix your passage back to Spain. You're free as the air."

Maw said frustratedly to Alonso, "Wished they'd speak up. Couldn't hardly hear a word they said. Kind of argument, the woman all on edge, the man kind of sleepy, not paying much attention, and then . . ."

Alonso felt his skin prick. "And then what?"

"Mister, you married?"

"I am a widower."

"Same thing. So you won't be shocked. You ever heard a woman cry out like a coyote bitch on heat?"

Alonso stared at her with horror. He could eat no more. He pushed away his plate.

"Was crying. I heard her. I says to Jake, that wife in there is crying. And he said, Maw, shut up, let me listen, she's all turned on." Alonso gathered the sexual sense of what he meant by "all turned on."

Alonso looked down. His instincts were at work. Indeed, from what he would gather subtly from Maria, he was very close to the truth. She must have lain there in the bed, shaken by something that tore at her, something she'd never experienced before. And he sighed. She was an Estremaduran and Spanish—the combination violent. She hadn't been constructed for virginity. Nature had built her, blood and loins and sex, to be a woman: not a saint. Perhaps . . . just perhaps . . . she was conscious of a sense of shared achievement. They'd been through so much together. And now: so tamely to end! Hypothetical, of course. In the end, Alonso shrugged, it all came back to sex.

He could picture her lying there in the dark, listening to his heavy sighs—the floor was hard and his leg sore, and he cursed both under his breath. Did she mean so little to him? To be so disdained! It was a physical affront. Alonso's overheated imagination could see her dark stricken eyes, curiously a-shine: her hot body wouldn't let her rest. She'd felt nothing like it in her life. As if a stream were carrying her along and she was too taut, too confused, to swim against it.

That, he guessed, was the moment she cried out. The simile of a coyote bitch on heat was disgraceful. But still she cried.

Jake said, "Curled the hair on my spine. I says to Maw, goddamn it, man ain't flesh that'd lie there and . . ."

"Only he didn't," Maw said. Unsavory eavesdroppers. To

285

think that they had lain there with their lustful ears clapped to the logs. "Got up. Heard the floor creak. I whispered to Jake: Hold everything, man. One of two things is going to happen. Either he hits her to let him sleep or else . . ."

Alonso sweated with embarrassment. This is fearful. No gentleman should listen to this prying, salacious pair.

Jake said with an awed cackle, "Mister, what happened on that bed was like the War of Independence. Everything but the cannon. Wall shook. That mattress took a pounding the like of which I thought'd bust it apart. Woman sobbing. Man whispering to her. And going on all the time. Wasn't so much a loving as a marriage battle. And was just one casualty. Our second-best bed. Fine brass bed I bought in El Paso. Fell apart with a clanking you could hear over in the barn."

"Woke up the chickens," Maw said. "Heard 'em squawking. Was damn near to squawking with excitement myself."

Alonso looked back at Charley the Indian. His eyes had a deep, deep gleam. He didn't seem too perturbed. He had three squaws who kept him busy. He probably thought it very ordinary beer.

Alonso said in a suffocated voice, "I do not wish to hear any more."

"Ain't no more," Maw said. "Was all done. She was whimpering like a child that's been overfed. And he was kind of smoothing her. Big, big man. Figured he could overfeed any woman," and it was enough. Alonso rose shakenly and went into the bedroom in which the final battle had been fought. Same brass bed. Miguel snored in it. I shall not sleep a wink, he thought.

He remembered something Francisco had said to him, that dreadfully deprived morning in the inn at Seville, "She's flesh. In the end she'll want it. She'll cringe. I'll take her when I'm ready, but she'll sweat for it," and she'd sweated. Poor Maria. Terribly assertive man! Was it necessary to be so cruel? And in the end it wouldn't work. He would always have trouble with her. It was a marriage that would "bust" every bed.

286

Frank Dibbler got up before dawn. He glanced thoughtfully at Maria, couched under the blankets, face creased baby-fashion in sleep, and went out. He was naked. He didn't mind the cold. Nobody, anyway, was about. He walked over to a ridge and stared south. Somewhere not too far over those slopes lay Amarillo. The ranch and the oil. He thought for a moment about Pablo, and then put him once and for all out of his mind. It was part of his personal explosive story, and too much of it remained to be told. The sun was just peeping up. Red, yellow fire, paling the stars. A chicken squawked.

His eyes grew fixed. His imagination edgy. Already he could see derricks sprouting, refineries, distillation plants, pipelines to tidewater, more and more of everything, branching out to territories overseas, for nothing would stop him . . . but, heated as his imagination was, standing nakedly on the windy ridge, nothing he saw matched the colossal reality that the boy, for whom Maria's womb had just moved, would one day see with his own eyes.

"Muchacho!" What made Frank Dibbler suddenly yearn for him that cold Texas dawn?

He grinned contentedly and went back to the warmth of his wife.